T0127477

## The Sou... ...g Building Coffins

"Louis Maistros has written a lyrical, complex, and brave novel that takes enormous risks and pulls them all off. He is a writer to watch and keep reading, a writer to cherish."
—Peter Straub, author of *Ghost Story*

"The Society of North American Magic Realists welcomes its newest, most dazzling member, Louis Maistros. His debut novel is a thing of wonder, unlike anything in our literature. It startles. It stuns. It stupefies. No novel since *A Confederacy of Dunces* has done such justice to New Orleans."
—Donald Harington, winner of the Robert Penn Warren Award

"Set in a meticulously researched, living and breathing Storyville-era New Orleans, *The Sound of Building Coffins* is variously an ultraviolet comedy, a family saga, and a meditation on race, class, and how those who think they're at the top of the heap seldom really are (more important points than ever in our post-Katrina landscape). Vividly drawn and frequently heartbreaking; a big, tremendously complex, absorbing, essential novel. Some authors live here all their lives and manage to write nothing but cliches about the city, but Louis Maistros gets it right the first time. *The Sound of Building Coffins* is easily one of the finest and truest pieces of New Orleans fiction I've ever read."
—Poppy Z. Brite, author of *Lost Souls* and *Exquisite Corpse*

"*The Sound of Building Coffins* is a soulful work from a writer of the weird. Maistros does more than make you feel for his characters and their twisted, damaged lives; he makes you want to feel."
—Paul Tremblay, author of *Head Full of Ghosts*

"This is a novel about love and life and death, New Orleans-style, when a cure can take the form of a healing or an abortion or an exorcism; where a hand on a heart can be a blessing or a burden; where the dead walk among the living and are known and listened to; where spirits live on and on, to torment or to love... Maistros creates a city that is part dream, part hallucination. His New Orleans embodies both the grim reality of a particular time and the city's eternal, shimmering beauty. And, with the book's title, he provides us with a new and unforgettable metaphor for the sound of hammers at work, whether boarding up for a storm or rebuilding after one."
—Susan Larson, *New Orleans Times-Picayune* and *USA Today*

"(*The Sound of Building Coffins*) is a macabre and utterly hypnotic feat of literary imagination, an extended tale of voodoo and jazz in the Crescent City, circa the turn of the 20th century. The novel is so fluently delivered that it sometimes feels as if it were being channeled via the same spirits—evil and good—that inhabit these richly drawn characters. Maistros, a New Orleans record-store owner and former forklift operator with no formal training as a writer, has crafted a work spiked with historical characters and events, so striking and original that it probably deserves a place on the shelf of great fiction from his adopted hometown."
—Philip Booth, *St. Petersburg Times*

"*The Sound of Building Coffins* is set in turn-of-the-century New Orleans, where, explains Maistros, residents have 'a long and curious relationship with death, a closeness, a delicate truce...' In spite of all of the death and violence and betrayal, *Coffins* is also filled with love. Love moves characters to commit terrible acts, but it also drives them to right their wrongs. Love offers second chances, sometimes in this life and sometimes in the one beyond."

—*Atlanta Journal-Constitution*

"For me, it was the perfect book, at the perfect time, and I will cherish it forever."

—Ray Shea, *The Rumpus*

"The multiple plot lines smoothly interlock like simultaneous horn solos in an early Louis Armstrong single, and the steady flow of closely observed details and dialogue are a consistent pleasure."

—Joab Jackson, *The Baltimore City Paper*

"One has to write with considerable authenticity to pull off a story steeped in magic and swamp water that examines race and class, death and rebirth, Haitian voodoo, and the beginnings of jazz in 1891 New Orleans. Maistros's gritty debut novel follows the interconnected lives of the Morningstar siblings–all lovingly named by their father after diseases—as they wrestle with a powerful demon, con outsiders, kill and die, die and are reborn. The plot is complex and magical, grounded in the history of the city, without being overly sentimental. There is a comfort with death as a part of life in this work that reveals deep feeling for the city and its past. Of course, every novel about New Orleans must have a good hurricane. Like the one in Zora Neale Hurston's classic *Their Eyes Were Watching God*, this hurricane destroys the city while making hope possible. Highly recommended for all fiction collections, especially where there is an interest in jazz."

—Library Journal

"Magical realism meets the seedy melting pot of early 20th-century New Orleans in this richly complex novel. The story has plenty of ghosts, magic, demons and, this being New Orleans, a 'Cajun bogeyman' named Coco Robicheux. It depicts a world where Jesus himself, speaking to a pastor busily wrestling with demons, would say 'Get the fuck out of this house.' It shows a place where outsiders are conned with elaborate scams that send them packing, none the wiser but considerably poorer. Those who survive this dangerous milieu are bound together by water, and the liquid becomes one of the novel's major leitmotifs. If all of this sounds improbable, it is. Yet this novel contains considerable wonders as well, and these wonders are more than enough to transcend the story's complexities."

—Publisher's Weekly

"*The Sound of Building Coffins* exhumes volumes of New Orleans myth and legend and folk-historical matters on death and rebirth and spirituality and epic storms. It's the story of a haunted family of five children named after dread diseases—Diphtheria, Dropsy, Cholera, Malaria and Typhus—out of their father's respect for the redemptive inevitability of death. Here, Buddy Bolden appears as Diphtheria's feckless love interest, but also as a teenage witness and musical accompanist to a searingly intense New Orleans-style exorcism. In that moment, Bolden sees God's face and begins to play cornet like a man who's experienced ungodly awe and terror. This Bolden, largely unsympathetic—at times unforgivable—feels very much the author's own. Louis Maistros' *The Sound of Building Coffins* is relentlessly absorbing."

—Steve Nathans-Kelly, Paste Magazine

"This book sings out in true jazz fashion—wildly inventive, oddly formed yet perfectly made, and never a sour note."

—*The Anniston Star*

"If Maistros was a traditional storyteller rather than a writer, he would be one of those gifted individuals that you would listen to raptly, late into the night."

—*The Roanoke Times*

"*The Sound of Building Coffins* manages to be surprising and deeply inventive through to the end. For those of us who were schooled in the refined belle-lettres traditions of American literature, this novel is a raw and unsubtle example of what it means to open a vein and write. To wit: 'Like a hurricane party or a jazz funeral, an embrace of some fast-coming and brilliantly inevitable (if unjust) end, an open invitation to the last and wildest party on earth, a high stakes gamble with neither certainty nor hope'."

—*The Alabama Press-Register*

"Maistros succeeds by populating the novel with hoodoo queens, jazzbos, tricksters, rounders, and various folks with one foot in reality and the other in the spirit world. A sprawling, complex, and ultimately absorbing work."

—John Lewis, *Baltimore Magazine*

"A writer of lesser ability would have been swallowed up in the swirling complexity of such a plot, plunging it to the level of a silly period piece regional novel. However, *The Sound of Building Coffins* is different. Maistros keeps his head above water and pulls off an admirable story because of his keen research into the history of New Orleans and his compelling style that is fired by his use of foreboding imagery. Readers can never guess what is coming next as the various threads are revealed and followed. The story, although complex, rings true because of its meticulous backdrop and immediate reader sympathy with the Morningstar family. Maistros' story is not a fantasy tale. It is about life and the timeless theme of how people integrate living with the good and the bad around them and how they can emerge with newness as a result. *The Sound of Building Coffins* is riveting."

—*Endtype: A Canadian Literary Magazine*

"The stories of *The Sound of Building Coffins* weave in and out 'like threads in a rug,' connecting in a lyrical prose that's as unique to Maistros as his story. In the back of your mind, you know that Maistros's absorbing tale will lead to a grand finale, one that will explain all. And he delivers."

—*The Times of Acadiana*

"Louis Maistros's novel, *The Sound of Building Coffins*, brings turn of the century New Orleans to life. Maistros masterfully interweaves tales of voodoo, hurricanes, the birth of jazz, and even demonic possession in an unforgettable book written in eloquent prose that draws the reader further in with every plot twist, turn, and character insight."

—LargeheartedBoy.Com

"This powerful novel set in 1890s New Orleans is a complex debut novel from Louis Maistros... Lyrical in its prose, the book deftly paints a world that is changing, a world where music fills the streets even as pain fills the doorways. A beautiful and compelling first novel."

—LiteratureChick.Com

# THE SOUND OF BUILDING COFFINS

## Louis Maistros

New Orleans, LA

Joseph S. Phillips and Susan J. Wood, Ph.D., Publishers
www.blackwidowpress.com

Cover design & text production: Geoff Munsterman

ISBN-13: 978-0-9986431-7-5

Printed in the United States of America

*for Booker*

# CONTENTS

*Foreword by Gary Krist*                                                    *xi*

## BOOK ONE: NEW ORLEANS, 1891

CHAPTER ONE: *Deliver the Children*                                           5
CHAPTER TWO: *The Note*                                                      11
CHAPTER THREE: *Man of God*                                                  13
CHAPTER FOUR: *Dominick's Affliction*                                        17
CHAPTER FIVE: *Gin Joint*                                                    23
CHAPTER SIX: *The Day Before*                                               35
CHAPTER SEVEN: *Run*                                                        37
CHAPTER EIGHT: *Beauregard Church*                                          41
CHAPTER NINE: *The Cell Has No Walls*                                       43
CHAPTER TEN: *Keep This Letter Should Misfortune Befall Me*                 47
CHAPTER ELEVEN: *The Tenant of the Tin*                                     50
CHAPTER TWELVE: *Night Fishing*                                             57
CHAPTER FOURTEEN: *Catfish Blues*                                           59
CHAPTER FIFTEEN: *Sky is Falling*                                           63
CHAPTER SIXTEEN: *The Note Revisited*                                       65

## BOOK TWO: BUDDY BOLDEN AND THE CHRIST KID, 1906

CHAPTER SEVENTEEN: *Calisaya Blues*                                         69
CHAPTER EIGHTEEN: *Up From the Crib*                                        75
CHAPTER NINETEEN: *Malvina*                                                 81
CHAPTER TWENTY: *Blackest Night*                                            85
CHAPTER TWENTY-ONE: *Emmanuel Fred*                                         87
CHAPTER TWENTY-TWO: *Djab*                                                  93
CHAPTER TWENTY-THREE: *Intentions Eversweet*                               95
CHAPTER TWENTY-FOUR: *Popcorn Ash*                                         99
CHAPTER TWENTY-FIVE: *All About Jim Jam Jump*                             103
CHAPTER TWENTY-SIX: *Typhus*                                              107
CHAPTER TWENTY-SEVEN: *Shoes*                                             113
CHAPTER TWENTY-EIGHT: *Christ Kid is Risen*                               123
CHAPTER TWENTY-NINE: *Dog*                                                131
CHAPTER THIRTY: *Recovery*                                                137
CHAPTER THIRTY-ONE: *Hattie's Cure*                                       143
CHAPTER THIRTY-TWO: *Fish and Buttons*                                    147
CHAPTER THIRTY-THREE: *In the Court of King Bolden*                       153
CHAPTER THIRTY-FOUR: *I Promise, She Lied*                                163

CHAPTER THIRTY-FIVE: *King Tat*     169
CHAPTER THIRTY-SIX: *What Dropsy Saw*     177
CHAPTER THIRTY-SEVEN: *The Nature of My Double-Blink*     181
CHAPTER THIRTY-EIGHT: *Night Whisperer*     185
CHAPTER THIRTY-NINE: *Two Seconds Past Now*     189
CHAPTER FORTY: *The Dependable Nurse Janeway*     193
CHAPTER FORTY-ONE: *Down*     195
CHAPTER FORTY-TWO: *Mourning Star*     197

## BOOK THREE: TROUBLED ABOUT MY SOUL, 1906

CHAPTER FORTY-THREE: *Deliverance*     203
CHAPTER FORTY-FOUR: *Reckoning*     205
CHAPTER FORTY-FIVE: *Lost Bayou*     207
CHAPTER FORTY-SIX: *Typhus' Dream*     216
CHAPTER FORTY-SEVEN: *Beware the Shoe Dove*     219
CHAPTER FORTY-EIGHT: *Blindfold*     225
CHAPTER FORTY-NINE: *Main Door*     229
CHAPTER FIFTY: *Malaria and Typhus*     231
CHAPTER FIFTY-ONE: *Rising Fog*     237
CHAPTER FIFTY-TWO: *Together All Three*     239
CHAPTER FIFTY-THREE: *Typhus' Cure*     245
CHAPTER FIFTY-FOUR: *The Twenty Tens*     247
CHAPTER FIFTY-FIVE: *Fathers and Sons*     251
CHAPTER FIFTY-SIX: *This is Blood*     257
CHAPTER FIFTY-SEVEN: *When a Cop Comes to Call on Poor Folk, Ain't Never Good News To Tell*     259
CHAPTER FIFTY-EIGHT: *Diphtheria's Cure*     265
CHAPTER FIFTY-NINE: *Ain't Nothin' Gonna Be All Right*     271
CHAPTER SIXTY: *A Contrast of Hands*     277
CHAPTER SIXTY-ONE: *Spiritworld*     283
CHAPTER SIXTY-TWO: *Rhythm Found*     285
CHAPTER SIXTY-THREE: *Malvina's Cure*     287
CHAPTER SIXTY-FOUR: *The Sound of Building Coffins*     291
CHAPTER SIXTY-FIVE: *Keep My Baby Down*     295
CHAPTER SIXTY-SIX: *How Long to Return?*     297
CHAPTER SIXTY-SEVEN: *The River*     305

## BOOK FOUR: APOCRYPHA

CHAPTER THIRTEEN: *The Last and Unexpectedly Final Words of Jim Jam Jump*     387
CHAPTER SIXTY-EIGHT: *Can't No Grave Keep My Body Down*     396

*Acknowledgements*

# FOREWORD

"When Aristotle notes that man is a rational animal," says Richard Everett, narrator of the novel *Expensive People* by Joyce Carol Oates, "one strains forward, cupping his ear, to hear which of those words is emphasized—*rational* animal, rational *animal.*"

The same can be said of the much-abused literary concept of "magic realism." Do we mean by that term magic *realism*—an essentially straightforward narrative shot through with elements of the supernatural or the marvelous? Or is it *magic* realism—a kind of alternative, counter-rational version of the world set down in a faithful manner as if no comment or explanation were necessary? The distinction may be subtle, but it's critical; it amounts to the difference between a work in which symbol and myth *comment on* reality and one in which symbol and myth *are* the reality.

I'm not sure that Louis Maistros would consider *The Sound of Building Coffins* any kind of magic realism at all, but I'd argue that his book embodies the latter variety. And for a historical novel about New Orleans, this is probably as it should be. Magic realism may be the single most appropriate narrative style for describing a place where, by the author's own admission, "the casual departure from reality" is an urban hallmark. "In New Orleans," he once told an interviewer, "what's true isn't always believable." This fact creates an interesting problem for the novelist, whose most authentic representation of the city's improbabilities might put undue strain on a reader's suspension of disbelief. But rather than worry about plausibility, Maistros wholeheartedly embraces the city's stubborn nonconformity with the usual boundaries. Thus we have a novel where as much of significance happens in dreams as in waking hours, and where, as one character puts it, "Dead people just as real as live ones, I reckon."

The line between death and life in this New Orleans is never sharp. "In this city there is a long and curious relationship with death, a closeness, a delicate truce," Maistros writes in his chapter called "The River." That closeness manifests itself in many ways. The most obvious one: you can't help noticing that an awful lot of people die in this book—by violence, disease, natural disaster, and various types of misadventure. (One character names his children after fatal diseases like Cholera, Diphtheria, and Typhus.) But the presence of death here goes deeper than double-digit body counts. There is a sense in this novel that the natural lifespan of its characters represents just a small part of their overall story, and that who they are is often determined by people and events belonging to a time long before their own birth. The dead of *Building Coffins* don't so much haunt the living as interact with them, influencing their actions and helping to determine their fates. So to say that death hangs over the New Orleans of this novel is perhaps not as dark an assertion as it sounds. After all, without death there can be no rebirth, and rebirth is really what New Orleans—and what this novel—is all about.

"As the city dies, the city is reborn," Maistros writes, and this is an idea that runs through the whole book. From its extraordinary first scene—in which young Typhus Morningstar brings aborted fetuses to the river to coax them back to life in new, piscine form—to its equally extraordinary finale—about which, since this is a foreword and not an afterword, I will say only that it involves a return to that same river—the novel abounds with resurrections of every kind. A pattern plays itself out repeatedly: Something is created, stillborn, then reborn. It's a progression we see not just in Typhus Morningstar's fetuses, but also in a young Buddy Bolden's teasing out of an expressive note on his cornet. For jazz, too, is about nothing if not rebirth, springing as it does from the rejuvenation of a spirit beaten down and nearly erased by centuries of oppression and sorrow. (Jazz as blood is a recurring metaphor in the novel.) And this is why New Orleans—no matter what some jazz history revisionists may say—was the birthplace of the genre: "The city has always had this miraculous gift for regeneration," Maistros has pointed out. "New Orleans has always been challenged by hard times and struggle, but it has always managed to improvise its way through these seemingly hopeless situations by harnessing its collective passion for life."

Given this overarching theme of rebirth, readers may be surprised to learn that the original version of *Building Coffins* was written before 2005's Hurricane Katrina, especially since the novel culminates with a brutal and hypnotic account of a 1906 hurricane. But Maistros actually ended up removing some of the storm elements from the not-yet-published book. "After Katrina hit," he said, "a lot of that stuff felt inappropriate or exploitative. It made me uncomfortable, so I trimmed out some of the more difficult scenes." But Katrina, of course, fits right into the history of New Orleans as we see it here—the latest iteration of the city's endless cycle of death and rebirth.

That impulse to avoid even the appearance of exploitation speaks to Maistros's empathy as a novelist, but also to his integrity as a historian. Because as fantastic as much of the novel's action may seem, it is actually quite faithful to

New Orleans history. Maistros takes plenty of artistic liberties, of course, but the touchstones of the city's story—the 1855 Yellow Fever epidemic, the 1891 Parish Prison lynchings, the 1918-19 Axeman murders—are all here. Before writing this book, Maistros already had a long resume as an artist, photographer, writer, and entrepreneur (he was proprietor of Louie's Juke Joint, a Decatur Street music-and-art shop that eventually was reborn—that word again—online). Here he adds historical researcher to the list. But the fieldwork he does is not just the kind performed in libraries and archives; he also puts in plenty of time pacing the city's neighborhoods and public spaces, absorbing whatever urban essences he can. "Research can be a type of séance," he has said, "a way to mine a spirit through that human link we all share." The result is a kind of street-level spiritual biography of the city, showing how the public crises in New Orleans history play out in the private lives of his cast of fictional characters.

That cast is pretty large, and there are times when *Building Coffins* can seem disconcertingly like the sprawling novels that Henry James once called "loose, baggy monsters." This is especially true with the new material added in this expanded edition (Book Three: Apocrypha), which carries the action into the 1930s. It's not a tidy book by any means; Maistros ranges through points of view, styles of narration, and levels of realism with a speed and abandon that can leave a reader dizzy. But somehow it all ends up hanging together, thanks in part to the continual reappearance of the demon force—whatever it may be—that manifests itself in little Dominick Carolla on the night of his father's lynching. It's a darkness that originated long before the child's birth, and that will go on long after his demise, resurfacing again and again like the shallowly buried bodies in the potter's field of the Girod Street Cemetery. For a time in the novel, it even looks as if this darkness may triumph. We reach a point where, as Maistros writes, "pain has healed no one, no one has done right by anyone, there is no saving grace."

But a saving grace does appear. Appropriately enough, it's tied symbolically to the Mississippi River, which assumes the importance of a main character in the novel—a little like Egdon Heath in Thomas Hardy's *The Return of the Native* or the Nebraska prairie in Willa Cather's *O Pioneers!* The river is the embodiment of the principle of regeneration, and this is what ultimately keeps the book—and the city it describes—from collapsing under the weight of its own despair. Yes, the characters in *The Sound of Building Coffins* do more than their share of suffering, but they somehow manage to go on, living life at a level of intensity unknown in other locales. Because as anyone who has spent much time in the city knows, New Orleans is no ordinary place, and it never was. "Here is where bad hands are played for all they're worth," as Maistros writes. "Here is where miracles come up from mud."

GARY KRIST
DECEMBER 2017

# THE SOUND OF
# BUILDING COFFINS

"*The river starts like a spring and the story just came out. The river starts like a spring and he's like a newborn baby, tumbling and spitting, and one day, attracted by a puddle, he starts to run. He scurries and scampers and wants to get to the marsh, and, after being followed by a big bubble, he does, and at the end of the run he goes into the meander. Then he skips and dances and runs until he's exhausted, and he lies down by the lake—all horizontal lines, ripples, reflections, God-made and untouched. Then he goes over the falls and down into the whirlpool, the vortex of violence, and out of the whirlpool into the main track of the river. He widens, becomes broader, loses his adolescence, and down at the delta, passes between two cities. Like all cities on the opposite sides of the deltas, you can find certain things in one and not in the other, and vice versa, so we call the cities Neo-Hip-Hot-Cool Kiddies' Community and the Village of the Virgins. The river passes between them and romps into the mother— Her Majesty The Sea—and, of course, is no longer a river. But this is the climax, the heavenly anticipation of rebirth, for the sea will be drawn up into the sky for rain and down into wells and into springs and become the river again. So we call the river an optimist. We'll be able to play the ballet in any church or temple, because the optimist is a believer.*"

—Duke Ellington

"*Medicine, to produce health, must examine disease, and music, to create harmony, must examine discord.*"

—Plutarch

BOOK ONE
*New Orleans*
1891

# CHAPTER ONE
## *Deliver the Children*

The short legs of the mulatto boy pedaled the rickety bicycle southeasterly down the bumpy, ballast-stoned streets of the French Quarter. A burlap bag, full of fresh fetuses, sat loosely at the center of a chicken-wire basket tied between handlebars. As the cobbled surface of Customhouse Street gave way to the rocky dirt of the levee, the bicycle slowed and sudden turbulence bounced the contents of Typhus' burlap sack. *Easy does it,* thought Typhus. Should have tied those babies in, he knew, but Doctor Jack had run out of twine. Simple problem, simple solution: Easy does it. That's all. See that? *Easy.* The bouncing diminished accordingly and the bag did not jump, fall, or spill. Typhus' children stayed with him.

Typhus Morningstar was only nine years old, but older of eye. Old enough to have suffered some, but young enough to know there are easy solutions to most types of suffering; solutions not too difficult to grasp and quick enough to be done with if a person had half a mind to. Typhus often considered the possibility that when a boy or a girl reached a certain age of maturity (or reached a certain physical height) that simplicity itself became a thing not to be trusted. Pain for grownups is easy enough to feel—their problem lies in the *whys, hows* and *what-nows* that always accompany such pain. Simple questions are bound to yield simple answers, but also; a thing too easy often feels like a trick. Typhus hoped never to reach the age (or height) of a person who could only trust the harder, more complex ways of handling life's trials.

Typhus maneuvered up the side of the levee, then down the slope towards the river, where the water's recurring kiss had hardened and smoothed the sand into a firm, grainy mud. It was tougher to pedal here, but a smoother ride. He felt safer on this side of the sloping embankment anyway, beyond eye and earshot of the busybodies and shady nighttime characters who roamed the Quarter when the sun was down and gone. It wasn't unheard of (or even uncommon) for a tan-colored boy with a package to be stopped by harbor police for no good reason at all.

Plus, it was so much prettier this near the river.

He followed the slow curve of the riverside until it ambled him up and onto the boardwalk that ran alongside the docks. The only light here was of the moon, bouncing off the water like a million lemon slices, shimmering and shining but yielding no useful illumination. Smudge pots bobbed atop buoys fashioned from beer barrels fifty yards offshore, warning ships of sandbanks too high for safe docking. Thick, black smoke from burning pitch—its powerful smell equally loathsome to man and mosquito—etched creases in the coal sky, quietly proclaiming that there's always something blacker. Only the fatigued crews of smaller vessels dared navigate between the hidden sandbanks, but even these few vessels seemed void of living beings tonight. Every porthole of every ship: black, black, black.

It was all so peaceful and still here.

Typhus loved his midnight bicycle rides. The sound of the water, the feel of night air against his skin, and the acrid smell of burning tar; it all conspired into a comforting sense of oneness with his father's God. And that's all his child's heart had ever really pined for. Not much else, anyway.

A block or so ahead, the shadow of a man cast long from the end of a narrow pier. The dark shape jerked grotesquely as Typhus rode past, sending a sweeping wave of warm gray across the river's yellow-sparkly surface. Typhus smiled and waved back to the elderly gentleman known to most as Marcus Nobody Special. He wished he could stop and talk to Mr. Marcus, but he had business to tend. Maybe after—but most likely, he'd be too tired to socialize after the errand. The business of the errand always took a lot out of him.

Mr. Marcus, who'd been caretaker of the Girod Street potter's field since before the War of the States, had either buried or overseen the burying of just about every man, woman and child of color who'd died in the last fifty years around here. Mr. Marcus was seventy if he was a day, but never complained of aches or pains and always spent the nighttime fishing off the longest pier at this particular stretch of levee. It seemed the old man never rested or slept at all.

Most of the locals thought Marcus crazy. Some even thought him a ghost, people saying he'd died, buried his own bones and come back; that he was on some kind of mysterious mission to find a particular fish that would let him go back to the grave in peace. That fish, they said, had stolen Marcus' soul.

But Marcus seemed alive enough to Typhus. The old fellow ate, drank, pissed, and laughed just like every other living person Typhus knew. So the one part was a lie, but he knew the other was true enough: Mr. Marcus did have a certain odd obsession with fish. Typhus had had occasion to sit alongside the old man on a few of these queer fishing expeditions, had even seen Marcus catch himself a perfectly good catfish now and then—only to throw it back in the water after a cursory examination. He'd simply shake his head and apologize to the wiggly, fat thing, saying; "Sorry, old man, didn't mean to interrupt yer nightswimmin'." Then he'd shake his head some more and say to himself, or to whoever was standing nearby:

"Not my dern fish. Not my fish at all. But I'll get 'im. Yessir."

Typhus liked Mr. Marcus very much. His behavior might not have made the plainest sort of sense, but Typhus understood as much as he needed to. No use being greedy about understanding people other than yourself. He figured people have a right to some privacy concerning the strange workings of their own minds.

Up ahead a hundred yards or so, Typhus spotted his destination. A morass of banana plants interwoven with tall, swaying saw grass signaled the presence of a large sandbank-turned-island just beyond the pier. People sometimes used the little island for fishing during daytime hours, but at night it was Typhus' spot.

Typhus slowed the bicycle.

Put one foot down, stopped the bike at a hard angle from the ground. Looked around slow. No lights. No movement but wind and low waves. No one around but Mr. Marcus looking for his elusive fish. Not another soul.

Typhus got off the bike and eased the burlap sack down to the moist wood of the boardwalk. Rolled the bike into hiding behind some shaggy codgrass near the pier. Slung the bag over his shoulder and lowered himself to the mud of the island. Walked the forty yards or so it took to get to the other side, the side that faced away from the pier and across the water. Out of sight, even from Mr. Marcus.

On the other side of the river was a place called Algiers. Typhus had never been there, had never had good reason to go across. By day it looked just like the pictures of Africa his Daddy liked to show him, but at night it was inky and wonderful, a huge and glorious dead spot where glimmering lemon slices stopped dancing. He took his shoes off and sat at the edge of the island's shore with his feet in the water and the bag at his side. Chewed a hunk of tobacco his father had given him that afternoon after chores. Looked at Algiers and wondered, resting his hand on the bag, spitting juice into the water.

After the tobacco in his cheek was reduced to the vile, juiceless lump it was bound to become, he pulled it out of his mouth and winged it as far as he could into the river, causing lemon slices to laugh and jump for joy. Typhus slung the bag over his shoulder and waded into the water, clothes and all. When the river came about knee deep he knelt down in it and brought the little burlap bag before him. Lowered it into the water, not letting go, just allowing the water to rush in through the thousand tiny holes that make burlap what it is. Unknotted the top. Peeked in. Babies. Three tiny, unborn children. Getting their first taste of nighttime air and warm, muddy river.

Steadying the bag on his lap, Typhus reached a hand in and stroked the tiny arms and neck of one of the children. Scooped his other hand inside the bag and tenderly—so tenderly—separated the little creature from its brother and sister. Let its tiny head bob at the water's surface. Its sweet face looked up at the moon, bathed in lemon light. There was no pain in this face. No tragedy or loss. But there was something missing.

Life.

Typhus' small hands looked huge holding the little creature. He held the baby steady at the surface and gently cleansed him, let the water wash over its pink and blue skin. Washing away the sticky blood and gelatin of birth.

Typhus Morningstar closed his eyes. Smiled.

"Come on, little fella. Time to be on yer way." Opened his eyes again. Looked down.

He held the baby's arms to its sides with the slightest pressure, his left hand moving up and down along the child's right arm in a sweeping caress. Its smooth skin yielded to his touch like clay, gradually melting to its side. Seamlessly. He repeated this process with the left arm until both sides were a perfect match. Then Typhus focused on the legs, stroking and smoothing the soft flesh into a single fat leg, his gentle hands molding the unborn child's figure into a swooning teardrop. Next were the shoulders. So smooth. So trusting. Blending into the neck so perfectly. Exactly like wet clay.

Last was the head.

Nose and mouth extending into one. Lips disappearing. Eyelids vanishing over wide, round, flat, staring eyes. Cheeks flattening. Smooth. Perfect. Warm.

Typhus held the newly shaped fetus underwater. As the head went under, there appeared a moment's struggle—but there's always a slight struggle in waking moments, Typhus acknowledged. The legs, now a tail, thrashed about. Mouth bubbling, horizontal slits opening where ears used to be, head bucking. Typhus held fast, stroking the creature ever gently till it calmed. Cooing. Said the thing that he always said at this point:

"They gave it to me, but I gave it back the best I could."

He sang as the baby finished its changing time, its water birth. The song he sang was of a religious nature, but he placed no significance on the words. He just thought it was a pretty tune, something sweet to sing as he delivered his children. It put them at ease, or so it seemed.

> *Jesus, I'm troubled about my soul*
> *Ride on, Jesus, come this way...*

The tiny catfish was pure pink and rapidly calming now, its tail experimentally flicking at the currents of the top waves with hungry curiosity. With a kind of yearning.

It was time.

Typhus let go. A tear rolled down his cheek. It was always hard to let the babies go.

Swimming now. Towards Algiers. Disappearing from sight. Beneath sparkly slivers of yellow light.

> *Troubled about my soul...*

Again, and with great love, Typhus Morningstar reached into the burlap bag. A light drizzle began to fall.

# CHAPTER TWO

## *The Note*

The song began like all melodies, with a single note.

On this day, at this hour and this particular moment, the note was E flat. Unaccompanied, the note betrayed key neither minor nor major, betrayed no key at all. Beginning soft as breath and held, gaining strength and definition with only the slightest quiver. Not *vibrato* in any premeditated way, just the lightest jangle of the player's nerves, his humanity, his heartbeat.

Then a fade.

As if the note were giving way to something greater than itself, greater than its own simple purity and strength; weakening ever gently. Giving up quietly, submitting to its own misinformed sense of futility, going back to earth, to the simple clay of dumb beginnings and answerless endings.

§

The player considers the note. He cannot sustain. There is no reason. But the weakening tone is somehow unfinished. Like a spirited pup born too soon, too small and too weak to live, knowing nothing of life but clinging to it anyway; stupidly, stupidly—fighting for its chance but not knowing why, not understanding what sort of thing the chance is. Not knowing anything. But knowing everything it will ever need to know. Its heartbeat struggles, weakens, slows—but does not stop. And then:

The fade is cut short, interrupted by a flurry of sound; a quick burst heading skyward, headstrong and unexpected, defying the futility of the E flat, exposing a minor key in the subtlest way, transforming the uncertainty of E flat into a belligerent D. Holding. Dipping. Leaping and crashing—but not crashing.

*Saved.*

Gliding back down to...E flat again? No. A. Holding again—but not holding. Bending, wavering, wanting to climb too high but resisting—spinning somehow without moving up or down, pulling something from deep within the player, bringing this thing out of the cornet, out *through* the cornet. All this in a single note. A single, simple, ordinary note.

A.

But not A. Something about the A is different. It is a different world from the world of the E flat entirely. Something about the way the player arrived at the A. Not *that* it was discovered, but *how* it was discovered. Something about the player's reaction to the note, the lightness of mind and intensity of spirit it brought him for just a moment. Something about the way the instrument reacted to the touch of his lips, the way it trembled in his grip. The note was A.

*A.*

But not A.

This is where things change; completely, irrevocably.

But with change comes clarity. And with clarity comes understanding. And with understanding comes questions. And with questions of this kind comes a sort of madness.

E flat. Transition. A.

Questions.

The player stops.

He is drunk. He does not know what has happened. His mind is not ready for the questions, he doesn't want to hear them. He reaches for his bottle of train yard-grade gin but only knocks it to the floor; the bottle doesn't break and he doesn't pick it up. He lays his horn on the pillow, he lays his head next to the horn; it is inches from his eyes. His eyes are red, he feels tears building there but doesn't let them through. They close. He strokes the horn. He falls asleep. Gin drips to the floor, the bottle on its side.

He will not remember the A. He does not know that he has seen the face of God.

Clarity. Questions. E flat. A.

Something is created but stillborn; promised but denied.

Awaiting rebirth, it has all the time in the world. What did not exist does now. An abortion dumped in the river, letting go of life for now but knowing that new life will come. In time.

Differently. Irrevocably.

Buddy Bolden snores.

# CHAPTER THREE
## *Man of God*

**N**oonday Morningstar named his children for diseases. From oldest to youngest they were Malaria, Cholera, Diphtheria, Dropsy, and Typhus.

There'd been those in the Parish who'd publicly chided Father Morningstar for the naming, declaring it cruel to name innocent children for that which reminded a body only of suffering and death—but to Morningstar the names were a tribute to God's glory, plain and simple. It didn't matter if nosy folk didn't understand or approve. God understood everything just fine.

Morningstar saw life as a trial and death as a reward, a bridge to paradise —and he saw God's mysterious afflictions of the body as holy paths to that salvation. Disease may be a source of pain and hardship on earth, but what can be kinder and more blessed than a shortcut to heaven through no fault of your own? What could be a more magnificent display of God's powers than the merciful, invisible insects that float through the air to infect the body, guiding you to your last breath and on to reward?

Plus, the diseases had such pretty names.

Strange name-giving aside, Noonday loved his children deeply and they returned his love in kind. He was a gentle and loving father to them and they, in turn, proved the wonders of God to him everyday. God had been generous, in His way, with every one of them. All were healthy and happy children—save for Cholera, who died after only two months on this earth, ironically, from cholera.Although he believed it wrong to admit a favorite, Father Morningstar secretly saw his youngest as the gem of the lot. Although Gloria had died on the occasion of Typhus' birth, Morningstar knew his wife would have gladly consented to that sacrifice to bring a creature so magical into the world. It was only a shame she hadn't lived to know her little Typhus, her reason for dying.

About a mile and a half northwest of Congo Square, the Morningstar family's tiny two-room house sat on a too-big piece of marshy ground too near where the Bayou St. John met the Old Basin Canal—a manmade waterway dredged from the bayou to the city's heart nearly a century ago. It was a poor choice of real estate, prone to flooding—but the Morningstars had few possessions to lose and, in a pinch, could always relocate to the little church near the Girod Street potter's field for the few days it took the waters to subside. Building a home on flood ground was something few were foolish enough to do, but the recklessness of the choice rewarded the family with unprecedented privacy in the fast growing city. Right out the front door was pure, wild beauty; dark, soft ground alive with salt meadow codgrass, water hyssops, and towering cypress trees—the latter entwined with boskoyo vines that proudly sprouted their sweet smelling violet and white flowers. At night there was only blackness, but if you ventured out with an oil lamp the ghostly trumpet-shaped blossoms of moonflowers would make themselves known.

The two rooms of the Morningstar house had their work cut out for them with five occupants to accommodate, so functionality was the rule. The larger was for sleeping and storing—the littler one for cooking, eating, and praying. The living water of the bayou could be strained then boiled, then used for washing or drinking. There was no real need for anything more—it was a fine place to live.

Tonight the timid hum of the children's sleeping sounds offered guilty comfort to Noonday's weary heart, and the stove fire failed to relieve his chill. He meditated on the glowing embers as they struggled to maintain orange— but meditation and prayer did not soothe on this night. He stabbed gently at the burning wood with a pointed iron, absently noting the fluttering patterns of white as ash broke apart and drifted to the stove's base.

Earlier today, Noonday had done a thing that had brought shame to his heart, having put his own well-being above that of an innocent. Called to the home of Sicilian immigrants, he had believed he was to perform the last rites for a fatally ill child, a common enough sort of call. But when he entered the house a smell like burning compost hung in the air and a heavy sense of dread settled into his bones. The child appeared asleep in its crib as Noonday read aloud from Matthew 18:

*"Whosoever therefore shall humble himself as this little child, the same is greatest in the kingdom of heaven.*

*"And whoso shall receive one such little child in my name receiveth me.*

*"But whoso shall offend one of these little ones which believe in me, it were better for him that a millstone were hanged about his neck, and that he were drowned in the depth of the sea."*

At that, the child's eyes sprang open to lock with his own.

It was in this moment of eye contact that Noonday heard the voice of Jesus telling him to leave, telling him that to stay would mean to sacrifice himself in vain, to make his own children orphans—and The Savior's tone had not been gentle in the telling. Noonday had often heard the nagging voice of God in his head, had never before questioned it. But the kind of blatant abandonment suggested by his God today felt wrong to him. The words of the reporter who'd stopped him outside the house had echoed his own thoughts; this was God's business—and Noonday Morningstar had dedicated his life to such business. It was not his place to turn tail and run, even at the insistence of Jesus Christ Our Lord and Savior Himself. What is a man of God to do when the clear instructions of The Savior conflict with the plain feelings of right and wrong that God himself has placed in his chest? If there was an answer to this question, he dare not seek it in the eyes of his children. This was a burden he must carry alone.

"Father?" Typhus was standing in the doorway. Noonday couldn't guess for how long; Typhus was such a quiet thing.

"Yes, son?"

"You're crying."

Noonday had been unaware of his own tears until that moment. "I suppose I am," he offered his son with an embarrassed smile.

"Can I help?"

These three words carried unintended poignancy, and, as always, Typhus' simple kindness offered simple answers. The boy truly amazed him.

"You already have, Typhus. I love you so much." He picked up his son in a hug. "I have to go out for a little while. House call. Unfinished business."

Typhus looked alarmed. It was unusual for his father to leave on "house calls" after dark.

"Bring me with you." Typhus' tone implied instruction rather than request.

"Not tonight, little man. I won't be long. I promise."

"Daddy?" Typhus rarely called his father "Daddy". It was his way of pleading.

"Son, I said no."

"But Jesus doesn't want you to go."

The words brought a chill to Morningstar's heart, but he was not surprised by them. Typhus had the gift of understanding.

"I know, Typhus. But He'll thank me later." "I think I should go with you."

"Listen to me, son. I need you to stay here and take care of your brother and sisters. Will you do that for me?"

A pause. "Yes, father."

"That's my little man. I'll be home before sun up. Now, get back to bed."

Noonday Morningstar kissed his son on the forehead, then went into the larger room where Malaria and Dropsy still slept. He noted with a frown that Diphtheria had snuck out again. He kissed the two before grabbing the family bible and lighting up a small lamp that was rusted red but perfectly functional. Walked out the door and into night.

Typhus threw some sticks on the fire, watched them turn white beneath the weight of orange flame.

He crawled onto the large, straw-stuffed mattress between his brother and sister. Found his homemade pillow; his own multi-purpose invention. The little burlap sack was originally constructed to hold coffee beans, but could also be stuffed with straw for sleeping—or filled with unborn babies for transporting and water-birthing. He held it tight to his face and smelled the river in it. He reached over and stroked the hair of Dropsy. It helped a little.

Typhus Morningstar did not sleep, but he did dream.

Although he knew disobeying his father would yield consequences, he emptied the contents of the pillow at the foot of the bed and stood up. Went outside without benefit of light, carrying the empty all-purpose sack with him. He sensed he might need it.

Found his bike in the dark.

# CHAPTER FOUR

## *Dominick's Affliction*

Caught in the dank grip of an unusually warm October, the City of New Orleans had already been on edge and looking for a fight when the murder of Police Chief David Hennessey brought things from a simmer to a boil in the fall of 1890.

Eighteen Sicilian immigrants were arrested that October, but not until March of 1891 did eleven of them stand trial. The trial itself had been a fiasco; peppered with threats and assaults on witnesses, jury tampering and more, leading to two dismissals for lack of evidence, six found not guilty, and three released through benefit of a hung jury. The acquitted men were scheduled for release on the following afternoon, but such reasonable resolution was pre-empted by an open letter that appeared in the morning edition of *The Daily Picayune*. Penned by the Mayor of New Orleans himself, the letter was, in essence, a thinly veiled call to arms against the soon-to-be-freed defendants.

Within hours of the paper's arrival at newsstands, an initial crowd of five thousand assembled at Clay Statue, where a host of dignified speakers eloquently whipped mild hearts into murderous lather. By noon the mob had made its way to the prison at Congo Square, its eventual number surpassing twenty thousand.

At Congo Square, a group of seven professional bounty hunters (employed, it was rumored, by the cronies of Mayor Shakespeare himself) enlisted an unfortunate prison guard by the name of Beauregard Church to act as their guide, at gunpoint, through the lightless jail. The vigilantes soon selected eleven victims; eight shot down on prison grounds and three dragged into the square to be hanged for the amusement of the mob. One of the hanged men, Antonio Carolla, appeared already dead—perhaps from fright—when the men placed the noose around his neck.

In effect, eleven men—whose guilt or innocence was never established—were tried, convicted, and executed by the local press and the Mayor of New Orleans.

§

Marshall Trumbo, a good man in his heart and by his nature, found himself deeply burdened by his own role in the slaughter of the Sicilians. A reporter for the *New Orleans Item*, Trumbo knew that to stir racial tensions in the sweltering city would be a reckless act—still, he had forged ahead with the rest and now lived with his guilty heart. But on the day after the massacre, Trumbo believed he'd found potential hope for redemption in the form of a sick child.

The one-year-old son of the twice-murdered Antonio Carolla had contracted a mysterious illness on the afternoon of his father's death. Hoping to lighten his conscience by somehow aiding the Carolla family in their darkest hour (and perhaps simultaneously satisfying his employer's thirst for saleable melodrama), Trumbo took to the home of the boy and his mother with pen and paper in hand.

Trumbo's gallant mood sank sharply upon his arrival. The boy was tiny and thin and the color gone from him, his eyes closed tight, an unnerving grin stretching his lips nigh ear to ear. It was explained to Trumbo by the doctor in attendance—who applied leeches to the child's torso with appalling calm—that the grin was merely a contortion brought on by recent fits of convulsion.

Due to the child's apparently dire condition, several men of the cloth had been called to the home since the day before—all staying briefly and leaving abruptly. The man of God currently in residence was one Trumbo knew from a prior assignment, a priest called Noonday Morningstar.

As Father Morningstar droned out a verse from his open Bible, the boy's eyes shot open with fear or rage or a mixture of the two. Trumbo thought he heard the child whisper something angrily at Morningstar. In apparent response, the preacher shut his Bible, crossed himself, then exited quickly, mumbling something about a forgotten prior commitment. While the doctor fiddled diligently on with his collection of leeches, Trumbo followed after Morningstar—supposing the preacher had made some private spiritual diagnosis.

Moving up quietly from behind, Trumbo placed a hand on Morningstar's shoulder; the unexpected touch causing the taller man to spin around with a gasp. Trumbo apologized for spooking him, then got right to the point.

"Pardon me, Father, but please tell me what you saw in that house that has alarmed you so." Morningstar at once pulled back, then took a breath and seemed to relax. Before speaking, he looked around to see if anyone else was close enough to hear.

"You a newspaper man, sir?" His voice was low and gentle.

"Yes, Father Morningstar. Trumbo's my name—I have interviewed you in the past if you will recall, regarding the sharp increase in cholera deaths last year. But you have my word that I will keep whatever it is you tell me today in the strictest confidence if you so wish."

"I don't believe that for one minute, sonny," the preacher said with a thin smile.

"I understand, Father." Trumbo's tone softened. "It's true that I came here for a story, but after what I've seen—I just want to help."

Morningstar's demeanor softened in kind.

"You seem like a nice boy," he said. "Do yourself a favor and stay out of that house. Those doctors can't help that young 'un. Neither can I. There's something wild in there. Something dangerous to the souls of men. Something absent of God—or too full of God. Stay away from that place, Mister Reporter. There's no story in there. Only death." He turned to leave.

"If you are a man of God, sir—"

Morningstar stopped but did not turn to meet the reporter's eyes.

"If you are a man of God—how can you leave that young child's soul in danger, as you say?"

Morningstar's eyes then met Trumbo's—and there was ice in the connection. "That boy's soul is lost, sonny. This is God's business now."

"But isn't *your* business God's business?"

The preacher stepped close—allowing Trumbo's full appreciation of his larger stature. His voice remained low and even:

"Sonny, I hear the voice of God every day of my life. Sometimes every minute of every day. Sometimes I wish the Good Lord would shut the hell up and leave me alone. But I answer his call, and I do his bidding. It is my lot."

An awkward pause balanced in midair between the two. After a few moments he continued:

"Sonny, listen to me. When I was in that place I did indeed hear the voice of Jesus Our Savior. Would you like to know what He said?"

Incredulous, Trumbo answered, "I would indeed."

"The Good Lord said, 'Get the fuck out of this house. Now.' Print that in your damn paper." He left without another word.

Finding himself unable to follow Father Morningstar's sensible example, Trumbo walked back to the house on shaking legs—and entered on an appalling scene.

The boy was sitting up in his crib, pulling leeches from himself and throwing them in the direction of the doctor. Shielding his face with one hand while hurriedly packing his medical equipment with the other, the doctor paused only to stomp a stray leech before running out the door. The mother was screaming.

The child then vaulted over the side of his crib and did what appeared to be a dance before stopping suddenly to face Trumbo. Said what sounded like:

"Lakjufa doir estay?"

Trumbo turned to the mother— "Madame, do you speak English?"

"Yes. Some." Her voice was shaken, but she made an attempt to calm herself for the benefit of her uninvited guest.

Trumbo spoke slowly and precisely: "Is your son speaking in a language that you know?"

"It is not Sicilian if that is what you ask."

"How long has he been speaking?"

"He only one. Before today, he no speak."

"Not at all?"

Tears flowed freely down her cheeks as she replied:

"Before today he no walk either. Only crawl. Now he run. Dance."

The pair looked back at the boy, who'd begun clucking like a rooster. Trumbo instinctively backed away from him—to his horror, he noted the child's mother had done the same.

The child interrupted his performance to take another step towards the reporter.

"Lakjufa doir estay?" His voice was high in timber, but still far too deep for a child his age.

"I...don't understand."

"Lakjufa doir estay? Lakjufa doir estay? Lakjufa doir estay?" the child insisted, stepping closer with each reprise. Trumbo felt a strong urge to make a dash for the door as the doctor and preacher had done, but the pathetically desperate eyes of the mother paralyzed his movement.

"I'm sorry," he said finally.

The child rolled his eyes and let out a final squawk before quickly extracting a piece of charcoal from the stove's belly with pink little fingers. Dropping to all fours, he rapidly scratched seemingly random letters and numbers to the floor with the coal:

U UERI NAD PTEL FUYQ LORD
EAF VULCFOL IYLRLCO AFN
EFEHDS SNUB STGSY ORTET
HSONU ETKDS BCSHE EOAOK
EREH ESRE PEYR EVWE
4X5X4/4X4X1

The boy then leapt into the air and back over the rail of the crib, landing in a fetal position with a soft thud, immediately falling into a deep sleep. Mutually dumbfounded, the two could only stare at the child's still form for several moments, not knowing what to expect next.

Trumbo took pencil and paper from his bag to write down, for the record, the nonsense message the child had so frantically scribbled on the floor.

After several moments of no new horrors, Anabella Carolla dissolved into a fresh wave of tears. Not knowing what else to do, Trumbo cautiously placed his arms around her. She did not resist; in fact, she hardly seemed to notice he was there. "Ma'am," Trumbo offered uncertainly, "I will summon another doctor..."

"No, no, no. It no use. This is third doctor. And fourth priest. Priests no longer come. Is why this one a negro. He my baby's last hope. And he go too."

"Listen. I will be back. And I will bring help. Trust me, dear, I will be back."

"You will not be back. Is all right. Understand."

"No. I will be back. I swear it." Trumbo turned towards the door and added, "My name is Marshall Trumbo, reporter for *The Item*." To his surprise he felt no sting of shame in stating his credentials.

She smiled weakly, "You are good man, Marshall Trumbo, reporter for *The Item*. You come back." And then, after a moment, "I am Anabella Carolla. My boy is Dominick. He is good boy."

"I know who you are, dear. Stay with your son and don't lose hope."

He left her, strange thoughts whirring in his head on the long walk home. Trumbo had gone to the Carolla house that morning in search of redemption, but the current workings of his mind seemed only to spell damnation.

He'd heard strange stories from reliable sources about an abortion doctor in the red-light district who went by the name of Doctor Jack. As the stories went, Doctor Jack was a medical doctor of the lowest possible esteem; not only was he a negro who made his living snuffing the hapless unborn from the wombs of whores, he was also a known witch doctor, catering to the superstitious needs of the city's voodoo-worshipping African population. Trumbo considered himself a good Christian who never took stock in such things, but what he had seen today was not possible. A witch doctor, he conceded to himself, may be this poor family's last hope.

Convinced it would be wrong not to help—by any means—an innocent mother and child victimized by matters so clearly beyond the reach of scientific or Christian methods, Trumbo resolved to risk damnation. Perhaps, he thought, it is not wrong to fly in the face of a God who would allow such an abomination to occur on this earth. Perhaps, he nearly concluded, God is not at all the benevolent being that his well-meaning parents had taught him to believe in so unquestioningly as a child.

Marshall Trumbo lowered to his knees. He wanted desperately to pray. He found that he could not.

Instead, he wept.

# CHAPTER FIVE

## *Gin Joint*

**F**urnished with crates meant for produce and one square table salvaged from a junked riverboat and bought with a dollar, Charley's gin joint always managed an empty feeling about it, even on weekends when the crowds pushed in. Wooden crates filled with barber supplies (along with others containing cheap booze) pressed tight and high against the back wall near a pump, basin, and pail; the three purposefully grouped together at the ready. The air was hot and hazy from home-rolled cigars, eight flickering oil lamps giving smoke an appearance of impossible weight.

A fourteen-year-old boy played cornet every night of the week at Charley's; the sound of it being mostly sour, unrefined, crazy in pitch. The kind of noise people don't get paid to make.

Real musicians played for real dollar bills in a section of town centering approximately around and gravitating towards the point where Customhouse Street met Basin. Played for real dollar bills while pretty girls danced with little or no clothes on, enticing rich white men from out-of-town to put paper money in a hat, make their choice, bring a girl up the stairs for an hour or a night. This boy was not a real musician—and too young to be a part of that scene, anyway. So he blew for nothing at Charley Hall's every night, infringing on the ears and sensibilities of card players who were just drunk enough not to care. A girl about the same age as the boy but three inches shorter sat cross-legged near his feet; the only female in New Orleans in-love-enough to venture into a joint like Charley's. The whites of her eyes: nearly as yellow as her dress. Her hair: long, straight, black. Her skin: the color of coffee with a generous splash of cow's milk. Sucking on a cigar butt and looking sick, she appeared utterly lost in the god-awful noise of the boy's horn.

Being payday, the players were betting real money. Some pulled up ahead and some kept losing, but even on payday there's never enough money to make anyone significantly richer or poorer in Orleans Parish. This was one of the few blessings of being poor in the Parish; not enough money to get mad about.

Marcus Nobody Special rarely had the cash to pay for his swallows, and so was fussing with Charley again. "This damn rotgut liquor ain't worth more than a gravedigger's bad credit anyhow."

"If ya don't like it ya can drink and not pay some-other-damn-where," countered Charley, who poured Marcus a fresh snort just the same.

*Bap. Bap-bap. Buh-bap, bap, buh-bap.*

A knock on the back door. A secret knock, a passcode for members. Gin joints like this were not strictly legal and faced away from the street for a reason. Charley unbarred the backdoor to reveal the imposing figure of Beauregard Church.

Pre-liquored up for reasons of economy and grinning like a skull, Beauregard carried with him an old leather sack containing a few odd items meant for luck, ready for a few hands with the boys.

"Damn, Buddy—cain't you play that thing any quieter? Have a little respect for the dyin', wouldja?" Beauregard pointed to a large bandage covering the left side of his head. The kid, Buddy Bolden, stopped blowing momentarily, and the sudden absence of sound turned the girl's face tragic.

"I think it's beautiful," she said, with eyes wet and dreamy. "Man, that's what I call true love!" one of the card players piped up. A round of wheezy snickers filled the room.

"Let the boy practice, Beauregard," said Charley, still smiling. "If he don't, he won't get no better—then we'll all be hurtin' for a much longer section of time."

Snickers blossomed into full out laughter as Buddy stabbed thick air with the loudest, most annoying note his skinny body could push clear of the horn. The girl smiled triumphantly and Beauregard winced mightily.

Like most in his profession, Charley the Barber possessed some basic doctoring skills and so walked over to Beauregard with a look of mild concern. "Let me have a look at that, old man." Beauregard sat low on a crate near the basin so Charley could remove his bandages and clean the wound, dabbing away dried bits of blood and skin with a dampened cloth. Marcus looked away—he saw dead folk every day, but the sight of real human suffering always made him uneasy. Charley applied fresh cotton and cloth to Beauregard's head and Marcus sighed with relief.

Before an hour could pass, Beauregard found himself down to his last four nickels and dozing off with a jack, two tens, a five, and a four held loosely in his right hand.

BAP! BAP! BAP! BAP! BAP! BAP! BAP!

A knock on glass, hard and fast and not in code. Beauregard's droopy eyes propped open, wide and quick. Buddy stopped playing; everyone instantly quiet without need of being shushed. Though it wasn't in code, the knock was familiar. A cop knock.

The girl jumped to her feet as a lone mosquito broke the silence; flying too near an oil lamp, crackling into oblivion.

"Goddamn," whispered Charlie, pressing extra hard on the "damn."

Marcus scratched thoughtfully at the hole where his nose used to be. "Prob'ly nothin', cap'n," he offered quietly to no one in particular, attracting a handful of irritated, nose-wrinkled glares. *Damn their noses*, thought Marcus.

Spell of quiet.

Then:

BAP! BAP! BAP! BAP! BAP! BAP! BAP!

This time accompanied by unintelligible, muffled shouting.

"Lord, Lord." Charley shook his head with casual dread before snuffing all but one of the hanging oil lamps. "C'mon, boy," he said, looking at Buddy. The usual drill was to march Buddy out, explain to the copper that Charley was giving the boy a horn lesson, that the time had slipped away and he hadn't realized the hour. Charley opened the door leading from the backroom to the barbershop, just enough for himself and Buddy to pass through.

The man outside was no cop. White fella; dressed nice, built thin.

Charley's mood dropped from nervous to put-out. *What's this dumb cracker want this time of night?* "Closed!" yelled Charley towards the assaulted but so-far-unbroken pane of glass positioned decoratively across the door's upper third—as if this fancy white cat might be looking for a haircut in the dead of night from a black barber who doesn't even cut white people's hair.

BAP! BAP! BAP! BAP!

Louder than before this time, near to breaking glass.

"Son of a *bitch*," Charley spat, barely under breath. Then, louder; "Don't be breaking my damn glass, now! I'm comin', I'm comin'!" He walked to the door quickly, turned the key, cracked it.

Turned on the Uncle Tom way of talking that grumpy white folks seemed to like so much:

"Sir, if we's makin' too much noise, I's shore sorry. I's just giving some music lessons to the boy." Charley motioned to Buddy who stood by the back door, smiling and waving his horn perfectly on cue, "and I guess we just—"

"Are you the one they call Doctor Jack?"

"Am I the…? Well, no sir. No, I ain't—"

"I was told he would be here. It's very important that I—"

"No one here by that name, sir. Just me and the boy—I's just giving him a lesson and we went a little late is all—"

"I swear to you that I'm not a police officer. It's very important that I talk to Doctor Jack. Please." The man's voice was fake-calm, panic leaking through at the edges.

"Like I said, mister, we was just—"

"I'm not a police officer, damn you, but if you try my patience I can be provoked into providing one." Getting that all too familiar I'm-white-and-you're-black-so-do-as-you're-told kind of huffiness—but there was also a cold desperation in the man's eyes, and this fact rang a bell of sympathy in Charley's cautious heart. "Now, please," the intruder continued, "understand that I mean you no harm. This is very important business."

Charley the Barber looked the man up and down, then asked, sans Uncle Tom, "What sorta business?"

The man let out a breath of relief, measured his tone, "Medical business. Emergency medical business. The kind that most doctors don't do. It has to be Doctor Jack. Please." He placed a hand on the door as if to push it open.

Charley softened his eyes, but held the door firm. Said:

"No coppers?"

"No. Absolutely not. No police. I swear it." The man offered Charley his hand, but Charley only looked at it—pretty, soft, white, spidery little thing; not telling of a single day's hard work. Charley couldn't bring himself to shake it—afraid he might scuff it up. But he did open the door.

"Follow me."

Marshall Trumbo followed Charley through the darkened barbershop towards the backroom entrance where young Buddy Bolden stood, horn in hand. "I could hear you playing from outside," said Trumbo.

"Sir?" Buddy's voice sounded nervous. Wasn't accustomed to white folks talking directly at him in soft tones.

"I heard you playing. Sounded nice."

Catching the compliment as he opened the gin joint door, Charlie broke into gentle laughter. "You really *do* need a doctor. Lord, Lord! Sounded *nice?* Ha!"

Buddy Bolden grinned.

The door to the adjoining card room opened wide, and the first set of eyes to meet Trumbo's were the ones closest to the surviving lit lamp; pale brown eyes pounding like cool sun into his own. Trumbo found himself staring at a weathered, coffee-colored face framed with white blotchy hair, a terrible scar where a nose used to be. The urge to shudder came and went quickly, Trumbo fighting it off through force of will and sheer good manners. Charley lit a thin stick from the remaining lamp before making the rounds again, relighting the seven lamps he'd snuffed only moments ago. The flames caught quickly, and the lamps illuminated just fine. The girl refocused on Buddy with loving eyes; still looking sick, still smiling.

Charley made a move towards breaking ice: "This nice gentleman wants to know where he can find a person called Doctor Jack. Any of you fellas know what he may be talkin' 'bout?"

A beat. Then: Heads turned down, card game resumed. Beauregard pulled some cards from his lousy hand, slapped them down, said, "Hit me three times," when he should've just folded.

"Gentlemen," Trumbo started, a crack in his voice, "I'm not here to cause any trouble. I only—"

"And who might you be, sir?" The question came from the dealer, a middle-aged dark brown man with peculiarly straight hair that just touched his shoulders. The dealer laid down three cards for Beauregard without looking up.

"My name is Marshall Trumbo. I'm a news reporter by trade, but that isn't why I'm here. It's about the Carolla child—maybe you've heard—"

"Newspaper man, eh?" the dealer said, still not looking up. "You fellas did a helluva job crucifying those Sicilians. Shameful stuff, that."

Trumbo paused, decided on honesty: "Actually, I agree with you. That whole ugly business made me reconsider what I do for a living." Trumbo got the impression no one was buying that line of talk, however true it might be. No matter. "But I'm here about the child of one of the Sicilians—the man's name was Carolla..."

Beauregard, now wide awake and stone sober, laid down his losing hand with a grunt, "I'm done." Gave the reporter a hard stare.

"I've heard about the child," said the dealer, making a mental note of Beauregard's reaction. "What interest would newspaper folk have with that sort of trouble—other than for a good ol' eye-poppin' story? Sell some papers, a story like that, I guess."

"I was there today—at the Carolla house—looking for a story, like you said. But the doctors left. The priest called Morningstar—he was there, too—but also left."

The girl broke her gaze from Buddy momentarily to throw Trumbo a suspicious glance. "No one wants to help—and I promised the mother I would try. The boy—he's...well, he's in a desperate state. You wouldn't believe me if I told—"

"How does this Doctor Jack person fit in to this goodwill expedition of yours, sir?" the dealer interrupted, still looking down, still laying cards.

A moment's pause, then: "I had heard, well, I'd heard stories…"

The dealer laughed. "Stories, eh? Well, don't believe everything you hear, mister. Lots of superstitious folks in Orleans Parish, y'know. Yes indeed."

"Yes, yes, of course—I know that. But today I saw things—that, well, that gave me pause." He pulled a folded paper from his inner breast pocket, began to unfold it. "That one-year-old boy, a boy who before today could neither speak nor walk, scribbled letters of the alphabet on the floor of his mother's house. I wrote them down here." Trumbo held the page up.

"Lemme see that, mister," said the dealer.

Trumbo pulled it back. "No. I need to find this Doctor Jack fellow." Refolding it. "So please, if you would only—"

"What if I were to tell you that I was this Doctor Jack fellow, mister?" Eyes hard, yellow, streaked with red. Green with black in the middle.

Trumbo turned to Charley the Barber who nodded. Trumbo's hand lowered, holding the paper out to Doctor Jack, the dealer.

Jack unfolded it and looked hard at the words. "A one-year-old baby wrote these letters?" he asked.

"Yes. On the floor. With charcoal."

"Hmm." A pause. Beauregard and Marcus were looking over Jack's shoulder, staring at the sheet with wide eyes. After about thirty seconds, Doctor Jack refolded the page and attempted to hand it back to Trumbo. Instead of taking it, Trumbo only stared. Jack answered Trumbo's stare:

"Means nothing to me, Marshall Trumbo. Ain't no magic or hoodoo I never heard of. Just gibberish. Sure is strange a little baby wrote it—but it means nothing to me. I'm sorry."

Trumbo barely had time to open his mouth in protest when Marcus Nobody Special spoke up:

"Means something to me."

Doctor Jack's eyebrows lifted in amusement.

Trumbo: "Excuse me, sir?"

Jack smiled, shaking his head.

Marcus repeated, but this time louder, "I said: *Means something to me.*"

"Crazy old fool," said Charley the Barber. "Have another drink for free and knock yer own dumb ass out."

Marcus bristled at Charley, wrinkling his nose-scar clear up to double-ugly. "Shut yer dumb ol' face, you poison-peddlin', bad-hair-cuttin' good-fer-nothin'…"

Trumbo was getting uncomfortable. "I think it's time for me to go, gentleman. Thank you for—"

Doctor Jack: "Hold on, Mr. Trumbo."

"Yes?"

"Why don't you ask him? Can't hurt. Marcus ain't pretty but he's harmless enough."

Marcus instantly shifted his verbal assault from Charley to Jack, *"Ain't pretty?* Who you callin' *ain't pretty?*—you pig-assed, ugly-two-time, stank-nose, witch-doctorin'—"

The room erupted into laughter, even Trumbo managing a smile. Beauregard laughed enough to re-awaken the pain in his head, wincing through a grin.

"Settle down, old soldier, I was only funnin' you," said Jack, patting Marcus on the shoulder. Marcus stopped his deluge of insults long enough to consider the favorable reaction of the card players. After a few seconds, he turned to Trumbo, pointed at the sheet:

"Civil War code, that."

Laughter faded from the room.

A beat. Two beats. Trumbo: "I don't understand."

"On yer sheet of paper. It's Civil War code. I wouldn't have caught it myself, 'ceptin' the key is written there at the bottom. The numbers is the key, see. Dass right, mm hmm. Key right there in plain sight. Usually the key is committed ta mem'ry, never writ down. Makes the code tougher to break that way. But someone done give away the code by spellin' out the key. Means someone don't want the code to be too good a secret. Civil War stuff. It's how they delivered messages in the old times. In case the messenger was kilt or captured along the way. Old-timey stuff."

"You can read...? —I mean, how do you..."

"Don't be so shocked, mister," Beauregard said in a perturbed tone. "Lots of us dumb niggras can read just fine. And Marcus may be ugly, but he's sharp as a whip. Old war hero, too."

"Why thankee, Beau—" said Marcus before the word "ugly" registered— "You no-good, fat-assed, pecker-lickin', jail-housin'..."

Another round of laughter.

"What I mean to say is," Trumbo continued, "I wasn't aware that men of color were privy to Confederate ciphers during wartime."

"Don't feel bad, young fella," Marcus smiled, displaying the absence of two formerly prominent front teeth, "lots of white folk—and black folk, too—have a hard time believin' there were plenny of proud black Confederates in the South back in them days. I was as free then as I am now, sonny. And happy with my life the way it was—like lots of free black folk was. Didn't cotton much to that double talkin' 'mancipation proclamation. Ol' Abe hadda mind to ship ever' last one of us back ta Africa—a place I ain't never been and never cared ta go. Worst yet, when Abe couldn't get that idear ta fly, he was talkin' bout sendin' us all to *Texas*. Lawdy *mine!*"

Trumbo shoved the conversation hard towards its original path:

"Are you saying you can decipher this, sir?"

The gravedigger looked up at him. "Why, shorely I can. Yes indeed. Hand it over ta here." He snatched the paper from Trumbo's hand and flattened it out carefully on the table. "Spare a clean sheeta paper and pencil if you please, sir." Trumbo pulled a blank page from the notebook in his satchel, found a pencil. Beauregard got up from the table, offering Marcus his chair—Marcus huffed at the big man, but accepted the courtesy.

"Well. Now. Let's have a look at this thing. Hmm. All righty now." The group of men and the young girl gathered close around the old gravedigger. Wide-eyed and curious, like kids at a circus.

Marcus stared at the nonsense words on Trumbo's original sheet.

```
U UERI NAD PTEL FUYQ LORD
EAF  VULCFOL  IYLRLCO  AFN
EFEHDS SNUB STGSY ORTET
HSONU  ETKDS  BCSHE  EOAOK
EREH ESRE PEYR EVWE
4X5X4/4X4X1
```

"Yes, indeedy," he began. "See, you gotta put the letters in a square. The key—these numbers down ta here at the bottom—tell you how to make that square. Easy as puddin' and pie. Like so."

He drew what looked like a too-tall tic-tac-toe board within a rectangular border:

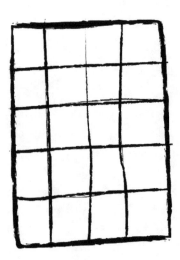

"See that? Says four by five by four. Means four times five—which comes to twenty—but four times. You kin tell yer on the right track cause the first four lines have twenty letters a piece in 'em if ya count 'em up right. Go ahead and count 'em. Tell me if I'm wrong, sonny."

Trumbo did the simple math in his head. Sure enough, the old man was onto something.

"And the second line of the key—four by four—but one time. Thass right, too," Marcus went on. "See? One row of sixteen letters right there at the bottom."

"Well, I'll be damned," said Beauregard. "You crazy, sly old devil..."

Trumbo stared at the nonsense words in wonder, counting letters: "Yes, I can see—but how do you decipher...?"

"I'm getting' to that, sonny." Marcus, slightly irritated, shot Beauregard a stern glance. "Watch and learn." Trumbo shut up. Beauregard tried in vain to conceal his amusement. Doctor Jack's expression lacked any trace of amusement at all.

Marcus methodically filled the boxes with letters in the same order as they appeared on the original sheet. "Trick is, you write 'em top to bottom, but read 'em left to right. See? And each individual line gets its own four-by-five box. Folla?"

The first line of letters filled its grid like so:

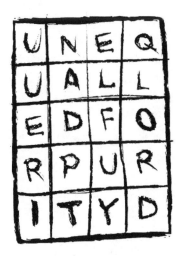

Marcus's eyes swung up to meet Trumbo's:

"Sir, I gotta ask again to be sure. A little baby wrote these letters?"

Trumbo said nothing. Only stared at the sheet in wonder. Nodded.

Marcus: "Lord, Lord."

The old gravedigger wrote the letters out in their new order beneath the rectangle:

UNEQUALLEDFORPURITYD

"Says, 'Unequalled for purity'. The 'D' at the end prob'ly first letter of the first word in the next box." Marcus drew three more boxes for the remaining lines containing twenty letters apiece, a smaller one—four by four—for the line containing sixteen letters. Then he began filling them with letters from the original sheet; from top to bottom.

By the time he'd finished, there was a dead silence in the room—soon broken by a small voice:

"It's an advertisement for coffee. Like this." Typhus Morningstar held up his multipurpose companion, a burlap bag originally made to hold coffee beans, manufactured and printed by the New Orleans Coffee Company. Doctor Jack smiled at the boy. "How long you been standing there, Typhus?"

"Just a little while—but long enough, I guess. Front door wide open."

Charley the Barber: "Shee-it!" Fishing through his pocket for keys, Charley scrambled towards the front door of the shop, cursing himself along the way for letting Trumbo's disruption distract him from relocking.

Typhus turned towards the little gal whose arm was still slung around Buddy Bolden's shoulder. "Daddy find out you in this place, he be mad," he told her.

The girl flicked the short remnant of her still lit cigar at Typhus with impressive accuracy, her arm arcing wide for greater impact, yanking hard against Buddy's neck in the process. "You tell Daddy and I'll whoop you good, you little runt. You shouldn't be out neither!"

Buddy winced, pulling away from the girl just enough to rub the afflicted side of his neck.

"I'm out *lookin'* fer Daddy. He gone," said Typhus, dodging the smoking butt with casual expertise and sounding not the least bit intimidated by his older sister.

Diphtheria Morningstar's anger instantly melted to worry. "Gone where, Typhus?"

"It's why I'm lookin'. Not sure."

Marshall Trumbo eyed Typhus' bag and held out a hand, "May I have a look at that, son?"

Typhus hesitated, but obliged: "I need it back so don't rip it er nothin', mister."

"I'll be careful."

Trumbo examined Typhus' bag. It was cropped at the top and the printing was faded, but the last two lines were clear—and matched the last two lines of Marcus' deciphering handiwork:

*Used by the best cooks*
*And housekeepers everywhere*

The bag smelled of river and fish, and Trumbo's arms were covered with goosebumps.

Diphtheria spoke, looking at Typhus but pointing at Trumbo. "That man said Daddy went to the place with the sick Sicilian boy today, Typhus."

Trumbo looked up from the bag and directly into Diphtheria's pointing finger: "Your father?"

"You said, 'the priest called Morningstar.' That's our Daddy." Her eyes were tearing with worry. "But you said he left?"

"Yes, he left. I'm sure he's all right, dear." Trumbo's eyes dismissed the girl's concerns and returned to Typhus' bag, as if mysterious answers might reside in its thick, rough threads.

Typhus gently pulled the bag from Trumbo's hands, said: "When he left the house tonight he said he had to take care of something unfinished. Said it was a house call."

"We best be going," said Doctor Jack abruptly, no trace of a smile left on his smooth face. "You know the way, Mr. Reporter. You lead. Typhus—you come, too."

"We're coming, too!" said Diphtheria in a clearly nonnegotiable female tone, holding tight to Buddy's arm. The young horn player resolved to his fate.

"All right then," said Doctor Jack—and then, to no one in particular, "come if yer comin' and stay if yer not. But let's git gone."

Marcus: "Well, I got me a date with a fish…"

"That's fine, Marcus. Go get that fish. We'll see you next payday."

"Sir, if I may ask," Trumbo began uncertainly. "If someone or something is trying to communicate through this child, why employ such peculiar method?"

"The method is the message," replied Doctor Jack. "Whoever or whatever wrote those words wanted the attention of certain people, and those people happen to be here tonight. The civil war code was for the benefit of our friend Marcus. The coffee advertisement was for Typhus. Could be someone else in this room connected, too—just ain't spoke up yet." He glanced quickly at Beauregard, then away. "No matter about that. Time to go."

Charley the Barber lifted the heavy wooden bar that secured the back door. "Y'all be careful, now. I don't like the sound of all this. Not one bit." The five made their way to the door.

"Wait." Beauregard Church talking.

Doctor Jack turned, raised an eyebrow.

"I got something belonged to the father. Might be what this is all about. It's in here." Bo-Bo reached into his leather pouch containing odd items meant for luck. Pulled out an old tin.

The square tin was graced with the image of a little white girl collecting pink flowers from a field where no flowers grew, just an endless landscape of yellow wheat stalks. Above her head were the words:

*Every drop's a drop of comfort*
*Is the verdict of all who drink out*

And she was surrounded by more words:

*Unequalled for purity*
*Delicacy of flavor*
*Fullness of strength*
*Used by the best cooks*
*And housekeepers everywhere*

Beauregard Church, longtime guard in the service of Orleans Parish Prison, was holding up a coffee tin in shaking hands. The tin was manufactured and printed by the New Orleans Coffee Company for the purpose of selling beans, but only Beauregard was aware that, at the moment, it contained the right hand of Antonio Carolla.

One of many odd items intended for luck.

# CHAPTER SIX

## *The Day Before*

The cells at Orleans Parish Prison are all exactly the same. Eight feet long, four feet wide, and seven feet high. There is a barred door exactly two feet wide. The cot is also two feet wide. A bucket, for toilet purposes, is the prisoner's sole companion, offering dubious and strong smelling inspiration for long hours in the dark.

It is always dark in the cells at Parish Prison. The cells are entirely without light, even of the artificial kind. Even when his eyes have adjusted to the complete lack of it, the prisoner cannot see from one end of the cell to the other. Can only smell his friend, the bucket.

Each day, the prisoner is locked in his cell at noon. He will stay there until seven-thirty the next morning. At seven-thirty, upon leaving his cell, he is given breakfast. Breakfast is a substance approximately the same color and consistency of the substance it will become when it is ready to leave his body later in the day. The smell of the food is different from the smell of the stuff that winds up in the bucket, but is equally inspiring.

After breakfast, there is work for about half the prisoners. Hard labor is what the prisoner hopes for at Parish Prison. Only the fittest are allowed work; the rest are placed in a large guarded room where the prisoner does nothing. There, he sits. He plays cards. He argues about things that don't matter. He talks about women. He talks about murder, rape, and assorted petty crimes. He laughs for no good reason. He boils from the inside out. He tries not to think. And thinking is all that he has.

65 hours a week are spent in the big room doing nothing. 103 hours a week are spent in the total darkness of the cell.

In one year, 5,356 hours are spent in the dark. 3,380 hours are spent on a bench in the big room doing nothing.

This is why morphine is in demand at Parish Prison.

Many of the prisoners have arrived with morphine habits, but many more will leave with them. You would think it would be the other way around.

The prison infirmary buys its various medical supplies, including morphine, from a drug firm owned by the warden's brother-in-law. There is good money to be made in prison pharmaceuticals. The pills are supposed to vary in strength so that the dosage can be decreased over time, gradually weaning the addict off the drug. This is a basic principle of rehabilitation. But the tablets do not vary in strength—in fact, the addict is given considerably more than he needs. Addicts only want their pain to go away, they don't want to die—so there are extra tablets floating around Parish Prison. They are like currency here.

5,356 hours in the dark. 3,380 hours doing nothing. One year.

Dark + Nothing = ?

In Parish Prison,

? = Little White Pills.

Antonio Carolla developed his morphine addiction at Parish Prison like so many others, but he is lucky. He has only been here for twenty-one weeks. He has not been convicted of any crime and was formally acquitted yesterday. Today he goes home to his wife Anabella and their one-year-old son Dominick. He knows the love of his little family will help him find the strength to beat the morphine in his blood. He knows Anabella's good Sicilian cooking will put the meat back on his bones. But first he has to get out of this place.

He is sitting in the dark now. Waiting.

# CHAPTER SEVEN

## *Run*

There's a dull throb in Antonio's head, an echo of this morning's white tablet. Reaching down, he feels around for the tiny goat skin pouch he keeps tucked at the insole of his left shoe. Pulls it out. Empties the contents into his right hand. By sense of touch he counts how many pills are left. There are two. He closes his hand around them. His most recent dose still dances at the fringes of his mind; he will save these for later.

A dull roar creeps into his cell. He assumes it's an effect of morphine, but it's actually the sound of shouting voices—in the thousands—outside the prison. The faint sound of gunfire crackles from beyond the walls of his cell as the barred doors of the prison begin slamming open, slamming shut; prisoners shouting, some in Sicilian, some in English, some in French. Antonio senses he will not be leaving Parish Prison today after all. In his heart, he knows it.

In consideration of this, he changes his mind about the two remaining pills. He swallows them quickly and washes them down with his own spit; they scrape down his dry throat painfully. This, he imagines, will numb the pain of whatever the mob winds up doing to him if it is not done quickly. It may even distract him from closely considering the inevitable.

He lies down on the cot. Thinks of his son, Dominick. Reaches up to the section of stone to his right where, twenty-one weeks ago, he etched his son's name with a sharpened spoon. Touching the letters brings a weak smile to his lips. Dom is a very bright and handsome boy. The morphine amplifies the wonderful memory of Dom's face, the way it used to light up when his father came home from the docks each night. Antonio knows he will not see his son's beautiful face again. His head spins from the morphine—Dominick and Anabella spin along for the ride. He does not cry. He is Sicilian. He will be strong for them. Even if they are only in his head.

Outside his cell door there is the sound of labored breathing. A key jangles in the lock. The door slams open.

"Go! Go! Go! Go! Go!"

The shouting comes from the guard called Beauregard, an African black as coal. Antonio has never heard Beauregard's voice in this excited tone and so barely recognizes it. It is usually slow, deep and smooth but now it is shrill and fevered. Beauregard only says the one word over and over, but still, Antonio doesn't understand. Then, finally, variation:

"You in here, Tonio? Answer, dammit!"

"Yeah." Beauregard negotiates Antonio's location on the cot by tracing his voice through the dark.

"Dammit, you stupid dago-wop, get offa that damn cot and get movin'! You got some visitors comin' that you don't *even* wanna know about! Get movin', dammit! *Now!*" Antonio has never heard Beauregard use words like dago and wop before, has considered Beauregard something like a friend in this place. He ponders the big man's pointed words and pauses just long enough for the guard to reprise his tuneless, one word overture—this time punctuated with a nervous stutter:

"GO! Guh-GO! Guh-GO! GO! Guh-GO!"

Something about the crazy rhythm of the stutter brings Antonio to his feet, legs rubbery from morphine and fear. He discovers he is exhausted though he hasn't significantly moved in hours. His own voice echoes off the walls of the cell, the sound of it detached—as if from a mouth other than his own: "Where…go?" Stupid-sounding echo.

"I don't know, dammit! *Hide!* Yer on your own. Just get movin' and find a place to hide till this thing blows over, *Ka-Peach?* Now, *go,* damn you!"

Antonio obeys, makes to leave his cell, bumps into Beauregard as he passes, mutters, "pardon." He is moving fast, but not too fast. The hallway is long and black—he has to brush his hands along the walls to find his way. After about forty steps, he reaches a familiar "T" in the hall—he knows this particular intersection. He knows that going right will lead him to the Big Room Where Prisoners Do Nothing 3,380 hours a year.

He goes left.

The shouting is louder now, but he can't tell if it is behind or before him. The stone and mortar of the prison hallway carries echoes funny, and the morphine makes it a carnival game. His recent double dose is kicking in hard now, raging and leaping in his brain. Antonio is running wildly through the hall, running without touching the walls for guidance, flailing his arms before him.

Antonio Carolla's eyes need more than what they are getting. They don't dare hope for light, but they do hope for variation in blackness, a slight difference in shade, a hint of depth. His pupils struggle to widen, convinced that if they can widen a bit more they may snatch up some elusive optic information. But there is no information for them to snatch. It is so damned dark in here. So goddamned dark.

Shouting is louder now. Voices closer. Without warning: information of the eye does appear.

The black carnival game of the prison hallway has acquired a slight orange glow. Antonio can now make out the texture of the walls. Dust and soot from some long ago fire are caked between the stones, obscuring mortar like creeping death, weakly gleaming with dull moisture. His eyes drink the orange glow greedily—though he knows it is bad news.

Behind him. They are coming close from behind. With torches and oil lamps. Orange light.

A rifle report booms through tepid air. Antonio feels it vibrate through the stone at his fingertips and the echo makes the sound as towering as a cannon blast. A scream. Another boom. The owner of the scream is now pleading. Antonio falls to his knees, crippled by fear, breathing hard. He knows this voice. It is his friend, Salvador Sunzanno. He hears Sallie cry in the wobbly, orange-tinted dark. Hears him whimper and beg. The men with torches only howl in response, a pack of wild dogs; they are out for blood, not for bargaining.

Another blast resonates along the walls, bruising wet air. Sallie cries no more. For a moment even the mob is silent. Then, whispering. Low tones. The voices twitter like feathers down the orangey curve of the wall. Sound carries well in this place, but not well enough for Antonio to make out the words. Even so, it is not difficult to understand their meaning. They are regrouping. They are planning their next move.

Antonio rises to his feet. Stares down the curve of the hall. The twittery whispers of the murderers almost comfort him; it's an oddly gentle sound. The orange glow is becoming duller now. The men are moving in the opposite direction, away from Antonio. He understands that they will be back this way again—there is not that much hallway to cover—but their error buys him time.

He spins around quickly; trying to get a good look at his surroundings before the bobbing haze of torchlight disappears. His eye catches something just before the glow is consumed by black.

About fifteen feet forward and to the left he thinks he's seen an anomaly in the wall; a smoothness in the midst of rough, irregular stone—probably a trick of the light or a phantom of morphine. He feels weird regret that the killers have gone in the other direction. He needs their light.

Carefully, he gropes his way towards where he thinks he saw the smooth spot. If it is real, if he didn't imagine it, it may be some sort of door or passage. This could be a good thing and it could be a bad thing, but at least it is a thing.

He runs his hand firmly against the wall as he moves forward, searching for the slightest change in texture. There is an abrupt transformation beneath his hand from sandstone to glass. He regards the transformation suspiciously and considers the morphine in his blood.

He tests the smooth surface with both hands, running his fingers against it, searching for clues to its purpose. Glass. It is exactly like smooth glass. He pushes against it. He slaps it with open palms. It is solid and thick. The anomaly is about four feet wide. It has no attributes of a door. It is *different* from the wall, but it is *of* the wall. Antonio Carolla wants to believe there is more to it than that. Needs to believe it.

*Does* believe it.

There is nothing in the glassy stone to pull or grip, so Antonio pushes hard. Throws his body against it. Again. Again. His shoulders and spine ache from the impact. It all seems so ridiculous, flirting in the dark with this weird bit of hope, hunted and cornered. This thing is not a door. It is simply a smooth spot in the wall. It may very well be a miracle, but it is not *his* miracle.

Antonio Carolla is lost. He is letting go. He can no longer entertain the possibility of escape. A useless smile stretches his cracked lips.

His legs buckle beneath him. He collapses, sobbing, against the smooth surface of the cruel wall, his exhausted body sliding easily to the dirty floor against it. He cries loudly now, not caring if Sallie's murderers will find him sooner, not caring that Sicilian men don't cry. Be done with it, he is thinking. "Come and get me, you bastards!" he shouts. He sits on the ground, his back against the smooth spot. Weeping. Lost. Eyes wide open for no good reason in the dark.

And then it moves.

Startled, he lurches forward and away. The glassy wall has moved approximately an inch and a half. He leans back against the wall, braces the worn soles of his shoes to the coarse dirt of the ground; pushes.

It *is* a door. Like the door of a tomb. It glides easily with a low groan, then stops. Just enough for him to squeeze his body through and in.

The door is about two feet thick. There's a greasy quality to it. Through the opening he sees the walls are turning orange once more; the mob is returning this way. He pushes the massive door from inside—incredibly, it shuts without a sound. It's possible they have seen him or the movement of the door. Antonio Carolla waits for long moments.

Long moments pass. He hears nothing. They have not come for him. He is safe for now. He believes he is safe.

# CHAPTER EIGHT
## *Beauregard Church*

"Which cell is it, niggra?" The butt of the Winchester rifle hits hard to Beauregard's blood-sticky head for the ninth time in less than five minutes. "Where's that dirty dago at, boy?"

Beauregard has no clue where Antonio might be. The last place he'd guess would be his own cell, but then you never know what a man might do with enough morphine jumping around his skull. Wherever he is, Beauregard has to take these crackers *some* place—he doesn't know how many more knocks to the head he can take.

With his head swimming from blows Beauregard pauses to rub his eyes, wipes some blood out. The gang's apparent leader mistakes Beauregard's pause for spite or laziness and lays another whack into him for luck or encouragement. The sound that comes out of Beauregard's mouth is so pained and pitiful that he fails to recognize it as his own:

*"There 'tis, dammit! There's the dago's cell! Now, have at 'im and stop smacking me with that damn thing already!"*

He indicates the open cell with a wave of regret. Though he knows it is far from likely, he fears Antonio might actually be in there waiting for them. *Dumb wop if it's true*, he thinks. Tears mix with blood on Beauregard's cheek as he crosses himself and watches the men swagger to the mouth of the cell, the rank smell of their murderous hearts sickening his own.

# CHAPTER NINE
## *The Cell Has No Walls*

The odor is foul in these new surroundings. Antonio's foot kicks against something that makes a dull clang and suddenly he understands the source of the odor. A bucket. Parish Prison standard issue. Recently used.

Theory: He is in an ordinary Parish Prison cell. Standard issue. He confirms this theory by sense of touch. Eight feet. Four feet. Cot. He stands on the cot. Touches the ceiling. Seven feet.

Standard.

The only difference is that there is no barred door. He steps down from the cot. Sits. His legs are trembling.

The cot is oddly warm, as if someone has recently slept here. He lies down on it—the cot feels good to him, it's almost like being home. He closes his eyes as if it matters. There is blackness either way.

Somehow, it is darker in this place than it was in the hallway. This is not possible. No light is no light. Blackness is blackness. But still, it feels darker. There is always something darker, he thinks. Idle thoughts. There is no time for philosophizing about varying degrees of total darkness. Antonio Carolla reflects purposefully, thinks of a plan.

He will stay here a day or two. He can go without food and water for that long. Then, after the authorities regain control of the prison, he will yank open the tomb-like door and surrender himself to the warden. The warden will have to turn him loose—he is, after all, innocent and recently acquitted of all charges.

Having a plan feels good and his heartbeat slows. His mind drifts in and out of sleep as adrenaline subsides and morphine transforms his tired muscles into pools of warm water. He curses himself for taking the last two pills so soon—he will suffer mightily in the coming days as the terrors of withdrawal begin. But it will be all right.

Drifting. The air and his skin join the warm water of his muscles. From force of habit, he reaches a hand up to the wall alongside the cot. Brushes his fingers against clammy stone. His fingers trace etched impressions:

D O M

He jerks awake. Adrenaline jumps back to life in his brain. This is wrong. This is very, very wrong. He continues to feel out the letters:

I N I C K

It is not possible that he is back in his old cell. He traces the letters again. He is wide awake. This is not possible. He must think.

He gets up from the cot. His legs wobble beneath him.

He walks to the other end of the cell. In this standard issue Parish Prison cell, he should only be able to take five steps. He takes six. Then seven. Eight. Nine.

Thirty.

Still, he walks forward. The cell has no walls.

*This is a dream of morphine,* he thinks. *It must be so.* He rubs at his eyes.

Upon lifting hands from eyes, Antonio Carolla sees the familiar starburst patterns that every human sees after rubbing his eyes in the dark. The pinpricks of phantom light within the confines of his eyeballs give him minor comfort. They are, at least, not black. He stares at the kaleidoscope designs that dance beneath his eyelids like will o' the wisps, focuses on them. He adores the light inside his eyes. It is light. Some kind of light. Its circles and patterns feel like silent laughter.

§

The torchlight of the seven vigilantes fills the cell with deep orange to reveal the body of Antonio Carolla, lying face down on the floor near his cot, not breathing. Beauregard stands back and away, still dizzy from blows, eases himself back into the hall. The men quietly tie Antonio's hands and feet, as they would any prisoner, and drag his body through the innards of the prison towards the light of day. In the square outside they fashion a noose, throw the long end of the rope over the low hanging branch of an ancient live oak. Their blood warms as the crowd roars its approval. Beauregard looks on, head in hands. He cannot believe they mean to execute a corpse. Neither the killers nor Beauregard realize that Antonio is not yet dead.

The noose is placed around Antonio's neck.

§

Light flares and spreads within the mind of Antonio Carolla. Bits of empty, dancing light explode and multiply, filling his eyes with a burning white. The light sears the backs of his eyes. Too bright. He rubs his eyes once more, hoping the whiteness will fade, but it only worsens. What was once perfect blackness is now perfect, excruciating light. It is all he can see. Is this what it means to go blind?

His eyes close and he feels the sun on his face. This is not possible.

He hears music.

§

The body of Antonio Carolla trails the comet of his skull, yanked up hard towards the heavens, noose snapping tight. His neck pops like a firecracker, his eyes fly open. The crowd shouts its endorsement. Antonio shakes and shudders but does not hear them. Does not see them. Only hears music. In his mind; he is not bound, there is no noose, strangers do not wish him dead.

The music in his head is that of a trumpet. Or cornet. A single horn chasing after a single elusive note. Holding. Dipping. Leaping and crashing—but not crashing. Saved. It is a trumpet that he hears. Or cornet. Like in a parade.

He sees nothing, only white light. Then a face. It's the face of an angel, the face of his baby son.

Dominick smiles at his dying father. Speaks: "Papa." His first word.

Antonio Carolla reaches up to touch him, finger to cheek. The skin of Dominick's cheek is soft as clay. The face is changing now.

Antonio Carolla watches as his son's face melts into the many shapes it will assume within its lifetime. From early childhood to adolescent boyhood to early manhood. The face becomes less sweet as it grows older. Lines form. Its gaze becomes complex and troubled. There is a longing in the eyes. There is a violence in the eyes. Antonio Carolla is looking into the face of a young man, a face that will someday belong to his now one-year-old son. The face has the pallor of death. It speaks:

"Jesus is mad, Papa. Wait for me. I will look for you in the water. I will find you in the storm. Jeeka bye boo." The future ghost of Dominick Carolla takes his father's hand.

The son leads the father to a wide green river. There are lights beneath its surface. The lights are dim but joyful, they are welcoming. Antonio is not afraid. He says to his son, "Goodbye for now."

§

The sun is going down on Congo Square.

Antonio Carolla is dead. His body dangles between those of two Sicilian compatriots, his wide eyes empty and blank. Trash and debris, remnants of chaos, give the impression of recent war. The square is empty of any living soul save for Beauregard Church.

Beauregard holds a dull knife in his hand, walks to the base of the tree, cuts the rope that suspends Antonio, gently lowers him to unsympathetic earth. The air is heavy and has no wind in it. Beauregard looks at the knife in his hand, stoops down to Antonio's body. Takes his hand into his own.

A hoodoo medicine man called Doctor Jack once told Beauregard of witches in Europe who refer to the severed right hand of a hanged man as a *hand of glory*—and that a *hand of glory* can work powerful magic. Beauregard figures Antonio might be due a little power in the next world—he'd certainly had none in this.

He slices into the wrist of his friend, finds it bloodless. From the ground beneath the hanging tree, liquid the color of rust bubbles up in a tiny spring.

In his mind he hears a baby crying.

# CHAPTER TEN
## *Keep This Letter Should Misfortune Befall Me*

621 Spain Street
New Orleans, Louisiana
March 18, 1891

My Dearest Brother,

I'm sure it must seem that I only see fit to write you when in a troubled state of mind. For this, I beg your forgiveness and tolerance, of which I know you will generously bestow. You have been so very good and patient with me, kind George.

I am afraid the story I must tell is one I cannot bear to convey in detail, even now, to you, my brother.

There are certain facts that I am obligated to pass on to the public as dictated by my duties as newsman, and yet I have not, and will not. To do so would, quite simply, at least, cost me my job; or, at most, my sanity. So keep this letter, dear brother, should misfortune befall me, that there may be at least some record of my deep misgivings during these dark days of Orleans Parish. And please accept my apologies for withholding any more detail than my shaken mind can now bear to impart even to you, my most trusted confidante.

The truth of actual events were never recorded by me or any other reporter in New Orleans, dear brother. To believe the evening editions would be to believe that such strange and final truths never occurred. And yet there were witnesses. Thousands of witnesses. But not one to my knowledge has spoken openly of it since. Only the tidy misrepresentation that has appeared in the papers have thus far passed the lips of the people at large. There is a palpable fear of the truth here that is frightening in and of itself.

The acknowledged events are these: The chief of police was murdered by a criminal group of Sicilians. The killers were apprehended, but were wrongly released on technical consider-

ations according to the letter of the law. Seeing the injus-
tice in the court's decision, the citizenry rose up and took
matters into its own hands, resulting in a most horrific
massacre on the prison grounds. But the devil, dear George, is
in the details. There is far more to it than mere mass murder.
I know, for I have seen. And yet, it is not the strange events
on the prison grounds or the subsequent dissemination of
misinformation that troubles me most.

On the day of the horrors, the one-year-old son of one of
the lynched Sicilians had contracted a mysterious and severe
illness. Before having learned this on the morning after, I
decided to meet with his mother, seeking comment on the death
of her husband. But there was no comment to be had. Instead, I
was subjected to happenings that are beyond my understanding,
both intellectually and spiritually. I do not know how to
explain the things I have seen. But I cannot forget, nor can
I do nothing. Decency calls me to action, even if such action
requires a perhaps graver indecency be committed.

I left this mother and child, but I gave promise to return
with help. And now I am here in my cottage on Spain Street,
writing to you, dear brother. Committing these thoughts to
paper gives me a moment's solace before I do what I know I
must do. I can hardly believe what it is that I plan, but I
must go forward for the sake of this poor mother and child.

To do God's work, I must dance with the devil. I do not know
if you will hear from me again, dear George. And if you do,
I cannot vouch for my future state of mind once the terrible
task is complete. Please take care in how you receive whatever I may say to you hence.

May God have mercy on my soul for even considering the
weird alliance I must now forge, albeit for the greater good,
with a man so clearly in league with devilish things.

Please pray for...
Your loving brother,
Marshall

## CHAPTER ELEVEN

## *The Tenant of the Tin*

Τhe band of six—Typhus, Diphtheria, Buddy, Beauregard, Trumbo and Doctor Jack—walked the nine blocks from Charley's barbershop to the Carolla house in silence, walked right down the center of Burgundy Street without passing a soul along the way. Uncomfortable thoughts zigzagged between them, unspoken. The street was slippery with recent rain and horseshit, little green blades of codgrass peeking up from between smooth rocks as if trying to fathom the wisdom in starting new life at this particular corner of the world.

No one had ventured to ask Beauregard about the contents of his tin. No one seemed to want to know. All they knew for sure was that Beauregard had been among the last to see Antonio alive, and that he now claimed to have something belonging to him.

In a coffee tin.

Uncomfortable thoughts zigged, then zagged. In silence.

The Carolla house sat not ten feet from the street, a small square of earth before it bearing only thin, wispy grass and a lonely date-palm. Sandwiched tightly between neighboring homes, the house was striking for the care with which Antonio had tended it during his short life. The interstices separating its joists were smoothed over flawlessly with mortar, the structure's flat, sturdy walls meticulously white-washed with lime. The roof shingles had been perfectly cut to the appearance of slate, the reflection of the approaching party's lamplights dressing their edges finely in dull iridescence. Firelight showed through the single window by the front door, its glow framing a figure on the stoop in hazy silhouette. A bible sat by the man's feet while the low moan of a thousand tree frogs warbled from afar.

Not one of the six could conceive of the turmoil in Noonday Morningstar's soul as he sat on that stoop, none could know what he had seen and heard in that place that night. Nor could they know that upon his re-arrival he had once again heard the clear and unmistakable voice of Jesus Christ Our Lord and Savior, and that those words had been: "I told you not to come back, stupid nigger. Now yer gonna reap it fer sure. You little shit. Himminy-haw-haw-hoo."

Noonday Morningstar sat with head in hands, his heart trying to reach beyond the cold words of his God, when a small hand laid down against his left shoulder alerted him to the fact that he was no longer alone.

"Jesus was wrong, Father," Typhus said. "You only come back because what's good in your heart told you to. Jesus is wrong. Jesus don't know. Even the Son of God can't know everything." Typhus Morningstar had the gift of understanding.

Morningstar did not look up, but his own hand reached up to his son's, gently covering it, pressing down firmly.

"Forgive me," he said; not to his God but to his son. On this night, Noonday Morningstar possessed a rare understanding that even Typhus was incapable of. He understood that not all in attendance would survive tonight, and he knew that the "who" and the "how many" of it would depend upon his own actions. He chased the useless thought from his mind, focusing on the matter at hand.

Morningstar stood up to scan the dull sparkle of eyes around him. Twelve searching eyes. Scared, confused. He didn't chastise Typhus and Diphtheria for not being home in bed with their siblings, but rather, addressed all six: "What the hell took y'all so damn long? We got ourselves a little job to do here." Then, after a pause: "It ain't too late. Not yet it ain't, no sir. Jesus be damned, this evil can still be fixed." Then to Beauregard: "What you got we'll be needing. So be ready with it." The fact that the preacher seemed to know Beauregard's secret brought a mixed chill of premonition and hope to the prison guard's heart. He nodded to Morningstar and took a step forward. Morningstar's gaze turned to the rest. Spoke softly:

"Each of you is here for a reason. This cast of characters ain't by chance. You all need to look in your hearts and do right by this mother and child tonight. When it's your turn to act, do so without thought. Act on instinct. And if God Almighty should speak to you directly, make like you don't hear. Follow your heart instead."

Buddy fingered his cornet nervously. He had believed his own reason for being here was to comfort a pretty gal worried about her daddy. But Morningstar's words struck a chord of truth for him—a simple truth that he didn't fully understand. But wasn't that the definition of faith? Simple truth beyond conventional understanding? Dumb truth believed for the sake of the belief itself? The question failed to fill his mind with sensible dread, but, instead, with odd purpose. Yes, Morningstar was referring to faith—but he was also asking them to turn their hearts from God. So what exactly was he asking them to place their faith in? Buddy's arm slipped around Diphtheria's shoulders and gave her a gentle squeeze. Pressed a bit of yellow fabric between forefinger and thumb, confirming to himself the existence of everyday stuff like yellow dresses.

Morningstar opened the front door and motioned the rest to follow. He left his bible on the stoop outside, the others carefully stepping over it as they made their way to the threshold of the house.

The tiny one room house was strangely cold inside, even with a fire in the potbelly stove that transformed black coal to raging white. Being a thin girl, Diphtheria instinctively wrapped her arms around herself. Buddy's arms took the hint and wrapped around her as well. Father Morningstar did not protest Buddy's familiarity with his daughter.

A few lamps hung from decorative chains, adding minimal light to the various grays that colored the walls. Expertly hung wallpaper displayed alien purple flowers, the paper hugging tightly to plaster except where a ravaged and peeling section turned up and away near the ceiling; evidence of ancient water damage. The floor was bare concrete except for an irregularly cut but beautifully stitched European rug that sat straight but off-center near the middle of the room, a defective scrap bought cheap at the French Market from a Sicilian colleague.

A bed for the parents stood two feet from the crib, separated only by a small table altar on which various religious icons were propped up in odd-shaped frames. Attached to the walls were brown-toned daguerreotype photographs depicting stony-faced men with thick black mustaches standing closely behind beautiful women with lost-looking eyes. The women in the pictures sat with hands folded carefully across their laps. Save for the bed and crib, there was precious little furniture in the home.

Anabella Carolla sat silent on the floor by the crib, her arms around her knees, her face down and buried between them. The only sound was a rhythmic tapping. The rhythm was familiar to Beauregard and Buddy—but out of its normal context neither could quite place it.

Doctor Jack recognized it immediately.

*Bap. Bap-bap. Buh-bap, bap, buh-bap.*

Over and over again. A secret knock. A desire for fun amongst friends. A plea for entry. Gentle but persuasive. Jack walked to the crib and looked over the edge of its smoothly polished, dark-stained rail. The child was lying on his back, eyes closed. There was rapid movement beneath the lids, flitting back and forth, telling of an urgent dream in progress. Thick red welts had risen behind the baby's ears. His little fist was rapping gently and absently, continuing the familiar rhythm against hard wooden bars. His breathing was labored, a film of sweat covering the tiny naked body that lay in a watery mixture of "chamber lye and tattlin'"—baby piss and shit. The smell of it was powerful and cut through the cold air like the blade of a dull, dirty knife.

Morningstar stepped alongside Jack. Motioned the root doctor to back away from the crib.

Rapid eye movement stopped abruptly. The child's lips contorted as his eyes shot open, connecting with those of the preacher. A harsh, adult voice came out of the tiny mouth:

"*Stupid fucking nigger. How many times do I have to tell you? This ain't yer scene, pops. Not for you. Not your place. I shall shit down your neck, Father. And I shall shit down the necks of your children as well. Mip kit wiggity fip fah—*"

Morningstar responded full-throated—his sermon-delivering voice—effectively cutting short the demon's rant:

"Go hence, thou who comest in darkness, whose nose is turned backwards, whose face is upside-down and who knowest not why thou has come."

"*But I do know why, Father!*" cackled the demon with a sleepy smile. "*Higgle biggle boo! Hot cha cha cha!*"

Morningstar continued undeterred, calm:

"Hast thou come to kiss this child? I will not let thee kiss him. Hast thou come to send him to sleep? I will not let thee do him harm. Hast thou come to take him away? I will not let thee carry him away." The preacher produced a small glass container two inches in diameter from his coat pocket, removed the lid and scooped out the majority of its contents with the middle and forefinger of his right hand. "I have secured his protection against thee with bloodroot, onions and honey, sweet to men but evil to the dead." He spread the sticky-sweet concoction over the child's sallow chest. Then, placing his fingers to his own mouth, Morningstar licked himself clean of it.

Doctor Jack, impressed with Morningstar's apparent knowledge of herbal magic, smiled weakly and looked at Typhus with lightly questioning eyes. Typhus only shrugged, suddenly wondering about the bible his father had left out on the stoop.

Morningstar turned to Beauregard: "The thing that you brought. Give it to me now."

Dazed by the scene before him, Beauregard snapped alert to remove the tin from his leather pouch and stepped towards the preacher quickly; nerves jangling, heart pounding. Dropped the bag with its remaining items intended for luck to the floor, freeing both hands so he could focus on the tenant of the tin.

Pulled the lid off. Dropped the lid to the floor along with the bag. Clangedy-clang on the floor. Reached into the tin. Looked around at the others. Looked at the two-dimensional, daguerreotype Sicilian faces that stared from the walls. Said:

"Don't ask me to explain this." No one did.

Zig.

Beauregard did not remove the severed hand of Antonio Carolla gingerly between thumb and forefinger, but instead grasped it firmly, as one might clasp the hand of a seldom seen friend. Spoke to the hand's former owner. "Well, old man, I sincerely hope this is what you had in mind." He gave the hand of Antonio Carolla to Father Morningstar.

Zag. A wave of doubt washed over Morningstar's mind—but he shook it off quickly. "The father will save the son…" he intoned with weary eyes. "The father will save the son. The father will save the son. This is not right. This must be made right."

Morningstar placed the severed hand of Antonio Carolla over the child's chest, covering the honey-mixed herbs. The demon let out a short, pained shriek, and then changed.

The face of the child focused on Beauregard with soft eyes, speaking directly to him in odd rhythm and gentle tone, nearly a whisper:

"*My brother, this, the second day of my birth, was not unlike your first—but of water—restrictive of motion till now, till this cutting of hand, this slicing of wrist, to deliver this now unto me with love in your heart as you have, this father's hand, this way out and above water in order to cleanse of the earth, in the form of this boy, the son of a friend, of father to son and to brother of brother and now for father once more, though first intent was desecration for luck and for hope of fortune not earned, the intent is now changed, a deed sharing sameness with sin born of love, committed in hate, by she who has birthed, of anguish and rage, respectively we, and now it is he who was born Thomas that must complete the circle today and tomorrow and tomorrow and tomorrow…*"

The cadence of the demon's nonsensical rant diminished eventually to a mumble and then to nothing, the child falling once more into rigid catatonia, eyelids fallen shut again; rapid eye movement returning with fresh vigor.

Lips, a straight thin line, betraying neither emotion nor reason.

Beauregard Church stood motionless, silent.

Morningstar offered a hand to the mother. "Stand up, Mother. So that you may watch your child be saved."

On wobbly knees, Anabella Carolla took the preacher's hand and pulled herself to her feet. She at once recognized the small heart-shaped birthmark below the middle finger of her husband's disembodied hand. "*My 'Tonio.*" She reached out to touch his pale index finger. Morningstar held her trembling hand back, his voice kind but firm:

"Shhhh. No. It will be all right. This is your husband's gift to your son." Then, after a brief pause: "He knew. Your husband knew. It will be all right now."

The child's breathing had become increasingly labored. Jack ran a finger across the smooth rail of the crib, looked down and in, whispered matter-of-factly and without expression, "*Babaku.*" A word for nameless African demons.

"No, Jack," responded Morningstar. "This is no pagan demon. A Christian one. And it has a name." As little Dominick's chest struggled to expand for air, the severed hand appeared to tremble of its own accord.

"The Christian demon has a name," repeated Morningstar. This time for his own benefit, a reaffirmation of things witnessed in dreams.

Dominick's chest stopped rising for air.

It was now clear that the autonomous movement of the hand was not illusion. A gentle massage of the child's chest. A caress from a dead father. Anabella Carolla wiped her eyes, allowing them to widen in terror or hope. Marshall Trumbo stepped directly behind her, sensing she may faint, ready for her fall.

Trumbo spoke up. "The name of the demon, Father?"

Morningstar looked at him blank-faced. "Knowing the name would do you no good, son. No good at all."The preacher focused his attention back to the child—who had suddenly begun thrashing violently against the barred walls of the crib. Head and feet taking turns whipping up then down, a blind see-saw. Rhythmically. Beating against the loose fabric of the thin mattress:

*Bap. Bap-bap. Buh-bap, bap, buh-bap.*

The rhythm's reprise erased whatever lingering doubt Morningstar may have reserved. He spoke to those in the room:

"It is the demon himself who needs to be saved tonight. Without the demon's redemption, the boy is lost. And so are we all."

"Lookit the hand," said Typhus in a whisper. "I don't like it."

The movement of the hand had picked up in speed, fingers kneading the taut skin of the boy's chest frantically—pushing through skin. No, not pushing through—sinking *in*. The flesh of the dead man's fingers was melting into and joining the flesh of the child. Fusing.

Anabella Carolla prayed something in Sicilian between lips barely parted, her hands flattening over her face, fingers spread just enough to allow herself fragmented witness, teetering on exhausted legs. Trumbo stood behind with his hands gently brushing her waist. Ready, once more, for her fall.

Morningstar faced the mother, laid a shaking hand on her shoulder. An imploring whisper: "Please, Mother. Leave God out of this. This business ain't none of His. God has His own troubles to tend. His own house to clean. Let Him be." Defying Morningstar's instruction, Anabella Carolla only prayed louder.

In the crib, a change had begun.

"This isn't right," said Morningstar. "This isn't supposed to happen. Ain't the way I dreamt it."

Dominick's body had begun a visible transformation:

*rebirthing*

Arms pressed to sides, legs pressed together. Ears receding, mouth stretching wide, eyes separating, nose flattening. The red welts that had risen behind the ears had turned to slit-shaped holes, sucking in a tortured, thin stream of air. Whistling.

*rebirthing*

Diphtheria gasped. Buddy held her tight.

Dominick was transforming rapidly, his perfect, soft skin changing.

The sound that flew from his mother's throat was a scream but not a scream; the note of an opera singer, high in pitch, full in tone, quivering with perfect vibrato, sustained. It was a beautiful sound, it was an ugly sound. During the mother's note the child momentarily stopped thrashing, transformation interrupted.

Anabella Carolla's note ran out of air. She fell to the ground, body and mind finally spent. Marshall Trumbo did not catch her.

The child began, once again, to thrash about.

*Bap. Bap-bap. Buh-bap, bap, buh-bap.*

Flesh resumed melting in on itself, the child's original form degenerating once more.

*rebirthing*

It only took Jack a split second to ponder and appreciate the interruptive value of the mother's note before turning quickly to Buddy:

"Boy. Blow that thing. Play loud and long and don't stop for a breath. Play like the devil, boy. Blow it." Buddy hesitated, perplexed. Jack, impatient: "*NOW! Blow, blow, blow, blow, BLOW!*"

Buddy Bolden raised his horn and sucked in air, lips encircling the mouthpiece.

*Blow.*

High in pitch, full in tone. Sustained. It was an awful sound, it was a beautiful sound.

The tune that came from Buddy's horn was a spiritual. Buddy blew from his very core, the root of the sound coming from a place in his soul he was previously unaware of.

The notes came out two octaves higher than he had intended.

The notes held, dipped, leapt and crashed. But didn't crash.

It took several moments before Buddy realized his fingers were splayed and spread wide, holding up the instrument with only the thumb and forefinger of his right hand, not touching the keys at all with the left. Only with this realization, and with the uncalculated sensitivity of a lover, did he lay his fingers upon the keys; following the path of their course in progress, paying attention to their meaning, feeling their odd warmth, interpreting their need, their apparent longing. Understanding the healing quality of the sound. The joy in it.

*joy*

Typhus recognized the song right away.

*Troubled about my soul…*

His rebirthing song. The one he sang to calm his babies at the river. The one that just felt right. And then he knew.

Typhus Morningstar moved to the edge of the crib, his eyes meeting Doctor Jack's for confirmation. Jack nodded, said:

"Yes, Typhus." And to Noonday Morningstar: "Let him work. Don't stop him. This is what he needs to do. What he's been practicing for, what he was born for. Let him."

Typhus lifted himself up and over the railing of the crib. Laid his hands on the body of Dominick Carolla.

Noonday Morningstar fell to his knees, face in hands, weeping; and then spoke to his God; "Damn you. Damn you straight to hell."

Buddy Bolden played on.

*Ride on Jesus, come this way*

# CHAPTER TWELVE
## *Night Fishing*

O n a pier off the levee less than a mile from the little house where very odd matters of the spirit were currently unfolding, a gravedigger and devout Christian known by most folks as Marcus Nobody Special had caught a fish.

The night was black and starless; the only light offered up to human eyes came from the bobbing smudge pots on the river, warning ships to keep away, to dock further up if at all. Turning the water into a million slices of sparkly lemon, embedded like jewels, loosely in darkness.

He held the catfish in two hands. It was a small one, maybe two pounds. He unhooked its mouth and stroked its rough scales gently, carefully. It squirmed and wiggled at his touch. Its flesh was brown with streaks of pink. It moved with a rhythm that struck Marcus as vaguely familiar.

"Sorry, old man, didn't mean to interrupt yer nightswimmin'." Shook his head sadly and added: "Not my dern fish. Not my fish at all. But I'll get 'im. Yessir."

He looked up at the lines of smoke that crept from the smudge pots, creasing the blackness of the sky into something blacker still. He was surprised to find tears in his eyes. Marcus hadn't shed a real tear in nearly forty years. Not since his Coffee Maria had taken sick and died way back in 1853.

"Always something blacker, I reckon."

He dropped the fish back in the water. Wondering if he had done right in his life.

# CHAPTER FOURTEEN
## *Catfish Blues*

**B**uddy Bolden played on.

*The devil is mad and I am glad...*

The small fingers of Typhus Morningstar caressed and pulled at the scaly pink flesh of Dominick Carolla, rebirthing in reverse. Tugging at ears, tracing at seams with fingertips: careful, sculpting the head and face back into human form. Sliding fingers between fused legs, separating. Pulling arms away from sides, gently but firmly. Massaging gills behind little ears, closing them, smoothing them over. Rubbing the father's severed hand, pushing down, melting the hand into the flesh of the child's soft chest, feeling the sticky mixture of honey, onions and broken crumbs of bloodroot. The flesh was warm and soft as clay, but its color was turning from pink to gray. The child had become whole again. The child was not breathing.

Typhus Morningstar had the gift of understanding.

He bent down and sucked his lungs full of cold, dry air: held. Placed his lips to the lips of the child. Blew. Steady, even.

*He lost one soul that he thought he had...*

As Typhus blew, Buddy Bolden's cornet flew from his mouth and slipped from his hands; clanking to the ground, denting the horn slightly and permanently at the rim. The instrument made a noisy fuss against the hard floor before settling.

Quiet.

Dominick Carolla's eyes slammed open. Little eyes filled with rage. Rage not human. Black rage. The demon blew back into the throat of the rebirther.

Typhus's small body shot back violently against the side of the crib like a rag doll, then bounced to the mattress in a small, tremulous heap. Typhus tried blowing the foul air back out, but could not.

A baby's cry filled the room. A normal, healthy, frightened cry. The sweetly tragic sound of a one-year-old jerked from deep sleep. Dominick's skin was pink again, shiny with sweat. Anabella Carolla scooped her son up and out of the crib, into her arms, muttering: *"grazie, grazie, grazie, grazie..."*

Typhus Morningstar lay unconscious in the corner of the crib, his eyes closed but moving rapidly beneath his lids. His lungs struggled for breath.

Father Morningstar lifted his son from the crib. Laid him down on the carpet that was not quite at the center of the room. Tore open Typhus' shirt, scraped once more at the small jar with trembling fingers, spreading remnants of honey potion on the boy's chest, shouting between sobs:

*"Hast thou come to kiss this child? I will not let thee kiss him. Hast thou come to send him to sleep? I will not let thee do him harm."*

Noonday Morningstar's hand began to fuse with his son's chest through the honey mixture. Typhus stopped breathing altogether, red welts rising rapidly behind his ears.

*rebirthing*

Buddy stood in shock, rubbed at his lips, stared at the grounded cornet. Motionless, useless.

Jack picked up the bruised horn from the ground and blew into it himself. The sound was low and deep; a soulless moan. Buddy didn't intervene: only stood, momentarily lost, trembling, rubbing at his mouth, eyes full of tears, exhausted, beat.

Down. Out.

Morningstar blew hard into the cold air of the room, profoundly exhaling, emptying his lungs with a determined wheeze. Kissed his son on the mouth. Then:

Sucking in.

Pulling foul air from the boy's chest. Typhus' small fists beat at the skull of the man he knew as Father and sometimes Daddy.

*Bap. Bap-bap. Buh-bap, bap, buh-bap.*

As bad air transferred from son to father, the hand of the father sank deeper into the chest of the son.

Two brown eyes focused on the scene; drying, crystallizing. A mind became clear.

Buddy Bolden snatched his horn from Doctor Jack. Drew in cold air once more, blew out hot with eyes shut tight. Blew hard. Loud.

*Troubled about my soul, Lord...*

Typhus crumpled in his father's arms. Hands lifeless, knuckles brushing against the floor. Father Morningstar's eyes became wide, enraged, black.

Doctor Jack searched his soul for answers and found none.

Beauregard Church reached into his worn leather bag, removed an old and dull-bladed knife that once belonged to his grandfather. Pearl handle with bits of glass polished to look like jewels. Cheap family heirloom. Good for nothing except maybe for luck. He leapt towards Morningstar and plunged the knife into the preacher's back up to the handle, the dull blade tearing straight into, then past, his heart.

Diphtheria screamed. Ran to her father as Buddy dropped his horn to intercept her, holding her fast. Whispered soft in her ear, feigning calm: "It's over." Held her tight, stroked her hair. "I think it's over."

Beauregard stood up, leaving his cheap family heirloom in the preacher's back. Picked up his leather bag full of lucky stuff and walked out of the house without word or expression, walked into the warm air of night. Walked down the steps. Kept walking. Didn't come back.

The dark red life of Noonday Morningstar spread across the floor of the Carolla house, bathing the soles of Anabella Carolla's shoes and evenly soaking the uneven carpet. Anabella Carolla had seen none of it, nothing past the release of her son. Nothing else mattered. She simply held the baby to her breast and repeated over and over: "*grazie, grazie, grazie, grazie…*"

Dominick Carolla was fast asleep in her arms. Breathing deeply and easily. Except for the grateful chant of his mother and the gentle sobs of Diphtheria Morningstar, the house was now silent, its temperature warming. Noonday Morningstar's lifeless body lay atop his son's. Father and son in a puddle of joined blood, swimming motionless.

Jack pulled Beauregard's heirloom free from Morningstar's back. Dropped it to the sticky floor. Put a hand on the preacher's shoulder, rolled him over and off of the nine-year-old. This would not be Typhus' day to die. His father had sacrificed too much to allow it.

Empty wrist: Noonday Morningstar's right hand was nowhere to be seen.

Covering Typhus' naked chest was a large, bright pink welt. A fresh scar in the shape of a hand.

Jack picked the boy up in his arms. Took him out of that place. Buddy and Diphtheria followed close behind. None of them spoke. Leaving as quietly as they had come. Marshall Trumbo stayed behind.

He looked at the mother and child, so strangely reunited. Quiet and calm as if no demon had ever visited them.

# CHAPTER FIFTEEN
## *Sky is Falling*

22 Customhouse Street
New Orleans, Louisiana
March 19, 1891 (2 a.m.)

Dear George,

All is Well.
All is well all is well all is well all is well all is well
all is well all is well all is well all is well all is well
all is well all is well all is well all is well all is well
all is well all is well all is well all is well all is well
all is well all is well all is the verdict of all who drink
out all is well all is well all is well all is well all is
well all is well all is well all is well all is well all is
well all is well all is well all is well all is well all is
well all is well all is well all is well all is well all is
well all is well all is well sky is falling.

Warmest regards from your brother,
Marshall

# CHAPTER SIXTEEN
## *The Note Revisited*

The song resolved like all melodies, with a single note.

A.

But not A.

§

Things change with resolution; completely, irrevocably.

From resolve to clarity, clarity to understanding, understanding to questions. And with questions of this kind comes a sort of salvation. But not salvation.

E flat. Transition. A.

Questions.

The player stops.

He is more sober now than he's ever been in his life. His mind isn't ready for the questions, but he listens to them intently. He doesn't want to hear them; he *needs* to hear them. He reaches for his bottle of train yard-grade gin, holds it firmly, reels back and tosses it through an open window. Listens to the tinkle of shattered glass outside. Lays his horn on the pillow, his head next to the horn; it is inches from his eyes. His eyes are red and he feels tears building, but he does not let them through. His eyes look up at the warped, rainwater-stained ceiling as he strokes the horn protectively. He cannot sleep. He wants a drink and recalls the recent sound of shattered glass. Out the window.

This time, he will remember the A.

He knows he has seen the face of God.

Questions. E flat. A. Clarity.

Something is created, stillborn, then reborn; a broken promise on the mend.

A rebirth in progress, it has all the time in the world. What once existed but left too soon has returned. An abortion swimming up from the river. New life. With time.

Differently. Irrevocably.

Buddy Bolden dreams with eyes wide open.

BOOK TWO
*Buddy Bolden and The Christ Kid*
1906

# CHAPTER SEVENTEEN
## *Calisaya Blues*

W ell, little miss, I do appreciate wisdom in the young. And that's just what you done showed me tonight.

Pretty little miss like you coming round to Doctor Jack asking about a cure, sure nuff. Not asking *for* a cure, but asking *about* a cure—the difference between the two being larger than you might expect. One question show caution—the other just quick and dumb. And I do appreciate you for it, little darlin', indeed I do.

Most gals come around to Doctor Jack just hoping for a quick fix to what they view as an imminent crisis or a state of impendin' personal doom. Figgerin' a cure is a cure and don't reckon much that a cure might turn out bad. But sometimes a cure can make things best for short and worst for long. So it truly is wise to ask *about* before asking *for*.

I'll answer your questions best as I can, little one, though, truthfully, my answers can't possibly be right for no one but myself. No, my answers are for me, but maybe I can point you in the direction of your own. Then, once you decide, we can go on talking 'bout curin' and such, if you still have a mind to.

The cure is a thing called calisaya. Bark off a shrub that come here on a boat from South America. Can grow pretty good in New Orleans, too, if you get it down in good so the roots take hold. Just grind up the right amount then put that powder in a tea. Once that calisaya get inside ya, little girl? The cure is on.

Sets your insides to contractin'. Might be some bleedin' and might be some dyin'. Lungs'll contract too, making it hard to breathe. Bladder too, making you wanna pee. Retina too, making it hard to see. Heart too, and that's where the real danger be. But if you get past all that, then past is past, and that—for some—is the cure.

But you didn't just ask on the how. You asked on God, too. What God might think of all of this curin' talk. Hmm.

Well, hell, I don't know what God thinks. But I do know this:

God has occasion to talk to each of us directly at one time or another—and all along he be telling us the same thing, to be sure. We just *listen* different is all.

Some folks turn away from God because he won't answer a peep when they ask him questions through diligent and heartfelt praying and such. He quiet as a mouse, that ol' God, when the prayers come out—almost like he ain't there. Well, maybe, just maybe, that's on accounta God waiting on *us* to answer a few of his own questions first. Bet you never even thought of that, eh? That's all right, little sis, not many do.

I see you scratching your head and I can't says I blame you. But let me go on for just a bit and maybe it'll make more sense by the time I get through. If you got a few minutes, why dontcha take off your hat and have a little sitdown?

Typhus? Be a good little fella and make a cup of tea for our pretty little company.

I'd say coffee, sweetheart, but I don't believe coffee to be good for a gal in the family way. In case you decide agen' the cure, that is.

So, I was talkin'. That's right. Thank you, Typhus. Thank you. Try this one on for size, little sis:

Try and think about God before he made the world. Before he made the saints and the angels and the puppies and the gators and the babies and the mothers. When all he had to mess with was planets and stars and moons made out of cold dirt and hellfire. Try to think of God as just a regular fella in that situation.

Now then. I bet you thinking he was powerful lonely.

He warn't lonely, sister. No, ma'am, he didn't *know* to be lonely. Before you can get lonely you have to miss someone, and if you're all there is and ever was then you never get the chance to pine—or even to imagine the pining.

But God's a smart feller and had plenty of time to think about all kinds of things out there in the universe all by himself with nothing to do except making stars and moons and swirlin' dirt. And I imagine somewhere down the line he mighta thought, "What if?" What if he *weren't* the only one? What if he *didn't* know all there was to know—as might be the case if there was another being he warn't aware of with thoughts he couldn't see. So God mighta considered the possibility of *not* knowing—and that possibility would be a foreign thing to someone like God, the only being ever was. And, to God Almighty Hizzownsweet Self, would such a possibility be a good thing or a bad thing, a right thing or a wrong thing? Which brings up another thing altogether.

When a creature is so utterly alone in the universe, such a creature got no use for right and wrong, good and bad. If there's only you and no one else, then there's only what comes to mind—and if what comes to mind don't affect no one but yourself, then right and wrong don't exactly apply. So right and wrong never occurred to God just as wings never occur to catfish in a river.

But when God got to thinking about the possibility of maybe not being so alone, then the idea of right and wrong logically sprung to mind—like the idea of wings might spring to the mind of a catfish plucked from the river and thrown up into the air. These earliest thoughts of morality didn't digest easily, though—for God had no way of knowing what morality might mean except in theory. I suppose this notion might've seemed more interesting than stars and moons and swirlin' dirt, so he hunkered down to business and threw some flesh and blood into the mix.

Flesh and blood. That'd be us; you and me and that little baby in your womb and ever'one else to boot on this big green earth. Ever'one ever was or will be, too.

And this thing that he put in our hearts might've been our very reason for being—the inner knowledge in each and every one of us about the difference between right and wrong. And the power to act on this knowledge in a meaningful way.

Y'see, little sister, God ain't a naturally moral being because he got no use for morality. It don't apply to his personal situation. But questions do arise and answers do beckon.

Now, being God might very well mean to know everything. But you must understand that *even for God* the knowing don't come easy. So when a question come up that stumped his big ol' God-brain, he set about finding an answer. And that's where we come in. He invented morality and planted it in *our* breasts. And only through our actions could he ever hope to learn about that particular thing.

Now, if this be so, then it'd be a maddening thing for the human race to reconcile such a notion in its collective heart and mind. But what I'm saying is this here. Might be this. Just might be.

Typhus, boy, where's that tea? Make mine special like always. Just a touch but don't be stingy. And keep it clean for the little gal. Hard liquor ain't good for a gal in the family way, I s'pect.

Now, where was I going? That's right. I was talkin' might-bees. Might be this. Might be this, indeedy.

Now, listen up and let your own self decide, little darlin':

Could be we're here to answer God's questions and not the other way around. Follow? God is learning from us, little sister. Giving us free will and waiting to see what we do with it. He don't give us no details, because the tellin' would taint the answers. He needs us to be straight up with him about this stuff. He don't even come right out and admit to being there, don't even supply us with proof-positive of his very existence. Just give us enough smarts to recognize the *possibility*, then let us ponder it out on our own. Folks call that sort of pondering "faith." Nothing wrong with that because, truthfully, it don't make a licka difference.

The problem of morality is something that God is inclined to know about, but can only learn from creatures with a need for it. So we must oblige. We've got to do our very best to show God what's right. Only a man can do right, little sis. Only a man can *save*. Jesus, little sister, was an earthly man. Could be Jesus was God's way of testing out the waters.

But the question of right and wrong that's been put to us by God is sometimes a tricky one—because right and wrong don't always wash as clean as black and white. All kinds of grays in the hearts of men, little sis. What feels right in the heart of one might feel wrong in the heart of another, and so forth and so on. But there are some exceptions that stay mostly constant. Some things stay mostly light—like loving. And some things stay mostly black—like killing.

And since you come to talk about a cure, I guess that means we're talking about both. The cure is the trickiest kind. Because the calisaya cure is surely killing—but it can be about loving, too.

You've got to ask yourself a question, little missy—and try to find the answer in the deepest part of your soul.

If a second life resides within your own body, a life that has no choice whether to live or die on its own, do you have the right to make such a decision by proxy? Is that second life close enough to your own life that you can *treat* it as your own? If that child is doomed to live a life of hurt, would it be truly right to keep that life from touching air and earth and water, never to draw a natural breath?

It's a question that only breeds more questions, for sure. After all, how can you know that the life of this child will not be a good one? How can a person know whether taking that life, before it's even had a chance to show itself, might be a right thing or a wrong thing? Can the morality that God put in your heart even begin to decipher such a thing? Of course, this might smell like a question best put to God himself. And now we're back to the beginning.

Because if what I say is close to true, then we're here to answer God's questions and not the other way around. And even if I'm wrong, well, do you think that God could even answer a question like that?

Hell, I don't know. But I do know this:

God ain't tellin'.

So the answering is left up to you, little sister. And when you make your answer then things do unfold, and then God might learn from the unfolding. And when God gets enough unfolding, then the unfolding might start to look like answers, and then, maybe, just maybe, from these answers he can make the next world a better one for every eternal soul that come back around.

But there you are with that little second life in your belly right in the here and now and wondering about a cure. Not even thinking about this world or the next. Stuck in a situation and wanting to know what to do. Right now, this very minute. And so you have a decision to make about killing—and it ain't a decision with an obvious answer, nothing purely black or white about it, child.

The decision must be a hard one. And it must be answered very carefully. So you must draw on that thing that God gave you, the thing that God has never felt for himself; that thing about right and wrong. You must teach God from your own suffering. And you will suffer.

You only get to decide how.

So close your eyes and listen deep, little sister. Listen to the thump of that second life in your belly. Try to hear if it's talking to you—and pay attention to what it has to say. And listen to your own heart, too. When you've pondered long enough, you come back here and see Doctor Jack again. If you're still looking for a cure, then I will gladly oblige. And I'll oblige just like so:

Your tea will be just as sweet, but it will have a bitter aftertaste and that taste will be calisaya. Typhus will make your bed and you will lie on it. Then you will be sick, as I have explained. The second life will come out of you, and then it will die. There will be pain for you and for the little one, too. Typhus will take good care of that baby, bring him to the river for nightswimmin'. And I will do my best to ease your suffering. It will be your saddest day. And there will be more sad days to follow.

If you go by that path, little sister, after listening to all the love in your heart, then you may take solace in knowing this one thing:

All life is eternal because all souls are eternal. Even little lives taken by calisaya tea. Little lives like that stay with you always, and sometimes even visit you in ways you don't expect. That's because even little lives come from the will of God, and there is a mysterious joy in that fact. For God is learning about love *from you*, little sister. And he is eternally grateful for the lessons that you give. Through your pain you teach God right from wrong.

It is never the other way around. Never has been and never will be. It's the reason we are here on this earth, little sister. We are educating God.

With a pain that he could never feel.

# CHAPTER EIGHTEEN
## *Up From the Crib*

**S**ix-dollar stockings and she went through them like kindling, but the right had been hard earned and so the small luxury brought her no shame. Pretty little whore pulled up a stocking nice and slow; not for worry of runs, just for savoring the slide of silk against skin. It had been a long road to the sweet life of whoring at Arlington Hall.

Opportunities of employment for young girls in the Parish came down to whoring or factory and field work. Whoring paid better than the others—and wasn't much dirtier all told—so the choice was bitter but obvious for pretty tan gals of color like Diphtheria Morningstar. So at the tender age of fifteen, Diphtheria had rented herself a crib on Marais Street and got busy.

When a gal is working the cribs, it means she rents a tiny room in a shotgun row house at the dirty inner crust of the district, puts out a red lantern and pays rent to a landlord who doubles as pimp. The room is so small that her bed must be narrow, so narrow that it can't hold two unless one is on top of the other, which is the idea anyway. A bed, a stove for heat, a washstand and two lanterns; one regular and one red. The red one to draw in flies.

Most of her memories of that place were reduced to blur by now, but the wallpaper in that crib had remained etched in her brain with perfect clarity all these years. Still had dreams about that wallpaper. Curved burgundy lines joined by small x's at the ends, making shapes that could pass for either edges of stormclouds or seagulls in flight or razor-wire fencing—depending on her mood and disposition. The paper itself was dingy yellow, curling brown towards the ceiling and warped from leaks. All the cribs had their leaks. "If it got no leak then it wouldn't exactly be a crib," Oscar the Pimp once told her by way of excuse for not fixing hers.

Money is short but steady in the cribs. This is the low budget world of whoring where sailors can have a go for a dollar or less, usually counted out in the form of nickels and dimes. "Crib-nickels" they called them—sailors rarely holding paper money in their pockets. The higher class bordellos of Basin Street are for the mid-to-high society men who want more than just to fuck; they want music and atmosphere and a woman's tender touch (along with tender lies) before their britches come down. It's the tenderness and music that costs extra—you can't expect such fancy things for no combination of crib-nickels.

In the cribs, the pay is low and tenderness is dispensed at the whore's discretion, but traffic is high and the nickels can really add up if a girl works long hours.

Five solid years in that crib on Marais.

Five years turning sheets over between customers because she didn't have time to wash. Five years of watching other girls get sick, then die of flesh plague, wondering when her own turn might come up—hoping, on some days, that it might be sooner rather than later. Five years of being handled rough by sailors, listening to their nasty mouths and feeling their fists when they couldn't get it hard after six months eating sea rations spiked with saltpetre. Five years wiping tears from the faces of women who had to decide between a "trick baby" and a visit to Doctor Jack for a "cure." Five years of phony smiling, leaning half naked through a window saying, "C'mon pretty papa, come take a li'l nap with mama." Drawing in flies. Needing their nickels. Hating their grins. Wishing them harm.

Sometimes doing harm. During her time in the cribs, Diphtheria Morningstar had kept a knife under her mattress. Seven-inch blade with a four-inch wooden handle, a knife meant for gutting fish. Just in case, for self defense.

Diphtheria knew better than to use a blade simply because a john might give her a smack on the jaw or skip without paying. Oscar would turn her over to the cops quick as a whip for cutting a john over something so small. But if her life was in actual and immediate peril, well, that was a different matter. A pimp can't make a red penny off a dead whore, and so Oscar tended towards sympathy regarding humanitarian plights that might result in lost profits.

The bruises around her throat had been proof enough for Oscar on the night she'd used the fish knife. The bruises were less from pressing than from the rub of rough, callused hands, but those hands had meant to kill Diphtheria Morningstar all the same. Oscar had been a real sport; dumping that sailor's body in the Bayou St. John and bringing around a clean mattress with a new set of sheets that same night. Oscar had snuffed out Diphtheria's red lantern while the night was still young, told her to rest up, feel better, don't worry about the cops—and even gave her a dixie (a ten dollar bill) to keep her mouth shut.

Oscar had taken care of everything the night she had killed the sailor—and by the next morning it was like it never happened. All gone except for the remembering.

Remembering his limp dick flop against her thigh, only getting harder as his fingers tightened around her neck, his eyes feeding on her terror, filling his terrible, handsome face with a look of cold confidence and dumb power, his complete control over her life and death being the key to his sexual success, to his defeat of the saltpetre in his veins. She remembered looking into those wide black pupils, eyes like a shark, and seeing death. A part of her beaten soul welcomed the sight.

She remembered the ease of giving up, slipping into sleep, watching those depthless eyes fade and melt into the flickering gray of his face, a concrete statue come to deliver her from the crib. Was this man her knight in shining armor? Come to take her from this awful place, to show her something better? No, he wasn't that. Wasn't that at all. But it was true he had delivered her from the crib. At least for a moment.

For a moment she was gone.

Diphtheria remembered touching death with her fingertips, caressing its cheek, kissing its nose, swimming in its thick waters, its music tickling her ears. The music was familiar and telling, its voice gentle and firm. It was the sound of Buddy's horn, the same strange sound it made the night her father died, the sound it made while Buddy's fingers splayed and stretched above the instrument, impossibly; not touching the keys at all. The music spoke to her dying mind the night she touched death; said that love was *life*, not death. Not now, not yet.

And so, before her heart had beat its last, she had reached beneath the mattress.

The sailor's grip on her throat didn't loosen right off, had even tightened some as the knife dug in, as Diphtheria cranked the handle back and forth, tearing at the sailor from between and beneath thick ribs. His cold look of confidence had slowly yielded to fear as his insides ripped and mingled, and she felt him go limp inside her before any meaningful biological transaction could be completed. As crimson and black spread from between his shoulders to touch warm air, the color crept from his face. Still, his grip failed to loosen—and Diphtheria's mind went black once more.

In time she awoke, the sailor cold and motionless, his weight a vast, dead stone across her body. With much effort she rolled him off of and out of her—wedging his naked bulk between wall and mattress edge. Sat at the foot of the bed, thinking. Not crying, not afraid, not proud, not feeling lucky to be alive—not feeling much of anything. Just thinking.

The sailor was still bleeding and therefore not yet dead, but she decided it would be best not to interrupt the dying process. She waited for the blood to quit its shimmering trickle, waited for its metamorphosis from shiny motion to shiny stillness. Watched him die there on the bed, watched the bright red life vacate his body and ruin her only mattress. When she was sure his life was done, she walked out slow and knocked hard on the door of her neighbor and crib colleague, Hattie Covington.

Diphtheria's pounding had caught Hattie in mid-trick. Upon opening the door Hattie looked mighty perturbed—until she saw the blood on Diphtheria's skimpy fuck-me-silly-in-my-crib-for-pocket-change dressing gown. Hattie's john had jumped up from the bed; riled as hell, buck naked, swinging his fists in the air and ready to let loose—when he too noted the bright red. Got quiet all the sudden—then got his pants on in a big hurry. Left a whole dollar on Hattie's washstand before leaving.

Hattie fetched Oscar. Oscar erased the night. Erased all but the remembering.

She had killed the sailor during her fifth year working that Marais Street crib. And so five years in the cribs had added up to that. A series of close calls, a long train ride called misery, and a pitiful, endless stream of dirty crib-nickels.

But in late 1896, before that fifth year was done, everything changed.

Buddy's band got booked out of Charley's Barbershop on South Rampart Street and into John the Greek's on 28 Franklin—right across the street from The Big 25, one of the most popular mid-priced sporting houses in the tenderloin. It was a good, solid gig that paid regular paper money—and Buddy's strange, super-loud way of playing had become a stone sensation. Then, as if to confirm the good omen of Buddy's big break, a miracle happened. Diphtheria got herself in a family way.

Buddy's first reaction to the notion of fatherhood was purest joy, but at the age of only nineteen there was plenty of room for waffling. As the idea sank in and Diphtheria's belly grew, Buddy's mind went wobbly and his eyes began to ricochet, returning the flirtatious glances given him by the almost-high-class whores of John the Greek's; pretty gals, nigh high-yella, who bought him shots of Raleigh Rye and fought to hold his coat. Soon Buddy did the inevitable and convenient thing, doubting out loud whether Diphtheria's child might be his own. This was understandable on a certain level—considering how she'd made her living for the past five years—but hadn't there been love and promises between them? Hadn't she stayed faithful to him (in her way) for all that time, five years in the crib? Didn't he owe her child a father and a good life—even a trick baby, if that's what it was, now that the good life had finally showed the crown of its head?

Diphtheria quit crib-whorin' just as soon as that baby stole her figure away, but she couldn't help but wonder if having that baby was the best thing to do. And she wondered what God might think of such thoughts, these thoughts of Doctor Jack and his cure.

When the pregnancy did end, Buddy disappeared entirely. But even without him, she'd managed to make it up from the crib on her own steam. By age twenty-five, she'd made it to the big time, a featured girl on Basin. And now, at twenty-nine, she had a regular customer base, a Blue Book listing of her own, and ten pairs of six-dollar stockings.

Still, she wondered if she'd made the right decision about Doctor Jack and his cure, that decision she'd made back when times were so hard.

# CHAPTER NINETEEN
## *Malvina*

"Goddamn shoes."

Malvina Latour loved her sister with all of her heart, but after more than a half century of living together she'd still not gotten use to Frances' habit of leaving shoes strewn about the floor. Frances' typical response to her sister's grumbling was nothing like an answer, but something like a question.

"Mother? Where my little Maria at?"

And so it went.

When their own mother died from cholera with Frances less than a year old, Malvina had found herself in the role of mother for the first time at age twelve. Frances had always called Malvina that, "mother"—it had been her first word.

Raised Roman Catholic, Malvina turned away from her parents' God by age twenty. By the time she hit thirty she was a full-fledged mambo in the Vodou religion. And when you are a mambo, you are a mother to many.

Now, at age ninety-nine, Malvina found herself still mothering Frances, now eighty-seven. Their relationship had turned bitter long ago, but neither ever considered leaving the other.

Frances' eternal response to her sister's ire (nothing like an answer, something like a question) was regarding this: In 1853 (fifty-three years previously), Frances' teenage daughter and only child had died during the worst yellow fever epidemic the city had ever seen. Maria's death had placed a pain in Frances' heart, the kind that stays long term. She gave her soul over to pain and resentment then—and never let go.

For her own reasons, Frances had blamed her sister for the tragedy. Or so it seemed.

For her own reasons, Malvina blamed herself as well. And so it was, in fifty-three years, not a single word had passed between the sisters. Which isn't to say there'd been no talking.

"Shoes."

"Maria?"

Frances talked to herself. And Malvina talked to *her*self. Always for the other's benefit, but in no way acknowledging the other's presence. Not directly. Talking under breath, between teeth. Sometimes whispered, sometimes howled.

Frances refused to look Malvina directly in the eye, but Malvina often looked into Frances'—and in those eyes she saw the baby she'd once raised. Remembered feeding Frances warm goat's milk, calming away tiny tears and goosing laughter from that frowning little mouth with funny sounds, impressions of swamp frogs and crickets. Remembered how that little baby would crawl up on her lap as she sat in their dead mother's big oak rocker, would speak in the wonderful fragmented language of babies, pleading for a song. "*Chanson tanpri, Mer.*"

"Song please, Mother."

Such sweet memories. Malvina kept these vivid in her mind and close to her heart, always, always.

And she would sing:

*Mo pap li couri la riviere,*
*Mo maman li couri peche crab*
*Dodo, mo fille, crab dans calalou*
*Dodo, mo fille, crab dans calalou*

Which translated approximately to:

*My papa has gone to the river,*
*My mamma has gone to catch crab,*
*Sleep, my daughter, crab is in the river*
*Sleep, my daughter, crab is in the river*

The daily penance paid by Malvina for the last half century, the penance of her sister's eyes, had succeeded (somewhat) in soothing her own sense of guilt. But even so, what was done could never be undone, and so she'd wondered. Could she have done more to save her sister's child? She wasn't exactly sure. In any case, she knew Maria had not died from yellow fever as she'd led Frances to believe. The truth was something she'd protected her *fille* from. The truth, she believed, would have killed Frances.

"Always under foot."

"Where my Maria?"

In 1853 Maria had been the toast of Rue Dumaine, a star attraction at Auntie Jin's Sporting House. But she'd given her heart to a common man, a lowly cemetery worker. The gravedigger left Maria brokenhearted and heavy with child, making things easy on himself—and so Malvina had seen to it that he paid for his crimes. Among other things, it was hard to be handsome minus a nose. The gravedigger's son had died during childbirth and Maria fell gravely ill shortly after. Malvina had tried desperately to save her niece—had done everything she could think of. Conjured cures of the body, cures of the heart—

*ground cinnamon, 8 parts; rhubarb, 8 parts; calumba, 4 parts; saffron, 1 part; powdered opium, 2 parts; oil peppermint, 5 parts; macerated with 75 parts alcohol in a closely covered percolator for several days, then allow percolation to proceed to obtain 95 parts of percolate, in percolate dissolve the oil of peppermint, dissolve the oil, dissolve the oil, the oil, the oil, powdered opium, 2 parts; dissolve, powdered, dissolve, powdered*

*dissolve...*

None of it worked. Nearly out of hope, she'd turned to otherworldly methods. A ritual of the spirit meant to mend Maria's heart, body and mind—and something more, something special for the gravedigger.

Malvina would always remember that night. That strangest of nights. That black, black night in 1853.

"Pickin' up other people's shoes."

"Where my Maria?"

*dissolve...*

# CHAPTER TWENTY
## *Blackest Night*

As Maria lay withering in the fall of 1853, Malvina had discovered her own bruised heart lacking in its former capacity for faith. As she prepared for the night's ritual she was unsure if she possessed the strength required to bring Maria back from death's edge—but she was quite sure she possessed the skills and wherewithal to ruin the one who had done her harm, the lowdown good-for-nothing gravedigger known as Marcus Nobody Special. Real faith, she determined, was easier to conjure from a heart bolstered by rage than from a heart damaged by sorrow. To fortify her faith, she must focus her rage.

Discarded corpses were plentiful in the killing season of fever, so it hadn't been hard for Malvina to locate one suitably resembling the gravedigger. The mulatto corpse now lay face-up in an open pine coffin near the foot of Malvina's altar. The altar itself was a beautiful collage of dried flowers, fine jewelry, gold coin, keepsakes from long-dead ancestors and bones of the dead collected up from the crumbling, shallow-bricked tombs of the poor—all artfully arranged around molded statuettes of Catholic Saints. Other various and appropriate amenities for the *lwas* (tenants of the Spiritworld) included a fine red rooster, omelets prepared with corn and hot peppers, a honey mixture of corn and black pepper, dried corn mixed with gunpowder, raw tafin liquor, pepper jelly, and a red candle intricately carved into the shape of a woman holding a heart. With all preparations in place, the big door of the tall, box-shaped coffee warehouse shut with a hollow *boom*; signaling the drummers to begin their slow, steady rhythm. Brands held by the dancers were lit aflame, then used to light the many candles of the crowded altar. The rooster responded by squawking and flapping nervously, its plumes bathed dimly in flickering light. Long shadows brushed gracefully up the twenty-foot ceiling's thick beams, painting various shades of radiant gray on wood.

The guardians of the Spiritworld gladly protect their earthly children from its more destructive tenants, but these same guardians must be specifically invited and given proper respects before such protections can be enjoyed. First was the evocation of *Legba*, who holds the key to the gateway. Then of *Loco*, who will sound a warning crow to alert *Legba* of any malevolent beings at his back. And lastly, *Loco's* wife *Ayizan*—who will hold at bay any dark being who attempts entry into the world of the living. However, with the gravedigger in mind, chaos and vengeance were not things Malvina wished to avoid on this occasion, so tonight *Ayizan*, the protective mother of the living, was not to be called—leaving unknown possibilities.

Malvina had drawn a large *veve* for *Erzulie le Flambeau* with powdered corn-meal twenty feet from the altar's base. A dancer called Rosalie now sat at the center of it, legs crossed and head down. A loose circle of dancers glided deftly around her, all of them dressed as she; immaculate white linen draping their lithe brown bodies, bright red headwraps hiding the black of their hair. Malvina raised a finger towards a barrel-chested man who nodded in response before sounding the conch shell. The sound of it was a low moan, a request for *Papa Legba* to open the gate. The drumming intensified as the dancers dipped and weaved with improvised elegance, and the salty wind of the Spiritworld gushed forth.

As the call for *Ayizan's* protection was bypassed, Malvina felt a guilty thrill. She breathed in deeply, a childlike smile coloring her face with wonder. *Anything* could happen now, she marveled. *Anything, anything.*

As the dancers continued their slow circle, Rosalie lifted herself into a standing position at their center. Arms held forward, head thrown back, eyes closed; an invitation for possession. Malvina reached into the bucket near the altar; threw a handful of dried corn and gunpowder towards the girl's shins, tempting the rooster to draw near. Rosalie lifted a foot to stroke its feathers. The fowl cooed.

Slowly, almost unnoticeably, Rosalie's face began to change.

# CHAPTER TWENTY-ONE
## *Emmanuel Fred*

**MARSHALL TRUMBO:** Mr. Fred, I thank you for agreeing to this interview. I'm sure our readers will be quite interested to hear your story, as well as your opinions regarding certain recent events.

**EMMANUEL FRED:** Well, it ain't much of a story, I guess. But ain't like I got nothin' else to do in this hellhole. Don't mind a little conversation, anyway, so you go right ahead with yer questions, mister.

**MT:** Fascinating, fascinating. Our readers will certainly be appreciative of your candor. If you don't mind, I shall begin the questions.

**EF:** Whatever. (subject yawns, scratches left armpit)

**MT:** Will you please state your name, age, and occupation for the record, sir.

**EF:** Uh, well...all right. Emmanuel John Fred, 61 years old, amateur lunatic. I only say amateur because it don't pay, but I guess you could say it's a full-time occupation. Used to be a bricklayer long time ago. That paid, but not much. Guess bein' a lunatic is easier work. Free room and board, too. Lookin' on the bright side, I mean.

**MT:** Number of years incarcerated?

**EF:** Guess it's somewhere near thirty by now. But I ain't really crazy. Just drunk and ornery is all. Well, I ain't been drunk since I got here, but that just makes me more ornery. So I guess it evens out. (more scratching, this time right armpit)

**MT:** So, would it be fair to say, in your opinion, that you've been wrongly incarcerated?

**EF:** Hell, I dunno. I used to hear voices that told me to do stuff. Probably was the doing stuff that got me locked up. Still hear voices sometimes, but there ain't much stuff to do around here. And if you even try doing stuff they put you in the cold water baths. Ain't worth it, so I don't do much stuff these days. Don't care what the damn voices want, I ain't takin' no more cold water baths.

**MT:** And what type of things did the voices tell you to do that resulted in your stay here at the hospital?

**EF:** Just stuff is all. Don't remember exactly.

**MT:** I see, I see. Mr. Fred, if I may be so bold, are you favored with a vivid recollection of your dreams?

**EF:** Sometimes, I guess. If I wake up in the middle of one I can usually remember it pretty good. Mostly, I dream while I'm awake, though. Gotta be careful about that. I ain't takin' no more damn ice baths.

**MT:** Certainly understandable. Of the dreams you remember—the sleeping variety, that is—are there any that spring immediately to mind? Give me as much detail as possible, please.

**EF:** Can't think of none right now.

**MT:** Do the words "Coco Robicheaux" mean anything to you?

**EF:** Sure. Boogie man from the swamp. Old fairy tale. Big fat Cajun supposed to eat kids who don't do what their mama say. Way I remember it, leastways.

**MT:** *You idiot.* Coco Robicheaux most certainly does *not* and never *has* eaten children. He specifically kills *fathers*. Fathers only. Any moron would know that.

**EF:** Ain't the way I heard it told. Anyway, there's no need to get testy, mister.

**MT:** Regarding this Coco Robicheaux, who you seem to know so much about— has he ever had occasion to visit you in dreams?

**EF:** No. Maybe when I was a kid, but I can't remember that far.

**MT:** Nothing recent?

**EF:** No, sir.

**MT:** You're sure?

**EF:** Yeah, I'm sure. I said I'm sure and I'm sure. (subject appears agitated)

**MT:** You mean to tell me that you don't recall Coco Robicheaux coming to visit you in your dreams just last night? Less than an hour after you fell asleep? At approximately ten-oh-seven in the p.m.?

**EF:** I got no recollection of that. Like I said, I don't remember much about my dreams unless I wake up in the middle. I slept straight through to sun-up last night. Anyway, how the hell would you know what I dreamt about last night? If I even dreamt at all?

**MT:** You mean to tell me, sir, that you don't recall the dream last night in which Coco Robicheaux himself grabbed you by the collar and pulled you down with him into a hellish bog of stagnant orange water, pulled you down through the shallow pool and into the mud, through the soft mud and into the rocks, the hard, unyielding underground stones that crushed the air from your lungs, pressed the blood from your veins?

**EF:** Why would the water be orange? Never seen no orange water.

**MT:** Answer the *question*, please.

**EF:** No, I ain't had no dream. I think I'm done this talk. I don't think I like you much, mister.

**MT:** Isn't it also true, sir, Mr. Fred, that you encountered a Creole Voodoo woman in this dream? The woman who calls demons into the bodies of little babies so that these defenseless innocents may encounter a lifetime of torture? That you aided and abetted this woman with your very tolerance of her? Isn't it true that you helped to spread her disease into this world through your very unwillingness to stop her? Isn't it true, sir? Isn't it true?

**EF:** Oh, for the love of Pete…

**MT:** Isn't it also true, sir…

**EF:** Here we go again. (subject rolls eyes)

**MT:** Is it not true, Mr. Fred? Is it *not*? Is it not *true*, sir, that you *also* came into contact with a third party in this dream which you deny having, a third party in this muddy, orange pit; a *third* party, Mr. Fred?

**EF:** You're out of your fucking mind, mister.

**MT:** A *third* party, Mister Fred? Do you not recall the man with one hand? A man wrongly imprisoned and executed in a most horrible manner? A man whose only wish was to be reunited with his infant son? A son whose body was invaded by a demon brought forth by this Voodoo witch? Isn't it true that this man, this innocent father with but one hand and but one simple wish, has languished for years in the orange pit of the *Coco Robicheaux* without mercy or relief? Can you not recall these simple facts, sir?

**EF:** Fuck you, nutbag. Orderly! Hey, someone calm this freak down. I may have to hurt him—and I don't want no damn ice bath, okay?

**MT:** Do you expect me to believe that you don't recall these things?

**EF:** Back off, mister. I'm warning you. *Orderly!*

**ORDERLY:** What's the problem, Manny?

**EF:** This whack job is getting' all crazy-like on me. Prissy son of a bitch slapped me on the cheek. Didn't hurt much, but that ain't the point. I don't want any trouble here, but he's getting right up close, y'know?

**MT:** This man is guilty, your honor! I'd swear my life on it! Have him arrested at once!

**ORDERLY:** Now, Marshall it's nice to see you up and around, but you can't go bothering the other patients like that. Just settle down, ok?

**MT:** You idiot! It isn't me! I am not the perpetrator! I am an investigative reporter! *Investigative* means to investigate! That's my job—to IN-vest-IG-gate! This man has witnessed the most heinous crime—again and again and again—every night for the last fifteen years and continues to do *nothing* to prevent it from occurring. Again and again and again and again —

**ORDERLY:** Now just settle down, Marshall. Everything will be all right. Dave!! Give me a hand here would ya? Marshall, now you just settle down and come along with me, all right?

**MT:** You get your god damned hands off of me! I want to see my doctor! Someone phone my attorney! *This* man is the guilty party! You're letting him get away!

**EF:** Crazy motherfucker.

**ORDERLY:** Watch that language, Manny.

**EF:** Yes, sir. Don't want no trouble.

**MT:** *No*! Dammit, let me go! Where are you taking me?!!

**ORDERLY:** Just gonna help you to calm down, Marshall. Ain't nothing to get upset about.

**EF:** Gonna getcher self an ice bath is what. Serve you right too. Better you than me, brother. Better you than me. Crazy fucker.

**ORDERLY:** Language, Manny.

**EF:** Sorry, boss. Don't mean no trouble. No trouble at all, sir. And that's a fact. God as my witness and that is a fact. God as my witness and I'll say it again. God as my witness, boss. Sure, sure.

**ORDERLY:** Get him by the feet, Dave! Dammit, hold on!

**DAVE:** Got 'im.

**EF:** God as my witness. (subject crosses self)

*end of interview*

# CHAPTER TWENTY-TWO

# *Djab*

osalie fell.

Her red headwrap loosened as her head hit warm, hard ground, her black hair flowing down like water against concrete. Tiny drops of blood dotted the rooster's beak as it pecked her head and neck. Rosalie's eyes opened; changed. This was Rosalie. This was not Rosalie.

*Djab.*

Malvina rushed forward to wave the bird away, but was interrupted by a fist to the jaw that threw her to the far wall between altar and coffin. The bird made soft chuckles.

The *djab* in Rosalie now turned to face the drummers, its newly acquired body jerking in wild spasms, instructing rhythm with alien motion. The men changed their beat to suit the movement of the *djab*, and as the new rhythm fell into place the *djab's* weird motion intensified—coaxing the drummers to push harder, faster.

*Bap. Bap-bap. Buh-bap, bap, buh-bap*
*Bap. Bap-bap. Buh-bap, bap, buh-bap*
*Bap. Bap-bap. Buh-bap, bap, buh-bap*

Rhythm changed, night taken.

Malvina ran towards the girl, but scooped up the rooster. Threw the bird towards the altar, jumped down upon it, held its body firmly between her knees. The rooster protested—pecking frantically at Malvina's hands and legs in rhythm with the drums, blood now pouring from the mambo's wrists. Malvina wrinkled her nose at the smell of her own blood before reaching into a small leather pouch she kept tied around her neck, quickly smearing a mixture of bloodroot and honey over the bird's feathers. Holding the rooster's neck in one sticky hand, she reached into the bucket by the altar and proceeded to push the dried corn and gunpowder down its gullet with the ball of her thumb. As the bird's neck bulged, its panicked squawks degenerated into sleepy whistles. A final pinch of hard corn and the rooster whistled no more.

As the bird slipped from her fingers, a wave of dizziness washed over Malvina and gravity urged her down. Lying on her side and facing the bird's honey-matted feathers, her head felt light, almost peaceful.

Drums pounded like thunder. Arms and legs of dancers flashed like lightening. A smell of burnt coffee hung rich and smooth in the air. The night hurtled on towards something unknowable.

*anything, anything*

Malvina's eyes focused hazily on the stomping feet of the congregation. Sound evaporated. Eyes clouded. Thinking.

Thinking of Maria's grief. Knowing her niece would soon die, that her sister Frances would suffer terribly at the loss. That Marcus Nobody Special could not possibly suffer enough for his crimes, and that any revenge she may bring would not undo the damage he had done. That her own reckless notion of justice had brought this terrible thing—this *djab*—into the world, with no idea of how to send it back—or even whether it could be sent back at all. This is what love has wrought, she mused. The love of a gravedigger. The love of a sister like a daughter. Useless love, wringing its fists at the sky. Tenderness corrupted by rage.

Love could go so terribly, terribly wrong.

The rooster woke from its death-sleep to let out a final crow—but not a crow. The sound of an immortal spirit terrified.

The warning crow of *Loco*.

A warning…

(too late, too late)

Lithe hands reached down to her and lifted Malvina's limp body upwards by the hair. Malvina sailed across the room, all of her hundred and twenty pounds expertly pitched into the mulatto's coffin. Malvina lay atop the corpse, felt its stillness, its lack of warmth, its chest that did not rise for air.

Drummers pounded skins and dancers flailed, human thunder and lightning intensifying—faster, wilder—hands and feet blistering with friction of speed. An oblivious foot kicked out at the bucket willy-nilly, causing kernels and black powder to spray waist high before distributing across the dirty floor with weird purpose; settling in lines like the rows of a field. As the *djab* spun and leapt to the wild beat, the touch of Rosalie's delicate feet somehow reduced hard kernels of corn to fine yellow dust. Gunpowder sparked and crackled.

Malvina lay in the coffin, the corpse beneath her no longer still.

A tremble.

Her soul began to tumble. Something had taken her. Leading her downward.

And down she went.

# CHAPTER TWENTY-THREE

# *Intentions Eversweet*

F alling.

She is falling. Through the dead mulatto, through the bottom of the casket, through the table, the concrete, and the ground below. Falling.

The sound of drumming becomes distant, then fades. Finally: To nothing.

Air turns dark and thick, but offers no resistance to the fall. Air assumes color and then is not air at all.

Water.

Green, smooth water. Beautiful, safe, caressing water. She is falling through the womb of the Spiritworld, the city of the dead. Where no harm can come, where finality offers nothing but time. She sucks green, perfect water into her lungs, holds; then expels. She can breathe—but slowly. Pulling the stuff into her lungs gives her a divine sense of relief, a profound serenity.

She closes her eyes. Imagines she is an infant, cradled in the arms of a mother. Now, for once, Malvina Latour is not the mother. She imagines a gentle hand stroking her brow, wiping away all the pain of her life.

There *is* a hand wiping her brow. Softly, gently. She opens her eyes.

A magnificent brown-skinned woman is cradling her at the floor of a deep green river, stroking her hair. "Shhh," says the woman.

Malvina looks into her eyes, into her troubled smile. She feels nothing but love and gratitude for the woman, wants to articulate emotion beyond words, but says only:

"Mama."

Malvina knows this *lwa*. She is *Manman Brigitte*.

The voice of the *lwa* is soft and rich, traveling through green water to caress Malvina's ears:

"Peace to you, child. This thing is not your fault. You have acted on your pain. Actions born of loss can never be truly evil. You have never experienced the trials and joys of true motherhood, but have acted as a mother to many. Your soul is damaged but pure. Your luck has been bad, my child, but your intentions eversweet."

Malvina watches as her own tears rise up through green water, tiny spheres of lilac, drifting upward.

Manman Brigitte smiles:

"Endure this night, then use what is left of your time on earth to heal the injured souls around you. Show your enemy the light of true pain and he will do right by you and yours of his own accord. The one you now hate will become your saving grace. Make him see, and let his work be done.

"This is your penance, for it will not be easy. You must leave here now, child. You can no longer breathe in this place."

The *lwa* Manman Brigitte raises a finger upward. Malvina's gaze follows it—sees.

She is in a deep grave. There is no green water here; she is dry and alone. Far, far above her is a rectangle of blue sky and white cloud. The faces of long-dead ancestors peer down from the grave's edge, watching her curiously, their expressions etched with concern. Their eyes meet Malvina's as they sprinkle dried rose petals into the grave; the petals flutter, glide—and, finally, tickle the mambo's face and hands.

She wants to speak, wants to stand, to reach up to them—but she cannot move. She lies flat on her back in the grave, looking up.

Her chest does not rise. Her eyes do not blink. Her heart does not beat.

Rose petals falling. There is a wetness at her back, water rising in the grave. It touches her ears, then fills her nose, covers her eyes. The water is neither green nor smooth. It is muddy and cold and not of the Spiritworld. It is good that her lungs do not crave it.

She watches the waterline rise quickly, but she does not float up. The water is corrupted with brown, but is just clear enough that she can still see the faces of her ancestors. Their features are distorted and grotesque through the water; abstract, monster-like.

She closes her eyes. Drifts off to sleep. Does not wish for death.

Through brown water she feels a breath on her cheek, an odor of sour swamp. She turns her head to see with eyes still closed, a dream within a dream. There is a man lying beside her, he is dressed in tatters, has long hair and a tangled beard, his body is trembling as if from intense cold. His face has no eyes.

*no eyes*

She's never seen him before but recognizes him as Coco Robicheaux, the bogeyman of children's tales. He slowly lifts a hand towards her. Her heart is pounding, she wants to get away but cannot, she is frozen with fear. His massive fingers wrap around the thumb of her right hand. He lets out a wail as he squeezes, the sound of it high in pitch like a baby or a cat. *Wake up, wake up, wake up*, she says aloud in the dream.

Her heart springs to life; beating fast, free from the second layer of dream but still trapped in the first. Her lungs pull in water; deadly, unbreathable.

The voice of Manman Brigitte screams in her mind, pours a harsh warning light over her soul:

*"Rise up, child! Now!"*

Malvina understands the *lwa's* urgency. It is not her time to die, not her day of finality. She must lift up and expel the death in her lungs. Quickly.

Her back no longer touches the muddy floor of the grave. She is rising. Hurtling towards rectangular light. Up, up, up.

Through misty brown the rectangle of blue and white expands above her. She sees silhouettes of heads lining the mouth of the grave, watching her approach. As she nears them, the faces become clearer. They are no longer the faces of her ancestors; they are the faces of Christian saints.

Her body shoots past them, and bursts into warm, waiting air.

## CHAPTER TWENTY-FOUR

# *Popcorn Ash*

Malvina flew upwards from the pine casket and fell hard against the concrete floor of the coffee warehouse. She did not recall the words, face, or touch of *Manman Brigitte* but she did recognize in herself a new (if mysterious) sense of resolve.

Resolutely, she pulled herself up on unsteady legs, crossed herself, and turned to face the *djab* in Rosalie.

"Gerouge! Serpan dezef! Arete sek!" The thing in Rosalie grinned in amusement and lifted what was left of the motionless rooster, its gullet still thick with dried corn and gunpowder.

Placing the rooster's head into Rosalie's mouth, the demon bit down then jerked away. The stump of the bird's neck shot white flame into its host's unguarded face, scorching the girl's lips, nose and chin with blackish purple blisters. Rosalie's ruined face cracked in the heat of flame; blisters swelling, bursting, running down once-perfect cheeks like clear, thick honey.

Rosalie's feet pounded the ground in relentless rhythm, the gunpowder no longer merely sparking beneath them but igniting into sharp, crisp flame; blackening the girl's soles. Flames spread quickly across the floor, dried kernels burst into fluffy popcorn, popcorn reduced to fiery ash. Ash dipped and jetted through the air, touching and infecting all in its path with hungry bits of orange, yellow and red. Popcorn ash: Wafting downward, landing on the white linen dresses of the dancers, invading large sacks of coffee, catching everything alight. The skin of Rosalie's feet blackened then peeled in the heat; tissue and muscle falling away in chunks to expose charred bone, cracking against hot concrete with sickeningly rhythmic smacks. The taut skins of the drums transformed with new color as the drummers beat on, undeterred, slapping at flame, hands oblivious, exposed finger bones whacking against the hard wood of the rims. The formerly rich, thumping drumbeat degenerated into ugly, hollow clacking:

*Clack. Clack-clack. Cluh-clack, clack, cluh-clack*
*Clack. Clack-clack. Cluh-clack, clack, cluh-clack*
*Clack. Clack-clack. Cluh-clack, clack, cluh-clack*

...somehow circular to Malvina's ear—*round and round and round.*

The warehouse filled with a sound like crackling gunfire as thousands of coffee beans exploded in the heat. The fleshless bones of the dancers whipped and writhed, drummers clacked ever on, and Rosalie's black ashes mingled with those of the rooster on the dirty concrete floor. Without so much as a whimper they all burned to dust.

Running through flame, Malvina reached the door.

Upon touching the cool air outside, she discovered her own dress partially alight and so flung herself to the wet November grass, rolling herself in dewy moisture till the last of the embers had smothered. She sat up in the grass, hugging her knees and sobbing quietly as smoke poured from the single open door of the windowless warehouse.

She had done this thing. She had killed these children. Had thrown them into the arms of unknown evil. Her excuse was less than pitiful; she had done it because she had loved.

Flames failed to consume the building. Did not punch irregular holes through the walls of it, did not angle up to melt the tar of the flat roof. Billowing smoke quickly reduced to a trickle—then, finally, evacuated completely into a handful of snake-shaped wisps. There was no smoke at all now. The sky was clear and full of stars; no trace of it remaining.

Malvina rose to her feet. Looked at the door. Quiet, smokeless. Squinted her eyes. Nothing. As if the awful night had not taken place at all. A reprieve from God? Malvina took a step forward. Still nothing.

Then. Something:

Orange water.

Streaming lightly through the front door, down the steps and onto the grass. Just a trickle at first—then more than a trickle. Bright orange with slender streaks of red and yellow. The color of flame. Pure, smokeless, liquid flame.

Orange floodwaters progressed along the ground with a low-toned hum, rushing towards Malvina's bare feet. The mambo held her ground, said a quiet prayer to *Ayizan*—begging forgiveness—and crossed herself once more. Closed her eyes tight and wished it away.

Prayer and wishing stopped nothing as the sound of rushing liquid steadied into a roar. Malvina Latour—a mother to none, a mother to many—opened her mouth to scream. Sound poured from her soul and into the night as orange water flowed to, around, and past her ankles. But there was no pain in its touch, no heat, not even warmth.

The sensation was of cool water. She bent down to place a finger in. Stared into it, noted nearly transparent streaks of pink, flitting past. Like wisps of human flesh, the pure flesh of the not-quite-born. Immortal, bloodless flesh.

Closing her eyes, she listened.

Beneath the thick drone of wet motion was a kind of music. Sweet, light music; a rich, tinny echo of happier times—times both past and yet to come. And the echo carried with it a familiar rhythm.

The carpet of wet surged onward from the yawning mouth of the coffee warehouse; covering the ground, running into and past the street, into and past Congo Square, soaking into the dry, coarse dirt of the yard at Parish Prison. She watched as the water headed towards the Old Basin Canal, kissing oblivious dirt streets as it passed.

It was beautiful, the most beautiful thing she'd ever seen. Tonight she'd committed grave error and witnessed resultant death, but in the here and now there was only epiphany—a culmination of mystical things beyond her understanding. Feathery tongues of recent dream continued to nag at the edges of her mind—wanting to understand, knowing that she would not, could not. She acknowledged a strange joy in the not-knowing. A voice interrupted her rapture:

"Keep yer damn mouth shut, nigger witch! People trine ta sleep!"

Malvina hadn't realized she was screaming.

She looked up at the irate pink face sticking out of a second story window, feeling oddly thrilled at the sound of a human voice, even an unfriendly one. She smiled and waved in his direction.

"Isn't it beautiful?" she cried.

"Crazy whore! Opium eater!" the man shouted before slamming the shutters.

As the window smacked shut, the sky drained of color, the humming ceased—and a series of recently loosened gears in Malvina's soul clicked and snapped into place. The door of the warehouse stood closed and silent as before.

Once again: no apparent trace of blackest night.

Suddenly: Aware of a lingering scent. The metallic, acrid smell of burnt coffee. Something remaining. In the air. And she knew that something else remained, too. Something that had gone towards the waters of the bayou.

"Shoes."

"Kilt her is what."

She would never clearly remember her journey through the grave that night, through the waters of the dead. Nor would she ever fully recall the gentle caress of Manman Brigitte. At least never in waking life.

But she did—and always would—remember the orange water with its thin streaks of pink. Would always remember the tinny music, its distant echo. These memories would become a part of who she was. That could not be changed.

She had called it. It was here. It remained.

She'd never sent it back, didn't know how. Wasn't sure if she would want to. It had been so beautiful, this thing that consumed both life and death before retiring to the stagnant waters of the bog. Maybe, she thought, it would eventually leave this world of its own accord. Maybe it would die in the swamp. Or maybe it was sleeping and biding its time.

Awaiting rebirth.

She decided that if it did return, she would be ready for it.

"Goddamn shoes. Always in my way."

"Where that little girl go?"

And so she had waited. Going about her day to day life, but always, in the back of her mind; waiting.

*Now.*

Fifty-three years had passed with no sign of the thing that had gone into the canal. And now Coco Robicheaux, the Cajun bogeyman of children's' tales, had seen fit to plague her sleep with dreams; old, sour memories mixed with something new, and something darker still at the creases of her mind. In dreams, Coco Robicheaux is looking for her—without benefit of eyes. Frances had known none of it. Had only walked around the house, leaving her damn shoes everywhere and searching for the ghost of her long dead Maria.

"Damn shoes."

In fifty-three years not a word had been spoken between the sisters. Not to each other.

"Maria?"

Not directly.

## CHAPTER TWENTY-FIVE
## *All About Jim Jam Jump*

My name is Jim Jam Jump—and this here is my story! Figgered I should write it down since Mama says I'm special and bound to do great things-liggity-bump. Normally I don't take much account to what Mama say, but I reckon she's right on that one.

Rat clap-a-tap map flap cut cat basic facts about myself being:

Sixteen years old fer now, handsome as heck, thin but strong and mighty quick, two times smarter than a whip, menace to my enemies and grim reaper to rodents who dare to cross my path.

Jippity jap hubadah gump flitty pritty stump.

Mama says I got me a good imagination, right about that too. Words come into my head and I just say em. Folks call it gibberish but I know it ain't. Means plenty to me and it feels good when I talk em. Sklip pap pah. The sounds just come outta me and it makes me real excited-like. I know dern well if something feels that swell it must *be* swell, too. Jeeka by boo.

What I say, Jim.

Mama says I'm a good lookin' fella, she right about that too. Mama's not right about ever-single-thing, though. She's poor Italian immigrant trash, full of superstitious ways and spoutin' broke-up English 'bout the Lord n'such. Never did learn to talk right, she. Mama tried teaching me Italian once but it never did took. Now, *that* sound like straight up gibberish to *me*, Slim; zigga higga jig is what. But she a good ol' gal and I mean her no wrong fer it. Nope-a-dope shippity shah.

Weren't born with the name of Jim, got that name from Crawfish Bob, same fella made me famous. Born with the super eye-tal-yun soundin' name of Dominick Carolla. But my hair is nigh yella and my eyes are fishy-blue, so no one need to know where my folk come from. Keep that to yerself, Slim. Jim jam scram hucka lucka zucka zig.

Ffffrit.

Fame and fortune come my way at the age of no more'n ten. Bored as fly in a glass box I pounded a nail straight through a heavy chunka wood, hunka hunka chunka wood-shy, and took to killin' rats in the alleys of the tenderloin district just fer fun. Lotsa good fat ones up-down-roun' thattaway. Best time fer huntin' rats being the twilight time when it ain't quite dark. I could score an average thirty-three in twenty minny, my personal best being forty-seven and I ain't even lyin', Sam. Flim flum flam.

The night Bob happened upon my killin' hobby I didn't even shy-lie know he was peekin' till he shouted and whooped and jumped up and down, fliggity mighty lighty lo and bee-hold, offering me a job 'fore I could shout jumbo. Paid me two full penny a night to kill rats lurkin' like grim fuzzy terror where the alley dark and damp as a sewer runnin' straight past and behind his place o' binness on Basin, a fight store named for Bob called Crawfish Bob's. Bob's place wasn't directly on Basin, more like in the alley behind, crunched up with a block of warehouses full of liquor and coffee beans. If you didn't know where to look you'd probably never know.

Anyhoo, I thought that a pretty good lotta-licka loot back then, but it only got better is what. Glam slap fly. Got better it did too, real right quick and then some, sho.

Got better 'tween fights at the fight store one night when ol' Bob took a slew of bettors out in the alley to see me in hellfire killin' mode. The bettors just stood with mouths all agape as I got ratties with the nail-stick, whackety crack smack freaky bop squeak, one right after the other just like fappy-tah. After none left fer movin' and I'm catching my breath, Bob speak up to the bettors:

"I'd bet a dixie that, in a controlled settin', that boy could kill thirty rats in ten minny." Tall order, that, thought me.

Little clicka silence before one of the bettors wrinkled up his gin blossom nose and spoke back sharp-like:

"I'd put a dixie agen' that, Bob." Unbeliever is what. Mama call unbelievin': Inf-*fuh*-dellin'.

And thus it begun, wallah wallah gallah hoo. What I say, Jim, jeeka bye boo.

The fight pit at Crawfish Bob's saw ever' kinda blood. Chicken blood from cockfightin', dog blood from pit bull fightin', and man blood from bare knuckle boxin'. Didn't seem such a stretch to add some rat blood in the mix. And so-wee 'twas.

Crawfish Bob put me in that pit with a cage fulla fat, hungry vermin collected up by the niggras who usually just sweep the floors and break up fights among the gin blossom gang. Bettor-getter-fly, say hoo. Well, them bettors still makin' bets when the cage door fly open, and I just go: whackety crack split bap-a-tap just like normal 'ceptin' with people shoutin' and a-whoopin—some rootin' fer me and some rootin' fer rats depending on where they money lie. That very first ratfight made ol' Bob a pile o' clean dixies right off the bat lickety splat. And I'm on my way to fame, just like that.

Bob say he gonna paint my name on a big wood board out front, and that I oughtta come up with a snappy show-folk name ta help sell tickets. Well, I just scratch my head and say "Jim jam jump, what kinda name ya mean, there, Bob?"

He just smile real big and say, "You said it, son. Jim Jam Jump, the Amazing Ratboy of Orleans Parish and Serr-ROUN-din' Terri-trees!"

The name of Jim Jam Jump got known far and wide lickety-quick, and the money rolled in fer Bob at the rate of one thin dime per tickee with a whole lot more from bets on top o' that. Rats got scarce so Bob started ta breedin', but it take a while 'fore pink baby ratties to fill out chubby-full-grown. It warn't long 'fore ol' Bob hadda spend some of his Amazin' Ratboy loot on hirin' more niggras to collect up street-rats fer the spectacle. Collected up so many rats that the Parish got mighty clean of em, 'ol Bob and Ratboy winnin' praise from Mayor Almighty Himself. Fap whap ding.

That's how I got to know my best pal, the niggra called Dropsy Morning-star, a fine rat collector and new good ol' friend of yours truly, Jim Jam Jump.

Dropsy an idjit; smilin' too big alla time and dumb as a stone, but he fun to hang around 'cause he do what I say and strong as an ox times two. I guess you could say we partners n' such. Mippity moppity jiggle wiggle wutch. Come to find; my family and Dropsy's got a connection too. This town shore is small, I say it to you and say it again. Small as a ball in a crack in a wall and that's all to the hall. Tickety-tall.

O'course, I got plans bigger'n rat killin'. Stuff of legends must go beyond mere rodent-blood induced fame.

I'm gonna learn to play the horn like Buddy Bolden. Better'n Buddy Bolden is what. Now, if I could just get me a dern horn! I'm savin' up fer one now, is how.

Slimmity-slam honk-a-tonk man, be I. Just shortly and around the corner. And that's what.

What.

I say.

What I say, Jim.

Jam-Jump!

# CHAPTER TWENTY-SIX

## *Typhus*

The sky was dark and moonless as the sound of footfalls thudded past. Nowhere near sleep, Typhus Morningstar heard them perfectly and ignored them completely.

The youngest of the Morningstar clan hadn't slept much since the death of their father fifteen years ago. With so many unanswered questions having plagued him since then, Typhus' youthful knack for understanding had long since left him of its own accord. Served him right, he figured, for being so smug in his judgment of grown-ups back then—their avoidance of bothersome truths being the last thing he really did fully understand nowadays.

In the now and so many years after Noonday's passing, it was just Typhus, Malaria and Dropsy who kept on at the old house—along with the occasional and welcome addition of young West Bolden. For lack of anywhere else to go, Diphtheria's nine-year-old spent most of his nights (and a great many of his days) here at the Morningstar place while his mother plied her trade on Basin Street.

Over the years Dropsy had grown from wispy and thin to thick and sturdy, but his inner transformation to manhood had been less plain. While the other Morningstar children allowed their spirits to harden at least marginally after the loss of their father, Dropsy had maintained a steadfast tenderness, never relinquishing his innocent fascination for everyday things. Some of Typhus' earliest memories were of his older brother's eyes examining the journeys of ordinary threads through ordinary fabric (be it shirt, rug, or sock) for long minutes. He imagined Dropsy's wide brown eyes searching for hints of code, probing imagined or hidden meanings within the woven color of fabric—as if the fabric of an old shirt might also contain answers to the fabric of the universe itself. Dropsy, now twenty-five, never lost this odd penchant for rug pondering—and Typhus often found himself grinning with envy at the sight.

Conversely, the trauma of their father's death had affected every inch of Typhus—or lack thereof. Quite literally: he had not grown an inch since that night—now standing no more than four and a half feet tall at age twenty-four.

With the coming of his own manhood, Typhus' interests had become decidedly adult in nature, and, having the body-size of a child, such inclinations proved problematic. In his twenty-four years, Typhus had only known one woman in the biblical sense—that being an act of charity, a gift from Diphtheria on his sixteenth birthday. Diphtheria had paid an undisclosed sum to a pretty crib colleague called Hattie to take young Typhus on a night-long tour of her worldly skills. Although the experience had proved educational, there had been neither love nor convincing tenderness involved, and so the encounter served mainly to underline the profound sense of longing in his heart. With this dull, bitter longing came a dull ache, and with the dull ache came a dull anger, and with the dull anger came dull fear—and that fear was of being alone. Typhus began to wonder if a man in the shape of a boy could ever realistically hope to attain the tender touch of woman neither sister, nor whore, nor whore-hired-by-sister.

Doctor Jack's keen spiritual radar picked up on the boy's blue condition shortly after its manifestation, and he wasted no time addressing the problem in his own unique way:

"The love of a face you'll never know is the purest love of all, Typhus," he had proclaimed with soft eyes as he handed Typhus a paper present intended as cure. "That's because the love you feel for an unknowing stranger has no conditions or demands. So, Typhus, give your love to Lily—and know that she will neither return your love nor break your heart. There is safety in a smile like hers." Doctor Jack's gaze shifted from Typhus' eyes before concluding, just under breath, "If safety is a thing that you require."

The gift was a picture of Lily—and it just happened that Lily was the prettiest lady Typhus had ever laid eyes on. So pretty, in fact, that Doctor Jack's final mumbled sentence failed to register its intended warning in Typhus' dizzy heart.

The photograph was printed on heavy, smooth paper measuring five by seven inches, with the following words imprinted in loopy French type along the bottom margin:

*"Daliet Aristo Finish, 517 Frenchmen Street, New Orleans."*

The paper itself was light brown in color, dressed in sundry shades of chocolate ink with light burgundy highlights. A ham-handed studio artist had filled in Lily's dress with pure white, giving the garment a detached and artificial quality. Its stark paleness provided an illusion of weightlessness, the dress appearing to drift a millimeter or so above the photo's surface just beyond the two-dimensional logic of Lily's chocolate-burgundy world. Anomaly of white aside, the dress infused Lily with an oddly virginal quality, complimenting her child's smile and sparkling eyes; a miracle of irony within her rectangle of existence.

Lily sat in her chair; knees tight together, right hand in a loose fist on her lap. Her hair was thick and piled high, wisps of it escaping their frilly ties, tickling pretty at the edges of her eyes. Exaggerated and round, her deep black pupils and gently drooping eyelids suggested the effect of opium as they gazed at an odd angle, apparently seeing something of casual interest just left of the man behind the camera. Beside her was a small round table holding two shot glasses (one half-full, the other half-empty), a bottle of Raleigh Rye, a small round clock, a circular metallic pillbox, and a few other small objects (cosmetic items?) which Typhus couldn't name. On the wall behind her hung several oddly shaped hand-carved frames tenanting images ranging from the vaguely religious to the vaguely obscene.

Diminishing to a thin edge of lace, the material of Lily's nightgown encircled her throat elegantly, its hem riding less than an inch above her knees. Her left hand cupped her right breast; a crude gesture filtering itself through an improvised taxonomy of grace, defending its existence in terms of dim-witted innocence. Lily's face was a tender juncture of perfect lines; slight curves converging and intersecting, swooping and gliding, her full lips barely meeting in an uneven smile, coaxing the slightest dimple from her right cheek, betraying the presence of any African blood that potentially swam beneath fair skin. In Storyville, they called girls with Lily's complexion "high yella." High yella also meant high-priced.

Typhus didn't know how old the photograph might be; there was no date assigned it by the *Daliet Aristo* photographic studio. Had no way of knowing anything of Lily's personal history—or even of the photo itself. He'd never seen her face in the flesh and didn't realistically ever hope to do so. There were many whores in the district and he'd only occasion to see a handful, all of whom were friends or associates of his sister. No matter, for he had no intention of seeking Lily out in person—concrete knowledge or physical contact with her, he believed, could only harm the perfect type of love which Doctor Jack had described to him.

Could be that Lily was an old woman by now. Maybe dead. Her name probably wasn't even Lily; just a pretty name for a pretty picture made up by

Doctor Jack. Maybe this photo had passed through many hands before it found its way to his own; Typhus only one in a long line of Lily's smitten admirers. Maybe Doctor Jack had been smitten himself at one time. No matter.

Typhus, of course, knew what pictures like this were for. They were meant as useful mementos for sailors preparing for long trips on high seas—for inspiration in moments of lonely, self-inflicted passion. No doubt this photo had seen its fair share of such inspiration—Typhus even noted a water stain near the lower left corner with a suspicious yellow quality about it. But he reckoned Lily to be passed around no more. She was his to keep, and he made a promise to always keep her safe:

"I'll take care of you, Miss Lily," he bargained sincerely in the direction of her perfect dimple, "I'll keep you from harm caused by fire, water, insect or other. And all you have to do in return is be what you are. Nothing else required at your end, Miss Lily. I promise you that and cross my heart so-help-me-Jesus-amen."

Which doesn't mean to say that Typhus never indulged a little self-inflicted passion of his own on her behalf—but he knew his paper Lily would bear him no grudge for such. When he felt good on her account, it was from the love in his heart—the feeling from down below being mere punctuation. Hattie Covington, a lady in the flesh with all attendant sweating and moaning and huffing and touching, had inspired nowhere near this kind of good feeling in Typhus on his sixteenth birthday. With his paper Lily it felt better, it was different.

Love was the difference.

§

Thoughts of Lily evaporated with the sound of sliding naked feet in the kitchen doorway. Typhus looked up to find an expression of sleepy concern animating his brother's squinting eyes.

"What's the matter, Dropsy?" Typhus said with his back to his brother, brushing bits of blackish dirt from the surreal white of Lily's dress.

Dropsy paused, wiping sleep from two eyes with one hand. "Heard a sound. Someone outside."

"No one's outside. Get back to bed." Typhus turned to face Dropsy with Lily held behind him.

Apparently startled by the sound of the two brothers, the owner of the footfalls outside broke into a run, crackling and thumping through grass towards a general fade.

Dropsy: "What that, then?"

"Whattaya think?"

A pause. "Think it's Daddy." A yawn.

"Mebbe so, Dropsy, mebbe so."

Dropsy's yawn introduced air into Typhus' nostrils, stale and awful smelling; a reminder of his brother's taste for chaw. Typhus crinkled his nose and narrowed his eyes.

"Shouldn't we go see what he brought this time, Typhus?"

"It'll keep till morning. Too dark now. Might go and step on whatever it is when it's so dark. Plus, might not be Daddy. Might be a bear."

Dropsy grinned and raised an eyebrow. Bears were pretty much unheard of around St. John's.

"Or maybe Coco Robicheaux," added Typhus with playful menace, referring to the Cajun bogeyman their father used to tell tales of when they were small. According to the stories, Coco Robicheaux was a beast of a man who bathed in foul swamp water, dressed in dismal rags, and kept a long, braided and filthy beard. Into this horrible beard had been woven many pockets, and in the pockets were little knives and mysterious tools. Their father had grimly informed them that Coco Robicheaux made it his life's work to pay terrible retribution upon children who stole cookies, talked back, and forgot chores. Although it was never entirely clear what Coco Robicheaux would specifically do with the little knives and tools kept in his beard, one thing was certain; if you ever lied to your mother, Coco Robicheaux would eat you. Dropsy's expression went sour with minor worry as he lowered his head and trudged slowly back towards the bedroom.

"'Night, Typhus."

"'Night, Dropsy."

"Typhus?" Dropsy turned in the doorway.

"Yeah?"

"I hope it's meat this time. I been hungry for meat. Ain't had any in a while."

Typhus smiled. "Well, I'll just bet it is. Now get on to bed and we'll have us a look-see soon as the sun come up."

Dropsy yawned once more before disappearing into the dark of the sleeping quarters. Typhus heard the crunch of straw as his older brother settled in.

# CHAPTER TWENTY-SEVEN

## *Shoes*

T he consensus among the Morningstar family was that their
mysterious benefactor and dead patriarch were one and the
same. Typhus secretly knew otherwise, while sympathizing
with his family's need to believe what could not be so. The
phantom's mystifying persistence had certainly offered more questions than
answers—and the idea of a fatherly ghost offered at least some token sense of
comfort. Typhus supposed such an explanation was as likely as any other if a
person didn't care to think things through.

Nine days after their father's death, the phantom had made its debut. In
that terrible time of grieving, temperatures had plummeted in South Louisiana,
stove coal becoming a scarce commodity. Then one chilly Tuesday morning,
Malaria opened the front door and let out a yell, "Lord God, thankee Jesus!
Amen, amen and a-*men* some more!" The rest of the Morningstars rushed to
bear witness. Shivering, hungry, and with hearts nowhere near mended, they
were in a vulnerable frame of mind where potential miracles were concerned.
But there it was.

A bundle of purple and white boskoyo blooms tied with a note, and beside
the blooms sat a huge crateful of beautiful black coal. The note was a small
square of paper (folded four times smaller) and, upon the unfolding, a single
word had been written in pencil:

*simpithees*

The phantom's gift of coal was enough to see the Morningstars through
every cold night for the rest of that year, and several of the next.

Time soon revealed the coal as mere introduction. In subsequent weeks the
Morningstar family found itself in need of basic articles for living, and as need

arose, answers appeared on their doorstep. If the quantity was any less than bountiful, the gift usually came with a note of apology,

*sory iffit ayn anuff.*

Blankets, coffee beans, grain, fruit, tools, clothes, animals for eating, and fresh water for drinking—nothing seemed beyond the generosity of the Morningstar family's phantom benefactor. If a conversation had taken place in the house regarding a particular need, that need would soon be satisfied. It was as if someone was spying on them; listening in, watching, taking notes and making sure. And the giving never stopped. Fifteen years later and the Morningstar family's benefactor had kept on benefacting.

Believing the phantom to be a ghostly representation of their own father had felt natural and good to the Morningstars—and the theory seemed approximately proven the first time the phantom passed over muddy ground, leaving clear, unshod footprints. Always first to rise, Malaria discovered the tracks at dawn, and she immediately retrieved a pair of her father's shoes from the house. Her face beamed as she compared the track's size to the length and girth of a corresponding shoe:

"See? A perfect fit!" Malaria announced authoritatively, at a volume intended for all to hear. The siblings were suddenly overwhelmed with a sense of guilt for burying their father without shoes on his feet. From that night on, Malaria made sure a pair of her father's shoes stood prominently by the doorstep with a note tied on, reading, in Malaria's perfect handwriting:

*Take these, Father, and thank you.*
*From Your Loving Children.*

The shoes sat unmolested with Malaria's note for better than a month. Then, when a particular bad growing season presented itself and the market price of corn went beyond the Morningstars' means, two bushels of near-ripe corn appeared, and the shoes were gone. A note had been left:

*mitee nis shoos thankee.*

Father Morningstar had owned and kept three pair of shoes in his adult life, so the remaining two pairs were left as offerings on subsequent nights. It was not long before all three pairs were retrieved—replaced with badly spelled "thank you" notes and fresh parcels of needed things.

From that point on, when the ground was damp and items appeared, tracks left behind were clearly made by the shoes of Noonday Morningstar. This only helped solidify the notion of ghostly intervention—despite the obvious truth of how the phantom had acquired means of such evidence. But the fantasy was made easier to believe—and the Morningstars desperately needed a thing to believe.

The truth had dawned on Typhus the morning Malaria left that first pair of shoes on the stoop. It struck him how Malaria's own "thank you" note had been so neat and perfect. This wasn't only true of Malaria; the whole family possessed first-rate writing skills, and their writing excelled because their father had taught them well. To the contrary, this phantom was clearly no good at spelling, and his handwriting was equally substandard. On the basis of this evidence alone, Typhus deducted the phantom could not be Noonday Morningstar. Typhus kept this observation to himself. The rest seemed so reassured by the idea of having their father back, even in this distant way, Typhus would not rob them of such small and harmless hope.

Before tonight, Typhus' sleeping troubles had provided him a single benefit—the right to bear exclusive ear-witness to the footfalls of the phantom. He had never considered sharing these nocturnal dramas with his siblings—to do so might encourage them to investigate or confront, which may be construed as ungrateful in the eyes of their benefactor—whoever it might be. After all, the phantom had given endlessly to the family, and all he seemed to want in return was his continued anonymity.

Tonight would mark the first and last time Typhus would violate that unspoken condition.

By the time the footfalls had returned, Dropsy was back in bed, snoring gently. Typhus found himself afflicted with a sudden and uncharacteristic curiosity. Why not put an end to a mystery so easily solvable? Impulsively, he kissed the hem of Lily's white dress with trembling lips and told her goodbye. Grabbed his multi-purpose coffee sack, kicked off his shoes for the sake of quiet, and went out.

Typhus' stunted size gave him the advantage of quiet steps, his bare feet hardly yielding a whisper from the moist codgrass blanketing the threshold to the brackish marsh. The sky was clear that night, moonlight barely trickling through tangled branches of towering cypress and black willow trees, not quite tickling stars. A crisp crush of blackberries beneath Typhus' feet gave him fair warning of nearby Devil's Walking Sticks—treacherous growths whose soft leathery leaves masked the presence of thorn-studded branches. The phantom moved ahead evenly without shadow or silhouette, his progress betrayed only by complaint of hard, spiny fruit balls crackling dully beneath his feet, freshly fallen from sweet gum trees that sprouted high above the marsh. Swamp-muffled moonlight distracted rather than illuminated, so much so that Typhus opted to remove light from the equation altogether; eyes shut tight, he walked on. Removing the want of light allowed a deeper appreciation for information of ear and hand. Typhus moved forward, fingers stretched before him, gently brushing rubbery leaves of unknown plant life. His legs and feet brushed and bumped against hard cypress knees, the height of which indicated how high the waters were prone to rise in a given section of swamp, but also giving some indication of how far he was from home. Nearer the house, the cypress knees were no more than six inches at their tallest—here he noted several in excess of three feet. He soon became concerned as to whether he'd be able to navigate his way back in the dark. Soon the sound of footfalls stopped. Typhus stopped, too.

Quiet.

Would have been perfect quiet if not for the low warble of a hundred lonely bullfrogs, hoping for love and getting none. Typhus waited. Still: No sound beyond that of lovelorn reptiles. With private embarrassment, he realized his eyes were still closed. When he opened them, a gentle illumination in the bog brought him a soft shock. It made no sense. It struck Typhus that this was not light as he understood it.

Light—but not light. That is, it wasn't so much light as it was a lighter shade of dark. Even this might have made sense had it been a variety of gray (as shadows tend to be)—but this shadow had color. Like fire minus the flicker and crackle; just warm, thick color, lightly painting plants, trees, and saw grass.

Orange. Everything orange.

No sign of the phantom, no sound, no telltale silhouette; nothing. The brightest area of swamp appeared twenty yards or so ahead where cypress knees stretched upwards of four feet. The center.

Center of what? Typhus considered turning back. Didn't. As he drew close to the light's apparent source, the ground became muddier and the desire to inch forward amplified. Typhus's toes wiggled in the slush, his feet sinking in, then pulling out; the quagmire lightly tugging at the soles of his feet like a living thing. He took another step. Another. And again.

Forwards.

In the swamp of Bayou St. John every inch of terrain is packed with unruly life, every grain of soil nourishing something that insists on being, and thus is, and so grows. This is the way of all wetlands. But the place where Typhus currently found himself didn't follow these basic rules. Typhus was standing in a clearing—a tacit impossibility where life only competes to push forward, mindlessly crowding in on itself in the name of dumb survival. As his brain struggled to accept the strange reality before him, it dawned on him that the odd light tapered and faded from the spot where he now stood. He was standing at its source.

A lone mosquito-fern drifted nearby, its mossy mats and two-lobed leaves bunched up death-still at the surface of the pool.

Here there was nothing—no sound or sensation, not even of frogs. But there was a certain power in this nothing, a power with no evident bearing on human senses. There was no feeling about it, no feeling at all; just a knowing. But this "knowing" did prod a feeling from Typhus' chest; a feeling of naked, new wonder.

*threads through a rug*

His feet were submerged, toes squishing in mud. He bent down to dip a finger in. Cool, orange water. Licked his finger. No odd flavor, only the rancid muddy taste of any stale bog. He bent down; inspected the water's smooth surface carefully by eye before realizing that, although he hadn't waded further, hadn't moved at all—somehow the water had crept to his knees. Idle thought: "I'm sinking."

Sinking. *sinking*

No matter.

The possibility of his body and soul being consumed by this (*nothing*) was unimportant at the moment. Typhus thought of Dropsy's knack for instant bliss, and now here was his own. His own uncomplicated, painless acceptance. If there was danger here, then danger was welcome. This was right now. This was his special reality. This belonged to him. This thing. His thing.

*bliss*

In the water. The water. Water.

*water*

But from this purest moment, the worst possible thing happened.

(...)

Lily. Removed from his mind. From his heart and his soul.

*(bliss)*

If she remained somewhere in his heart, he was simply unaware. She was gone from him now, and he didn't miss her. Her eyes forgotten, impossible white dress forgotten, Raleigh Rye forgotten, mysterious yellow stain forgotten, hand in a loose fist forgotten, promises made and rewards rendered: forgotten, forgotten, forgotten.

*water*

The water was a kind of false light—but not light—and, really, not even water. There was something in it. Something living in it.

*the journey of*

Streaks of reddish brown and tiny wisps of pink: jetted and swam, soared then dipped, shot then faltered. *threads through a rug*

The pinkness was familiar to him, the familiarity a calming thing, the color of rebirth, the color of his babies. The babies he'd sent off on their way into the river, for second chances, for the tender mercy of childless mothers. Typhus didn't know whether to feel joy or dread at the familiarity. He didn't know whether to feel at all. There was nothing more to feel.

No matter.

As his eyes followed pink motion, a tinny music positioned itself at the back of his mind, the sound of a horn through a ghostly filter; not a physical sound. The water snuck to his waist—but he didn't care, couldn't pull his thoughts from the sound in his mind and the image in his eyes.

So beautiful. Haunting. Lovely. Final.

Bliss.

*Troubled about my soul...*

Sinking.

*No matter.*

As the water (*not water*) reached his chest, Typhus realized he no longer needed to bend at the hips in order to view (*adore*) the divine movement of pink. As orange gradually (*not gradually*) rose to the level of his throat, a fear of drowning failed to present itself. The thought of being submerged forever here was not a threatening thing.

Typhus Morningstar was, like his faithful friend the mosquito-fern, now perfectly still. His trusty burlap sack slipped from his fingers.

Typhus waited for the bag to float up to the top. It did not. It was lost. A nominal price for bliss, he thought. Goodbye, old friend.

A stray thought. Unwelcome. Bliss = loss?

Now Typhus thought about loss. Thoughts of loss brought Lily to mind; promises he'd made her, the guilty fact that she'd always lived up to her end of the bargain without question, complaint, argument, or negotiation.

Unexpectedly, something like fear materialized in Typhus' chest.

What had been pink and lovely had become vaguely dreadful. The gliding grace of alien music stretched and tore into a colorless wail.

Loss = death?

He could not do this thing to Lily, would not do this thing.

*sinking*

Paper Lily. The girl who would neither return his love nor break his heart. The girl he had promised to keep and protect.

Death = absence of pain?

Life = ?

Just as the water reached his lips, Typhus threw his head back, pulled his arms above his head and frantically clutched at warm air.

*pain?*

A violent splash. Two heavy hands clasped Typhus just above the elbows, pulling his feet and legs up through cool, smooth mud, provoking a gaseous squeal from around his waist and below, the sound of resistant suction. Typhus looked down and saw his own muddy feet kicking above angry orange. Now thrown back and away from the lake of cool fire, his body smacked into a patch of moist saw grass. Typhus' eyes blinked hard, then darted—searching for the owner of the saving hands. Finding: A black silhouette. Hearing: "Typhus? Typhus, you all right, boy?"

It was a voice from his past—one he couldn't quite place.

A hulking shadow of a man.

"Typhus?"

The face was a murk of swamp grays.

. Fuzzy sparks of recognition triggered in Typhus' mind as the phantom leaned closer. The man was kneeling. Dressed in ancient, filthy rags; nothing but the shoes on his feet offering any functionality. Typhus didn't recognize the man, but he recognized the shoes. His father's shoes.

The hair and beard of the phantom were long; copious grays braided and flecked with traces of green and brown. The beard stretched past his naked belly with weird purpose; little curved bumps in various shapes and sizes disrupting its thick mass from chin to tip, suggesting lumpy cells of concealed code. With a sleepy sense of dread, Typhus realized the anomalies in the phantom's beard were, in fact, a series of woven pockets, and from their mouths gleamed the edges of mysterious implements.

"*Coco Robicheaux,*" Typhus whispered dimly.

The phantom's shadow-saturated features ignited upwards from concern to amusement, his voice deepening with a rumble of low laughter; "*Temps moune connaite l'aute nans grand jou, nans nouite yeaux pas bisoen chandelle pou clairer yeaux!*" The words were a Creole proverb his father had been fond of, the approximate meaning; "When a man knows another by broad daylight, he doesn't need a candle to recognize him at night." The phantom cleared his throat with a cough, managed to collect himself, then let his smile settle into a soft grin before switching back to English:

"Can't go standing in the orange water, Typhus. It'll sing to you first, then suck you down second if you ain't careful."

Typhus's eyes struggled to decipher the man's face. He knew this face. It was not his father, but it was someone his father had known.

"You okay, Typhus?"

He knew this face. He knew that laugh. He remembered. Now, he remembered.

"Typhus, say something. Say anything."

Typhus meant to thank the phantom. Might have thanked him for all he'd done for his family over the years. Might have thanked him for saving his life just now. Might have thanked him for saving his life fifteen years previously. Might have apologized for having betrayed all past kindnesses by following him out into the bog on this night, for choosing not to respect the phantom's simple and single condition of privacy.

Typhus said none of those things. But he did say:

"It ain't right to wear the shoes of a man you kilt."

Beauregard Church fell still and quiet; breath hushed, warmth drained from his eyes as pain and regret felt their way through the gray. His heavy head lulled, then dipped. He stood, looked at his feet; at the perfectly fitting shoes of Noonday Morningstar that warmed and protected them. Turned. Walked into darkness, crunching grass and twigs beneath the shoes. Shoes once belonging to a man whose back had held and bled from a family heirloom.

So many years ago.

*away*

Orange dimmed, its smooth color inaugurating a fade, then dying completely. The swamp: now black. The ground: uneventfully damp. Typhus closed his useless eyes. A thousand lonely swamp frogs warbled on. He made his way home quickly. Despite the dark and without moon or stars to guide him, Typhus found in himself a near miraculous sense of direction. To find his way home, he simply followed the brightest thing in his troubled heart.

Lily, on a high shelf in the kitchen, was his North Star.

§

The phantom returned to the Morningstar home soon thereafter, on a night when mist stifled starlight and sky reached its richest shade of coal. Moist air corrupted the travel of sound, and so Typhus did not make note of footfalls.

That morning, the traditional bundle was found on the doorstep. No note was attached.

Malaria, always first to rise, joyfully carried the lumpy package through the threshold, gaily chirping, "A present from Father!" Typhus and Dropsy dragged themselves from straw mattresses, wiping sleep from dry eyes. Dropsy goosed a groggy smile from his lips, spoke in a cracked whisper:

"Well, what's in it, Malaria? Dump it out already."

Before the contents fell, Typhus recognized the wrapping. A burlap bag made for holding coffee beans, but also good for any number of functions, including rebirthing babies in muddy rivers. Malaria held the bag from its bottom corners, pinching fingers and pulling up; spilling its contents to the floor.

Malaria screamed. Typhus' eyes filled with water. Dropsy accepted, stating simply, "I was hopin' fer meat."

On the floor, lay exactly six shoes.

Fresh tracks outside betrayed the recent presence of a large man with bare feet.

# CHAPTER TWENTY-EIGHT
## *Christ Kid is Risen*

The oversized and square right fist of the big white man arced wide to connect with the unguarded cheek of the Christ Kid—and Eugene Reilly felt a twinge of panic tickle his bladder.

The Christ Kid was looking punchy and incompetent—this had not been the plan, had not been the agreement, not at all in accordance with promises made by Crawfish Bob's allegedly disenfranchised right-hand man Stiffy Lacoume. Still, Reilly held out a hope. Maybe this was all part of the act. Just to make it look good. Believable. Everyone knew Windmill Willie was the easy favorite, a win from the Christ Kid was near unthinkable—and a *quick* win would smell like the rat it was.

The Christ Kid ducked a second windmill—but a hard right jab to the midsection followed shortly. The Kid flurried in return; sending six but delivering only two.

On the bright side, the Kid did manage the occasional connection. On the grim side, the white giant hardly seemed fazed. The bulk of the crowd, having gone with shorter odds and smarter money, whooped and hollered for the Christ Kid's inevitable demise. Reilly tried to ignore his nagging bladder as he fantasized of slow and creative ways to end the life of that double-crossing Cajun charlatan who'd suckered him with every sucker's favorite bait: the words "sure thing."

Then, as if Reilly's distress was spelled out across his forehead, Stiffy materialized in apparent response. Placing a hand on Reilly's shoulder, he bent to the Irishman's ear, "Pretty good show, eh, Mr. Reilly?"

"I think our boy's in trouble," Reilly grumbled.

Stiffy made an injured expression. "Have a little faith, my friend. Those boys both know the score—and neither has an ounce of love ner loyalty for that shameless skinflint Crawfish Bob. They were told to make it look good, and that's just what they're doing."

Reilly, unconvinced: "I dunno. The Kid looks like he's losing his footing. Like he's losing *consciousness*, fer chrissakes."

Stiffy smiled wide, exposing large brownish teeth, two of which were chipped enough to expose blackened centers. "Of course he does, pardna! Of course he does!"

"If this is Willie's idea of a dive, I don't like it. Not one bit, I don't."

"Well, perhaps business of this sort is conducted more subtly in the Great State of New York, Mr. Reilly. Here in the South we enjoy adding a little dramatic flair to everything we do."

*Shit-grinning swindler,* thought Reilly. "If this is a double-cross, I swear to Christ…"

Stiffy gave Reilly another firm pat on the shoulder, followed by, "Just relax and enjoy the show, friend. You'll see." Stiffy vanished into the crowd, waddling with confidence.

"Smug bastard," Reilly hissed under breath, although he had to admit the old coot's confidence had bolstered his own somewhat.

The Christ Kid failed to block a quick succession of brutal blows to the ribs and fell hard to his knees, gasping for air. The pudgy, balding man who functioned as referee angled his body between the two fighters and began the count:

"ONE…… TWO……THREE……."

"Goddamnit," said Reilly through clenched teeth.

"FOUR……"

If this was part of the show, it was too damn convincing. A one-sided workout at best, Willie was only slightly winded, a thin sheen of sweat lightly coating him from forehead to ankle. The white boxer easily caught his breath and casually examined his swollen knuckles while the Christ Kid wheezed in apparent agony on the canvas. This couldn't be happening, Reilly thought. He had five thousand dollars riding on this "sure thing." Someone would pay for this, by God.

"FIVE……"

He couldn't look. Reilly's eyes surveyed the room, eventually settling on the kid they called Ratboy, who immediately preceding the boxing match had dispatched a record forty-three rats in three minutes with a wide, nail studded stick. Ratboy was now sitting on the floor near the bar dabbing a collection of small, bloody ankle wounds with a moist cloth. At first glance, Reilly mistook the expression on Ratboy's face for a pained grimace—but after a moment he deciphered the expression more accurately: The kid was grinning from ear to ear. *Holy Jesus Harold Q. Christ,* thought Reilly. *Does the whole state of Louisiana need to be fitted for a rubber hat?* Oh, how he longed to return home, to the place he'd always considered the toughest, most dangerous place on earth, his beloved New York City. Up north, at least, the dregs of society retained the smallest crumb of dignity. Up north, they only pitted dogs and niggers against rats in the fight pits. Not light-haired children snatched from the looney bin.

In his prime, Reilly had been considered one of New York's finest short-con operators. His game had been faro, and he was damn good at it—hell, he practically invented its modern version. In its early days, faro was considered the fairest of all gambling endeavors, the dealer's advantage being a mere two per cent. Reilly had single-handedly coupled creativity and skill to subvert this fairest of games, his innovation being the manufacture of a special dealing box—a handcrafted steel and brass affair complete with hidden levers, plates, and springs—that allowed the dealer to not only preview the deck's order, but to manipulate it. It was the physical beauty of the box itself that had the marks lining up; its shiny authority and fine detail reflected upon its owner—a thieving shyster could not possibly own such a beautiful gadget.

That was long ago, though, before the game's reputation had been tarnished by the hundreds of tag-a-long imitators and their own clumsy variations and ham-fisted executions. The new generation of unimaginative bums had ruined the system for dignified entrepreneurs like Reilly. He'd made his fortune, but had spent it too fast—and now he was looking for a quick way to multiply what remained. This trip to New Orleans was supposed to be a simple holiday—like so many Northerners, he'd been enticed by tales of Storyville's legendary feminine delicacies. But a trusted friend had urged him to contact Stiffy Lacoume while in town, had assured him Stiffy was a reliable man and an excellent source of quick investment opportunities. And so here he was.

"SIX......"

Goddamnitall straight to hell.

Reilly's dumbfounded eyes located Stiffy's puffy mug across the ring; poker-pussed and unblinking, looking straight at him. Then: the slightest nod, followed by an almost imperceptible wink.

In an instant, everything changed.

The Christ Kid had risen.

"SEV—"

The body of the Christ Kid trailed the comet of his fist, barreling forwards, knocking the ref over backwards along the way. Windmill Willie hadn't seen any of it, had missed the shriek of the ref and the gasp of the bettors, missed the swoosh of the Christ Kid's breeze. Even the impact to Willie's jaw failed to register until his bulk reeled against gravity, losing to sharp physics; crashing to the mat.

The crowd held its collective breath and Reilly let out a too-audible sigh. Stiffy threw him a wide grin, shaking his head as if to say: "I told you so, mister." Dazed but uncursing, the ref picked himself up and solemnly went about a new count, this time to the detriment of Windmill Willie.

ONE...

Somewhere behind Reilly there was a commotion.

TWO...

Shouting, slamming doors. Could be the jig was up—perhaps a disgruntled bettor had smelled something rotten in this farfetched comeback, setting off the sparks that would blossom into full-out brawl. This, Reilly had to admit, was probably not the case. What he had just witnessed was the most convincing dive he'd ever seen—even *he* didn't believe it would actually happen till after the fact.

THREE...

From the general direction of the commotion, a deep, booming voice of Irish extraction shouted, "Nobody move!"

Coppers!

A rush of men went for the back door, a gun went off, a man fell—spitting blood and coughing loudly. No one else followed the bleeding man towards the door, a second rifle blast sending a dozen trembling men to the floor with hands clasped behind blubbering skulls.

FOUR...

As if insulted by the ref's continued count, Windmill Willie rose to his knees, then to his feet. The Christ Kid bobbed and danced, ready for Willie to mix it up again. The fight was not yet over.

Enraged by the tenacious boxers, The Irishman's baritone raised to near tenor; "Stop this motherfucking fight, goddamn you! This is a raid. Game over, you *shits!*"

The Christ Kid let out a sigh, and let both arms droop to his sides. Willie just stared at the Kid, muttering something between clenched teeth. Reilly was just close enough to make out what was said:

"You sucker-punched me, boy. Can't let you get away with that."

Willie wound back for a final swing, a swollen right fist connecting directly to the center of the Christ Kid's unguarded chest. Unprepared for the blow, the Christ Kid dropped like a sack of bricks, flat on his back, his head hitting hard to canvas. The Kid let out a gasp and a cough, then a fountain of thick phlegm and blood shot upwards into the air.

*"Goddamn it, I said stop this fucking fight!"* The Irish cop's cheeks were reddening rapidly.

An ungodly shriek pierced the air. Reilly's head turned to the source: "Scriminee-HEE-HEE-HEEEEE! *That's my partner!* Dropsy, get up!"

It was Ratboy, jumping to his feet and charging towards the ring. The little white kid jumped under the first rope and slid to the side of the Christ Kid, pulling off his own rat-bloodied shirt to tuck under the Kid's head for a pillow.

"*Dropsy!* Dropsy, say something!"

The Christ Kid looked into the eyes of the Ratboy, gave a little smile, said, "I'm hurt bad, Jim. Where's that doctor?" His eyes went cloudy and rolled to white.

"*DOCTOR!!*" shrieked Ratboy. "They done kilt him! They kilt my best partner Dropsy!"

A paunchy man with a stethoscope dangling from his neck ducked beneath the ropes and climbed onto the canvas. "Now, boy, stand aside. I'm sure ol' Dropsy's just got the wind knocked out of him."

Ratboy edged aside, refusing to let go the boxer's swollen hand.

Cops wrestled with distressed bettors; some fighting like wild animals, others offering only nervous smiles and futile negotiations. The big Irishman stood near the ring: "He gonna be okay, Doc?"

The Christ Kid's eyes, no longer purely white, stared upwards. His lips sputtered no more, and Reilly noted odd-shaped ovals of blood adorning the canvas around his head.

"Well, Officer, what we have here is an accidental death," said the man with the stethoscope.

"*Death?*" The cop: Incredulous, eyes wide.

"Yessuh. Deader 'n fried chicken, I'm afraid."

Ratboy shrieked.

The Irishman's eyes narrowed. "Well, doc, what we have here is *manslaughter.*" Then, turning from the ring with his loudest authoritarian voice: "Bad news, you surly bunch of law-breakin' sons o'jackals! Your 'illegal gambling' charge just got upgraded to 'accomplice to manslaughter.' That'd be a felony in the great state of Louisiana, so the first of you to make a move for the door gets a bullet in the back. Do not doubt my sincerity in this matter."

*Holy shit on a shingle,* thought Reilly, rapidly calculating the odds of his own awful luck.

The New Yorker edged his way up to the Irish cop-in-charge, fine-tuning in his mind a burgeoning angle.

"Officer, may I have a word?"

"Stand aside, scum." The scowl of the Irishman brought Reilly a chill.

Needfully persistent, Reilly flashed his most winning faro-smile; "Officer, I'm a businessman from New York, and I have a train to catch in thirty minutes. I assure you that I was brought here under false pretenses by a tour guide whom I've only just met. I had no idea—"

"New York, eh?" The cop was smiling.

"Yes, sir," Reilly offered hopefully. There were lots of Irish families in New York; maybe this cop was from one.

The cop sent a backhanded smack across Reilly's prickly cheek, throwing him backwards into the arms of a second, conveniently located police officer.

"Listen, you high-brow Yankee dirt bag. Your big city bullshit don't wash with the Louisiana law. What's your name?"

Reilly saw another card to be played and went for it, "Eugene Reilly, officer. Of Irish decent just like yourself. How about giving an Irish brother a break?" Reilly gave his faro-smile another workout. "Whaddaya say, Captain?"

"Well, Mr. Eugene Reilly of Yankee nativity and Irish descent, I will make a note of just who and what you are. We have special fun with Yankees down the precinct, but I'll make sure the boys leave a bone or two unbroken on account of your fine Irish bloodline."

"But Officer, I'm certain we can work something out if you would only…"

Reilly's pleas were interrupted by renewed commotion near the front door. A group of desperate gamblers had tried to smash the padlock with a crowbar smuggled from behind the bar. A corresponding group of beefy men in uniform responded with corresponding brutality.

"Stand against the bar, Reilly!" The big Irishman grabbed Reilly by the back of the neck and shoved him towards the bar. Fearing another blow, Reilly meekly complied. This was clearly not a good time to explore further negotiations. Perhaps at the jailhouse, after temperaments had a chance to cool. There was nothing Reilly could do now—except stand with his back to the bar as the pathetic black circus of his life unraveled around him.

Suddenly a new distraction presented itself—this time from within the ring. Reilly stared in weak amusement as Ratboy chased Windmill Willie around the ring in a surreal blur—waving his ratkilling stick and shrieking gibberish like a wounded hog. The big man and the skinny boy somehow managed to avoid trampling the corpse of the Christ Kid in the course of the wild chase, Willie bellowing threats at the boy but fleeing just the same. The thin lips of the Christ Kid seemed to curve at the edges—most likely a trick of the light, Reilly deducted—or perhaps a minute muscle contraction related to the dying process. Either way, this image of smiling death made the tiny hairs at the back of his neck bristle and stand. Reilly practically jumped out of his skin when a hand grabbed his shoulder from behind. He turned to look.

Stiffy Lacoume stood behind the bar with eyes wide and finger to lips. Before Reilly could think to question, the old Cajun displayed surprising strength and agility by yanking all two hundred pounds of the New Yorker over the bar top and onto the sticky concrete floor behind. The two men crouched alone on all fours as the room beyond exploded into a new wave of violence, Reilly's disappearance going unnoticed.

"If you want to get out of this mess, you'll keep your mouth shut and follow me," said the Cajun. Reilly quickly nodded. Stiffy wasted no time, turning around and crawling towards the deep end of the back of the bar. Reilly followed Stiffy's sizable backside, glimpsing salvation in its frantic waddle.

The bellow of Crawfish Bob rose above the din, "He got 'em, goddammny! Ratboy done got Willie! Got 'im with that naily stick o' his! Now we got ourselves *two* bodies!" Bob's excited tone was a weird mixture of horror and amusement.

"Holy Christ almighty!" Reilly yelped.

"*Quiet,* damn ya!" Stiffy scolded.

Reilly looked up to see Stiffy fiddling with a section of wall near the back end of the bar. Miraculously, a rectangle measuring approximately two and a half feet wide by three feet high came loose in the Cajun's hands. Stiffy shoved the rectangle outside and bounded out and after it. Reilly followed fast.

Once they were both safely in the comparative cool of the alley outside, Stiffy reattached the rectangle, got to his feet and brushed himself off.

"I devised that escape route for in just such a case," said the Cajun, with no small amount of pride.

"You're a genius," Reilly exclaimed in genuine awe. "Now what?"

"Now what?" Stiffy grinned. "Now ya git gone, sunnyjim. Catch the next train north. You done made a big impression on that mick copper." He took a deep breath before amending, "No offense meant by that, my Irish friend." Continuing, sans grin, "Good chance he'll notice yer gone once the dust settles. Git yerself to that train station and keep low about it. Cops might try'n nab you there since you were dumb enough to mention yer travelin' by train. So be careful, palley. Goodbye, and good luck."

Reilly did some quick faro-math and figured Stiffy's plan an eighteen-to-one favorite. He had to get on that train and pray it was leaving soon, before the Irish brute had a chance to notice his absence. Reilly clasped Stiffy's hand in both of his own, said, "How can I thank you? You saved my life."

"Ah, puh-shaw," said Stiffy with pronounced humility, exposing a top row of yellow, brown, and black. "I don't leave my business associates hangin' out to dry if I kin help it. No, sirree."

"What about you?"

"I got places to stay 'round here. Don't you worry none about yer old friend Stiffy Lacoume. I'll be just fine. Now, you best git, pardna." Then, after two breaths of awkward silence: "Go on, now. *Git.*"

Reilly nodded, walking briskly southwest in the direction of the train station.

In the heat of the moment, neither man mentioned the five thousand dollars Reilly had left behind in the fight pit. After he was well on his way to safety there was a very good chance Reilly himself would write the money off as an acceptable loss. After all, things had gone amazingly wrong and he had at least managed to escape with both his skin and freedom intact.

Thanks to his dear and thoughtful friend, Stiffy Lacoume.

§

In the alley behind Bob's, Stiffy whistled low as he strolled leisurely to the alley's mouth. When he hit the stone pavement of Franklin Street, he turned left, and walked to the corner before going left again. Half circle.

Upon arriving at Crawfish Bob's front door, which was currently padlocked from inside, Stiffy stopped briefly to ponder the night's events as he listened with amusement to the muffled chaos raging inside. He shook his head and let out a chuckle, scratched his greasy head and said out loud, "Lord, lord, lord." After an additional second or two of meditation, Stiffy raised a gnarled right fist and knocked with just enough force to be heard over the ruckus, not quite hard enough to break the skin of his knuckles.

Bap. Bap-bap. Buh-bap, bap, buh-bap.

The sound of chaos faded, then all but ceased.

A mass of muttering. Almost quiet. A small burst of laughter. An admonishing shush. Finally: Near total quiet.

The fresh silence was gently broken by the clickety sound a key makes in a padlock.

The door creaked open slow, just enough to expose one very serious-looking mug.

"Well?" inquired Crawfish Bob.

Stiffy: "Cooled out and on the broad, Bob." That being con-man talk for:

*The mark is on the train with piss in his pants and nary a clue.*

# CHAPTER TWENTY-NINE

## *Dog*

**A**t six-foot-one and two hundred twenty pounds, Dropsy Morningstar certainly had the looks of a killer—especially with his face freshly bloodied on the job at Crawfish Bob's. In truth, Dropsy was nothing more than a large child and incapable of hurting a fly. At the other end of the spectrum, Jim Jam Jump looked harmless enough at sixteen years of age and ninety-six pounds, but most certainly was a killer. So, between Dropsy's unsettling looks and Jim's unsettling inclinations, the two believed they didn't have cause for concern as they walked through the dark alley behind Marais Street, their pockets stuffed with equal fair shares of Eugene Reilly's recently plundered life savings.

"Think that Yankee fella done got what he deserved, Jim?" Dropsy was prone to feelings of remorse after a good touch—and counted on Jim's uncanny ability to soothe his dented conscience.

"Hell, Dropsy, that New York mick was as crooked as they come. Only got beat because he was aimin' to beat out Bob, ain't that right? Fella lookin' ta cheat deserves to be cheated—ain't that right, too?"

"S'pose so, Jim." Dropsy's internal conflict melted only slightly, but enough for now.

With half his face swollen and a cut above the left eye, Dropsy was as exhausted from his performance as the Christ Kid as he looked. Rest, however, was an unlikely option, for Jim didn't have it in him to let a good night of larceny end at such an early hour. After thirty more strides of walking and thinking, Jim had formulated a fully detailed scheme with which to fill the night's remainder. His keen ears detected an alien hum coming from somewhere up ahead—Jim made a quick mental note of it, but refused to let it break his train of thought.

"Dropsy, my goodly and bestest partner, yer old pal—Jim Jam Jump myself, that is—has been thinking hard on these many strides, thinking in terms of continuous and profitable fun on this night, a night blessed thus far with luck and substantial financial reward."

Dropsy winced lightly.

"Limmity-hay, whaddaya say, ol' pal o'mine, my buddy, my friend, my partner in time and jiminey-crime?"

Dropsy let out a sigh. "Damn, Jim. I'm thinking in terms of my busted-up head resting its poor self on a nice pillow 'bout now. Down for the night is what." Wishful thinking was more like it. Dropsy knew better than to argue, but watching Jim turn the angles had become a sort of pastime of his, even if Dropsy himself was at the receiving end of the current angle in question.

"Well, sure—sure you are, Dropsy. I understand that." Jim could barely conceal his amusement. Dropsy's game was to supply the obstacles upon which Jim thrived—and they both knew it. Continuing with faux concern, and the all-important-never-ending-angle-in-progress; "That's why I figured on fun with minimal physical labor on your part, old pal. Have a looky here."

With the precise and edgy movement of an alley cat, Jim shot a hand into his left breast pocket to extract two small, white objects. Jim held his hand close to Dropsy's face—in case moonlight proved insufficient to their revelation. Dropsy knew before looking that Jim held two sugar cubes marked with black dots from a fountain pen. Homemade dice. One was straight, the other tat. Crooked die.

"I swear by almighty, Jim, I ain't a clue as to where you find the energy. After killin' that buncha rats and all."

"New world record is what!" Jim Jam Jump the Astounding Ratboy of Orleans Parish and Surrounding Territories beamed brightly with hard-earned pride for a moment before returning to the topic at hand. "Dang, Dropsy, that was hours ago. I'd caught my breath up and was ready fer more before you was anywhere's near dying in that second round." Jim put on his most fetching who's-yer-pal? smile. "So whaddaya say? How's about a little tat? Rat a cat tat map flap whap tat? Eh, ol' pal? C'mon, Dropsy. Don't be an old woman about it." A look of mock distaste spread over Jim's face.

"Dunno, Jim. Mighty tired is what I surely am."

Dropsy's half-hearted protest trailed into a growl, but the source of the growl came from twenty feet ahead, towards the alley's mouth. Both stopped cold, looked up. Two eyes reflected red from the sparkle of moonlight. Two eyes and lots of teeth. Not long ago this same growl was far off enough to be perceived as a hum; that same hum being an integral part of Jim's already-figured calculations.

"Well, looky there," said Jim with twitchy glee. "We got ourselves a foamin'-at-the-mouth doggie-higgity-hog lie-shy, times..." Looking around to see if there might be a "dog" in the plural sense— "...times one!"

"Dang, Jim, hold still and talk quiet. Dog like that'll kill a person. Mostly pit by the looks of him." With only dull moonlight through low hanging fog, Dropsy couldn't see the dog well enough to determine breed—but he figured to err for caution, and assumed the worst. Pit bulls in Louisiana were mostly bred to kill black folk.

In apparent empathy of Dropsy's jangly tone of voice (but really just weighing out the situation), Jim scratched his head quietly for a moment. The dog's rumble raised in pitch, a spiky whine of pain quivering beneath it.

*Sick dog, mad dog, devil dog,* thought Dropsy.

Jim spoke in hushed tones, bloodlust nipping the edges of his throat like hungry rats: "Dropsy, my good man, I'll tell ya what I'm gonna do-wockahoo-hicka-shang-a-la do." Dropsy could feel the grin in Jim's voice, his friend's unreasonable air of confidence temporarily affording him an equally unreasonable sense of safety. Dropsy let out a sigh, unsure if the sigh was of relief or in acceptance of danger newly compounded. In any case, the dog was close enough now that making a run for it was no longer an option.

Dropsy, slow and shaking: "What might that be, pardna?"

"I'll bet ya a fiver I kin take that dangerous animal down with my bare hands before ya count to twenty is what."

"Jim, ya know I ain't a bettin' man. My daddy taught me agen' it." Dropsy's eyes narrowed in terror as the dog's pitch lowered, its back end lowering in kind. Dropsy continued in barely a whisper, voice shaking, blood on the chill; "Plus, it ain't a bet I'd feel good about winning. If I win it means the dog win, too. Meanin' Jim Jam Jump either hurt or dead."

"Puh-shaw, Dropsy. All that fight store loot in yer pocket and you scared of losing a fiver?"

A gob of white gleaming foam caught moonlight and plopped audibly from the dog's trembling snout to the alley floor.

"It's the principle, Jim." Dropsy held his chin in the air, thinking mightily on principle even in this moment of mortal danger. His daddy would be proud of such righteous resolve, Dropsy reckoned. But Jim had counted on Dropsy's high sense of principle, and so continued right on schedule:

"Fair enough then, my honorable companion. We'll make it a bet without monetary consideration. If I manage to take down that mangy and vicious beast, an animal who obviously means us nothing if not ill will and utter destruction, then you accompany me to the nearest fresh-face clip-joint where we can have us a little tat. If I don't, just leave my bloody body in the alley for that diseased animal to chew on while you head home for a nice nap. Ya can't lose, Dropsy Morningstar. If I win, we both scare up a little loot on the tat; if I lose, ya get to lay down and dream about it. Either way, this animal ain't yer problem."

"Dunno, Jim."

The rabid dog wobbled down low with pointless rage, readying to jump. Dropsy said a quick prayer in his head, struggling to keep still. Jim bounced a dangerously percussive chuckle off the walls of the alley before whispering through clenched teeth, "Considerin' we's pressed fer time in this sitchy-ation, I'll count that as a yes, Mister Dropsy Morningstar, my dearest and very friend." Jim gathered his concentration, sharpened his focus, and calmly articulated his unique brand of countdown:

"Shy......lye......*HOO!*"

Before Dropsy's lips could part to protest, Jim beat the dog to the jump, feigning a leap to the right and throwing the dog off his game—away from himself but in the general direction of Dropsy's unguarded throat. Dropsy dove right with a yelp as Jim pulled back and away, spun around to the left and, in one quick motion, let gravity throw his body hard towards the dog's airborne back-end—putting him in a position to grab a hind leg in each hand. Jim yanked the animal to the ground before its snapping jaws could do anything, but spray spit against Dropsy's neck, ear, cheek and eye. The dog's body landed with a soft, muffled slap as Jim angled its fur-matted body beneath him, all ninety-six pounds of the boy pressing squarely through his right shoulder into the dog's wiggly midsection. The animal's fury dissolved into shock, communicating such through a series of quick, panicked yips before rediscovering its rage in the scent of Jim's ratblood-specked pant legs. Resuming the attack, the dog snapped furiously at Jim's legs and feet—but the boy kicked himself away expertly, suffering only a single-toothed scratch along the back of his left calf."

Holy crimeny, Jim! Be careful!" Dropsy gasped with a tentative move forward. With blood still fresh on its tongue, the dog was in a frenzy now; snarls and snaps ricocheting like moist bullets off the soft red brick of the alley walls.

Jim: "Hold yer ground, pardna! I got 'im! I got 'im! Come anywhere near the head and he'll bite ya but good! Stay back!"

Dropsy wasn't sure where the dog's head might be in the whir of shadows—and so did as he was told, holding ground but ready to intervene if Jim's presumed advantage suffered obvious setback.

"Damn, Jim," Dropsy whispered, slackjawed at the spectacle of this skinny white kid wrestling a rabid pitbull without benefit of weapon or meaningful light. He strained and squinted to tell the combatants apart, coming up with nothing except murky, darting, soft shadows and a tangle of hateful sound.

Jim kept his legs forward out of the dog's reach while grouping both of its hind legs together in his left hand—thereby freeing his right arm to reel back and send an elbow to the back of the dog's neck. A sharp yip shot up through its throat, piercing warm air. The battle turned an important corner as the dog gave in to its pain; choosing retreat, frantically squirming to get away. A second hammering elbow left the dog partially stunned, its struggle reduced to a spasm of shivers and shallow whimpers. Jim tightened his grip on the dog's hind legs, its surrendering body firmly pinned beneath his weight as he reeled up to deliver another well-aimed elbow.

The animal lay silent. Jim took two slow breaths before rolling off and away. Uncertain if the dog was dead or just stunned, Jim rose warily to his knees—then, slowly, to his feet.

Jim Jam Jump and Dropsy Morningstar stood perfectly still—listening to the sound of each other's breathing and half expecting the dog to snap awake and have another go. After twenty seconds of uneasy quiet, Jim edged forward to give the dog a nudge with his toe. No response. Breathing hard, Jim let out a whoop and kicked the dog hard in the belly, sending it shortways along the alley into the backdoor of an anonymous crib, goosing a muffled, "What the fuck?" from a startled john inside.

Dropsy wiped dog spit from his eyes in disbelief. "You sure are crazy, Jim."

A stream of giggles floated from Jim's lips into warm, dark fog as he conceded merrily, "'Tis my claim to fame, pardna. My claim to fame."

"Did he getcha?"

"Just a scrape, old pal. Not to worry. Biggest thing I ever kilt, that dog. Guess you could say ol' Jim Jam Jump's movin' up in the world." Another round of giggles drifted into the night, transforming quickly into chuckles, chuckles into whoops, whoops into hollers. The alley mist wobbled in response.

"Need to get that washed up, Jim. That dog-disease could get in yer blood. Then you be snappin' and foamin' too." Dropsy silently wondered if mad-dog-disease might actually constitute some improvement on his friend's unpredictable temperament.

"Indeed, Dropsy. That I will. Will get it cleaned up at the first clip-joint we take a tumble to…fer *tattin'*, that is." Wink. "This little episode might even make for a good dramatic introduction to a nice juicy mark." Always working a new angle was the way of Jim Jam Jump.

"Y'know, Jim, I never did take that bet. Didn't even count to twenty." Dropsy: still playing the game, throwing up a challenge to Jim's angle-calculator.

"Only since you didn't have time to, pal. But I took care o' that dog just like I said, bare hands and all. Don't go mooching now. Might make a fella mad is what."

"All right then, Jim. I reckon you win. Any idea where to go?"

Jim just smiled. "'Deed I do, Dropsy. 'Deed I do."

Dropsy marveled at the able mind of his young friend. Always a plan in mind, always an angle smoothed to fine. Dropsy figured Jim was destined for great things, as predicted. A mind so sharp and focused could hardly go wrong.

# CHAPTER THIRTY
## *Recovery*

Insane Asylum of Louisiana
Jackson, Louisiana

March 3, 1902

My Dearest Brother,

I am sure it is with some surprise that you receive this
letter. After all, it has been over fifteen years since our
last communication and my prognosis at that time, I assume,
was not good. More surprising still might be my apparent
rediscovery of the English language, as I'm sure you've heard
all about my extended state of utter silence. In all fairness
to myself, though, I must tell you that I would have very much
enjoyed seeing you once or twice over the years. As you know,
I am rendered immobile by my current situation, and so could
not venture in your direction. You, on the other hand, have
certainly been free to move about and pay your only brother a
visit had you so wished. No need for concern or guilty feelings, though, as I fully understand your decision to stay
away from this wretched place. I am sure it was with great
heartache that you placed me here in the first place, and
perhaps the thought of revisiting the scene of my total mental
collapse would have only caused you further pain. And, yes, I
admit that I would have made a limited conversationalist (to
say the least) and poor company (generally speaking) until
recent weeks.

I am writing today to lighten any burden of lingering
guilt that you may harbor regarding my incarceration, for, I
believe (as do my stunned physicians) that I am presently on
the fast track to recovery. Although it may seem that these
many years I have been "away," I assure you that my particular
type of catatonia was not a complete inactivity of brain function (though I'm sure it must have seemed so at times), but

rather, a necessary phase I needed to experience in order to reclaim my life, my thoughts, and my understanding of reality itself. The things I have learned internally while "away" were indeed instrumental to the recovery of my ability to speak, think, and live in a normal manner once more. So, dear brother, know that your decision to have me committed will not ever be a source of ill will from me, as I must admit that I cannot think of a more practical alternative in the interest of any potential recovery for myself.

If I am less than completely forthcoming in this letter, dear George, please understand that there is some lingering concern regarding the way my previous letters to you were used against me as "evidence of my instability" in the past. Consequently, I can not help but be cautious in how I put things, especially since this letter will no doubt be reviewed (and perhaps censored) by hospital staff before it is allowed to reach your eyes. With this in mind, I will be brief but, hopefully, clear, as I try to explain what I believe led to my breakdown -- and how I managed to reach my current improved state of mental facility.

The surreal quality of my last series of letters to you, I believe, were, in part, a product of my own state of severe depression resultant of my disappointing and lonely experiences after having moved to New Orleans. That, coupled with any number of diseases that may have found their way into my blood system via impure local water and/or impure local women, must surely have compounded with said depression in such a way as to cause the initial hallucinations recounted to you in past letters. After witnessing the murder of Father Morningstar (whose assailant, I understand, was never found) my mind suffered total collapse, rendering me unable to form coherent thoughts or sentences. My insistence to you that "all is well" as put forth in my final disturbing letter to you may very well have been my mind's attempt to convince itself that the traumas it had suffered could simply be suppressed through the simplistic action of redundant positive thinking. This latter theory is supported by our Dr. Baxter, who, by the way, seems quite thrilled with my recent progress.

Although this may be hard for you to comprehend, Dear Brother, while in my previous long-term state of catatonia, my dreams have been largely investigative. Images and pictures in my mind have had an illuminating effect on my very soul -- and, indeed, have managed to put me back on the road to rational thought. The things I have learned while asleep have afforded me great insight into myself, my affliction, and -- dare I say -- a deeper understanding of life in general and God Almighty Himself. By way of dreams I have learned, Dear

Brother, that I must <u>awaken</u> in order to return to society at large and do God's bidding -- as is the duty of every moral and thinking creature on this earth.

I believe, Dear Brother, that with your support and endorsement, Dr. Baxter and his colleagues might be convinced that I am ready for immediate (or at least imminent) release. I beg you to journey to this institution at your earliest convenience so that we may reacquaint ourselves, and mend whatever there is between us which may need mending. After all, we are brothers and always will be.

In closing, my dear George, please know that I bear you no ill will whatsoever for my many years of incarceration. Quite to the contrary, I thank and bless you for the wisdom and love you displayed in having me put here, and I pray that there will be equal wisdom forthcoming as you play the necessary instrumental role in returning me to the outside world.

With warmest belated affections and highest respects,
I am your brother,
Marshall

ADDENDUM

My Dear Mr. Trumbo,

As mentioned by your brother, hospital staff is obligated to review all outgoing letters. It is not our practice to censor such letters (unless the content is hurtful, threatening, or socially irresponsible in some way), but it is indeed our responsibility to clarify any informational points as to the condition of our patients, so that family members may not be misled.

It is quite true that Marshall's progress has been astounding in recent months. He has progressed from his long semi-catatonic state (limited movement, rare speech, inability to eat, vacant staring, etc...). He has recently displayed unprecedented energy and enthusiasm towards improving his condition, as well as having developed a welcome interest in social interaction.

However, I must alert you that his condition is not entirely regulated or grounded, as his letter may have you otherwise believe.

Although he now takes regular baths, he insists on keeping his hair long. I have declined to force the issue as I am afraid that to restrain him for purposes of a simple haircut may prove traumatic or even physically dangerous. I believe, in time, that he will suggest proper grooming for himself, when and if his sense of reason is more fully restored.

Also, although it is very heartening to see him take a social interest in other patients (as well as hospital staff), his method of doing so is quite unusual. He seems to imagine that he is still a news reporter -- he does not hold conversations with others so much as he interviews them, asking questions at times bordering on the bizarre and scribbling notes on tablets (sometimes imaginary tablets) as his "interviewees" give answer. In addition (and more disturbingly), he occasionally conducts these interviews with people who are not there at all. This may very well be a positive sign, possibly indicating a desire to return to the familiar normalcy of his old life, but it also speaks plainly of residual dementia.

Although, obviously, I cannot recommend his release at this time, I do support your brother's request that you come visit him at your earliest convenience. Although medical science has made much progress in recent years, mental illness is still a condition cloaked in mystery for the most part. It is entirely possible that your presence here could contribute greatly to his ultimate recovery.

I look forward to your response.


Yours truly,
Herschel H. Baxter,
Medical Doctor and State Certified Alienist

# CHAPTER THIRTY-ONE
## *Hattie's Cure*

Hattie Covington lay on her side in the shape of a Z, her head in the lap of Diphtheria Morningstar—just as it had every night since the bitter evening of her cure.

Diphtheria and Hattie had risen from the Marais Street cribs to Arlington Hall together, and so had become like sisters. As Diphtheria stroked Hattie's hair and looked into her half-closed eyes, she found herself mildly alarmed by what she saw there.

"I know, I know," Diphtheria said in a whisper.

"You know more than me then, I guess," said Hattie, with hardly a movement of her lips, idly watching Diphtheria's boy play with a handful of buttons near the door. West had been methodically stacking irregular round and oval shapes for the last two hours. Stacking until they fell of their own accord, then starting over—and over and over—never quite able to stack them all in one freestanding button tower. "Might be I coulda made it like you. Raised me a nice little boy like West. Or a girl maybe. Might be. Could be. Won't know now."

"Shh. Things was diff'nt for me. I was just out of the crib—with nothin' at all to lose. Had me a man to fall back on, too—least thought I did." Diphtheria's nose crinkled slightly at the memory of Buddy's callous desertion so soon after West's birth. Buddy had gotten his first whiff of notoriety in the district back then—a wife and baby just didn't figure into the life of a rising star. When it became clear to her that Buddy would not be coming back, Diphtheria let go the notion of putting the whore's life behind her, focusing instead on becoming a *better paid* whore. With a child to raise on her own she would need money; better money than she'd been accustomed to in the cribs.

With Doctor Jack's help, Diphtheria had managed to lighten her skin a shade closer to high yella. Doing so had required daily, painfully stinging skin treatments (a mix of hot yellow wax, cocoa butter and a type of bleach Doctor

Jack called "petrolatum"), and in two months time she'd paled up nicely. In the interim she'd worked the rice fields of Assumption Parish to make ends meet; the hard work making her body toned, muscular and ready for selling. Ten dollars saved from the rice fields bought her a fancy dress, the kind she believed was required in the fancy brothels of Basin Street.

Her first big break had come in the form of Lulu White's Mahogany Hall, where she discovered no such fancy dress was required—at least not at first. At Lulu's she was hired on as the house "goat"; and to be a goat meant to prance around the first floor parlor naked as a jaybird save for high-heeled shoes. Lulu's goat was *lagniappe* for her high-class clientele. It was the job of the goat to award "five minutes of undivided attention" to any man who requested such— usually on her knees and free of charge. A nasty and thankless job it was, but a solid first step towards the good-paying career Diphtheria had dreamed of since Buddy's departure. If nothing else, Mahogany Hall offered a safer working environment than could be found in any crib.

Diphtheria had been a trusty and popular goat for Lulu, and so it wasn't too many months before her promotion to an upstairs room of her own. Eventually she moved down the street to the Arlington House, where she was given her own listing in the Blue Book under the name "Dorothia Morningstar." It was Josie Arlington herself who had insisted on the name change, pointing out that even an exceptionally pretty girl named for a disease might tend to inspire costly hesitation in the heart of a wealthy upper-class patron. Whatever the name, a listing in the Blue Book was the big time. Diphtheria had made it, and so had Hattie.

The process of coming up in the district had been all about hard times, but Diphtheria and Hattie had gone through the worst of it together. Now Diphtheria doubted if Hattie (or herself, for that matter) could summon the strength required to start again from scratch. Hattie's skin was naturally light, her lips thin and her nose narrow—fine Creole looks that made her own transition from the crib a smooth one. But that could all change fast if a baby ruined her shape.

"Your situation is diff'nt," Diphtheria continued. "Gettin' full-blown pregnant woulda lost you yer job in a high-class joint like Arlington Hall—and you know it. Woulda got kicked back down to the cribs in ten seconds flat. How you woulda raised a child in a crib with no man to look after ya? And no money? Cain't raise a baby up proper on no crib-nickels."

"I know, I know," answered Hattie, a delayed echo to Diphtheria's earlier whisper. "Still, I wanted that child. That was *my* child. Even if it was only from being selfish, I wanted that child. Maybe I coulda found a way. Might be, could be."

Diphtheria stroked Hattie's hair, ever gently. "Shush now, girl. You ain't selfish like that. It was your love for that child made you get cured. Knowin' his life would be so hard. Your own life be hard, too hard to care for him proper. It ain't like you didn't think things through. You tortured yourself over it. You gave it every consideration—which is more'n most girls do. You loved that baby in yer body and done what you thought best for *him*. Ain't no sin in doing what you think is right. Being selfish woulda been more a sin. You ain't selfish like that, girl. You know you ain't."

That much was true. Hattie *had* tortured herself over the thought of bringing a child into the world, and in the end decided the timing couldn't be worse. So she had seen Doctor Jack *about* (and later *for*) a cure, but she'd also committed herself to saving up a year's worth of wages; enough money to survive her next pregnancy, get her figure back, then get back to work.

But she knew she would never have another chance at having *this* baby. This baby was gone and gone for good; except in her heart. Its little pink body taken away by Diphtheria's brother, Typhus, to be buried or sunk God knows where. The next time it would be a whole other baby. A newer, luckier baby—allowed to live. But not the same baby at all. This baby was dead—and dead is forever.

"It ain't fair," said Hattie. "*I* ain't fair."

Diphtheria had no words for response, and so stroked Hattie's hair some more. Wiped away her tears.

"Shhhh," Diphtheria cooed again. "You and me best be gettin' to work now, girl. Try to put on a little smile for the customers."

"You go, Diphtheria. Tell Josie I ain't well."

Diphtheria's soft expression toughened slightly. "You keep that up and you'll be back to cribbin' after all. You *know* that. Josie's got some tenderness in her heart for you, girl—but you keep it up and she'll rent yer room out to someone new." Diphtheria let out a sigh, remorseful of the harshness in her voice. "Get dressed. And put on that smile." Diphtheria demonstrated a smile as if Hattie might have forgotten what one looked like. Then, after a pause, and with calculated tenderness, "So's you can put some money away for that *next* little one."

Hattie sat up slowly, her spine aligning gradually with the sofa back.

"Yeah. Guess you right, Diphtheria."

"'Course I'm right. Now, you get yerself gussied to make yerself a little killin'—you and yer natural high-yella skin tone set to breakin' hearts—Lord, *Lord!*—and I'll be back in my room doin' the same. Lotsa fancy men in town fer a fraternity meetin', they say. Meet you at the parlor room, all right?"

"I guess," said Hattie, unable to get excited at the thought of fancy men— she'd suspected (or at least hoped) it had been a fancy man from a fraternity who'd knocked her up in the first place.

Hattie felt her mood darkening. Thinking about taking a bath. Thinking about the straight razor in her washroom. Thinking about hot water turning pink. "Might take a little bath first," she said quietly.

"That's it, you take a bath." Diphtheria spoke brightly, but something in Hattie's eyes rang an alarm, so she added on for safety's sake, "But make it a short one. Got to get to work. I'll be back to check on you if you take too long."

"Yeah, a short one," Hattie monotoned. "All right then, Diphtheria."

"Got that new piano player ya like downstairs, girl. Mr. J.C. Booker, the one that plays them rags. Get yer mind offa things I bet, them rags." Hattie smiled some, almost forgetting about hot baths with pink water at the thought of J.C. Booker and his gay piano rags.

"Damn, that boy sure plays good," Hattie agreed. "Least he don't play them stuffy classics like the last boy." A little laugh escaped her lips; a tiny miracle. "Them Beethoven suh-nattas just put me clean outta the mood."

"That's right, dear." Diphtheria smiled. "Let that pretty piano boy lift yer spirits some. Skip the bath and come down quick. Playin' already, I bet."

"Yeah, maybe so."

"All right, then. See you in a few minutes," Diphtheria said, practicing her man-catching smile, grabbing West by his little hand, pulling open the door.

"All right then." Hattie echoed. And then: "Diphtheria?"

"Yeah, baby?" Half-way through the door, West's wrist wriggling in her grip.

"Thank you." Another little smile.

Big smile in return: "Stop talkin' crazy and getcher self dressed up, girl. Gotta go break some hearts and make some market." Diphtheria left, beaming at her success in brightening Hattie's eyes—a difficult accomplishment these last few days.

But the sound of the closing door felt hollow and echoless in Hattie's ear, and the room's sudden emptiness weighed heavy. A vision of J.C. Booker—his smile, his music, his passion for living—did manage to lighten a dark corner of her mind, but another corner stayed dark and dwelled on visions of pink bathwater. Hattie Covington stared hard at the pile of buttons West had been playing with. Neatly stacked by the door. One perfect tower. A child's success.

Hattie got up and went to the washroom. Put the stopper in the drain of the tub. Let warm, clear water flow. But before the tub was full, there was a rapping at the door.

The knock was small but firm. The sound of a tiny fist.

CHAPTER THIRTY-TWO

## *Fish and Buttons*

"Now, git on to the ante-room to see Miss Bernice double-quick," Diphtheria told West as soon as they stepped into the hallway outside Hattie's room. "Mama's gotta make us some groceries." Bernice was a sweet-tempered midwife hired by Madame Josie to watch over the little ones while their mothers were otherwise disposed.

Sudden concern distorted West's eyebrows: "Mama, oh no."

"What's a matter, child?"

"Forgot my buttons in Miss Hattie's room."

Diphtheria sighed. "Well, don't you worry. Miss Bernice got plenty of toys fer you kids to play with. You can getcher buttons back later."

"Can't I just knock on Miss Hattie's door and get 'em now?" West found his mother's knack for doing everything the long way both annoying and perplexing.

"Don't you even think about it, little man," Diphtheria held firm. "Miss Hattie's getting dressed now—might be taking a bath, too. You go barging in for your buttons and you might be walking in on a naked lady is what. That what you want?"

"No," West conceded timidly—the idea of walking in on a "naked lady" being a universally terrifying concept in the world of pre-adolescent boys. West much preferred his grown-ups fully clothed whenever possible.

"Now, off to see Miss Bernice. We'll worry 'bout them buttons later. You just let me worry about them buttons, hear?"

West's eyebrows raised, bunched, then spread—he knew full well his mother lacked the ability to worry properly over such things. But smart kids can be relentless when the fate of shiny buttons hangs in the balance—and West was certainly a smart kid. Grown-ups just didn't understand such things, and children don't have the patience to explain every little thing.

Diphtheria, knowing it was not in West's nature to give up so quickly, didn't have time to ponder any potentially devious intentions he may have. With a sigh she rolled her eyes, hoped for the best, and darted down the hall so she could get down to the serious business of making herself irresistible to strangers.

Having no desire to walk in on a naked lady, West's plan was to wait for Miss Hattie to finish dressing and come out under her own steam. As soon as she opened the door he'd simply ask for his buttons and be on his way; off to the ante-room like a good boy. In West's mind, being a "good boy" didn't necessarily mean doing every silly thing your mother told you to do in the correct order. He parked himself outside Hattie's door with his arms wrapped around his knees.

After about five minutes of waiting, West noted the sound of running water inside. Miss Hattie was drawing a bath after all—this might take a while. No matter, thought West, it wasn't like he had anything pressing to attend. Resolved to a longer wait, West let the water sound coax his mind into a daydream.

The daydream began with the topic at hand: Buttons. Red buttons, blue buttons, purple and pink, shiny and flat, square and round. Little buttons, big buttons big as a house, flying buttons, talking buttons, and buttons that could swim. But dream-thoughts of buttons can get old pretty quick even for a small boy who obsesses on such things, so the daydream soon turned to other fun things, the funnest non-button thing he could think of being his Uncle Dropsy. Uncle Dropsy had a rare comprehension of things important to little kids. He understood about wrestling and sneaking and playing tricks and hide and seek and doing slightly dangerous things without tattling and laughing over the serious things that mostly made mommies just cry.

Uncle Dropsy was different from other big people in another special way, too; when he played with West it wasn't just for West's benefit, wasn't any kind of babysitting chore at all. Uncle Dropsy actually *liked* playing with West. When the two of them were horsing around together, Uncle Dropsy's smiles were real. Uncle Dropsy honestly enjoyed West as much as West enjoyed Uncle Dropsy.

West knew in his heart that his uncle would have understood perfectly the importance of buttons left behind. Would have understood without explanation or debate. West spent the remainder of his waiting time imagining a big, button-filled house where he could live with Uncle Dropsy, just the two of them. Wrestling around and kidding all day long, building immense button towers that could never fall down. *Boy, that sure would be a time,* thought West.

Lost in his imaginings, West had no idea how long he'd waited before the sound of footsteps began clicking up the hardwood of the stairwell. West frowned at the noise; most likely some fool grown-up loaded with questions about what a kid might be doing sitting all by himself in the upstairs hallway of a whorehouse. West held his breath with one eye closed as the steps got louder. Finally, the owner of the footfalls came into view.

"Hiya, West."

West brightened, and his chest blew out nervous air in relief. "Hey! Uncle Typhus!"

Typhus was no Dropsy by any means, but he was easy enough to get along with and had never been the bossy kind of grown-up. At four and a half feet tall, Uncle Typhus wasn't even much taller than West.

"Here to see my mama? You done passed her door. She in there." West pointed helpfully.

"Nope, ain't here to see yer mama tonight," said Typhus. He walked right up to West before stopping.

"What ya got there?" West noticed a heavy looking bulge in Uncle Typhus' burlap coffee bag.

"You sure got a lot of questions, mister." Typhus smiled. "Got something for Miss Hattie." He raised his hand to knock.

"I think she takin' a baff."

Typhus rapped hard three times anyway. "That's all right. If she don't want to answer, I imagine she won't. Can always come back later on."

"Well, if she comes to the door," West said hopefully, "tell her I left my buttons in there. I be needin' 'em so I kin get on back to the ante-room like Mama said."

"All right then, Mr. Buttons. I'll see what I can do for ya." West's deadly concern over a bunch of old buttons gave Typhus a chuckle—but as Hattie cracked the door he lost the smile out of respect. He knew Hattie was having a hard time since the night of her cure. In fact, Hattie's pain was the reason Typhus had come by tonight.

"Evenin', Miss Covington."

"Diphtheria done left, Typhus. She's in her room—"

"Didn't come for Diphtheria, Miss Covington." Typhus searched the questions in her eyes. "Brought you a little something might put a smile on yer face. I hope this ain't a bad time."

Hattie's face softened some. Seeing the man who'd taken her baby from her as she lay miserable and bleeding on Doctor Jack's examining room table was exactly what she didn't need right now. But she couldn't blame Typhus for a

decision she'd made of her own free will, and he certainly was a pathetic creature; a grown man in such a small body. It was hard to be anything but kind to
a man who so resembled a child.

"Well, Typhus, it's mighty nice of you to call on me, but I be doin' just fine.
I have to get dressed now." Typhus just stared as if she'd spoken in Chinese, and
so she added, "if you don't mind, please."

Typhus' stare wasn't from lack of understanding, though. Hattie had been
the only real woman he'd ever had occasion to lie down with in his life, most
likely the only real woman he'd ever lie down with now that he had Lily to
tend to. As empty as his experience with Hattie had been, he now found the
sight of her slender, perfect body dressed only in a robe an unexpected catalyst
that connected certain previously unconnected things of heart and mind. The
robe she wore was pure white, nearly as pure as Lily's gown, and the contrast of
Hattie's smooth, light skin against the robe sent a shiver all the way to Typhus'
knees—caused his heart to skip a beat, his ears to boom. Hattie stood patiently
while Typhus took a deep breath to compose himself.

"Oh, that's all right. I'm sure sorry, Miss Covington. I did catch you at a
bad time."

West tugged at Typhus' shirt; a gentle reminder to mention his buttons
before the door closed.

"That's all right, Typhus," said Hattie. "Nuther time maybe." She made a
move to shut the door but Typhus had wedged a foot in its path.

"Trouble is, ma'am—I mean, I hate to be a bother...."

"Well, what then?" Hattie's eyes had lost their softness. The idea of pinkening
your own bathwater took some courage and getting used to and Typhus' inter-
ruption had begun to weaken her resolve.

"Ya see, I got something here for you that won't keep proper." He pointed to
the bulge in his burlap sack. "Perishable item."

Hattie's curiosity stirred. Something about the sight of the bag gave her
pause. "Well, what is it, then?"

"May I come in?" Motioning again to his burden: "Awful heavy, this."

Hattie eased out a defeated sigh as she swung the door open wide. Typhus
stepped in quick, fearful she'd change her mind and slam it before he could get
all the way through. West followed close behind.

"All right, now. Yer in." Her tone no longer made attempt to hide her annoyance. Still, she couldn't take her eyes off Typhus' bag; trying to recall where she'd
seen it before. Then she remembered.

This was the same bag he'd put her baby in that night. She stared at its bulge
and wondered if there was a baby in there right now. *Perishable item.* But the

lump was too big to be a thing so small. *Crazy thought,* she reprimanded herself, holding back angry tears.

"Thanks indeed," Typhus said, lugging the sack over to the thick, wooden table near the stove. "I have me a hunch you ain't been eatin' right lately."

This was true, she hadn't eaten in days.

He laid the bag on the table ever-gently.

"Been eatin' just fine, Mr. Busybody. As if it's any of yer damn to-do what, when, or how I eat." This talk of eating made Hattie uneasy. She'd decided she didn't care to know what was in the bag. And she was quite certain it wouldn't be anything she'd want to put in her mouth.

Typhus just grinned. "Well, you'll be eating good tonight, that's for sure." He held the bottom corners of the bag between thumb and forefinger, then lifted upward—dumping its contents onto the cutting board before Hattie could protest further. "Ain't it pretty?" said Typhus. On the cutting board lay the strangest looking catfish Hattie had ever seen. Pink skin instead of brown. Green eyes instead of black. Rubbery, thick whiskers. She took one cautious step towards it.

"What kind of fish is that?" she asked, surprised at the crack of emotion in her own voice.

"Catfish, Hattie." It was the first time Typhus had called her by her first name. "Your catfish."

"Well, I s'pose it is." Hattie couldn't fathom the meaning of her own acceptance. Her catfish? What was that supposed to mean? And why did the idea give her such a strange, warm feeling? What kind of feeling *was* that?

"Now, I know you was getting ready for workin', but maybe you could save yerself some time by skipping that bath." Typhus seemed to know about her bathwater-pinkening intentions. Not only knew, but understood. This couldn't be possible, but was so just the same. "Skip that bath and have yourself a little mealtime. You just sit back and let Typhus do the cooking. Just relax now. All right?"

West had already resumed his button stacking ritual by the door. As he worked, West grimly resolved to never, ever leave his buttons behind again. They were his buttons and he had a responsibility to take good care of them. He would not be so careless again.

*so careless*

"Sure, Typhus," said Hattie. "Cook it up. That'd be nice."

Without another word, Typhus lit the stove and placed the fish in the center of a large pan. He didn't gut or dissect the fish, but left it whole. Neither did he grease the pan or bother to search the kitchen for herbs or spices. In a few moments the fish was gently hissing on the pan, filling the room with its smell.

It was not a fishy smell. The smell was the sweet perfume of sunny days and freshly cut grass, of dreams lost but renewed. The smell of long lost children splashing in a fresh water pool on a hot, clear day.

When the cooking was done Typhus retrieved a white plate from the cupboard over the sink. He pulled the meat from the bones without a knife; the flesh of it fell away easily. After carefully placing the bones back into his burlap coffee bag, Typhus proceeded to cut the meat up into small, bite-sized cubes on the plate.

The squares melted in Hattie's mouth so smoothly that she barely needed to chew. She ate silently as Typhus made mono-directional small talk, West stacking buttons by the door, oblivious. The flavor of it was sweet and light, tasting vaguely of fine chocolate and cotton candy. It didn't weigh heavily in her stomach and she was able to eat it all, save for the last bite which she left on the plate. To make it disappear entirely would have felt *rude* to her somehow. She put the fork down and leaned back in her chair, watching the gentle rhythm of Typhus' lips as he babbled on. Her hand ran over her belly and she imagined movement there. A kick?

*yes, a kick*

Vague feelings of guilt washed over her heart at the sensation. She had no right to feel whole. No right to feel safe. No right to believe everything would be all right and always had been. She was perfectly aware that no catfish on earth tasted like cotton candy or chocolate or any of the things that gave comfort and joy to small children.

But all of these things were true. At this moment, they were all true.

She went on watching Typhus' talking head, not hearing a word, watching the quality of his smile. Watched as he got up and made for the door. Didn't hear him mumble strange words as he left:

*"They gave it to me, but I gave it back the best I could."*

West scooped up his buttons and carefully placed them in his pocket. He was a little hungry and the fish smelled so good that he stealthfully snatched the last square of meat from Hattie's plate, popping it into his mouth before leaving. What had been sweet on Hattie's tongue was bitter to his own, but he swallowed it just the same.

Typhus and West were gone. Hattie lay down on the couch, belly full, alone. Feeling fine. Not understanding why, not caring why.

*Fine*

# CHAPTER THIRTY-THREE

# In the Court of King Bolden

B y "fresh-face clip-joint" Jim meant a concert-saloon or barrel-house where the outsiders were clean. By "clean" he meant they were foreign enough to have little or no previous knowledge of Jim and Dropsy's special bag of tricks.

Of course, the short-con routines of Jim and Dropsy were commonplace enough within the local criminal community of Orleans Parish, and the boys knew they could count on the support of their criminal brethren in a pinch. A general truth of the South was this: Your neighbor may be your enemy in the now, but when a Yankee came to town, The People of the South Stood United For Better Or For Worse.

"Where we headed to, Jim?" Dropsy was pooped enough to jump into the first dive with lights on, but Jim being a young man with a distinct sense of purpose in nearly everything he did would no doubt have something more particular in mind.

"How'd you feel about paying a visit to your dear brother-in-law, pal o'mine?"

"Guess so," Dropsy sighed, too tired to throw up a challenge. Dropsy knew Jim's dream was to graduate from the rat killing business up to the music business, so Buddy had become something of a hero to him. It seemed Jim was always looking for an excuse to see that mean-spirited drunken scoundrel play that damn cornet.

Buddy's band was indeed playing a fresh-face clip-joint tonight—having recently retained weekly work at the Odd Fellows Hall, located at the corner of South Rampart and Perdido. Situated two floors above the Eagle Saloon (and sandwiching the Eagle Pawnshop & Loan Company directly below), Odd Fellows was a concert-saloon masquerading as a private society club peopled mainly with local musicians, gamblers and thieves. "Exclusive invitations," however, were often issued to potential marks spotted by lookouts in the saloon below. These hand-picked suckers might as well have worn signs begging

"SHAKE MY TREE"—their reliable presence constituting substantial cash flow to the local criminal economy. With plenty of suckers to go around for everyone, the resident smooth operators didn't mind if Jim and Dropsy stopped by to pick a few berries of their own—as long as the boys minded their manners and didn't horn in on someone else's game. Many of the old hands even found it charming to watch the youngsters in action. As an added bonus, Dropsy's oldest sister, Malaria, worked at Odd Fellows as a waitress on most nights. A fellow couldn't have too many allies nearby and on hand in this business.

As the alley behind Marais Street opened out onto Perdido, Buddy's bleating horn could be easily detected from four blocks away. Jim filled Dropsy in on the details of the night's scheme as the two walked in the general direction of Buddy's noise, Dropsy listening and nodding along the way.

The boys strolled casually through the front door of the Eagle Saloon—a few heads turning warily in their direction before nodding with recognition—and proceeded to climb the straight, narrow stairwell located at the rear of the bar and leading upwards to Odd Fellows. Upon reaching the top platform, Jim gave Black Benny a nod. Benny was a truly frightening individual who acted as doorman, bouncer and occasional house drummer. Jim greased the big man's palm with a five-dollar bill before sticking his head through the entranceway for a quick survey of the crowd.

"Easy pickins tonight," grunted Benny. "We'll call this fiver a down payment depending on the take at the end." This was not a suggestion but a statement of fact.

Even Jim knew better than to dicker with Black Benny. "Of course, my good man. Just a hint of greater things to come, this humble fiver."

Jim yanked his head back into the stairwell and presented his partner with a broad smile. "Dropsy, my friend, I believe Mr. Benny is dead-on correct in his summation. If I'm not mistaken, I've spotted a party of five been awaitin' on our arrival. Probably ruin their good time if we failed to give 'em a good goin' over. Let us not disappoint, old pal. Shall we?"

Dropsy couldn't help but give up a grin. "Well then, let's have at 'em, Jim Jam Jump, Amazin' Champeen Ratboy of Orleans Parish and Surroundin' Terri-trees."

A switch flicked on in Jim's brain that lit his face with instant agony. Faux-misery in place, Jim pushed past Black Benny:

"*Oooh*—my leg! Somebody get a doctor! That dog done got me! *Mad* dog is what! Foamin' and snappin' and done got me *good!* Saved by this fine gentleman here, the bravest niggra I ever knowed! *Ooohhh!* The pain! The *pain!*"

The air of the hall was a heady residue of things consumed, a living thing shaped by the racket produced by King Bolden's Band. Supporting Jim from around the shoulders (as recently instructed during the duo's Perdido Street stroll), Dropsy tugged his dramatically limping cohort through the crowded hall.

"Stand aside, gentleman! Sick youngster comin' through here! Bit by a rabid animal and needin' of medical 'tention!" And then louder: "*Is there a doctor in the house?* Jesus *please*, is there a doctor in this house?" Dropsy's heart-rending performance was enhanced nicely by his authentically rattled nerves and genuinely throbbing head.

The band charged furiously through Buddy's signature tune, Buddy himself standing authoritatively at the edge of a six inch platform serving as stage. Holding the cornet in his left hand, King Bolden belted out the lyrics with the passion of a back-o'town street preacher:

*Way down, way down low*
*So I can hear them whores*
*Drag their feets across that floor…*

Buddy interrupted himself with a quick, nasty phrase from the cornet, blinking hard in mid-verse at the commotion stirred by Jim's wailing. Annoyance transformed quickly to amusement as Buddy recognized the boys—and with a wink in their direction he lowered the cornet once more to resume verse:

*Oh, you bitches, shake your asses*
*Funky butt, funky butt*
*Take it away!*

Dropsy pulled Jim through the sorry looking throng of lowlifes and slicks; an unlikely mixture of race and class—from black to white and from high to low—that Buddy's unique style of playing managed to draw together in the district with astonishing regularity. Despite the diversity, the locals and out-of-towners were easy enough to tell apart—nearly as easy as telling cats from mice.

With steadily escalating imagined agony, Jim knocked his genuinely dog-injured calf hard against an empty stool to coax out a few additional drops of blood, just for show. "The pain! *The pain!*"

"Somebody please help this poor boy!" Dropsy was now so anxious that his eyes produced genuine tears. Nice touch, that—but his concern was well founded. The out-of-town element in Odd Fellows tonight had a distinctly hardened air about them, clearly not the type accustomed to playing mouse. This was often a good thing; the more worldly the prospect, the more likely the prospect would consider himself immune to tricks perpetrated by under-aged white kids and slow-minded coloreds—which meant a lowered guard. But also: one misstep with this bunch could prove disastrous or deadly. Not that the locals wouldn't bail the boys out in a crisis scenario, but some of these tourists carried pistols—and there wasn't enough Southern Loyalty in the whole of God's green earth to stop a bullet.

Dropsy pushed onward towards the bar until Jim signaled with calculated resistance. He led Dropsy leftwards with a staged shudder and low-pitched moan—mere preamble to an artful backwards fall. The cards and drinks of Jim's chosen party took the intended tumble, causing ten droopy, alcohol-fogged eyes to widen with surprise.

To Dropsy, the five out-of-towners looked like a postcard straight out of the Wild, Wild West: a crew of red-faced, hardened outlaws dressed in their Sunday best. As drinks splashed into laps and glasses chimed then tinkled musically to the floor, two of the men cursed and jumped up, while two others just sat looking confused. The fifth man looked only mildly startled—and somewhat concerned. This least perturbed member of the party stood up soberly, giving Jim a hand up from the ground and offering him his chair.

"You all right, boy?" said the man, crouching down to meet Jim's eyes.

*Paydirt,* thought Jim Jam Jump.

"Thank you, *thank* you so much for the kindness, sir. I'll be all right. It's just that it hurts…so…*aaahhh!*" A dazzling demonstration of sobs sprang from Jim's throat. His aim was to melt the hearts of the remaining four, but the immediate results were mixed at best.

The two who'd remained seated—one as fat as the other was skinny—got to their feet just long enough to right the table, then quickly reseated themselves with narrowing eyes. The two who'd jumped up wore put-out expressions—but were already on a slow cool, both standing with hands on hips as if awaiting formal invitation to rejoin their own party. The Good Samaritan who'd given up his seat had already full-out taken the bait, now placing an arm around Jim's shoulder while the boy responded with meek, artificial gratitude; trembling and fighting to hold back fake tears.

"There now, you'll be okay, son," said the Good Samaritan. Then to Dropsy, "Well, don't just stand there, ya stupid nigger, go find a doctor!" Dropsy scrambled off, hardly able to conceal his relief.

"I'll pay fer them drinks I done knocked over, sir. I got some money…" But the act of reaching into his own pocket caused Jim a freshly imagined stab of pain. "Aahhhh…*ow! ow! oweeee!*"

"Nonsense," said the Good Samaritan. "Don't you worry 'bout that, son. Tell me yer name, now."

"Nick Clay, sir." Jim's spur of the moment identity for the night.

"Well, Nick, you can call me Walter. Now, tell me what happened."

"Well, Mr. Walter…this rabid dog roamin' the street done cornered me. I tried ta git away, but he came up fast and bit me on the leg—wouldn't let go, just shakin' and growlin'. That niggra came out of nowhere and kilt that dog with his bare hands. Bravest thing I ever seen."

"Well, I'll be damned, is that a fact?" Then, after a beat: "What happened to the niggra's face? He get bit too?" The question revealed an angle Jim had neglected to work out in advance. Walter's question was a trap—Dropsy's head injuries bore no resemblance whatsoever to a dog bite, and Jim knew it. "No, sir," Jim improvised. "In the struggle…ya see, uh…the dog tripped him up and knocked him on his head. Hit the ground hard but kept on fightin'. That niggra saved my life, I tell ya!"

"Well, I'll be damned," the Samaritan repeated with apparent satisfaction, as he pulled a clean white hanky from his breast pocket to wrap around Jim's bleeding calf. "Anything I can do for you, son?"

Jim hesitated expertly. "Well…ah, nevermind. You already been way too kind, sir…" Jim squinted in actual pain as Walter wrapped the hanky too tight.

"Out with it, son. This ain't no time fer shyness."

"Well, maybe if I could get a little snort…for the pain, I mean."

"Well, of course! Sure thing, little fella!" Walter was clearly delighted at the prospect of reintroducing liquor to the table. "You betcha! *Waitress!*"

Dropsy had already shoved his way through the crowd to the far end of the bar, beyond easy visibility of Jim's table of marks. From across the bar he made brief eye contact with Malaria, who gave him a scolding glance but hurried herself in the direction of Jim's table of marks just the same. She didn't approve of the boys' thieving shenanigans, but neither did she wish them harm and so intended to keep a close eye. Dropsy wedged himself against the wall near the back end of the stage in just the right way, finding a good vantage point from which he could catch Jim's eventual signal indicating the commencement of phase two.

Buddy's horn was awfully harsh at such close range, but Dropsy decided it would be rude to jam a finger in for relief so close to the stage where people could see. And just then, with a quick motion of Buddy's hand, the band stopped all at once—the sudden absence of sound leaving a tinny whine in Dropsy's ears. Buddy took the opportunity to berate the crowd, imploring them to "not be so dern cheap and how about a tip for the band and nevermind the dern waitresses, they make good enough money around the block when they whorin'." Finally stepping down from the low platform, Buddy took two quick strides before throwing an arm around Dropsy's shoulder.

"How's my favorite cuz tonight?"

Buddy's grin made Dropsy flinch.

"Not yer cousin, Buddy. Just a plain old brother-in-law."

"Such a stickler for detail, cuz. Impressive talk coming from an idjit."

Dropsy knew good and well Buddy awarded no favoritism in this world whether brother, cousin, or casual acquaintance. "Doin' just fine, Buddy. Yerself?"

"Looks like you boys gotcher selves a little tat on, eh?"

"Tryin' to keep low here, Buddy." It's hard to be invisible when the bandleader is chatting you up. "If you don't mind."

"Ah, no, I don't mind a'tall, Dropsy." Of course Buddy not minding was no indicator as to whether he might do a fellow a favor by shutting up and moving on. "How's that pretty little sister of your'n, cuz?"

"Got two pretty sisters, Buddy," Dropsy said with a sniff and a glance in Malaria's direction, not liking the direction of Buddy's banter, smelling the whiskey on his breath and knowing how whiskey made him ugly.

"You know the one I'm talking about, cuz. Not the barmaid. The whore. The one I married. The one bore me a son."

Before Dropsy's brain could formulate a response, two attractive working gals—both light-skinned but only one with light-skinned features—surrounded Buddy from either side.

"Well, ladies!" Buddy's patented lady-killer glow poked sparkling pinpricks through the red of his eyes.

"Hi, Buddy!" the two chirped in giggly unison.

"Such beauty in this ugly world. Almost makes life worth livin', knowin' such creatures as your fine selves exist." *Café au lait* cheeks flushed rosy pink, giggles fluttering onward and upward with rising pitch.

Giggling whore #1: "Want I should hold yer horn fer ya, Buddy?"

Giggling whore #2: "Want sumpin' ta drink, Buddy?"

"Well, you ladies shore are kind to a working man. I'll just hang onto my little baby," stroking his horn, "but I admit to bein' mighty dry. My usual, if you please."

The girls scampered off competitively for the right to retrieve Buddy's famous poison of choice, a double shot of Raleigh Rye. Dropsy's eyes rolled—Raleigh was also Jim's drink, as a direct result of Buddy's example.

"Yer little cracker pal seems to be giving those gents a mighty good show, cuz. If they don't pay out on the tat, they oughta pay him for sheer entertainment value."

Dropsy was fully aware that Jim's adulation for Buddy failed to dilute the musician's contempt for him.

"I 'spect there's still a little bit of that devil left in him yet."

"Jim's the smoothest tat operator ever was," Dropsy monotoned in proud defense of his friend.

"Still ain't answered mah first question, boy." Buddy's lips had flattened, the red of his eyes regaining control. It could chill a person's blood when Buddy's mood dropped like that—and Dropsy gave a shiver to prove it.

"Diphtheria just fine, Buddy. Just fine."

"Look me in the eye when you talk to me, boy."

Dropsy kept his gaze in place. "Watching for a signal, Buddy. You know that. Gotta keep lookin' at Jim. Got a tat on."

Buddy grabbed him by the bicep and spun him around till Dropsy's eyes left Jim and locked with his own.

"You lippin' me, boy?" Buddy low-toned through clenched teeth.

"Nah, Buddy. I's just workin'. You know that." Buddy bore into Dropsy's eyes five seconds more before releasing his grip and coughing up a particularly ugly laugh. Dropsy brushed his arm as if ridding himself of ants before directing the compass of his nose back to the night's True North. He wasn't completely sure he hadn't missed the signal. Dropsy felt his heart thump with worry: *Damn that drunken, horn-blowing fool.*

Buddy whinnied some more at the sight of Dropsy's newly flared nostrils, "Just funnin' with ya, cuz. Don't get all excited now."

"I ain't excited, Buddy," Still steaming, but in control.

"I tell ya, cuz," Buddy switched gears from plainly mean to transparently tender, "If you see that pretty sister of your'n? The whore, I mean." Grinning like a Cheshire cat now. "You tell her I'm pinin' hard. Tell her I long for her sweet touch. Tell her I can't rightly live without her. Tell her I could use a good *fuck.*"

Dropsy struggled to keep his rage in check. There was business at hand; he had to keep a cool head and an eye on his partner.

"You need to get yerself a sense of humor, cuz! Lord o'me you do, indeedy-do. *Ha!*"

"I'll keep that in mind, Buddy."

"Looks like my lucky night, cuz." The two pretty octoroon hookers were making their way back to Buddy, each holding a double shot. Buddy placed a hand on Dropsy's shoulder, noting its tremble. "Now, if you'll excuse me, cuz. These fine ladies require my immediate and undivided attention." With a girl on each arm, Buddy crossed the hall, past Black Benny, and down the stairs to the Eagle Saloon—presumably to go around the block for some quick crib-time before the next set. Dropsy silently conceded that, all things considered, it really wasn't hard to see why Jim looked up to Buddy.

Newly undistracted, Dropsy re-sharpened his focus on the business at hand—just as Malaria reached Jim's table with a small circular tray balanced expertly on three fingers.

"Sir?" she addressed Walter, avoiding eye contact with Jim.

"Yes…um, another round of your fine red ale for my companions and I. And a shot of scotch for the youngster. And clean up this mess if you would, pretty darlin'."

"Rye, if you please," corrected Jim weakly. "Raleigh Rye if you got some."

The Samaritan seemed unfazed by the youngster's specific taste in liquor, saying only, "Raleigh Rye it is then."

Malaria's eyebrows narrowed in Jim's direction, her expression causing Walter to add, with measured indignance: "It's for *medicinal* purposes only, young lady. So don't give me no huff about his age. As you can see, our young guest has suffered injury and is in great pain."

"Of course, sir. Pardon." Malaria gave the table a quick wipe with a rag before disappearing back into the crowd.

One of the marks, a large bellied man with an unkempt black beard, peeled several alcohol-soaked playing cards from the floor. "Well, Walter, it looks like we're done with cards for the night."

Good Samaritan Walter shot the fat man a scolding glance: "I just bought you another round, Tommy. All you got is complaints? Well, ain't that just fine."

Cautious laughter crept up the throats of the other three but was swallowed back, leaving residual twinkles in six bleary eyes. "Sorry, Walter. Thank you, Walter," said Fat Tommy, with a sudden rosiness at the cheeks. Jim noted that Walter held some authority over the others. This was useful information, as it indicated they might have a tendency to follow Walter's lead.

After a few minutes Malaria returned, bending down to expose maximum cleavage as she laid out drinks. Walter paid, then tipped a nickel. She thanked him with a gracious smile then spun around quickly, her shoulder accidentally connecting hard with the bony chest of an old man with white hair and no nose.

"I got my eye on you, devil." Marcus Nobody Special stood on trembling legs, extending his right index finger in the direction of Jim Jam Jump. "Sent here by that Voodoo witch to make my life a hell. I know you." The noise level around the table dropped to a murmur. "Listen, devil. I got my eye on you. Don't think I don't. I watch yer every move." Jim stared at him blankly.

"What in the name of Pete…" Walter looked at Jim suspiciously. "Do you know this man, son?"

"No sir, never seen him. Sure is giving me the willies, though."

"Clear out, old timer," said Walter, clearly rattled. "Take yer drunken nonsense elsewhere."

"Look at his eyes," Marcus went on. "Don't you see? Red as summer cherries!"

"Look blue enough to me," Fat Tommy offered after a cursory examination of Jim's eyes.

Malaria put a hand on Marcus' shoulder but addressed Walter and Tommy. "Don't mind Mr. Marcus. He's just been drinking more than his share tonight. C'mon now, Mr. Marcus. Let's take us a little walk and get some fresh air."

"Ain't drunk," Marcus protested weakly. "Not too drunk, anyways."

Malaria gently took Marcus by the arm and guided him towards the door, whispering something in his ear as they went.

Jim scooped up the small glass of rye and downed it in a gulp, anxious to erase Marcus' disruptive performance from the minds of the marks.

"Gosh*amighty!*" he coughed.

"Easy, son," said Walter with suspect concern.

"No, it's all right," Jim assured him. "Feeling better already." His chin dropped to his chest as if to relieve the weight that his head suffered upon his neck. Jim's eyes widened dramatically upon meeting the floor. "Sir, perhaps you lost a charm from your watch chain."

"Come again, son?"

"Down there. On the floor."

Walter the Samaritan bent down in the direction of Jim's pointing finger and picked something up from a conspicuously dry spot on the alcohol-muddy floor. "Ain't mine," said the Samaritan, eying each side of the dice carefully. "Sugar cube dice. Lost from someone's game, I suspect."

Fat Tommy's eyes brightened. "Well, the cards are soaked through, but that dice looks all right to me, Walter. Have ourselves a little game?"

"Well, why don't we just take it easy a spell, Tommy." Walter offered a discreet nod of concern in Jim's direction.

"No sirree, Mr. Walter," Jim piped up with heroic fortitude. "I done wrecked yer card game and I sure as spit ain't gonna keep you fine gentlemen from having a go with that little sugar dice. Y'all don't mind me at all. Maybe watching you fellas play will take my mind offa this pain in my leg. That and another shot of Raleigh Rye, mayhap."

"Waitress!" Walter barked with a wink. Jim smiled feebly in return.

Fat Tommy snatched the sugar dice from Walter's paw, eying it as carefully as had Walter. The dice was as straight as a ruler. "So what'll it be, gentlemen? Craps?"

"Need two dice for that, Tommy," reminded Walter, the other men nodding in affirmation.

Jim looked up. "You fellas ain't from 'round here, are ya?"

"Why, no, sonny," the skinny fellow to Fat Tommy's left answered with a dopey smile. "What gave us away?"

"Craps is old hat in New Orleans. Best dice game I know is a game my Daddy taught me. Before he died, that is." The mention of a deceased parent is always good for effect. "Little game called 'tat'. No dice game better anywhere in the world, he used to say." Then, reiterating for emphasis, "My poor, dead Daddy used to say."

"Ain't never heard of no tat," said a jacketless man next to Skinny. His rolled up shirtsleeves revealed a green tattoo across one forearm declaring love for a girl called "Mavis" in dramatically loopy font.

"Finest game ever was fer dice, sir. Easy to learn, too—if you want me to teach it to ya."

Walter's broad smile set off a chain reaction around the table. "Well, sure, son," Walter cackled warmly. "Why don't you show us your little game of tat?" The drunken laughter that erupted around the table communicated to Dropsy that the signal was close.

"We usually play for sticks or straws or buttons," dead-panned Jim. "Got any straws we can use? Maybe the waitress might—"

"Well, son, you'd be playing with grown-ups tonight, and we're used to playing for dollar bills."

Jim's expression turned tragic. "All I got's two dollars and some nickels, sir."

"Well, I tell you what, son. What'd you say your name was?"

"Nick, sir. Nick Clay. Pleased to meetcha."

"Well, my young injured friend, to thank you for teaching us weary Pennsylvanian travelers your fine new game of tat, I'll give you three crisp dollar bills to have a go with. What you win you keep; what you lose is my loss alone. How's that sound?"

Jim scratched his right ear with his left hand thoughtfully before speaking. Dropsy caught the signal.

"Well, that'd be mighty nice of you, Mr. Walter. I'd be pleased and honored to teach you my Daddy's game of tat. And I thankee for the kindness of the three dollars."

A new waitress, not Malaria, brought around a second shot of rye which Jim dispatched quickly. Walter seemed pleased with Jim's newly relaxed demeanor— and with two shots of Rye in his blood, Jim didn't have to act to make it real.

The tat was on.

CHAPTER THIRTY-FOUR

# I Promise, She Lied

"**E**asy now, Mr. Marcus."

In the relative calm of the stairwell Malaria's husky coo was hardly audible to her own ears above the racket of the music hall above. With the subliminal guidance of her touch to his elbow, Marcus' whiskey-addled brain negotiated the steps before him, his labored breathing mixing with the cacophony of voices in his head, a combination that fogged all else.

"Not too fast, Mr. Marcus. Don't wanna go 'n trip," Malaria scolded, as he thumped heavily onto the second floor landing. His eyes brushed momentarily over the frosted glass window of a door that announced EAGLE LOAN AND PAWN before inching towards the precipice of the final flight down. The air did not significantly cool as they reached the ground floor where the Eagle Saloon sat nearly empty, but a muggy breeze through an open window offered mild relief from the stifling night. Malaria led him to a high stool by the bar where he slumped and let out a sigh.

"Barkeep," Marcus brightened marginally. "Couple shots of yer finest scotch for me and my fine young friend. No ice, if you please."

The bartender known as Larry Man Larry raised an eyebrow to Malaria for confirmation.

"Now, Mr. Marcus, could be you done had yerself enough for tonight," Malaria offered hopefully.

"Nonsense, my dear. I'm just gettin' paced is what. Night is yet young." She bowed a nod of surrender and Larry poured out two shots, blank-faced and muttering something about not having no ice anyhow. Marcus smiled and laid a hand over Malaria's. "All the fuss about your famous sister and I always thought you was the pretty one, Malaria. True and true."

Larry's dog, an effeminate poodle named Outlaw, emitted a decidedly un-intimidating trill of a growl from beneath the bench of a nearby and vacant upright piano.

"You're so sweet," she said without smiling, petting his forearm as if it were a cat. After a few moments closely examining the untouched glass before him, he pulled both of his hands down to his lap in a gesture akin to defense, interlacing his fingers into a nervous ball before looking at her sideways with wet eyes.

"Malaria, I know you think I been talking crazy up there, but when there's something ain't right in the world a fellow has to step up and do something 'bout it."

"You always done right far as I ever knowed, Mr. Marcus." She was wondering to herself if it would be okay to just leave him here like this, to skip back upstairs and squeeze out a few more tips while the night was still ripe and raging.

He locked eyes with her softly. "Do you think I'm crazy, Malaria?" He asked her this as if the question carried grave weight. "And I'd appreciate it if you told me true."

"No, of course not. You're my good friend, Mr. Marcus. Always have been, since I was small. You know that." Fact was she thought him a nutty old kook, if endearingly so.

"I'm much appreciative of kindness even when it ain't necessarily true, so I thank you, my dear." He smiled.

Malaria considered arguing but didn't want to appear rude or disrespectful, and so she only returned the smile in kind. Larry refilled Marcus' suddenly-empty shot glass without being told.

"Let me ask you something, Malaria." Marcus meant to go somewhere with this talk of his own sanity or lack thereof. "When you look in that kid's eyes, what color are they to you?"

"You mean Jim?"

"That's right."

A pause. "Well, I guess I'd say fishy blue."

"Fishy blue. That's good. It means he ain't got his sights on you. Not yet, leastways. Do you know what color I see in those eyes?"

"Upstairs you said 'red like summer cherries.'"

"That's right. Red. Red as can be."

"Glowing red? Like lamplight?" She was mildly fascinated by the notion of seeing whatever it was Marcus saw, even if it was a thing imagined.

"No. Like *painted* red. Dull in color, like dried blood against old smoothed wood. But red just the same." He reached for her hand again. "Malaria, I'm usually just fine with folks thinking me a fool, an old feller with a wild imagination and strange ideas about the world, but I need to come clean with you about certain things—and for good and particular reason. Now try to keep an open mind 'cause some of this gonna sound damn strange."

"All right."

"That Jim Jam Jump kid ain't quite human, darlin', and he done latched onto yer brother Dropsy. This is a very serious thing." His eyes told her he meant it. "Dropsy's a good kid, but this association gonna get him hurt. Or worse. So you need to know certain things."

Now he had her full attention. She had never liked Jim, though she couldn't exactly say why—she just felt a hollow, sinking feeling whenever in his presence. It made her very nervous the way Dropsy followed the kid around, even seemed to idolize him.

"What kind of certain things?" She failed to conceal the worry in her voice and so Marcus softened his tone.

"Well, dear, neither you nor I were in that house on that night, but we both have an idea what happened there. And I happen to know there's a lot more to it than what's been said around town in the barbershops and sewing circles and such."

Malaria understood which night he referred to. The night her father died—and almost took Typhus along with him. The night a demon was supposedly cast out of one-year-old Dominick Carolla, the boy currently known as Jim Jam Jump.

"Some folks say that boy was suffering from an illness, others say from demons. But I know it warn't exactly neither." An avalanche of irrelevant laughter erupted overhead—Marcus waited for it to pass before wheezing in a deep breath, then out, then continuing on. "The thing inside that child was invited by hoodoo most foul, brought on by that crazy old fool Malvina Latour. She set that thing into motion, brought it into this world many years back, before you was even born—and it was meant for me, that thing. Meant to right a perceived wrong I done against her kin."

"What kin?" She'd heard many stories about Malvina the Vodou mambo over the years, but this one was new to her.

"I can't get on that right now, and it don't rightly matter by this late date anyhow."

Malaria watched a bead of sweat roll down his cheek that could have passed for a tear.

"What matters is this: that old Malvina didn't know then what it was she brought on, don't know now neither, and likely won't know never. It was a *djab*, that thing. Now, *djab* is a Haitian word that translates as 'demon,' but really just means any kind of unruly spirit with a need to be kept in check by Papa *Legba* and Mama *Ayizan*—if allowed into this world at all. Whatever it might be or might not be, it don't see itself as no demon. It sees itself as some kinda savior of the human race. And, hell, maybe it is." He glanced over by the piano to avoid the burn of her eyes. "But its methods are suspect."

Unnoticed by any in the saloon, Outlaw told a silent tale of caution and dread beneath the piano bench with wildly expressive ears.

"But my daddy cast that demon out." She never really believed those old stories, but when the nights got black enough she sometimes wondered. "That's what they say at least."

"It was Typhus cast it out," he corrected. "And took it into himself. Yer daddy just hung up in the crossfire. But those two boys each got a part of it that linger on. Jim got the part what means harm. That kid was too young to fight it off or even know what was happening. He been living with that thing so long now he can't see no other way, he's become what it made him. I 'spect it's too late for that boy now. But Typhus was older, smarter, more skilled in spiritual matters. I suspect he's having a tough time with it in his own way, though." His eyes returned to meet hers. "Malaria, this gonna be hard to hear but important, so try and take stock. I believe this thing to be more dangerous than some old demon. I'm afraid we're talking about a danger so strong as to bring about a change in the weather. This thing means to clean the world of sin if it can, and the tryin' won't be kind nor pretty."

"Clean the world of sin," she echoed under breath. Malaria found herself fighting a powerful urge to laugh out loud. The urge passed quickly. "I thought you said this thing was after you in particular, Mr. Marcus."

"No, that was the plan of the mambo alone. The thing in Jim couldn't give a hang about that crazy witch's vendetta against a beaten old gravedigger like me. But it knows *that I know*, and so it's got its sights on me. I know this to be true when I look into those red eyes. And I plan to keep my sights on it, too—I mean to watch its *every* move. Now, don't be scared ner overly worried, but you need to keep an eye on it yerself—because this thing has positioned itself as a direct threat to your kin." He let his voice deepen nearly an octave before finishing: "Malaria, promise me that if those eyes ever go red on you that you'll be careful."

"I promise," she lied.

§

The strange confessions of Marcus Nobody Special had gotten Malaria to thinking about the dual forces that had set her life so firmly and cruelly on its current course; the forces of father and of God. Of what she'd hoped to learn from both or neither her whole life long—and how those lessons had remained so maddeningly unlearned yet so dearly paid for. Tonight she suffered new clarity as she came to realize such answers might come if only she dare indulge a secret wish to fail them both.

Being the oldest in a family of orphans had carried with it certain responsibilities. Her father's death had effectively preordained the rest of her days—or so she'd believed—handing down a life sentence with no hope of recourse or appeal, a sentence allowing her only to give of herself and never truly to receive.

Now here she was, standing at a crossroads of regret and thankless servitude, with no sign of relief or rescue for as far as the eye could see. This had been her lot in life. Never having had time nor inclination to find a man—let alone a child—for herself, never having closely considered the possibility of a career or a higher purpose, never having confided to a soul on earth that all she'd ever wanted was to sing.

The bitterest pill was that her commitment to self-neglect went wholly unnoticed—certainly unchallenged—by the ones she'd loved most, the very beneficiaries of her sacrifice. They seemed content to accept her love as a matter of course and get on with their own lives. She assumed her eventual death would be deemed a similar matter of course; briefly to be mourned, soon to be forgotten. She would outlive none of them.

Marcus had been right about Diphtheria. She'd made her mark on the world. She was a beautiful and well-respected commodity at the world-famous Arlington Hall, had gotten her own listing in the Blue Book, had even borne a child by the locally famous musician Buddy Bolden. It was a grand life she'd been permitted to lead.

Malaria's existence was ordinary and unadventurous by contrast. At her job she served drinks. At home she served the family; fretting over their well-being, their successes, their disappointments, their fears. Making sure there was always enough to eat. Worrying about Typhus and his lovesick ways. Keeping an eye on Diphtheria's boy when his mama was otherwise disposed; off having fun, making her own way, acquiring the things she desired and doing so without guilt or shame.

Tonight Marcus had brought her a new concern regarding Dropsy and his unwholesome affiliation with Jim Jam Jump. But it was more than a mere item of concern to her now, it was a new twist on an old tune, an idea that instantaneously fermented in her mind a challenge of lifelong principles regarding duty and honor, principles thrust upon her at such a young age by her long dead father and his invisible God.

Tonight she understood the attraction of things unsafe. It was true there was something insidiously not right about Jim, something evil and dark—but she saw also a thing exciting and seductive. Like a hurricane party or a jazz funeral, an embrace of some fast-coming and brilliantly inevitable (if unjust) end, an open invitation to the last and wildest party on earth, a high stakes gamble with neither certainty nor hope.

A new name on an old and forgotten dance card. Though she'd previously believed herself doomed to always do right in her life, she now discovered a secret part of herself deeply attracted to Marcus Nobody Special's drunken fantasy of evil and intrigue, to this unnamable adventure he'd painted of the world barreling like a comet towards imminent destruction in the form of a mean little boy.

# CHAPTER THIRTY-FIVE

## *King Tat*

Faithfully responding to Jim's signal, Dropsy Morningstar dutifully made dramatic reappearance—huffing and puffing with artfully-artificial dread. In between huffs:

"Sorry little fella. Ain't a doctor on the whole block, but I sure did look. Best ya climb on my back and let me take ya to the Charity Hospital. Ain't too far, I reckon."

Walter, still intent on displaying concern for his new young friend's welfare (but not so much that he'd sacrifice learning a game as intriguing as this "tat"), worked his own angle in Dropsy's direction; "Boy, it would seem I owe you an apology for handling you so roughly earlier. Our new little pal has declared you quite the hero."

"No, sir," Dropsy offered with exaggerated humility. "Just doin' what anyone'd done. No more'n that is what. No more a'tall."

"Well, have a seat and let me buy you a drink just the same. The patient is in good hands, the bleeding done stopped."

Jim displayed his handkerchiefed leg to Dropsy in confirmation.

"Young man's 'bout to treat us to a local dice game. You ever hear of a game called tat?"

"Well, who hasn't, sir? Best game of dice ever was, the tat."

"That's what I been hearing."

Dropsy changed the subject for sake of authenticity: "You sure you okay, little fella?"

"Feelin' just fine," Jim answered with a sleepy smile. In fact he was feeling downright warm.

"Ain't been drinking, have ya?" Dropsy persisted. "Skinny little guy like you might get sick is what."

Walter answered defensively on Jim's behalf. "Young Nick's had a little snort is all. Just to ease the pain. Medicinal purposes only, you understand."

"Well, all right." Dropsy yielded to the clearly-better-educated-white-man's-expertise-in-such-matters, as was proper.

"How 'bout that game, now?" The Man Who Loved Mavis sounded eager to lose his shirt.

"Well, then…" Jim slurred, clutching the three dollars. "I'm thinking this might be my lucky night. Got my life saved by this kind niggra, met you nice fellas, now I got me three whole dollars and might turn it into more."

"That's right, son," Walter affirmed. "Luck has smiled on you today. Unless you count getting bit by that dog."

"Yes, indeed," agreed The Man Who Loved Mavis.

"Nuff talk, now," continued Walter. "How about them rules, young Nick?"

"This is the game," said Jim. "We put this little sugar dice in a hat." Skinny offered his brown bowler in response. "Each player takes a turn shaking it three times, then the first man up gives it a roll. Then everyone gives it another good shake before the second man gives it a roll—and so forth and so on. After everyone's had three turns at rollin', ya just add up the number of dots each player got—and the one with the most wins the buttons or straws…I mean, the dollar bills."

"Nice little kiddy game is what we got, then," said Fat Tommy. "Kiddies and simple niggers, I guess," said the Man Who Had Not Yet Spoken, whose most remarkable trait was his very unremarkableness.

Dropsy, with slight indignation: "That ain't the way I'm used to playing no tat. Skipped over the most important rule is what."

"What might that be, Hero?" spat The Least Remarkable Man. Dropsy noted the man spoke with the venom of a dyed-in-the-wool nigger-hater.

Without looking Least Remarkable in the eye, Dropsy replied, "Winner buys a round of drinks for the table."

"Oh, I *like* that rule," said Fat Tommy.

"My Daddy never told me 'bout that rule," Jim offered suspiciously.

More laughter. Walter put a hand on Jim's shoulder, "Well, Nick, your Daddy was a fine man indeed, then. A fine man fer sher, I'd say!" Walter gave Jim's shoulder a fresh squeeze. "Well, whaddaya say, little fella? Yer friend's rule does make this little game of tat a bit more interesting."

"Gee, Mr. Walter, I dunno. Already had two shots and I'm just a youngster."

"Well, you ain't no little kid tonight, Nick. No kid I ever seen could knock back shots of rye like you just done."

"Anymore and I might be sick, Mr. Walter." Calculated reluctance.

"Best not get sick now. No, sir," agreed Dropsy, attracting disapproving glances all around—but most severely from The Least Remarkable Man.

"Nigger might have a point," Jim offered—his word choice specifically designed to earn the confidence of The Least Remarkable Man.

"Nonsense, son," said Walter. "Can't hurt to have a little more *medicine* now, could it? For the pain is all." Jim hesitated—staring at his shoes and sniffing at his soul for the precise length of pause. Then:

"No sir. Reckon not, I guess."

The tat was progressing better than expected. Jim's timing and execution had been perfect, and Dropsy had not missed a beat.

Walter got down to business straight away. "I nominate our nigger hero friend to pass the dice and hold the hat, being he has no conflict of interest here. Any objections?"

Jim just smiled. This wasn't going to be much fun if Walter did all the work for him. Took the sport out of it.

On the first round, each player (including Jim) examined the dice carefully before throwing. Six one dollar bills were won by an ecstatic Fat Tommy, who piled up four in front of him and ordered another round for the table with the remaining two.

Second round went to The Least Remarkable Man, resulting in the first non-malicious smile to appear on his face that evening. Dropsy sighed inaudibly and Jim made mental note of the fact that no one thought to double-check the dice on this second round. Shot glasses emptied and the room wobbled accordingly for the marks, Jim keeping his mind clear through sheer force of will. There would be time for room-wobbling later—maybe even a good puke. Now was the time to concentrate.

Jim had only one of Walter's dollars left.

Dropsy passed the hat, the dice fell six times. Least Remarkable won again, now grinning like the idiot Jim and Dropsy figured him to be.

"Well, I guess I'm out of money," said Jim with measured disappointment. "Thanks fer lettin' me play, Mr. Walter. Shore was kind."

"Ah, well, that is a shame, my little friend. But then again…" Walter paused.

"Sir?" Jim, as if he had no clue where Walter might be leading.

"Ah, never mind, son. Nothing, really."

"What is it, sir?" Imploring eyes.

"Well, there is that matter of two dollars and various nickels you'd mentioned in your pocket." Walter put on his best fatherly smile.

Jim and Dropsy's eyes met for a split second—just long enough. Having intimate knowledge of Dropsy's high-principled tendencies towards the golden rule and whatnot, Jim recognized this moment of revelation as crucial to Dropsy's state of conscience. This Good Samaritan, Walter, had not only bullied what he perceived as a fragile and injured young boy into excessive liquor intake, but was now angling to pick his pocket as well. The man was *asking* to be fleeced, and deserved whatever he got—even in the eyes of a righteous-minded preacher's son like Dropsy Morningstar. The way Walter was carrying on, Jim could conceivably convince Dropsy it would be a sin *not* to teach him a humbling lesson. Refocusing on the business at hand, Jim extracted a one dollar bill from his left front pocket.

Dropsy kept the tally and passed the derby—but when Jim's turn came this time, Dropsy made the switch. Dropsy was good at the switch, always subtle and smooth in the execution. But even had he been clumsy there was now enough liquor in the Pennsylvanian travelers that they probably wouldn't have noticed. The last thing they expected was to be taken by a simple nigger and a boozed up sixteen-year-old.

Jim took the win this time, squealing like a stepped-on kitten and drawing congratulatory applause from everyone at the table—save for The Least Remarkable Man. Jim made note of this fact as well; sore losers could often cause undue difficulties in the course of an otherwise smooth touch.

Now Jim had seven whole dollars in front of him; two gone for another round, five remaining. Walter patted Jim's hand, genuinely pleased that the boy was still in the game. Malaria came back and delivered the men another step into the clouds. Jim struggled mightily to keep his mind clear. He could do this. He was in control. He was Jim Jam Jump, World Famous Ratboy of Orleans Parish and Surrounding Territories—but not so famous, it would seem, in some place called Pennsylvania. *There'll be time enough for increasing my national fame status later,* thought Jim with a faint smile. *Right now I got a tat on in full force.*

Jim cleared his throat in a way that warned he might get sick, chairs squeaking on the painted wooden floor as Skinny and the Man Who Loved Mavis eased back warily.

Jim's eyes glowed at the five ones before him as if he'd never seen so much money in his life. "Hot dang if I *don't* feel lucky," he slurred brightly. "Tell ya what. I got five whole dollars now, how about we double the stakes on the next turn?"

"Sounds like someone done got bit by the gamblin' bug." Walter kept in touch with his fatherly tone, but added a hint of the devil. "And at such a tender age, too. Well, if you insist, little fella. Guess you ain't got much to lose seein's you better than broke even already." Another round of chuckles bubbled up—but in Jim's alcohol-blurred frame of mind the sound was of chortling pigs. *Clear mind,* he urged himself without speaking. The sound around him sharpened and focused upon internal command:

*CLEAR.*

The heads of the marks bobbed with a mutual nod regarding the increased stakes. Dropsy collected up two dollars from each player this time. The hat went around. Dice hit wood six times. Twelve times. Eighteen.

*Tat*

Jim lost this time.

"Maybe I ain't so lucky as I thought. Maybe used up all my luck meeting you nice fellas and surviving that dog attack."

"Well now, my young friend, don't fret. You're still up ahead from where you started. Started with two and now got three. One more round for luck, little buddy?"

Jim knocked back his shot, winced, faked a cough. Dropsy feigned concern with levitating eyebrows—but Jim's own eyes brightened suddenly.

"Yes, Mr. Walter! One more round! And if it's my last, then let me bet the whole farm. Three dollar ante!" It was now imperative that Jim make clear his intention to play until he'd lost every penny in his pocket. This was another important element to the process—for it assures your marks that they will eventually get back what they have lost.

Skinny giggled like a schoolgirl, "Hey, high roller! All hail, King Tat!"

Good humor took another lap around the table—but stopped conspicuously where The Least Remarkable Man sat, the nigger-hater squinting suspiciously. Jim: Making note.

*Tat*

Eight more rounds occurred, the stakes being raised on each turn, Jim winning all but two. Dropsy intentionally failed to switch the die in Jim's favor exactly three times, Jim winning by actual luck exactly once.

By this point, the suckers were so incapacitated they could hardly keep their drunken asses from dripping out of their chairs. Jim: Ninety-six pounds and holding firm.

*CLEAR.*

On the ninth round, a problem developed. Just as Jim was about to throw, The Least Remarkable Man lurched forward—tipping the table slightly and snatching the dice from Jim's hand. Sitting back down with the dice in his fist, Least Remarkable locked eyes hard with Dropsy. Dropsy silently wondered if his last switch had not been as clean as it could have been. Between forefinger and thumb, The Least Remarkable Man gave each side of the dice a penetrating squint.

Jim was not sure if Dropsy had even switched the straight dice for tat on this last round. He delicately glanced up into Dropsy's eyes, trying to get a read. The read was easy, Dropsy unable to mask his panic. The Least Remarkable

Man was onto them. The jig was up. The dice currently being examined by The Least Remarkable Man had five dots on four sides, and six dots on two. You would have to be drunk to the point of blindness not to notice—this is why the constant rounds of alcohol are so important in a good game of tat.

Jim and Dropsy attempted bored expressions as The Least Remarkable Man continued to squint with the occasional low-toned, angry grunt; rubbing his eyes, then squinting some more. Finally, Fat Tommy bellowed with drunken impatience, "You quite through there, Otis? You ain't bein' cheated by no kid. Get this game back on so's I can win summa my money back, damn ya!"

The Least Remarkable Man, whose name was Otis, saw wiggly dancing dots on the surface of the dice and nothing more. With a defeated slump, he handed the tat back to Jim. "Yeah, I reckon it's all right," he said, visibly flustered by the lack of cooperation he'd received from his own two eyes, too proud to admit the weakness. Dropsy had come to know in his lifetime that unremarkable people are usually the proudest.

Otis grumbled something under his breath, indecipherable words that reached Dropsy's ears as, "double double toil and trouble."

"How's that, Otis?" asked Skinny, operating the numb muscles of his mouth with great effort.

"Double up that damn bet, I said! First night in town and I'm damn near outta cash. Gotta win some back now, hear? Double it up!" Otis looked hard into Jim's eyes and saw red. "Damn, Otis," said Walter, "Prob'ly not such a good idea, I reckon. Kid's on a regular streak here."

"That gold horseshoe up his ass gotta shake loose sometime, Walter," pitched in Fat Tommy. "I'm with Otis. Double it up!"

"Ain't sure I got nuff left to go double," said Skinny meekly.

"Then I guess you'd be out, Roy," Otis barked without looking up.

Nervous nods dipped around the table, no one asking young "Nick" if he minded doubling the stakes—no one particularly caring whether he minded or not. This was as it should be with any good touch. Make sure the mark makes as many bad decisions as he can of his own design and free will. Nudge only when necessary.

Being the only sober mind left at the table, Dropsy had no further need of cleverness in the switch. He could have put a pig's ear in the hat without raising an eyebrow. One of the few advantages enjoyed by colored persons in this business was that white folks prefer not to drink with you—and, therefore, rarely protest if you choose not to partake. A white man's own sense of natural-born privilege could often be used against him in this way—you only need be aware of the fact, Dropsy had learned.

The hat went around until the inevitable occurred, Jim cleaning up once more. Drooping drunken faces stretched longer still as Otis slammed his fist to the table, the impact of the blow causing Skinny Roy's shot glass to bounce noisily to the floor.

Timing was everything:

Jim stood up quick, wobbling mightily, with both hands on the table for support.

Dropsy casually scooped up his partner's winnings as Jim spoke in a drunkenly disabled voice that no longer needed faking: "My ma will be so happy for the groceries I done made!" Without warning, the kid keeled over, flopping face first onto the table, then bouncing backwards onto the floor.

Dropsy dove down to retrieve him, stuffing his pockets with more bills along the way. Slapping Jim gently on the cheeks: "Y'okay, little fella?"

"Don't feel so good. Think I gonna be sick."

Walter rolled his eyes, peeved at the inconvenience. "Ah, crap. Why don't ya take ol' Nick outside, hero. Then come on back in and we'll have another go or two. Let us weary travelers have a chance at winning some of that money back."

"Just what I was thinking, sir." Jim began to heave as Dropsy pulled him to his feet.

"Hurry fer chrissakes!" Otis, the Least Remarkable Man, was concerned that the sight of Jim puking may trigger the contents of his own destabilizing gut.

As Dropsy and Jim neared the door, Jim's retching got louder. The second to last thing Dropsy heard from the table of used-up suckers was the voice of Skinny Roy:

"Dang, Walter, maybe we shouldn't have made that youngster drink so much whiskey. Ain't sure how such a little guy drunk so much without droppin' over dead."

And the *very* last thing Dropsy heard was the sound of the Pennsylvanians' own dumb laughter—laughing at what they believed to be the misery of a poor, sick boy just sixteen years old.

Dropsy couldn't have hoped for a cleaner getaway. He slipped Black Benny a wad of currency before helping Jim down the stairs. Benny gave up a rare smile witnessed by no one.

Upon reaching the dark Perdido Street alley outside, Jim did indeed vomit for the best of two solid minutes. In the aftermath of sickness, he wiped chin to sleeve, then brushed sleeve to hand. The night's winnings came out of Dropsy's pocket for a final tally in the shadows. The split was fifty-fifty—fair and square just like always.

"Nice little take there, fellas?" The voice of Buddy Bolden startled the two. Cigar clamped between teeth, and horn in hand, Buddy's tall frame conspired with the light of the alley's mouth to form a long shadow.

# CHAPTER THIRTY-SIX

# *What Dropsy Saw*

"Thought you was gettin' busy with them girls," Dropsy deadpanned.

"Howdy, Buddy!" Jim grinned with yellowy eyes. "Some mighty nice playin' tonight. Sorry we can't stay for the next set."

"Reckon that wouldn't be too safe, all things considered and such, eh Jim?" said the silhouette of Buddy Bolden.

"Ah, hell, I'd keep on going but them fellas tapped out. Ain't as fat as I reckoned." Then, after a moment's consideration. "From some place called Pennsylvania. Not much money up there, I guess."

"Well then," Buddy sounded tired. "What'll you be spending all that hard earned cash on, Ratboy?"

"Funny you should mention, Buddy." Jim smiled, a patch of dried vomit on his cheek cracking into a dozen smaller pieces. "I was thinking of buying that horn of yours offa ya. If yer willin', I mean."

"Didn't know you played, Jim." Pretending he didn't know all about Jim's grand notions of graduating from the rat killing business in favor of musical stardom.

"Well, if I had a horn I might." Smile gone, vomit bits reassembled.

"Lots of horns besides this one around, I reckon. Better ones, 'n cheaper too, I s'pose."

"I like that one," Jim insisted, eyebrows nearly joined. "Ready to pay top dollar fer it, too."

"That makes some sense, I guess. This horn does have some history. But it's also got sentimental value can't be bought. Anyway, after I'm done with it, it's already spoken for by some-other-body."

"Spoken for? By who?"

Dropsy had never seen such plain disappointment on Jim's face. The sight of it made him uneasy.

"That little boy of mine," Buddy answered coldly. "This horn got some of his daddy's magic in it, I guess. Some other kinda magic too, most likely. Figgered on hanging onto it fer awhile then pass it on to West one day. Least I kin do fer the little guy 'sidderin' I left him to be raised by a whore."

"That horn may be worth twenty dollars brand new," Jim angled. "I'll give ya sixty fer it right now." Jim's eagerness tipped his hand. One more thing Dropsy had never before witnessed Jim do.

"Sixty, eh? Well, that's a mighty tempting offer, son." Playing with the player is what Buddy had in mind. "But I'll have to pass."

"Eighty?" Jim's desperation brought Dropsy close to tears. Buddy smiled but shook his head, stroking the horn like a kitten.

"Hunnert, then," said Jim firmly with beaten, angry eyes. "Final offer."

Buddy's expression softened with a thing approaching genuine remorse—or, more likely, pity:

"I'll tell ya what. I'll give you a little blow fer free. Just so's you can see if you like it. Playin' horns ain't fer everyone, y'know. Might not be fer you once you have a go."

"Really? I mean, ya wouldn't mind? Ya ain't kiddin'?"

"Normally I'd mind plenty, sonny. But truth is you and this horn have a special history—though you was too young then to remember 'bout it now. Sang to you when you was a little baby, this horn. Put a breath in yer chest and a smile on yer mama's face. Only seems right you should have one little blow on it. Fer old time's sake." Buddy, unlike Dropsy, was aware of Jim's true history. Knew that Jim Jam Jump was a stage name invented for him by Crawfish Bob, and that his real name was Dominick Carolla, son of Sicilian immigrants in spite of fair skin and blue eyes.

"Well, all right then." Jim wasn't exactly sure what Buddy was talking about, but it was true he'd felt a certain connection with this particular horn. It wasn't just in the way that Buddy played it; there was something about the horn itself.

Reverently, Jim took the cornet from Buddy's outstretched hand. Dropsy suddenly realized that, until this moment, he'd never seen Buddy not holding the damn thing. The man looked surprisingly thin and vulnerable without it in his hand.

Jim drew in a deep breath and closed his eyes, then: lips to mouthpiece.

The sound that came out wasn't a note of music so much as it was a toneless scream. Jim's fingers depressed random keys, searching for the ones that might make sense to his ear, sending a trail of dissident, brassy coughs on a choppy journey through charcoal-colored air, the sound of it lightly amplified by dull mist. Finally, Jim seemed to find a note that suited him.

The lonesome, pitiful wail of Jim's chosen note echoed through the tenderloin. The sound went on and on without benefit of second breath. Dropsy pressed both hands against his ears to shield his mind from its brittleness, the pressure of his left hand enraging the tender ear recently punched hard by Windmill Willie.

Buddy Bolden stood expressionless, looking at his feet, knowing certain things. Jim Jam Jump was in church. In rapture. The scar of his chest was burning, the scar in the shape of a hand.

The ugliness of the note's journey was something Jim recognized at his core, an unwelcome and damning thing, a primordial reflection in a forgotten mirror. This thing was undeniably his, though, and so he didn't turn from it. He took it for what it was—and embraced it absolutely. Hearing the sound of your own soul can be an enlightening and satisfying thing, even if it isn't a pretty sound.

The cornet's howl gradually tapered and finally did end, leaving perfect quiet—except for a rustling sound.

Dropsy Morningstar: "Holy sweet Jesus, what's that?"

Not aware till now that he'd closed them in the first place, Jim Jam Jump let his eyes fall open.

Twinkling red lights dotted the cobbled floor of Perdido Street through thickening mist. The lights were in pairs, and behind each pair was a dark oblong shadow ending in a thin, whipping tail. Among the smaller pairs was one much larger set of red dots with its own accompanying shadow. The tail of the bigger shadow wagged happily—the tail of a dog.

*biggest thing I ever kilt*

The sight of it put a feeling of dread in Dropsy's stomach, a sensation of unpleasant things consumed but not yet passed—but for Jim it was a satisfying thing. It was a thing he'd made all by himself, the *biggest* thing he'd made yet. And it suggested to him the possibility of things *bigger still.*

Jim's face was as expressionless as Buddy's now, something in his soul shaken loose, drifting into night. Even the cherished horn of Buddy Bolden slipped from his conscious mind—its fall from his limp hand triggering a series of hollow clickety-clacks against the alley floor.

"Careful, dammit," hissed Buddy, bending down to retrieve the dropped cornet, whispering, "My baby. Shhhh. Poor baby."

The sound of Buddy's whisper brought Jim round, his eyes suddenly fluttering with twitchy double-blinks. He turned to Dropsy with flushed cheeks, "Guess I'll see you 'round tomorrow, pardna. How's about ten o'clock at our regular spot? Tomorrow be a bigger day, my friend. *Bigger.*"

Turning to leave, Jim strolled casual as you please down the dead center of Perdido Street, red twinkles and tiny shadows following westward.

"Hold up, Jim," said Dropsy. "Wait for me." Jim didn't seem to hear, so Dropsy took a step forward.

Buddy placed a hand on Dropsy's shoulder, said quietly: "No. Let him go."

Dropsy and Buddy watched in silence as Jim disappeared from view, followed by twinkly red.

Dropsy stood blinking, single blinks, not double: "Damn, Buddy. What just happened?"

"Nature happened, kiddo." Ever-expressionless.

"Nature?"

"Listen, up, cuz." Buddy was unprepared to venture into this conversational territory at that moment (or ever)—especially with an idiot like Dropsy Morningstar—and so changed the subject. "I want you to give yer sister a little message."

"Huh?"

"Tell her I ain't given up on her yet. Ain't given up on my little boy, neither."

Buddy Bolden turned away before Dropsy could think to reply. Swallowed up by the backdoor of the Eagle Saloon, off to play out the fifth set of the night.

Nighttime could be an endless thing for musicians in the tenderloin.

# CHAPTER THIRTY-SEVEN

# The Nature of
## My Double-Blink

What started as a minor annoyance is now officially full-fledged bothersome.

You. Thinking this relationship ain't no two way street. Smug is what. Thinking without proper considerin'. Not knowin' jack-doodly-squat-times-one. Damn if you ain't just a regular smuggle-dee-bug so and so. Smugbug is what. Thinkin' you know.

Think I *don't* know? Think you kin read these words offa page and make deductions 'bout where I been and where I'm gonna go, what *I'm* about? About who THE FUCK I am, even? Puh! Thinking you know All About Jim Jam Jump just 'cause ya read a chapter with such a title. Thinkin' once you put the bookmark in and wander off to the toilet that I somehow cease to exist, maybe even never really *did* exist. Well, maybe it ain't exactly the way you figgered, smugbug. Or maybe it is, but maybe there's somethin' more. Maybe when the bookmark goes in it's yer own dumb-thinkin' self that stops bein' and not me. Maybe *fer me* that's exactly how it is.

Maybe without each other ain't neither of us fer nothin'. Maybe the book bein' open is all that either of us got. Maybe ever was. Maybe you n' me need each other in a way. Two twins sharin' a heart. Good and evil, like Ida Mae and Becky.

Yeah, go on. Keep bein' so smug. Bein' smug don't change nothin'.

What you think you know:

You think ol' Jim Jam Jump is just a diseased fictional varmint pickin' the pockets of drunks and splattin' innocent rats fer fun and profit. Think I ain't got a natural sense fer fine music, think I'm some kinda hanger-on to Buddy Bolden, trine to soak up some glory by hangin' round 'im with too much rye in my belly, tootin' his worthless horn in the street for a pity blow only ta make a screechin' bunch o' rat-ghost-drawin' noise.

Thinkin' you know the nature of my double-blink.

Think I can't look straight back atcha when these pages held open, figgerin' you out just like you think ya got me figgered. Think I can't see yer hair ain't sittin' on yer head exactly how ya like it. How yer weird lookin' thumbs got a nail slightly longer on the right one. Clip that damn thing, wouldja? 'Bout ta make me sick so awful damn close to my eye, sittin' right at the edge of this page. Yuckety duck hissy-pissy hucklebuck n'fuck. You, with that folded up phone number tucked away, the one without a name written above or below it, scared to throw it out 'cause it might be important. Well, I'll tell you what; it *is* important. Call that number, smugbug. Never know who might answer. Might be some fictional boy pick up the phone. I await yer call, right here, right now, Dear Reader. Bein' that you need proof o' what I say.

What I say, Jim.

Thinkin' when the book done closed I can't bother ya no-more-no-how; that I can't open my *own* damn book anytime I want and have a peek inta yer own greasy-pink soul. *You.*

Presumin' to peek into my own little soul and thinkin' that fact puts you a step above yers truly. Yers truly, Jim Jam Jump. The fictional boy. Harmless little wisp of imaginary man. Just a character in a book by a two-bit hack. Finish reading it or don't; slam it shut, toss it in the trash or pass it to a friend or sell my cranky psycho ass on the market o' fleas for a dollar and a dime. Fuck you.

You see me, Smugbug. My dreams is stupid and thin, my future bleak, the fabric of my bein' not even fer real. Sure, sure. My methods might be nasty and mean, ya just might be right about that. But I'm only lookin' out fer number one like every other son-of-a-gun on God's green earth. Can't get by in this hard world without such a way. Just like you, is what. Jim Jam Jump weren't born with no privilege slippin' back on his pink-baby tongue. My Daddy dead, dead, dead; this scar over my heart, down and kicked around, fightin' back the only way I know how, killin' sometimes if I gotta—and even if I don't gotta but just feelin' ornery. Got plenty of shame and a tiny little remorse 'bout all that. Just like you. But just maybe now I be mad enough to develop a method beyond the random. *Modus operandi* the coppers call it. Frequency modulation say me.

You see that devil lingerin' in me,—but don't be so proud, 'cause I see one in yer own sweet self. You ain't so pure, Smugbug. You done killed some rats. You done wronged a friend. You got the taste of blood and went back for more.

On the sly.

Thinkin' no one looking. You've pissed on innocence; yer own and of others. You smelt yer own shit and pretended it ain't yers. Yer fingernails is dirty. You got blood. In yer veins, on yer hands. You done worse than me a hundred times over, only with less style. You got yer own damn frequency modulation of sorts.

Sayin' it ain't so don't make it not.

When you close this book I'm gone fer you, but yer gone too. Figment of my imaginary imagination. Gone. You and yer ugly, lopsided thumbnails, yer funny hair, yer spooked eyes, and yer smirkin' lips.

Think I can't see?

Clip that damn thing.

What I say, Jim.

Well, damn then.

If this ain't just too damn much.

Damn, damn, damn.

Clip it. Someone 'round here got themself a whole lotta nerve is what.

And I thought we was friends.

Poo times two.

You done pissed off the wrong hunk-a-lunk, Dear Reader.

Jim.

Jam Jump.

Say hoo.

# CHAPTER THIRTY-EIGHT

## *Night Whisperer*

Beauregard Church had long been aware of the long, muddy trail that stretched from behind the prison to the Old Basin Canal and up to the bayou's heart, had known about it since the days of his tenure at Orleans Parish Prison when he'd often used it to deposit the unwanted remains of prisoners who'd died bereft of other arrangements. The dark path had felt haunted to him even then, and he remembered imagining the sounds of the loveless dead wandering its length in search of last reward. But now the trail was his alone to haunt, and he haunted it well.

Ghosts were plentiful enough at Parish Prison, so it was no shock to guards or inmates when Beauregard's huge, creaking form began appearing in its halls. The presence of shadowy figures—gliding, stumbling, sometimes flashing—through the walkways of the compound hardly raised an eyebrow in a place so wrought with terrible things, inmates and guards alike often trading ghost stories just to pass the time. Beauregard rather enjoyed being in a position to inspire such tales—and was quite pleased to have once heard an old friend identify him as "The Ghost of Beauregard Church." The recognition gave him a sense of place.

Beauregard's excursions to the prison had supplied the Morningstar Family with many happy dawn-time surprises over the years; various foodstuffs, tools, coal, and blankets to name a few—but more recently the prison had supplied a thing of value to Beauregard himself. After many years of paying penance, Beauregard had recently discovered himself unwelcome and unforgiven in the eyes of Typhus Morningstar—the son of the man he killed—and so decided such penance was a thing that could never be paid in full. The prison's ready supply of morphine tablets provided something of an answer—or at least an escape from the prison of his own guilty heart.

The first tablet brought Beauregard near bliss—but along with this comfort came a hollow feeling at the center of his chest. The warm light of morphine gave him a sensation of untainted conscience, but guilt cut through bliss as a separation of body and spirit, and with this separation came an understanding that peace and emptiness may really be one and the same. He sat at the edge of orange-tinted swamp water pondering such circular thoughts as his eyes followed the lance-shaped leaves and small white flowers of alligator weed that floated at its surface. A voice broke the uneasy silence, his own:

"Got no business feelin' good 'bout nothin'," he reassured himself. "This morphine like ta test ya is all. Want to make sure you can keep a hold of yer own pain, Beauregard Church. Pain's all ya got left, old man. Gotta hang onto that. Pain is yer only reason for bein'. Don't forget that, now."

Tugging at his hair and beard with trembling fingers, he focused hard on the task of recapturing his heart's former heaviness. Gradually, his conscience refilled with regretful memory, but the god of morphine insists on extremes, and so the burden of his soul grew rapidly past capacity, a *physical* thing now, his heart swelling painfully under the pressure. The bubble of remorse pressed outward against his ribs, causing tears to fill his eyes that failed to blur, the jagged spines of alligator weed only sharpening in focus.

At first Antonio's ghost had been no more than a wisp floating up from the bog like a blue ball of lightning, speaking in throatless, unintelligible whispers. The Cajuns called this kind of light *un feu follet*—meaning "a spirit always moving." Beauregard had heard people refer to the lights by many names over the years, including foxfire, will o' the wisp, marfa lights, corpse lights, St. Elmo's fire, night whispers, Jenny burnt-tail, hunky punky, irrbloss, *les eclaireux*, and *ignis fatuus*. There was even a poem about the lights by the Acadian writer Annie Campbell Huestis. Beauregard liked the poem because, in contrast to most mythology surrounding the lights, Miss Huestis's poem told of longing, not dread:

*Flit, flit, with the hurrying hours,*
*In shadow and mist and dew*
*Will-o'-the-Wisp, O Will-o'-the-Wisp,*
*I could I would follow you,*
*With your elfin light for a lantern bright*
*The bogs and the marshes through*
*Will-o'-the-Wisp, O Will-o'-the-Wisp,*
*I could I would follow you*

Now there was a whistle of breeze where there was no breeze, the voice of the night whisperer. A dry whistling coming up from the orange water, solidifying and stretching from tin to brass. Music of some kind, vaguely familiar.

"Just the morphine is all," he said aloud. "It'll pass soon enough."

"Mister Beauregard, can you hear me?" A voice not his own brushed past his ear. Like the music: *familiar.*

"Just the morphine," answered Beauregard, unable to believe anything save for the terrible weight in his chest.

"Step down, old friend. Into the water." Antonio's voice was clear now, no longer a whisper. "Step down. It'll be all right. I have something to show you."

Beauregard placed a foot in the water. Something at the back of his mind warned of quicksand, told him not to go too far and be damn careful if he did—the wispy roots of alligator weed would not keep him from being sucked down and in if he faltered. He took three steps and stopped, lowering himself to his hands and knees to distribute his weight, to avoid sinking. Quiet. Nothing. Then:

"Don't be afraid," said Antonio.

The left hand of Antonio Carolla shot up and out of the water with a splash, hooking firmly behind Beauregard's neck, pulling him down, under. Beauregard struggled; slapped at the hand, pulled at it, writhed in the water—uselessly.

"Open them," Antonio whispered into Beauregard's ear. Beauregard's thrashes lessened as he pondered the instruction—wondering what might be closed that could be opened. Snatching the thought from Beauregard's mind, Antonio amended:

"Your eyes. Open your eyes."

# CHAPTER THIRTY-NINE

## *Two Seconds Past Now*

With the opening of eyes, there is change. The change is not in raw perception; optic, tactile, or other. It is dark with eyes closed, but darker still when truly opened.

There is no hand hooked behind Beauregard's neck. No sound of splashing, no feeling of panic in his heart, no water, no need to hold breath, nothing left to struggle against. He is kneeling on a hard surface, a stone floor. There's a terrible odor in his nostrils, a smell rushing forward from his personal history, a familiar smell. He pulls himself to his feet, takes a single step forward, hands groping before him in the dark. On the third step his left shin knocks painfully into something hard, angular.

"God*damn*," he complains aloud, reaching down to rub his leg. The pain is a small miracle, taking his mind off larger concerns in the now. But *now* exits too quickly, strange new reality rushing forward two seconds past now.

"'Tonio!" he bellows loudly, irritated. "What the hell, man? What's going on?" No response, not even an echo. He draws down a hand to investigate the hard object that knocked his shin. Hard edges, soft on top. He places both hands on it. Leans on it. Its voice is a creak. The sound of rusty springs.

*Cot.*

The meaning of the smell reveals itself:

*Bucket.* His hands trace the walls around him, measuring their distance from one to the other. Eight feet from here to there. Four feet from there to here. He reaches upwards, touches finger to ceiling. Seven feet from floor to ceiling, give or take.

*Standard.*

"'Tonio!" he shouts once more. Then: "AN-TOE-KNEE-OH!" for good measure. No response.

"Think," he insists of himself. A sob creeps slowly up his throat. "This is the morphine," is the only answer he can imagine. "Just the morphine. Took too much is all. I just have to sleep it off. When I wake up, I'll be back in my swamp. With a big, fat headache maybe, but back in my swamp. My bayou, my beautiful, beautiful bayou." He sits on the cot and rubs roughly at the wetness of his eyes.

Upon lifting hands from eyes, Beauregard Church sees the familiar starburst patterns that every human being sees after rubbing his or her eyes in the dark. Pinpricks of light poking tiny holes through internal darkness, exposing little bits of artificial white, dancing grains of electric salt. But the pinpricks are not all white; there are grays and colors among them. The white is not artificial: there is purpose, there is revelation, they are stripping away blackness a crumb at a time. They fade, disappear—too soon, too soon. He rubs his eyes once more, pinpricks resurrected. This time they don't fade. This time they widen and multiply rapidly, eating away at darkness like a cancer, tearing away blackness, stripping its skin. There is meaning in the grays and the colors. They are combining to form the figure of a man.

The cell is now illuminated with bright, sourceless light. Beauregard examines his naked feet. He'd never imagined how godawful the inside of these cells might be in bright light. He decides utter darkness had been a mercy for the prisoners after all. He looks up.

The figure revealed is Antonio Carolla. Antonio stands by the bucket, leaning against the far wall of the small cell. His eyes meet Beauregard's.

"You can see me?" Antonio asks calmly. "Yeah. Yeah, Antonio. I can see you just fine."

"Sorry about the trouble, old friend," the ghost of Antonio Carolla says with soulful eyes. "Being born can be as painful for the child as for the mother. Well, not *born* so much as reborn. Or *rebirthed,* as the Mulatto kid says." Antonio is smiling. "Kid thinks he's an orphan." Antonio is laughing. The Sicilian's words mean nothing, but his smile puts Beauregard at ease.

"Guess so," says Beauregard, without the slightest idea of what Antonio is talking about, feeling suddenly exhausted. "Antonio, I think I need to sleep."

"You are asleep, old man." Antonio steps forwards, sits next to him on the cot. Puts his arm around him, the arm minus a hand. "Listen, Mister Beauregard." Beauregard prefers it when Antonio calls him Bo-Bo, "Mr. Beauregard" being what the prisoners used to call him. "I know this is hard for you to take in. It was hard for me too at first. But listen to the song; it's a familiar tune, a good tune."

"I don't understand," he replies, but he does hear music. It's not so much a sound as a feeling.

"You don't need to. Not yet. You just need to understand that you've lived for a reason, and now you're moving on for a reason. You need to fix some hearts, make things right."

"I'm dead?"

"Bo-Bo, I'm worried about my boy. He grew up bad, but through no fault of his own." Antonio pauses then says in a low voice, "My wife, she tries, but she is weak and he is strong-willed. She can't control him."

"I don't know nothin' of your boy, Antonio. I been in the swamp since that demon got pulled out of him. Since I killed that man. Since I made those kids orphans."

"He grew up bad," repeats the Sicilian, ignoring Beauregard's confession. "His heart struggles with demons. My own hand struggles within his heart. It burns. And Typhus is no orphan. Didn't you know that?"

Beauregard's head is swimming, unable to understand, and so he cuts to the chase: "What do you want me to do, Antonio? What *can* I do?"

"There's a woman who brought a destructive thing into the world, and into my little Dominick. She's not a bad person, this woman. She did this thing through misguided love, would like to send it back but doesn't know how. She sees you in her dreams, but doesn't understand why. She thinks you are Coco Robicheaux. She fears you because she doesn't realize your destiny is to bring her peace. You must bring her this peace, though she may resist."

"You want me to kill this person?"

"I want you to bring her peace. She has ghosts."

## CHAPTER FORTY
# *The Dependable Nurse Janeway*

H aving studied the tedious intricacies of hospital routine for several months, Marshall Trumbo had taken care in acquainting himself with the every day activities of its denizens. Being perceived as insane had been his greatest asset in a way, for it allowed him to engineer certain changes in his own physical appearance without undue attention. This behavior was discounted by staff as merely symptomatic and, as far as he could tell, his true intentions were never suspected. With such extraordinary freedom of odd behavior, it took a surprisingly short amount of time for Trumbo to complete his transformation into Nurse Janeway.

The real Nurse Janeway (who had the redundant first name of Jane) worked the night shift every Monday, Wednesday, and Friday. She was thin and tall with unusually broad shoulders for a woman, and her hair was brown in an average sort of way (straight, thin, shoulder length). She was partial to pink (as evidenced by the lipstick and flush on her cheeks), her eyes were big and brown, her nose substantial and hooked. She was actually very attractive in a dignified yet homely way—the awkward definition of a "handsome" woman. But to Trumbo her most attractive quality was her dependability.

Nurse Janeway could be depended upon to always arrive on time and never miss a day's work. She could be depended upon to always wear the same distinctive coat when the weather cooled; a thin, woolen affair of red and yellow featuring exotically tacky stitchwork on the back that crudely depicted teepees, tomahawks and other icons of Indian culture. She could be depended upon to sit at her desk by the door with a single lamp lit, endlessly flipping pages of novels that detailed imaginary lives of beautiful but endangered women invariably rescued by square-jawed heroes with wavy, blond hair. Most importantly, she could be depended upon to leave her station between three and five times a night, dependably disappearing into the nurse's station to re-apply and touch up her various shades of pink.

Who Nurse Janeway wished to impress with her diligently maintained handsomeness was a mystery to Marshall Trumbo. Surely it wasn't for benefit of the beefy orderlies whose own lack of personal hygiene rendered mosquito repellant obsolete on hospital grounds. And absolutely not for the benefit of the inmates, most of whom drooled incessantly or shat themselves regularly more out of laziness or spite than of actual infirmity. Trumbo speculated that Nurse Janeway's relentless self-beautification was nothing more than a charming nervous habit. Perhaps she was simply vain. Whatever the case, there was a deliciously mundane mystery about her.

Nurse Janeway's neck had snapped easily on the night of Trumbo's escape, rendering all womanly mystery immediately irrelevant. She had been examining her own face too intently—and so didn't notice when his own face appeared quickly at the mirror's lower right corner.

As Trumbo put the finishing touches on his own (and decidedly less mysterious) make-up job, he paused to marvel at his work. He decided with some satisfaction that he actually made a much better looking woman than she, his own features more delicate and appealing. He even worried that his excessive beauty might give him away.

Not nearly dependable as the personality recently consumed and replicated, the brute known as Dave the Orderly spotted Trumbo in the long corridor that led to the front door.

"Where you headed to, little Janey?" Dave called out flirtatiously. Such an encounter was inevitable, but Trumbo found himself startled just the same. The only reasonable course of action was to keep walking, to pretend not to hear, just as he had seen Nurse Janeway do on numerous occasions.

"C'mon, pretty mama. Don't be that way," Dave called out in a hurt tone.

Trumbo walked on, closing the gap between himself and the door one measured step at a time, knowing that to run would be to tip his hand and throw the night into unknown directions. Killing Nurse Janeway had been easy enough, but he wasn't sure how easily Dave's neck would snap, or if he'd even get the chance to try.

"Well, aren't we high class? Stuck up whore," Dave muttered this last under breath, just loud enough to be heard.

Trumbo breathed a sigh as Nurse Janeway's key clicked easily in the lock. The door opened wide; cool night air penetrating the heavy makeup of his face, the Indian jacket hugging his shoulders but quickly losing the trapped warmth of the asylum.

He noted how well the white stockings warmed his legs while the rest of him struggled against the cold. It struck him as unfair that such practical comforts should be reserved only for women.

"Someone should so something about that," he whispered to himself. "It isn't right, isn't fair."

# CHAPTER FORTY-ONE

## *Down*

Beauregard Church had occasion to visit Antonio often since then, mostly to alleviate his own crushing loneliness. And although Antonio never again mentioned the woman he spoke of on that first trip, Beauregard never forgot her. He'd hoped that his dream-self had done right by her if she did dream of him, hoped that he'd brought her some kind of peace—and maybe helped to put whatever ghosts she might have to rest. Beauregard was pondering these very things on his final night in the swamp.

On that night, he sat staring into orange, listening to a familiar tune, waiting for the morphine to open his inward door. A rush of sound from behind momentarily broke his trance, but he attached no significance to it— it was, presumably, some random illusion of morphine, or, perhaps, a brother swamp creature dutifully hunting a meal. But when the blade sunk into his back and pierced through his heart, he understood it was neither.

Beauregard's body flopped forwards into orange water, his blood mingling with and deepening the color of it. Pushing up against soft mud, his head struggled to remain above water, still breathing at this moment.

"Good," said the voice of Antonio Carolla. "This is all right. This won't hurt." Beauregard felt a tickle at his right hand—a hand caressing his own from beneath the mud, a hand that came *up* from the mud, up *through* the mud, its thin fingers interlacing with Beauregard's thick ones; squeezing, pulling.

Down.

## CHAPTER FORTY-TWO

# *Mourning Star*

The carriage driver called Orr had taken pity on what appeared to be a solitary female walking alongside a lonely road in Jackson, Louisiana. Always the gentleman, Orr had not presumed to inquire why a broad-shouldered lady in a nurse's uniform would have call to visit the Cypress Grove Cemetery in Orleans Parish, so far away and in the dead of night. Headed in that direction anyway, on a mission to deliver tomatoes to the French Market, he dutifully dropped his passenger where requested—a mile or so east of a place Marshall Trumbo had previously known only in dreams.

In 1891, the initial year of Trumbo's incarceration at the Jackson Asylum, this cemetery had marked the edge of civilization—between it and the bayou had been only rough terrain and the occasional stray rice field. Trumbo found himself astonished at how drastically the area had changed since then, how the city had managed to creep so close to the muddy lip of the swamp. Had he guessed such a thing possible or likely, he'd have asked Orr to drop him nearer the bayou itself.

The pungent odor of the swamp coupled with a high chorus of tree frogs provided a vague sense of direction as he walked—but as the lights of the city behind him dwindled then faded to nothing, the sensation was more of walking out of wakefulness and into dream. After twenty minutes Trumbo lost confidence in this weird new faith he'd found in the utterance of frogs. He stopped, stood perfectly still. Took in a deep lungful of tangy, rancid air. Hoping to exploit any hint available to his limited senses, he pulled off Nurse Janeway's shoes and stockings to let his toes wiggle in the bog, feeling for clues. Closed his eyes.

A sort of clarity came. Not of sight, but of mind. The night was still black, but with eyes closed his mind came alive and into focus with a newer, more unfettered kind of dark. A simple truth occurred: When a man's eyes are closed there is no *expectation* of revelation—and when the burden of expectation lifts, a man is much more likely to see.

Holding his right hand outward as the arm of a compass, he turned in a slow circle, believing his arm may stop of its own accord. To his surprise, it *did* stop, and he found his finger pointing in the direction of a single sound, a sound buried beneath many others, a particular sound made by a particular tree frog, shriller than the rest and uniquely pronounced. The sound was nearly a wail and there was a mournful quality to it; a potential source for troubling dreams. This rogue reptile's tuneless song was to be Trumbo's own North Star. It would, he believed, lead him truly.

The sound smoothed as he walked in its direction, its drone gradually acquiring the shape of thin, sharp smoke in his mind's eye. He soon became less certain it was the sound of a frog—or of any living thing at all. Driven by curiosity and absurd faith, Trumbo quickened his pace only to trip on some half-buried root of some sort, perhaps of bamboo; falling sideways, his head hitting something hard. He lie still for a few moments, seeing stars. He waited for the stars to fade as his mental bearings shook off the temporary shock of impact.

The stars failed to fade, intensifying instead; bobbing up and down, drifting globes of bluish light. Entranced, he no longer hoped for their eventual disappearance but instead embraced them. The sound of his North Star became smoother still. No, this was not the sound of a frog—but it was a sound that he knew. The bluish globes decreased in size, moving forward and away from him, urging him to follow, multiplying in number as he walked. The sound that led him tugged gently at a thing in the back of his mind; a lost memory, waiting—like all lost memories—for its turn to be recalled.

*cigar smoke, lamplights, a square card table, a man minus a nose, a young boy holding something shiny to his mouth, a glint of brass, a sound, this sound; louder, louder, louder…*

Marshall Trumbo was not insane in this moment, not haunted, not enraged, not tortured. Marshall Trumbo was only enraptured, enchanted, redeemed. Soft mud introduced the sweet sting of sawgrass, but the pain of it failed to break his focus.

Nothing mattered now but the matter at hand.

Dull silhouettes of trees took shape before him. Light offered by the bobbing globes illuminated nothing; the revelation of trees coming from a separate source, an orange light from deeper within the bog. The sound that once was a tree frog had become mournful brass, and the pale lights now burst one by one; momentarily blinding, leaving only stringy trails of gray smoke. Trumbo walked past the trees. Looked down to find himself ankle deep in orange water.

Felt a tremendous urge to drop to his knees, to fall face forwards and into it, to let it take him—but the mournful sound of weird brass said

*no.*

Trumbo's wandering field of vision glided past the immobile form of a mosquito fern:

Twenty yards ahead was the figure of a large man. Dressed in rags, kneeling in bog water, perfectly still. Without seeing his face, Trumbo knew who this was, had seen him many times in dreams.

*coco robicheaux*

The wailing sound of brass increased maddeningly at the sight of the kneeling figure, and Trumbo's grip tightened around the handle of a stolen knife, stolen from the kitchen asylum early this morning, which he had brought for a purpose not yet fully known to him. Quietly, he crept towards the kneeling man. The sound penetrated his bones; urging him on, bringing him to glory, rendering him blind.

Marshall Trumbo was not aware of his hand as it fell quickly upwards, but he noted the breeze against his forearm as it fell downward into the back of the kneeling man. Felt it stop hard shortly after entry.

Warm, wet, sticky:

Felt that, too.

# BOOK THREE
## *Troubled About My Soul*
# 1906

# CHAPTER FORTY-THREE
## *Deliverance*

**T**he short legs of the mulatto man peddled the rickety bicycle northwesterly down the cobbled edge of the Storyville District. An empty burlap bag (most recently having held the body of a child; rebirthed, matured, and found again—then, finally, returned to its mother in the form of a meal) did not bounce at the center of the homemade chicken-wire basket tied between the bike's handlebars.

Two miles upwards of the district, the bicycle slowed of its own accord as the rocky surface of Saint Louis Street gave way to the pliant codgrass and mud that led to the bayou's tip. It had recently rained hard; the ground so soft and wet that Typhus had to get off and walk it the last half mile.

Typhus imagined that from the heavens this tip of bayou might look like a finger pointing away from Lake Pontchartrain and towards the river. His father once told him the five fingers of the Bayou St. John had long ago stretched all the way to the river, draining the high tides of Lake Pontchartrain straight through what had since become the City of New Orleans. Since then, and through the course of centuries, the bayou's fingers had grown stumpy and fat; a series of deadened waterways doomed to swell without relief when the rains came, causing the lake to puff at the base of its great hand. But Typhus knew the Bayou St. John still made that connection in its way, still managed to join lake with river. The two bodies of water were cut of the same cloth; limbs severed but still sharing the same blood, still able to draw together in spirit. Still one, always one. The bayou made it so. In its way.

Mosquitoes nipped Typhus' ankles as he walked the last stretch of muddy ground to the house. Dead tired, he found himself without energy to bend and swat them away from or against his skin. Rebirthing always knocked the wind from his soul, but returning the children to their mothers could be much more draining. There was a certain pain involved in the act of rebirthing; the assignment of lost children into a cold, vast river could be a troubling and thankless task, near tragic at times. He had no way of knowing whether they might survive long enough to fatten and mature at all—and the belief that they would eventually find their own way back to Typhus' fishing line was an enormous leap of faith. But if they did make it back, then they could be returned; and there is nothing happier than the reunion of a mother and child—even if the mother doesn't fully understand the nature of the reunion. What she fails to recognize by sight, she knows in her heart.

So when Typhus served Miss Hattie her lost child this night, there was joy in the act. He had seen the transformation of her eyes as she swallowed, the pain melting away, acceptance taking hold. The idea of eating children may seem an ugly thing, but not this. This was a beautiful thing, a proof of God's tender mercies. Miss Hattie would no longer have thoughts of pinkening bathwater. She would go on living, have more children, and do it right next time. Typhus had learned from Doctor Jack that sometimes nourishment is the only thing a child has left to offer—to itself, its mother, or anyone else. Things consumed are not wasted things, they're merely things sacrificed so that life might go on in another form. This cycle of life was good, and whether or not Doctor Jack himself believed in things holy, Typhus believed he was doing God's work.

The house was dark and quiet. Tiptoeing into the sleeping room, Typhus dropped to his knees quietly and began filling his coffee bag with soft straw. Laying the pillow against a cold spot between Malaria and Dropsy, Typhus Morningstar was half asleep before he was fully horizontal.

Not ten minutes into sleep, Typhus was visited by a dream he'd not encountered since a child. Not since the night his father was killed.

A dream almost forgotten.

# CHAPTER FORTY-FOUR
## *Reckoning*

"**G**otcher buttons."

Give 'em back.

"OK, but first I gotta show ya sumpin."

I'll tell Dropsy ya took my buttons. He'll whoop ya good.

"Tell him in person 'cause that's where we're going. Ta see Dropsy. He's your uncle, but he's my best friend. Ya think I'd do anything to harm my best friend's best and only nephew? He loves you more than life, West. It's why I'm bringin' ya."

Show me what?

"Sumpin by the river."

Mama be mad if I'm gone 'fore she get up.

"I done told Miss Bernice who's s'posed ta be watchin' ya I'm takin' you to see Dropsy. I bet yer mama'd be glad to sleep in a little late. I know she'd be."

Where's Miss Bernice at?

"Home to get some rest. She been up all night watchin' you and them other kids. I told her I was takin' you home, she thanked me and went on."

Them other kids left already. "I know. Their mamas up early. But yer mama worked extra hard and slept extra late. Onna counta she love you so much. More than those other mamas love them other kids."

I reckon.

"'Course ya reckon. Ready to go?"

I dunno.

"I think yer mama be mad atcha more if you stayed here with no one to look after ya proper."

I should wake her.

"Madder still if you woke her, I reckon. She worked hard all night pleasurin' them fraternity men. Needs her beauty rest is what."

Well, I reckon.

"'Course ya reckon. Let's go. You kin ride on my shoulders. It'll be fun."

I reckon.

"'Course ya reckon."

Kin I git my buttons back?

"Soon as we get there. Yer old buttons plus some new ones on top. But I better watch what I say though, cuz I don't wanna spoil ol' Dropsy's surprise."

New buttons?

"I reckon."

Shiny ones?

"S'posed ta be a surprise. But o' course they shiny. New, too."

The buttons are a surprise?

"I reckon. Ready ta go?"

I reckon."

'Course ya reckon. Now hop on."

All right, Jim.

# CHAPTER FORTY-FIVE

# *Lost Bayou*

Algiers lay across the water, green and golden below a perfect sun kissing cornflower sky. Marcus Nobody Special stood alone on his special pier, not early to rise but late to bed. Out all night looking for his fish, and decided to stay for sunrise. From where the boys stood he appeared about six inches tall.

Carrying West the five blocks from Storyville had been no strain on the shoulders of Jim Jam Jump, who was thin but wiry and not easy to wear down. When the two reached the boardwalk Jim stooped down to pull West's small body up and over his head, placing the boy gently on his feet.

"Well, here we are, little fella. Helluva a beautiful morning, wouldn't you say?"

"Don't see no Uncle Dropsy, Jim. Thought you said he here." West could be very serious for a kid.

Jim just grinned. "Oh, he's here, my good man. We got ourselves a secret place. Part of the surprise. C'mon."

Jim ran ahead of West, southwards in the direction of Marcus' pier. Marcus looked up at the two running children, shielding his eyes from the sun. West gave him a nervous wave.

"C'mon, slowpoke!" Jim goaded with a whoop.

West picked up speed as Marcus returned the wave. The cautious hesitation in Marcus' wave was barely perceptible, but West acknowledged it with mild relief. West watched as Jim jumped from the boardwalk and into the river. Miraculously, there was no splash. Carefully walking to the edge where Jim had jumped, West looked down.

"C'mon, kiddo! It ain't much of a jump. I'll catch ya!" Jim hadn't jumped into the water after all. He'd jumped onto a large sandbank about four and a half feet down. It wasn't so much a sandbank as a tiny island, overgrown with saw grass, banana plants and other plant life lanky and wild. Like a little piece of bayou that had lost its way.

"Uncle Dropsy! You there?" shouted West, still nervous. *"Uncle Dropsy!?"*

"Hell, yeah!" Jim joined in, "C'mon out Dropsy! Just me and little West here, come for his surprise! C'mon out, pardna!"

Dropsy failed to appear—and neither Jim nor West noticed Marcus putting down his fishing pole to walk as quickly as an eighty-five year old man can walk down the length of the pier, toward the boardwalk. The pier went further south before it hit the boardwalk—momentarily reducing Marcus to five inches in height, had either of the boys looked up to see. Marcus' shouts were too weak and too far to be heard over the constant, smooth applause of the river's waves.

"Well, my little friend, looks like yer old uncle done fell asleep. Can't say's I blame him—the two of us been up all night gettin' yer surprise ready. C'mon and jump down here and we'll surprise him first!"

"Why don't you go get Uncle Dropsy 'fore I jump. He's real big and kin catch me good."

"Ah, c'mon now, West. Don't be a little baby about it. I'll catch you just fine. You ain't no little kid anymore. Ain't no baby."

At the age of nine, a worldly child like West Bolden did not like being called a kid, much less a baby. "You catch me now, all right?"

"'Course I'll catch you. C'mon." Jim stood with legs spread and arms wide, looking fit to catch a small horse.

"All right then." West stooped down and jumped, hands reaching out for Jim as he fell.

Jim jumped back and out of the way as the young boy touched ground, his feet slipping forwards in rough sand and landing hard on his backside. Jim Jam Jump whooped and yelled.

"Hot damn, West, ya shoulda seed yerself! That's about the funniest sight I seen in my whole dern life! *Ha!*"

West, embarrassed, got to his feet brushing sand from his clothes. "That was plain mean, Jim. Know what? I don't think Uncle Dropsy's here at all. I think yerra meanie and a liar to boot. I'm goin' back to my mama." West put his hands on the boardwalk, ready to swing his leg up and pull himself back up. Back on the boardwalk, West noticed Marcus had reached nearly ten inches tall, limping briskly in their direction.

"Well, you go on and be a crybaby then, Baby Bolden. Some folks don't even know how to take a joke is what. Sheesh."

"That joke ain't funny. When someone says they'll catch you, then they oughta." West stood on the boardwalk looking down at Jim. "I coulda got hurt, then mama'd *really* get mad."

"Well go on then, Baby Bolden," said Jim, with his hands raised in defeat. "Oh, now wait a minute…" Jim looked down. "I think you done forgot something. These yours, West?"

"Hey gimme back my buttons!" West's little face scrunched up in little-kid-rage.

"Well, sure, West. I'll give 'em back. But first you gotta catch me! *Scriminee hee hee hee!*" Jim wrapped his fist tightly around the buttons and pushed his way into the tall vegetation of the lost bayou, disappearing from view.

Tired and out of breath, Marcus was relieved to see West back up on the boardwalk. He stopped to catch his breath, wiped the sweat from his forehead and looked over towards the boy with a smile and a feeble wave. West waved back once more—but then, inexplicably (and to Marcus' horror), jumped back down to the sandbank. The old gravedigger opened his mouth to scream as West disappeared from view, no sound of substance issuing from his beaten lungs. West was in grave danger, Marcus knew.

"Give 'em back, they mine!" West shrieked as he pushed through leathery leaves and sharp, tall grass.

"Gonna throw 'em to the catfish, Baby Bolden! Better move fast!" Jim's voice was a disembodied taunt, invisible but close by. *"Scriminee heeeeee!"*

Dressed in knee pants, the saw grass chewed viciously at West's ankles and legs as he pushed his way through. The sting of thin cuts and the feeling of warm sticky blood against his shins filled his eyes with blurry wetness. Stopping for a moment to investigate the damage, he put a hand towards a shin, which sent a tall, sharp blade of grass between middle and index finger, slicing the webbing of his hand with a shock of pain that barreled up to his elbow. No longer wishing himself brave beyond his years, West fell to his knees—sobbing like the frightened nine-year-old he was. West jerked his head around with wide eyes only to find green and yellow shades of swamp. This kind of fear was new to him, and for the first time in his life he considered the possibility of things more worthy of protection than shiny buttons. The revelation was cut short by a rustling sound from behind, a sound framed by labored breathing. Trembling, West turned to look.

"You all right, boy?" It was the gravedigger, Marcus Nobody Special, fighting for breath with wide, worried eyes. He bent down to put a hand on West's shoulder.

West sobbed freely now, no longer worried if anyone thought him a crybaby. "He got my buttons," West said as he took Marcus's hand. Marcus' scraggly, noseless face was a frightening thing to most children, but, at that moment, West felt certain he'd never seen a more beautiful sight.

"Don't you worry 'bout that, little one. That mean white boy'll get what he's got comin', sure enough. And you'll be reunited with them old buttons before you can say bippity-bop."

Marcus' warm voice calmed West some, but when the old man reached down to take his hand, he never pulled back up—just kept coming.

Marcus fell forwards and onto West, the two of them descending into razors.

"That old gravedigger be right on two counts, West," said Jim Jam Jump, still holding the large rock he'd used to hit the back of Marcus' skull. "'Cause here ya are ain't even said bippity-bop yet and reunited with yer precious button collection. And I *always* get what I got comin'. Just so happens on this particular beautiful morning what I got comin' is two dead niggers—an old one and a baby one."

Jim dropped the rock and grabbed West by both wrists. The saw grass didn't cut West as Jim pulled him up. Saw grass only cuts when you move down into it, not when you lift up and away. Only sharp in one direction, like the skin of a shark.

After twenty yards or so, they reached the section of pebbly sand that faced Algiers, the same piece of beach where Typhus brought unborn babies for rebirthing. Jim pulled a length of packing twine from his back pocket, stood West up against a tall banana tree and tied the boy's hands behind his back around its fleshy trunk.

"Now about them buttons, little fella," began Jim with a grin.

"You kin keep 'em, Jim. You just go on and keep 'em. Just let me go, all right?"

"Can't do it, West. You oughtta know that by now."

"I won't tell, I promise."

"Won't tell? Well, that's a different story completely then. Might as well just let you go if you ain't gonna tell." Jim burst out laughing, dancing madly in the sand, kicking little explosions of rocky white and broken seashells in the direction of Algiers. He suddenly stopped; smile gone, fishy eyes locked onto West's. Took a step forward.

"I'll tell you what, West. I'll let you go if you can answer me a little question. Just one question. You answer right, you go."

"Please, Jim. I said I won't tell—"

"*Goddammit, shut up!* Like I could give a damn bout whether you'd tell. I ain't no child and I ain't no nigger. Who'd believe your word over mine, anyhoo? Nobody is who, and you kin bet ever' goddamn shiny button on earth on it."

West closed his eyes, imagined how it might feel to be brave in a situation like this. Trying not to cry, failing miserably.

"Now, now, little fella. Don't be so upset. I done made you a fair proposition, ain't I?" The mock-tenderness in Jim's voice gave West a sick feeling in his stomach. "Just got a little question for ya is all."

West collected himself a little. "What if I don't know the answer, Jim?"

"Well, let's just say you *have* to know the answer."

"I-I-I'll try…"

"Fair enough! Can't ask for no more than that, West." Jim took another step forward, bringing his eyes less than three inches from West's. Jim's lips pulled back over tightly clenched teeth:

*"Lakjufa doir estay?"*

West just stared. "What's it mean, Jim?"

Jim threw his head back in a howl. After a moment, he reached into his pocket to retrieve an assortment of shiny, colored buttons, holding them in open palm so West could see. Bending slightly at the knees, he crept towards West again;

*"Lakjufa doir estay? Lakjufa doir estay? Lakjufa doir estay?"*

"The answer to that question would be *yes*, pardna." A deep voice came forward from the morass. "Yes, yes, *yes*. But you knew that, Jim. Dintcha know? 'Course you knew. Reckon you *did* know all along. Yes, indeed."

West watched as Jim's eyes widened, his lids raising high enough over eyeballs to make his lashes disappear entirely.

"Yer late, Dropsy," said Jim. "Told you to meet me here at ten. Can't ya fallah the simplest instructions, now? I declare."

"Watcha doin' with my nephew, pardna?"

"It's like I said, Dropsy. Moving up to the next level."

"Not with him. You want to move up, move up with me. I'm bigger than he is."

"Gotta be him, pardna. I got me a multi-purpose angle running here. You oughta know that. I always got angles runnin' all over the damn place. That's who I am."

"He's just a kid, Jim. Ain't sportsman-like."

"I thought about that, friend—and I appreciate your concern. But he's bigger than a dog, just like a dog's bigger than a rat. And then there's the other angle on top."

"What angle?"

"I need his daddy's horn, Dropsy. You know that. How'm I supposed to get that horn when old Buddy won't sell it for ten times its worth onna counta him? Plus, I need you to be here when it happens. Need to know we're truly friends. Need to know I kin trust ya. Trust ya good and deep, pardna."

"What's to keep me from snapping yer scrawny white neck right here and now, then toss yer fool-ass in the river, Jim?" West had never seen such coldness in Uncle Dropsy's eyes. If he hadn't seen it for himself, he'd never believed such a thing possible.

"This thing ain't gonna happen, Jim. So git it out yer head."

"Pardna, you just done hurt my feelings. And I thought I could rely on you through thick and thin. No matter, no matter. This don't change much."

"Git movin' Jim. I mean it."

"I don't think so, Dropsy. You may be bigger'n me, but I'm quicker. Kin swim good, too—just like a fish. Take another step in my direction, I'll jump inna water and swim to the closest ship er shore, tell em how you killed that old nigger then how ya come after me, chased me right into the river. Now, who'll take the word of a simple-minded nigger and a nine-year-old nigger baby-brat-*punk* over a poor, skinny, beloved and regionally famous white boy like myself? You'll be in jail awaiting execution 'fore supper time—then I'll have all the time in the world to come back for little West."

Dropsy didn't answer. He put a hand on West's head, stroked his hair, tried to calm his sobs.

"Now, pardna," Jim started again, the cockiness in his voice grating in Dropsy's ears. "You know I'm right. That boy's a goner no matter how you slice it. But your part is easy. You just stand there and watch me cut his throat. You ain't gotta do nothing a'tall. Just keep our secret—like you always done. But this secret is special—secrets like this can keep people partners for life." Dropsy's expression failed to soften, so Jim continued with less spit in his timber. "I need you, Dropsy. Don't you know that? You may not realize it, but you need me, too. Keep this secret and we'll always be friends. So whaddaya say? Partners?" Jim held out a hand for Dropsy to shake.

Dropsy Morningstar knew that Jim Jam Jump had won, that this was checkmate. Dropsy had never won a game of chess in his life, never could get the hang of thinking that far ahead. The only thing he was sure of right now was that there was nothing he could do to save his little nephew. He wasn't strong enough, smart enough, or fast enough.

Dropsy turned to face West, placed strong but gentle hands to the boy's trembling cheeks. There is a certain peace in knowing when you're beat, and Dropsy looked into his beloved nephew's eyes now, wanting to share that peace.

"West?" said Dropsy.

"Yes?" said West.

"I love you."

"I love you too, Uncle Dropsy."

"I'm so sorry. See you soon."

The boy's neck snapped with one quick motion, his death immediate and painless. Dropsy kissed him once on the forehead before releasing the head, letting it flop to an unnatural angle at the shoulder. Dropsy turned to Jim, looked him dead in the eye, said:

"*Tat.*"

Dropsy wasn't any good at chess, but he always was expert at the switch.

Jim Jam Jump's jaw fell open in horror:

"*Ya kilt him!* Ya weren't s'posed ta *kill* him!"

"Now ya kin git that horn, I reckon, Jim."

"*Hey!* You weren't supposed to do that! I ain't got no angle worked out fer *that!*"

"Guess we got no secrets, you and me, Jim. Nothin' to keep us friends now." Dropsy was walking towards Jim with deadly eyes. "Checkmate, Jim."

"You keep away from me, you big ape! I'll holler and someone'll come!"

"No secrets to tell, no secrets to keep."

To Jim's surprise, Dropsy wasn't coming for him after all, walking right past and into the river.

"Whatcha doin', you big fool? You cain't swim!"

"You tell this anyway you want to, Jim. Tell 'em the truth. Tell 'em I kilt my own nephew. Probably make you into some big hero once ya figger the right angle."

Dropsy Morningstar didn't lay a hand on Jim Jam Jump. Just kept walking. Walking in the direction of Algiers, which lay across the river.

# CHAPTER FORTY-SIX

# Typhus' Dream

There are four children—two boys and two girls—all tied to chairs and sitting at the edge of a wide pit ten feet in diameter. Flames and smoke lick upward from the pit's mouth. The children are sweating, their shins blackening and blistering in the heat. They are all about the age of eight or nine and bear a family resemblance to one another.

Typhus stands across the pit. He is untied, he is his father. The prison guard's knife twitches in his back as if alive. His right hand is freshly severed—but where there should be blood there leaks only water.

An old woman is standing behind the children, her head and face wrapped tightly in chicken wire. The woman stares at Typhus—her eyes fill him with cold fear. He should run to the aid of the children but is paralyzed by the woman's eyes. He knows she is capable of much worse than the mere harming of children.

"Hast thou come to kiss this child?" the woman asks him, pointing to the girl who sits between the two boys.

Typhus cannot form thoughts but hears himself say, "What child?" The sound of his own voice startles him; it is not his own voice, it is his father's voice. Typhus looks down and sees his father's old family bible in his left hand. It trembles in his grasp and is cold to the touch. The woman responds, "I will not let thee kiss her." She tips the girl's chair forward, sending her downward into flame. The girl's eyes are wide with terror as she plunges headlong. Her screams make no physical sound but reverberate through Typhus' chest. A part of him recognizes the girl as she falls—it is his sister, Cholera. But the recognition makes no sense; Cholera died at only two months old—and years before Typhus was born. This was not Cholera.

*This was Cholera.*

He now recognizes the rest of the children, but the ages are all wrong. They cannot all be nine years old.

"Hast thou come to send him to sleep?" The woman points to the boy at her left.

"Wait!" Typhus bellows through his father's throat. He opens the bible, searches its pages for answers. This is difficult with only one hand, and the paper is like ice. It takes a moment before Typhus realizes the pages are all blank.

"Uncle Typhus, please! I can't find my buttons! Someone took my buttons! Help me!" West is squirming beneath the old woman's hand.

*"Hast thou come to send him to sleep?"* she repeats patiently.

Noonday Morningstar's heavy tone rumbles through Typhus' narrow throat, "No! *No!* I haven't come to send him to sleep!"

The old woman's face contorts into a half-smile as she replies, "I will not let thee do him harm."

She tips West forward and into the pit, leaving one boy and one girl. Typhus realizes the girl is a child-sized version of Diphtheria—and that she has just witnessed the death of her own son. Her screams issue with such force that her neck bulges then splits. Blood spatters her perfect yellow dress.

The old woman points to the bleeding girl now. *"Hast thou come to take her away?"* Suddenly, Typhus recognizes the old woman.

"I know you!" he hears his father shout.

She repeats, "Hast thou come to take her away?"

The woman is a hoodoo mambo. She visits Doctor Jack two or three times a year to trade herbs. She has always seemed so timid and kind on her visits. Her name is Malvina Latour.

"Why are you doing this?" The voice of Noonday Morningstar trembles.

"I will not let thee carry her away." The child-version of Diphtheria tips forward and down, but her eyes are no longer afraid and there is relief in them as she falls. She will now, at least, be with her little West.

"Typhus," says the remaining child, a boy. His voice is calm, reassuring, unafraid. "Don't feel bad. You done no wrong here. You can't help that you lost your faith. People don't choose to lose faith. Faith leaves them, not the other way 'round." The child version of Dropsy Morningstar droops his head towards the pit, staring into smoke and flame with a grin. "I ain't never seen a thing so lovely. Ain't it pretty, Typhus? Pink threads, orange water, pretty music…"

*journeys of threads through a rug*

Typhus' eyes fill with tears as the woman deadpans through chicken-wire, "Has thou come to *crucify* him?"

"*No, no, no!*"

"But you have," says Dropsy with a smile. "It's okay, now, Typhus. Let me go."

Malvina Latour is screaming, "*Hast* thou come to *crucify* him?"

Typhus searches the weird peace in Dropsy's eyes for answers. He knows answers are there, answers to all the questions he could ever ask—but he can't find them.

"Forsake me, Typhus. You have no choice," says Dropsy. "Forsake me… please?"

Typhus Morningstar' heart is breaking: "*Yes*, yes, I have come to crucify him!" The sound of his own sobs chill his blood; he has never heard his father sob before.

The face of Malvina Latour is smoothing. Rage has vacated her eyes. Without another word, she steps forward and into the pit, her dress fluttering in flame as she falls. Dropsy remains seated and bound, his grin ever-widening.

"That's right, that's right," Dropsy says. "Ain't yer fault, Typhus."

"I'm dreaming," says Typhus, his voice now miraculously his own.

"Yes, you're dreaming. But the dream means something."

"What does it mean?"

Dropsy's grin evaporates. "It means you are out of hope."

Unable to accept this simple truth, Typhus opens the bible once more, searching. This time the pages are not blank, but are filled with gibberish. The same group of words are repeated over and over:

*Zedn Nasicb Uqmao Tuoyn Raioe Htvae Emayi Uodonri Ine Encpd Aq Plimu O Ano Oarce Unthar Dead Iu On Ere Hurt Ecibuotor*

Nonsense words. Unpronounceable. Stupid. Useless.

He slams the book shut, looks down to see two small feet. No longer in the body of his father, he is himself again entirely. A man in the shape of a boy. Old of eye, older of body, oldest of heart.

Dropsy is teetering back and forth in the chair, tempting the pit to take him. Typhus looks into the eyes of his brother, wanting to say something, an important question at the tip of his tongue. He is only able to say:

"Dropsy…"

Dropsy smiles one last time before rocking forward and over; "Goodbye," he says.

## CHAPTER FORTY-SEVEN
### *Beware the Shoe Dove*

D octor Jack regarded superstition as a luxury reserved for the weak of mind. He was a man of science first, so when confronting fresh mysteries he always considered the scientific possibilities first. However, when uncanny or illogical patterns presented themselves, he took care to make note and attach credence to such—even if the scientific basis behind these occurrences was not immediately evident. One such pattern he'd noted in his lifetime was this: Nights absent of sleep usually precede catastrophe. This was not a scientific theory, was not even a realistic hypothesis, but the truth of it had become apparent to him over the years. So when eyes stayed open and mind stayed alert—as they did on this night—it felt a warning.

Jack had been taught by experience and the passage of time that to lie alone in the dark can make you a prisoner of your own thoughts. Such quiet solitude can put a person in a mind to examine what he's done in his life, what he's doing, and where his life may be pointed. What a person might've done, should've done, could've done, couldn't do and wouldn't do.

But the worst were always the *should'ves*.

Annoyed with the workings of his own mind, Jack attempted to distract himself with things imagined: *a brown leather shoe with white-feathered wings, flapping above his head in the dark; soaring and dipping, hovering and zagging—whispering with grinning laces, "Beware! Beware!" One flying shoe divides and turns into two, two to four and four to eight. A dozen flying brown shoes gracefully weave in and around each other, never touching, whispering warnings:*

*Beware.*

Doctor Jack grinned then laughed into black, cool air. *Beware the shoe-doves,* he thought. Shoe-doves.

Should'ves.

Funny how the mind works.

He lightened at this weird poetry of the subconscious and so relaxed, the fantastic dance of shoe doves evaporating as quickly as they'd materialized. Sleep was now a possibility, but before his mind could escape into dreams, one last tenacious shoe-dove whispered then clawed its way back into his mind. This shoe-dove's name was Noonday Morningstar.

Morningstar's face had often visited Jack in dreams, sometimes in waking hours. The preacher's face was a reminder of his own inability (or, perhaps unwillingness) to act in moments requiring courage—just as he'd failed to act on the night of Morningstar's death. The prison guard Beauregard had acted that night. Young Buddy Bolden had acted. Even little Typhus had acted. But he—a medicine man, doctor, and spiritual leader—had merely looked on. Helpless and afraid, he had done nothing.

But what could he have done? What should he have done? He didn't know the answers, but he knew there *were* answers. Maybe it was something *yet* to do and not merely *would've, could've, should've—*

*Shoe dove*

Doctor Jack had always liked and admired Morningstar even though the two men had agreed on very little. There was never any bad blood between them—except for the one thing.

Shoe dove

Jack closed his eyes tight, rubbed at the lids, then opened them wide. Watched the dancing pinpricks explode from within, willed the pinpricks into shoe doves. Soaring, weaving, dancing. A tiny smile formed in his soul.

*This night is over for me,* he quietly conceded in the dark. *Time to bring on the morning.*

Doctor Jack sat bolt upright with thoughts of hot chicory simmering in his head, felt for the lamp, found a box of matches. The smell of burning saltpetre was pleasantly wakeful to him. He breathed in deep with eyes closed.

Three quick raps at the door gave him a start. Nocturnal intrusions were not unusual in his line of work, but Jack's recent sleepless premonition of bad-things-coming-soon had put him on edge. He hurriedly touched match to wick before seeing to the door.

Typhus Morningstar nodded to Jack and walked in casually, as if this were a thing he did often at four in the morning. "Sorry if I woke you," Typhus said, clearly troubled.

"That's all right, Typhus," said Jack. "I was having trouble sleeping anyway."

"Me too."

Jack pulled up a chair for Typhus who only stared at it and remained standing. "Trouble sleeping, eh? Well, that's a shame. But what brings you here at this unusual hour?"

"I'm sorry. Didn't want to wake Malaria and Dropsy, and didn't want to sit up in the dark no more all alone. Bad dream. I'm really sorry to bother you, Doctor Jack."

"That's all right, little pardna. Gonna take care of you just fine. Dreams can be worse than most sicknesses. There's no shame in dreaming." Typhus dragged his feet to the corner farthest from the door, eased himself into a sitting position with his head leaning leftways against the wall. His eyes were sleepy but unblinking.

Jack nudged him gently: "You feel like talking about it? This dream of your'n?'

"Not sure how."

"Well, just start at the beginning. If you remember, that is. Sometimes dreams can rush out of your head on the waking."

"I remember." Typhus' eyes told Jack that not only did he remember, but that he may spend the rest of his life trying to forget. "Don't know if I can talk about it, though. Hurts to even think about it."

"I see," said Jack.

"No, you don't see, Doctor Jack. No one can see."

"True enough, little pardna. Be plenty of time to make me see tomorrow morning. After you done got some rest. And only if you want."

"Guess why I come is on account of how the dream made me feel. Like I'm all alone in this world." Doctor Jack laid some sheepskins behind Typhus, who reclined against them.

"Dreams can't make you alone, Typhus." Jack walked over to the medicine counter to mix one of his secret sleep remedies in a small steel cup. The taste gave the so-called secret away—its alcohol content being in the neighborhood of ninety proof. He handed the concoction to Typhus.

"More alone than I ever felt since you gave me Lily." Typhus sat up enough to take a sip and then a full-blown swallow. He lay his head back down without wincing.

"Well, I guess even Lily has her limitations, son."

Typhus liked it when Jack called him *son*. "It doesn't seem fair," said Typhus. "I give her every bit of me, but she leave me alone at such a time. I guess that sound selfish, but I can't help thinking it. It's hard to talk about it."

"Try." Jack didn't want to press, but had a strong feeling Typhus needed to get something off his chest.

Typhus paused to arrange his thoughts, trying to decide between outright lying and half-truthing. He decided to talk straight. Lying wouldn't make the sin any less, and he knew he could trust Jack to keep his secrets.

"Had this dream." Typhus paused long.

"Gathered that much already. Listen, if you'd really rather not talk about it, we can just leave it for another—"

"Woke up hard—down there." Typhus swallowed heavily, too far gone to turn back now. "In my privates."

Jack raised an eyebrow and looked on expectantly.

"It wasn't the kind of dream supposed to get a reaction like that. There was no pretty lady in the dream. No Lily. There was only bad stuff in the dream."

Jack's eyes softened, moistening imperceptibly. "What kind of bad stuff?"

"Evil bad. People dying. Burned alive. People I know. People I love." Typhus discovered he was physically unable to recount any more detail than that—he hoped Jack wouldn't push it. "I couldn't make it go down. I tried and tried. Finally I got a knife...thought about cutting it...got scared...then I got on my bike and came over..."

"Well, now, boy. Ain't no crime to have a bad dream. And sometimes a person's lower body region can act in mysterious ways. Don't mean you was sexually interested in the bad things you saw in the dream."

"But I was."

"Was what?"

"In-trested." A pause, a glance down, a whisper: "Seck-shully."

"I think there's a good chance you're confused about that, son."

"I was," Typhus insisted in a whisper, closing his eyes in shame.

"Well, let's say you were," Doctor Jack said firmly. "Still ain't no crime. And the fact you're so bothered about it shows you got a good conscience."

"But there's a part of me that ain't ashamed. A part of me enjoyed it. A part that wanted it to happen."

"Nonsense, boy."

Typhus got to his feet, wondering whether he should go on talking or just let the conversation end there. More words left his lips before he was aware of his decision to speak:

"I felt this way one other time, Doctor Jack."

"I see." And he did see. He knew exactly what Typhus was talking about, there was no need for Typhus to go on explaining.

But the talking was a release for Typhus, so he continued:

"When I was nine. When that thing was in me. Before Daddy took it out. That bad thing I took out of the Sicilian baby—"

"Shhhh…" Jack got up to put an arm around Typhus' shoulder. "You ain't gotta say another word about that."

"I gotta say one thing…"

"No you don't."

"It's just that…"

"Shhhh…"

"…it ain't all gone."

"Of course it is."

"No. It ain't."

"Don't talk like that."

"It's still in me, that thing. I know it."

"What's in you is a *memory* of a bad thing. Not the bad thing itself."

Typhus broke into sobs, wanting to believe Doctor Jack. Unable.

"Typhus, now listen," said Jack as he rubbed Typhus' shoulder. "That thing you went through way back when, that'll always stick with you. But it's a memory now, nothing more. This thing that happened tonight—well, I reckon that'd be the result of a combination of things. Bad memories mixed with natural feelings of longing. I 'spect if there's a cure for yer troubles, it'd probably be by fixing the latter. Having all them longings done opened a big ol' window for those bad memories to come rushing out at you."

"Ain't got no longings like that, Doctor Jack. Not no more. Not since you give me Lily."

"What I gave you was a pretty piece of paper, Typhus. I thought it might be enough, but looks like it ain't."

"Don't want no one but my Lily, Doctor Jack. Thanks anyhow."

"Didn't say nothing 'bout no one else."

Typhus looked up, startled by the implication.

"That's right, boy. I believe it might be time for you and Miss Lily to meet in person."

Typhus' expression changed quickly from joy to hope to suspicion to something like anger. "You playin' games with me, Doctor Jack? Could be I ain't as gullible as you think."

Jack's own expression performed a similar succession; shock to anger to barely concealed amusement. "I know yer in a bad way, so I'll let that pass. Can't says I blame you for not believing—but it's true enough. Lily's alive and well and not at all far off. Now, I ain't saying she looks just like in the picture. That picture was took long ago. If you want her to be young and pretty, then I guess I oughtn't bother. But if you really love her, then what she looks like shouldn't oughta matter much."

Typhus considered this new possibility. Could he trust his own heart if Doctor Jack was telling the truth, if he was really able to meet the real Lily, the flesh and blood version? If she wasn't beautiful like in the picture, would it matter to him? Would he recoil from her? The questions didn't seem fair at first—but then he considered her eyes. How he'd always longed to see them in person, how he'd wondered about their color. He'd always imagined them green. He *knew* they were green. Green like his mother's eyes; eyes he'd never seen, that he'd only heard described by his father. In any case, Typhus figured Lily's eyes wouldn't have changed much, however old she might be now.

"It doesn't matter," Typhus said at last.

"Well, then. It's settled. You get yourself some sleep here tonight, then go on home in the morning and get cleaned up. Come back when the sun down. 'Tween now and then I'll have had a chance to talk to her, maybe make some sort of arrangement."

Typhus stood silent with a cautious grin on his face. Dr. Jack's sleep remedy was swimming madly in his blood, doing battle with a rush of adrenaline. His swirling thoughts focused loosely around an image of his best shirt, the one he'd wear to meet Lily the Real Live Girl tomorrow evening.

"Typhus?" Jack was smiling.

"Yes, sir?"

"There's a possibility, you know, that she won't come. I don't want you to be too disappointed if she don't." Typhus was disappointed at the mere thought. Still, he was high on this bit of hope. Sometimes hoping feels the same as winning. Sometimes hoping is good enough.

"No, sir. I understand."

"Good. Now, go on and git some sleep," said Doctor Jack.

"All right, then," said Typhus simply.

"All right, then" agreed Jack.

"Dr. Jack?"

"Yes, Typhus?"

"Thanks."

"Don't thank me yet."

"All right, then."

"All right, then."

"Good night."

"Good night."

# CHAPTER FORTY-EIGHT

# *Blindfold*

The sun was down but the air still hot when Typhus began his walk back to Doctor Jack's office the next day, and along the way he began considering the possibility that he'd put on his best shirt for nothing. Right now, these were things he nearly believed: the hope he'd felt last night was born of sleep medication, Doctor Jack had played a trick. But anger and suspicion calmed into acceptance and melancholy by the time he reached his destination. Typhus' knock was followed by a *click* then a *clack* as Doctor Jack removed the padlock from inside.

"Well, aren't you looking fancy for your big date." Something about Doctor Jack looked out of the ordinary, but Typhus couldn't quite place what. He looked *cleaner* somehow.

"Thank you," Typhus answered, taking in a deep breath before adding, "Did you talk to Lily?"

Jack just smiled. With the door closed behind him, Typhus found his question answered by the heavy scent of perfume. Sweet, fancy, lady fragrance. She was here, or recently had been.

"Of course I talked to her, Typhus. Told you I would, didn't I?"

"She coming?" Typhus asked with wide eyes.

Jack's face turned serious. "Have yerself a seat and I'll explain." He motioned for Typhus to take a chair. "I told Lily all about you, Typhus, and I was completely honest with her. Told her about that picture of yours, the one I gave you. Told her about your devotion to her. About your longing. Everything. I left none of it out." Jack's voice stayed low and even as Typhus' eyebrows raised in horror.

"Ah, Doctor Jack," Typhus said with shaking voice. "You shouldn't oughta done that. Might think I'm some kinda love-crazed fool."

"Like I said," Jack said, "I was dead honest with her. She a friend of mine just like you a friend of mine. How would you feel if I went on lyin' to you about important things?"

Typhus faced the ground. "Not so good, I guess."

Jack's tone softened at the concession. "'Course not, son. 'Course not. Always be honest with your friends if you can hep it." The truth did little to console Typhus. His head hung ever-lower, his eyes fastened to his shoes. He couldn't imagine Lily would think much of him if she knew the truth about his relationship with her picture.

"Ah, now, buck up, Typhus," Doctor Jack continued. "That ain't the end of it now, not by a longshot it ain't. Lily was touched by it all, just like I knew she would be. She told me in her whole life she never meant so much to anyone as her picture means to you. Your love for her without even knowing her is a thing that touched her very deeply. And she does indeed wish to make your acquaintance." Typhus' eyes regained light, but before they could light all the way Jack managed to splash some cold water on: "Of course, she has a few conditions before she will."

"Conditions?" Typhus didn't like the sound of that.

"Well, yes, Typhus. Conditions. You have to understand that this is a strange set of circumstances to be thrusting upon poor Miss Lily out of the blue and all. She being a bit older now than she was in that picture of your'n. And her being so much older than you anyway, old enough to be your mama. She doesn't expect the two of you will be able to carry on a proper relationship, so she wants to take things slow."

"How slow? What do you mean?"

"Well..." Doctor Jack paused, smoothing the lines of his forehead with the rough palm of his left hand. "Typhus, it's like this. She wants to meet you. She wants to meet you very much. But she doesn't want you to see her."

Mortified, Typhus whispered, "I don't understand."

Jack stepped behind Typhus and placed a hand on his shoulder. "She doesn't want to betray your image of her, the way you know her. She wants you to keep that. So she asked me to bring you here—but she'll only come in the room if you're sitting in that chair. With a blindfold on."

"A blindfold?" This couldn't be happening. "Doctor Jack, are you playing some kind of trick on me?"

"I thought you might say that—told Lily you might, too. But this ain't no trick. You can leave right now if you don't like the idea. Lily said she'd understand if you did, and I'd certainly understand, too."

Typhus lowered himself to the chair. Put elbows to knees and head in hands; thinking. After a few seconds he spoke without looking up, "I still want to meet her. Even if I can't see her."

The lines of Jack's forehead disappeared without the help of his palm. "She didn't think you'd feel that way, but I knew you would. I said, 'Lily, you don't understand how much you mean to that young man.'"

"So when's she coming? Tonight maybe?" Typhus hoped she might be waiting right outside the door. He didn't think he could stand to wait another minute.

"She's here already, boy." Doctor Jack pulled a length of dark blue cloth from his hip pocket. Typhus watched his hands as he did so, noticing a small bloody cut on Jack's forearm about five inches up from the wrist. Before tying the blindfold on, Jack gave Typhus one last opportunity to back out. "You sure this is what you want, now?"

To turn back now was unthinkable. This would be his moment of truth, his coming of age. No matter what this thing was to be, it was a thing he needed desperately. He couldn't fully be himself, or even know who he was, without it.

"Yes," replied Typhus.

Jack tied the blindfold tightly. After two minutes of quiet darkness, Typhus heard the door to Doctor Jack's storage room swing open, followed by the sound of bare feet padding lightly against the hardwood floor. Typhus' nostrils filled with perfume, the smell of it wonderfully overpowering. A bright image of Lily sprang to life in Typhus' darkened mind. In full color, living and breathing, and wanting him—wanting to see him, to be with him. Typhus believed it was all true now. She was here, standing before him. Here. She was really here. His Lily. His love.

Here.

"Well, boy, ain't you gonna say nothing to the love of your life?" Jack asked.

Typhus imagined he could feel a smile radiating outward from Lily's soul. But along with the smile he sensed her fear, her shyness, her caution at the idea of this meeting. He could feel her tremble through air.

"Hello, Miss Lily," started Typhus calmly, wanting to say so many things but not knowing where to start. "Don't be afraid. I only want to do right by you. I've made many vows to you that you don't know nothin' about. Vows about keepin' and protectin'. Vows about giving to you everything I can give. You might not know it, but you've given me so much already. So very, very much. I only want to give back to you. To know you, to be with you, to be good to you. I want for things to be right with us. In any way you want, in any way that makes you happy—"A finger touched his lips; shushing. He was not sure at first whether the finger belonged to Lily or Jack—it was soft, but rough in texture. Then Typhus heard what sounded like a gentle sob—and he knew it was Lily who'd touched him. The finger withdrew, and Typhus spoke again, "No, don't be sad. Don't be sad. There's nothing sad about this. I have no expectations of you. Nothing, *nothing*—"

Again Typhus was shushed, but this time by the touch of soft lips. He dared not kiss them back, allowed himself only to revel in their warmth. Like the finger, they lacked the smoothness he'd imagined and hoped for—but then, he knew this could not be the young woman of his picture; a picture taken long, long ago. Still, her lips were soft and her breath was sweet, almost too sweet— like the excessive sweetness of a peach too long in the sun; a hint of baked-in decay lurking beneath perfect skin. For all its imperfections it was still the most wonderful breath he'd ever smelled, and Typhus gently inhaled the air of it into his lungs. Her air was his air now, and if he never received another thing from her, at this moment he'd acquired a touch, a kiss, and a breath. These were things he'd never dared hope for before this morning—and if he gained nothing more, it would still be enough.

"I love you, Typhus." And now he'd heard her voice. A whisper.

"I love you, Lily," he said in return, too emotionally exhausted to really feel the meaning. He lifted up a hand to touch her hair; it was coarse, soft, and straight.

Once again, Typhus heard the sound of feet padding softly across the floor, back towards the storage room. As he reached up to remove the blindfold, Doctor Jack's voice stopped him: "No. Not yet. Wait." A few moments later, Typhus heard the storage door reopen, followed by the sound of quickly stepping feet, this time shod. The front door opened, then slammed shut.

She had gone.

She'd left without saying goodbye, but that was all right. In Typhus' mind she owed him nothing, not even that. He found himself dimly wishing he could keep the blindfold on forever.

# CHAPTER FORTY-NINE

# *Main Door*

From the moment of Lily's departure, a change in Typhus' demeanor and overall personality became evident to Doctor Jack. Typhus was clearly in love. Not the confused, obsessive love a boy might feel for a photograph of a pretty girl; this was the kind of love a grown man feels for a woman who's unlocked his main door, who has shown him that real happiness is a real possibility. The scary kind of love. True love. The kind that can cripple or kill or heal or make whole. This was big, maybe too big.

Jack wondered what Typhus would dream of tonight, how things were unfolding in his soul with so many of the old questions still unanswered and so many new questions freshly born. Maybe Lily's touch had really been enough, the cure for a troubled heart. A cure for the son of a shoe dove.

Though the encounter seemed a success, Jack still wondered if he'd done right by the boy—bringing Lily into his life at all, whether flesh or photograph. Could Lily's presence in his life offer any real spiritual nutrition? Perhaps such comforts were actually detrimental, a type of poison for the soul. If this new peace in Typhus' heart was a fleeting thing, was it only bound to lead him towards greater misery? Mostly, though, Jack wondered what it would do to Typhus if he ever discovered the truth about Lily.

Typhus must never, ever learn the truth.

Typhus let himself out without saying goodbye. Jack could hear him singing outside, sad words sung in a happy way.

*Jesus I'm troubled about my soul*
*Ride on Jesus, come this way.*
*Troubled about my soul.*

The lyrics of the song bore no meaning or purpose to Typhus on this morning other than to provide a hook on which to hang melody.

# CHAPTER FIFTY

# Malaria and Typhus

M alaria Morningstar sat shivering dead center on a five foot cypress bench located just outside and left of her front door. The bench held certain memories for Malaria that brought comfort during troubled times.

Father had made the bench for Mother with his own two hands when Malaria was still small. She recalled the painstaking construction of it, remembered the cursing, the measuring, the hammering, the sawing, the sanding, and the silly look of joy that adorned his face upon its completion. Most of all, she recalled the tender memory of her Mother's eyes as she nursed baby Dropsy on the exact spot where Malaria now sat.

Sitting here always gave Malaria a sense of calm when things went bad in her life. Mother and Father still existed in the wood of it, or so it seemed—still reached out to stroke her hair from its pores, still reassured her that all would be taken care of, that everything would be all right. Recognizing such comforts as fleeting and false by their nature didn't keep her from placing great value in them just the same.

But this morning she'd been unable to squeeze a drop of comfort from its stubborn pores and cracks. At the moment, things were not right in a very big way—big enough to defy even the sanctuary of the bench. Malaria had recently learned of a trouble which could be resolved neither gracefully nor painlessly, and the nature of this trouble was betrayal. She knew that betrayal of this kind couldn't be ignored—and called for immediate and decisive action on her part. Although such a confrontation could only serve to tear her world apart, she knew that to do nothing would be much worse.

The sun had begun its slow ascent less than an hour earlier, mist of morning still hanging heavy at the lip of the bog. Malaria let her eyes focus on the blur of it, imagining that to stare into it just right might cause the mist to scatter at her will. The mist failed to recognize the authority of her gaze, but that was fine. She had every confidence it would lift in time, of its own accord. Then again, maybe it wouldn't. What proof was there that this particular fog on this particular morning would lift from the *cipriere* just because it had chosen to lift in such a way on every other morning of her life? It wasn't inconceivable that a morning may eventually happen along to mark the beginning of a new era, the beginning of things never the same, ever again.

In a way, such a morning had already come. Amazingly, the realization consoled rather than frightened Malaria, though a part of her still wished the mist might play along. She wanted badly to get on with a new series of impossibly different mornings. *Who's to say such a thing is impossible?* she thought. She ran a hand across the bench, the texture of it smooth from years of use and moist from dew. It was perfect wood, a perfect object—but only that. Mother and Father had gone from it upon their deaths, and she'd suddenly grown too old to believe otherwise.

A rhythmic crunching mingled with birdsong, first faint then louder, coming nearer through the fog. Eight more crunches and she could make out the silhouette of a child. Not a child, but a man shaped like a child.

"Where's your bike?" she asked the silhouette.

"Left it at Doctor Jack's," said Typhus. "Morning, Malaria." Malaria failed to return the greeting. "Out all night again? That's two nights in a row. Starting to think you gotcher self a girlfriend."

Typhus was close enough now that she could see he was grinning. "Well, what would be so surprising about that?"

Malaria's eyebrows raised in amusement. The idea of Typhus with a regular girlfriend seemed about as likely as the fog's refusal to lift from the swamp. Maybe this really was a new kind of morning after all.

Typhus stopped with hands on hips and chin to chest, his grin evolving into bashful chuckles. "Well, Malaria, you wouldn't believe me if I told you. I surely doubt if you'd believe a word. Hell, I don't believe much of it myself."

Malaria's eyes remained sad, but her lips returned the smile. "Well, now, little brother. Sounds like some long overdue good fortune come your way. That's good, real good. I'm happy for you." And then, with a tone of parental sternness: "You be careful now. Those French Quarter women'll give you flesh plague and a broken heart to boot, you ain't careful."

Typhus shook his head and laughed some more as he walked past and inside. "Don't believe much of it myself," he echoed through the doorway, still laughing.

Typhus' high spirits were nearly enough to change Malaria's mind about bringing up the trouble. Maybe it could wait—one more day of nothing much wrong, one more day of fog lifting on schedule—but in her heart she knew this wasn't an option. The damage had been done and must be addressed—and the sound of Typhus' alarmed shouts from inside only confirmed these things.

"*Malaria!*"

She stayed on the bench, hoping for ghostly comfort.

"*Malaria!*"

Typhus stood in the doorway directly behind her now. She needn't turn to know there were tears in his eyes—they were plainly evident at the edge of his voice. There would be a particular something clenched in his hand.

"*Where is it?*"

Malaria turned to face him. "Sir?" she said.

He waved the coffee bag at her violently. "Where is it? There was something in this bag and now it's gone! You got no right going through my things!"

"I washed it for you, Typhus. It was stinking up the house with that old catfish smell. Thought it was empty at first." Malaria felt silly defending herself on this point, all things considered.

"I want it back," said Typhus evenly.

"Can't have it back," said Malaria, turning her gaze back to the swamp mist now rapidly thinning. The sound of her brother's shallow breath made her feel cruel.

"It's mine," said Typhus, in a cracked voice. He sounded beaten and resigned, as a child might sound upon having a favorite toy taken away as punishment. As Malaria imagined West might sound if Diphtheria ever got mad enough to take those damn, precious buttons from him.

Thoughts of West's love for shiny buttons softened Malaria's heart unexpectedly, and so she altered her course slightly. Perhaps confrontation regarding such sensitive and scandalous matters would not be the best thing. Could it hurt to simply keep his secret, to help him hide from this one devastating truth? Maybe that would be best.

"I'm not even sure what it was. Didn't see it till after I washed. Just blobs of brown paper bunched up and crumbling." She paused, giving Typhus a window to speak if he chose. He remained silent, so she added, "Looked like it mighta been a photograph. Hard to say for sure."

Typhus' voice fell to a whisper. "You didn't see it?"

"No, sir. Just went to wash the stink out yer bag, and found the crumbs after it was too late. I guess whatever it was, it must've meant something to you. Sorry I wasn't more careful."

Typhus studied his shoes in the doorway, a little bit of that smile from earlier creeping back to his lips. Malaria felt a wave of temporary relief.

"I see you gotcher nice shirt on," she said with a reassuring smile. "Must be some kinda extra special girlfriend you got."

Typhus smiled bashfully. "Yes, indeed. I guess you could say that. Hell, I don't need that old picture anyhow no more. Got me the real thing now. The *real* thing is what." He turned to go back inside.

Malaria stared at her left hand, closed in a fist. The smile lingered at her lips, but her brow furrowed. This trouble was not yet through, she sensed. "Typhus?" she called out, her voice slightly higher in pitch than she'd intended. "Typhus? What do you mean when you say you got the real thing?"

Typhus returned to the door, gnawing on a hunk of dry bread he'd found in the kitchen. "Well, I'll tell you, sis. You was right about that thing in the coffee bag. It was a photograph. Picture of a girl. I been keeping that picture a long time—but now I don't need it no more. Know why?"

"Why?" Malaria's eyes were burning.

"'Cause the girl in the picture—well, I found that very same girl in real life."

The words made Malaria light-headed.

"And, turns out, we got ourselves a little thing going on. Might even get married, I guess."

Malaria stood up to face her brother. "What did you say?" Gone a shade paler, she suddenly looked very old. Both of her hands were balled into fists at her sides as she repeated, "What did you just *say*?"

Typhus struggled to decipher what error he might have made. "Well, I mean...we might not get married at all. I mean we just met...I was just saying..."

"The real thing? You said you got the *real* thing?"

"Well, sure, I found the real thing. Is that so hard to believe?" Switching from defense to offense. "Is it so hard to believe that your little half-a-man, freak-of-a-brother might've found a real live woman? Someone who might love him back? Is that so very hard for you to comprehend, *big* sister?"

It dawned on Malaria that Typhus truly didn't know. Didn't realize. Someone had played a trick on him. A cruel trick. Unable to completely shake her rage, she forced her voice to soften, "Typhus, there's something you oughta know."

"Who you been talking to?" The anger in his own voice was mounting. This was a type of jealousy, Typhus decided—what else could it be? Malaria had been a spinster so long that she now wished to throw some rain on his own little bit of joy. "What are you doing, Malaria? Why you gotta ruin this for me?"

"Typhus, I seen the picture."

"Why are you doing this? I don't care if you seen the picture. Don't matter, you can keep it. I got the real thing."

*"Stop saying that!"* she screamed.

"Don't you ruin this for me, Malaria. I swear to God I'll never forgive you if you ruin this for me."

"Typhus, please," Malaria was fighting back tears now. "Listen to me. Listen to me." She waited for their eyes to meet before continuing: "Typhus, I know the lady in that picture. I recognized her. I know who she is."

Typhus, incredulous: "Lily? You know Lily?"

*"Lily?"* Malaria's eyes widened. "That ain't no Lily, Typhus. No, no, no. Oh dear God in heaven, *no…*" Malaria crumpled into sobs. "Dear God, Typhus. Someone been playing a trick on you. Someone done played a trick on you. My poor, poor little Typhus." She stroked his temple soothingly, but he recoiled at the word *little*.

"I ain't no little boy. I'm a man." His teeth clenched, his lower lip jutting firmly.

"You are a man," she said.

"And you ain't my mother. You're my sister."

"I ain't. And I am."

Typhus regained a degree of composure. "What are you talking about, big sis? Listen, whatever it is, it don't matter. I ain't never been happier. I met the real Lily and she loves me back. It's okay. I swear it's okay."

"Her name ain't Lily, Typhus. It's Gloria. And you ain't met her cause she dead. Been dead twenty-five years."

Typhus smiled uneasily. "Now, you just confused is all. One thing I know is she ain't dead. I—" he almost said *saw her*, but corrected himself before the words came out, "was with her last night. I…I…I—"

"Her name ain't Lily, Typhus," Malaria repeated, "it's *Gloria.*" She opened her fist and let the torn pieces of Typhus' photograph flutter to the ground.

Things began to fall together in Typhus' mind, and he understood what Malaria was trying to tell him, what she couldn't say flat out. His face went slack as he studied the wetness of his sister's cheeks and the pieces of Lily on the ground at his feet. Malaria put her hands on Typhus' shoulders as if fearful he may fall.

"Typhus, the lady in that picture," she leaned down to whisper in his ear, "she's your mother. My mother. Our mother."

# CHAPTER FIFTY-ONE
## *Rising Fog*

"Typhus, my brother, I do love you so."

"This ain't right." Typhus spoke as he collected up pieces of Lily from the ground, dropping them back into the coffee bag one by one. "And what ain't right gotta be made right."

"Typhus…" Malaria's tone was guarded. She was well aware that anything she might say could make things worse as easily as better. "Typhus, who did this to you? Was it that man?"

"What man?" Not in the mood for vague questions.

"Was it Doctor Jack who fooled you? Gave you that picture and…the rest?"

With the last piece of Lily in the bag, Typhus got to his feet. "I don't know if what you're saying is true, Malaria. But I can tell you that Lily is alive and well. If it's Mama—then *Mama* alive and well. *Somebody* alive and well. I was with her last night, Malaria. Whoever that a picture of, I was with her simple and true."

"It's a trick, Typhus. Might be someone looked like her. Even if she was alive, she'd be old now. Wouldn't look nothing like that picture."

"I didn't see her. I was *with* her." Typhus' eyes cast away from his sister, towards rising fog.

"What do you mean you didn't see her? What are you talking about?"

"It was her. That's all I know."

"The lady in that picture is *Mama*, Typhus. Don't you understand?"

"What if it is? If it is, then Mama ain't dead—that's all I'm sayin'." Typhus was coming to terms with the possibility that the woman he'd been with only hours ago might have been his own mother. That, in a way, would at least explain her unwillingness to let him see her.

"Now you're just talking crazy, Typhus."

"How about you? Did you see her?"

"What do you mean? Of course I seen her. She was my mama too, and didn't die till I was seven years old. I remember her like it was yesterday. I remember her sitting right here on this bench. I remember her face all the time—I see it in dreams and even when I'm awake. She stays with me every day, Typhus—"

"No, I mean did you see her dead? Do you know for a fact she *died*?"

Malaria hadn't considered this point. Truth was, Mother had died during childbirth, died bringing Typhus into the world. During the birth, Father had arranged for a friend from church to watch Malaria and her siblings. Doctor Jack had performed the delivery himself and pronounced Mother dead shortly after. The funeral had been closed casket because Father wanted his children's final memory of their mother to be of a living and vibrant woman, not an empty shell in a wooden box. Or so he had told them.

"No," she responded. "I ain't seen her dead."

"Well, how about that?" said Typhus. "You ain't seen her and I ain't seen her, but we both know what we know even though what we know ain't the same thing."

"Typhus—"

"Well, I'm about to find out which is right." Typhus turned his back and began walking briskly in the direction of the district. "I already know which is right," he added as he walked, "this is for your benefit, Malaria, not mine."

The fog had lifted completely now. It was looking to be a clear and brilliant day.

"Typhus—"

"What?"

"Be careful."

# CHAPTER FIFTY-TWO

# *Together All Three*

Doctor Jack was already brewing the morning's second pot of coffee. While the kettle struggled to boil, he sat down with the morning's *Bee* and glanced out the window. Jack smiled suspiciously at the beautiful, sunny morning—suspicious because in New Orleans beautiful mornings never guaranteed beautiful days. When the door eventually creaked open, Jack looked up from his half-read newspaper.

"Typhus—everything okay?" Jack noted immediately that Typhus no longer exhibited the symptoms of a man in love.

Typhus walked past him and emptied the contents of his burlap coffee bag on the examination table without a word. Jack's heartbeat quickened as Typhus began the process of piecing together the puzzle of Lily. After a moment Jack stood, unsure of what to say.

"Oh my. What happened to your little girlfriend, Typhus?" Typhus ignored the question, calmly continuing Lily's reassembly. Jack's tone became stern: "I trusted you with that photograph, boy. What do you have to say for yourself? You were sworn to protect her. You made a promise, and a promise is a serious thing."

A small fist slammed to the table causing the reassembled pieces to jumble away from each other. "Promise?" Typhus' eyes widened. "*Promise*? *I* made a promise? What about you? Or maybe it's all right to tell lies as long as you don't attach no promise. That how it works, Doctor Jack?"

"I won't have it," said Jack, trying not to sound shaken. "I won't have this talk."

"Yes, you will. You will have this talk."

"Well, son, if you were to put a brake on this nonsense maybe I could get to the bottom of whatever it is that's got yer goat."

"Ain't my problem. Not no more. It's yours."

"All right, son—"

"And stop calling me 'son.' I ain't yer son."

"Typhus—tell me. Tell me about *my* problem. Get it out already."

Another small fist met the table, sending pieces of Lily fluttering to the ground. "Who is this?" he said through clamped teeth. "Who *is* this?" pointing to the remaining pieces of Lily. *"Who is this? Who is this? Who is this? Lakjufa doir estay?"*

Then Doctor Jack knew. He knew that Typhus knew—and that there could be no more lies. As Typhus' anger melted to grief, Doctor Jack placed a hand on his shoulder.

"Listen, son—"

Typhus jerked back and away: "I am not yer goddamn son!"

Doctor Jack flinched—but still, his eyes stayed soft. He deserved Typhus' anger, maybe even his hatred—and he knew it. This was to be his lot. Jack allowed himself some small comfort in knowing that years of deceit would soon dissolve into truth—for better or worse.

"Don't call me that," warned Typhus. "Not now, not ever."

"All right, Typhus," said Jack, then, after a moment's pause: "But what if I was to tell you that's just what you are?"

Typhus stared, jaw trembling.

"Would that make a difference?" Jack whispered this last.

"What—?" Typhus steadied himself against the heavy table with both hands. "What are you talking about?"

"Maybe you should sit." Jack pulled out a chair for Typhus, the same chair Typhus had occupied during his encounter with Lily. Filled with fresh rage at the sight of it, Typhus kicked it away—and spun around to yank open the drawer containing Jack's surgical tools. The bulk of the implements spilled to the ground, and Typhus examined the gleaming pile of scattered silver briefly before bending down to scoop up the longest blade visible—a scalpel just two and a half inches long. He stood in a defensive posture with the knife in hand as if Jack's words were deadly weapons from which he needed to protect himself.

Jack raised both hands in a gesture of truce. "Typhus, you asked me a question and I mean to answer it. But I do want to warn you that what I have to say won't set well."

"Just stop," said Typhus. "I don't want to hear this."

"You came for answers, Typhus. Am I wrong about that?"

"I changed my mind. Just stop."

"Typhus, I think you already know the hardest part of this. The woman in that picture—Lily—her name ain't really Lily. Do you know her real name, Typhus?"

"*Stop it!*" Typhus slapped his hands forcefully over his ears, the scalpel making a small puncture wound to the right side of his neck.

"Typhus, I loved her. And she loved me."

"Please..."

"Your mother didn't have green eyes like yours, Typhus. But I do."

"Oh God..."

"When you were born, your father took one look at you, and he knew. He'd suspected her infidelity before that day, but it was in your green eyes that those ugly suspicions became reality. His rage was fleeting, but the result was regretful. He took your mother's life that day. Bloody, but quick."

"*Stop it, stop it, stop it...*" the scalpel was digging deeper into Typhus' neck—he either didn't notice or didn't care. Doctor Jack continued:

"Your father calmed quickly and was instantly remorseful—devastated by what he'd done. But her death was as much my fault as his—more so, in a way. So I helped him to cover it up—it was the least I could do. I wrote up the report as 'death during delivery, natural causes.' Your father never forgave me, but he was a good man in his heart and always meant to do right. He thought it wrong to keep you and me apart, Typhus—being blood kin as we were then, are now, and always will. So when you were old enough, he let you come work for me..."

"*Jesus...*"

Jack wanted to press on with the story, get it all out, purge himself of every detail—but it was evident to him that Typhus had already taken too much in. It was too much all at once—there'd be time for details later. Jack returned his hand to Typhus' shoulder and, this time, Typhus didn't shake it off.

"Son—" Jack started again.

"Don't call me that," Typhus whispered.

"Typhus, I know these are hard things to hear—"

"No. No more. It's my turn to talk."

"Typhus, please listen—"

"Who was here last night? Some hooker? Did you hire a prostitute? How much do I owe you for that?"

Jack had hoped Typhus wouldn't ask this question straight away. Hoped he might be content to process things a little at a time. "Typhus, there's plenty of time to talk about that later. Plenty of time for anger. Then a time for healing. Maybe even reconciliation."

"*Reconciliation*? Who was she, you bastard? Did she get a good laugh out of the pathetic, lovesick midget? Did you have to pay extra? Do *freaks* cost extra?"

"Typhus, nobody laughed."

"Who was she, damn you? Answer me goddammit or I'll kill you, I swear it." Typhus held the scalpel up in Jack's direction.

"Typhus," Jack wasn't sure how to continue. All he knew for certain was that he would never again lie to the boy. His boy. His son. "Typhus, there was nobody here last night except for you and me." There. It was out. All of the ugliness, out on the table.

The truth crystallized slowly but surely in the mind of Typhus Morningstar. Pieces of a puzzle assembling, urged on by formerly insignificant scraps of memory, now significant. He remembered how Jack looked differently to him that night—*cleaner somehow* he had thought. Remembered the smell of perfume and how it smelled strongest after Lily had emerged from the storage room, after the blindfold had been securely tied in place. He remembered the bloody knick on Jack's forearm—and realized now that he had shaved his arms (*cleaner somehow*), probably his legs as well. He remembered the texture of Lily's coarse, straight hair—he looked at Jack's hair now, wanting to touch it, to confirm.

Typhus fell quiet, his knife hand lowering while the other rose to the back of Jack's head. He touched the hair and looked into Jack's green eyes. The hair felt wonderful, and filled him with the memory of his most wonderful night—and it *had* been that, there was no denying.

For a moment, nothing else mattered. Didn't matter it was all a lie. Didn't matter that the man he'd always known as "Father" had killed his mother on the night of his own birth. Didn't matter that the man he knew as friend and mentor was really his father, and that this man had lied to him his whole life, had violated his heart and soul so unforgivably. At this moment, the lies and horrors didn't matter at all—all that mattered was that he had loved. He looked deeply into Jack's eyes, searching.

"My love?" he asked.

"Yes," answered Jack.

"My Lily?" Tears were clouding his eyes.

"Yes," answered Jack.

Typhus' hand closed around a clump of Jack's hair, then pulled it downward till they were eye to eye. He touched his lips to Jack's: gently, experimentally, warily. Jack's tongue slid out to brush against Typhus' upper lip, inviting reply. Typhus took the bait eagerly, pulling Jack's hair forward now, returning the kiss deeply.

Backing away slightly: "I loved you," said Typhus.

"I will always love you, son," said Jack with a weak, exhausted smile.

This last word squeezed like a hand at Typhus' heart, forcing blood upwards, filling his eyes.

*Son.*

A single word hissed through Typhus' teeth: *"Liar."*

Typhus felt real fingers press and pinch within his chest now; pure agony, slowing his heartbeat, clouding his soul, flooding his mind with blood and rage. He feared his heart may explode where he stood, and for a moment he went dizzy. His mind gone gray, headed for black.

There *was* a hand on his heart. There had always been a hand on his heart—ever since that night fifteen years ago.

Typhus yanked Jack's head downward hard by the hair, bringing the knife upwards three times fast into his chest. With an expression more of surprise than of fear or pain, Jack collapsed against the side of the water basin and slid to the floor.

"The boy told you not to call him that," said Typhus in a voice not his own.

*shoe dove*

Jack recognized the voice. Breath came hard—two of the puncture wounds had pierced the right lung—but he managed to say, "Typhus, I did these things for a reason."

On instructions of the thing in his chest, Typhus kicked Jack squarely in the crotch before responding verbally. "Of course you did. We all got reasons, I reckon. Some reasons are more wholesome than others is all. Some self-serving, others not so."

Jack tumbled to the floor. "Typhus, listen. Please."

"Go on speaking at your own risk, Jack."

"Can't you see what I gave you? What I gave her? It wasn't easy to do this thing that I did."

"You gave me nothing, old man. *Father.*"

"Try to understand, son." Jack no longer cared if the word carried repercussions. He knew he was dying—this was his last chance to unburden himself with the truth. "Last night—on that beautiful, beautiful night—we were together all three. Father, mother and son. For the first and last time, yes—but *together*. Just once, but enough."

Typhus brought the scalpel in line with Jack's throat.

Jack continued. "In your mind you were with *her*; with your Lily—the image of your mother. But in truth you were with me, your true father. And so, in your heart of hearts—and whether you knew it or not—we were all together for one perfect moment. A family at last."

With his lungs rapidly filling with blood, Jack struggled to speak. "Together," he repeated. "Together all three."

Typhus suddenly found himself feeling pity for Jack, pity for the man who'd deceived him so heinously, had wrecked his life so thoroughly. As Jack's eyes shined their last light, they watched Typhus' lips move—mouthing a single word that his ears could no longer hear.

"Sorry," said Typhus, immediately before cutting Doctor Jack's throat from ear to ear in one smooth motion.

# CHAPTER FIFTY-THREE

## *Typhus' Cure*

T yphus' best yellow shirt had been ruined, splashed with bright red that would never completely wash out. Rising to his feet, he caught a glimpse of himself in the mirror, his face moist with blood and tears.

Although the hand of Noonday Morningstar had loosened its painful grip on his heart, the inside of Typhus' chest felt bruised and strangely warm. Maybe he was bleeding from inside—didn't matter, he knew his time would now be short. Staring hard in the mirror, Typhus tore off the ruined shirt and examined the scar in the shape of a hand. Its color had deepened from pink to bright purple and was bleeding along the bottom edge.

Typhus lit the stove and put a teapot over the flame. He had mixed and delivered many a cure for others at Doctor Jack's behest, but today would be the day of his own cure. His day of abortion and hope. He would mix the calisaya tea at double strength and deprive himself of honey.

The poison went down quick; hot and bitter, stinging his throat and blurring his vision immediately. He felt a sharp pain in his gut—this was good. But also it was a signal to move fast or not at all.

He collected the scattered pieces of Lily from the table and floor, put them in his trusty, all-purpose, burlap coffee bag. As he began this final errand, the lyrics of a song marched through his mind like a line of diligent ants. A song whose melody he could no longer recall.

# CHAPTER FIFTY-FOUR
## *The Twenty Tens*

**B**uddy Bolden was sleeping the remorseless sleep of drunkards and angels.

*Bap bap bap bap bap bap bap bap bap.*

"Damn," he whispered. Then, not loud but neither a whisper: "*Whoever that is, get lost!* Man trine to get a little shut-eye in here." Buddy pressed his eyes closed once more, muttering, "Working man, too. Hard working man just needin' a little sleep is all. People knocking in the middle of the damn night ain't got no manners 'round here. True, true. Sad but true."

*Bap bap bap bap bap bap bap bap bap.*

"God*damn*it." Buddy's eyes stayed defiantly shut. More muttering: "Ain't answerin' that damn door." Then louder, for the benefit of the knocker, "*Ain't answerin' that damn door, ya hear?* Come back in the mornin' if it's so doggone 'portant!"

"It *is* morning," said a high-timbered voice that Buddy struggled to recognize. "*Past* mornin', Buddy. Nearly one in the afternoon."

Buddy wasn't in the mood for arguing such minutiae. "I don't hear ya and I *won't* hear ya! Now git gone!" Then, diminishing from angry to desperate: "I work late and need to sleep in a little. Have a mercy now and leave me be. *Please!*"

"Up *drinkin'* late is more like it," said the voice. "Get up now, Buddy. The world is passing you by."

"Let it pass, then!" Buddy shouted, his head settling back into the pillow, his mind drifting rapidly towards unfinished dreams. The would-be intruder's persistent knock turned into a dream of knocking; mercifully pounding Buddy deeper into dreamland. It wasn't till the rhythm changed that Buddy found himself coming back around.

*Bap. Bap-bap. Buh-bap, bap, buh-bap.*

It was a knock he hadn't heard in years—the secret knock from Charley the Barber's old backroom gin joint. To hear that particular knock all the sudden and from out of nowhere was a curious thing; so curious that Buddy found himself fully awake and in a sitting position, staring at the door. Suddenly, he placed the voice.

*Bap. Bap-bap. Buh-bap, bap, buh-bap.*

He got to his feet, undid the latch; the door swung wide.

"Where'd you learn that knock, boy?"

"Didn't learn it. Just made it up," said Jim Jam Jump hopefully. "You like it? Mebbe you can put it in a song."

Buddy rubbed his eyes and let himself believe Jim doing Charley's old knock was a product of his own rye-soaked imagination. "Dammit boy, what in hell is so allfired important you gotta stand out there beating my damn door when you know damn well I'm trine ta sleep? I'd do good to whip yer damn hide and there ain't a judge ner jury who'd convict me fer—"

"Settle down, now, Buddy. I come to make you a richer man. Just let me speak my piece, wouldja?" Jim extracted a thick wad of ten-dollar bills from his back pocket.

Buddy eyed the wad suspiciously, figuring the top bill to be hiding a roll of ones or, more likely, just plain newsprint. Still, the sight of that top bill alone was enough to bring him near sober. "What's this about, sonny?"

"Gotcher curiosity up, have I?" Jim unrolled and flipped the money between thumb and forefinger like a deck of cards. All tens. Buddy didn't respond, just raised his eyebrows some.

Jim went on: "I expect you'll be interested in selling that horn of yours now, Buddy. I mean considering all that's transpired of late. In fact, in a gesture of sympathy towards yer loss, I've decided to double my final offer. What you see here is not one but *two* hunnert American legal tender U.S. dollars." Jim flipped the roll again for punctuation.

"Goddammit, if I done told ya once I told you a thousand differ'nt times that horn ain't fer sale. I'm handin' her down to my boy when I'm through with her. Now if you would only get that through yer thick—"

"Oh dear," Jim interrupted. "You haven't heard. Well, gosh, of course you haven't heard. You been asleep all afternoon. I guess I just thought maybe they'd-a sent a copper out to tell ya. Well, hell, I'm truly sorry, Buddy. Mebbe I should just be off and on my way. We can talk about this at a better—"

"Fer the love of Christ Almighty what in hell are you goin' on about, kid?"

"Well, I hate to be the one to break it—"

"Fine, I'm going back to bed." Buddy wasn't in the mood for games.

But before the door closed, Jim managed to get out: "West is dead."

The door held at six inches, and opened no further. In Buddy's fragile, hung-over state of mind, to open it wider might make the words more real. "What?"

"Kilt dead this morning out by the river. Murdered. Seen it myself."

"What are you saying? Murdered? My little boy was murdered? I don't believe—"

"Seen it myself. Seen it happen. Sorry."

"Yer lyin' to me. Why would you make up something like that? Fer a damn horn?" There was a part of Buddy unable to believe West might really be gone—but another part filtered the truth from Jim's eyes.

"Yer brother-in-law the dummy did it. Dropsy. Snapped his little neck with one quick twist. Real coldhearted-like."

"Now I know yer lyin'," said Buddy. "Dropsy ain't much fer brains but he loves my little West."

"Ya mean *wasn't* much fer brains. Dropsy dead, too. Killed his own self right after. Walked in the river with a blank expression on his face, like one of them hoodoo zombies. Like to make my blood run cold the way—"

"Yer lyin'."

"Coldest, weirdest thing I ever seen."

"Oh my God..." Buddy could no longer pretend—breaking into sobs, backing away from the half-open door. Jim walked in as Buddy lowered himself to the edge of the bed, reaching for the cornet that lay to the left of the pillow, stroking it for comfort. The tender display of flesh against brass made Jim's mouth water.

"Now about that horn, Buddy..."

Buddy's eyes went blank as he got to his feet, waving the cornet at Jim. "You want this horn? This what you want? Will all the evil in yer black little heart'll just lay down and die if you get yer hands on *THIS. DAMN. HORN?*"

"Buddy, now, take it easy. I'm just talking about a simple business transaction is all. Pretty lucrative one for you, I gotta say..."

"You want this horn?" Buddy was shaking at the knees. "Well, I'll just go and let you have it then."

Jim Jam Jump, who prided himself on quick reflexes and a keen ability to work out most any angle well in advance would kick himself later for not having seen this coming. He honestly never expected Buddy might do anything to put his beloved cornet in harm's way. As it turned out, Buddy's grief and anger were just strong enough to put him over that edge—and now here he was pounding Jim's head with the cherished instrument. Got in three solid hits before Jim managed to collect himself, to twist away and out of range.

"Now, Buddy, that ain't no way ta—"

"I'll kill ya. I'll kill ya, ya little shit."

"I believe you would…"

Jim executed an artful dance around the shaky swings of Buddy Bolden, staying close but dodging further blows, trying to figure a way to throw a few of his own. A quick, right fisted jab to Buddy's groin caused the horn to drop, another dropped Buddy to his knees, the musician sucking in air with bulging eyes. Jim snatched the cornet from the ground—immediately spinning it longways in a horizontal circle till the wide end connected with Buddy's temple. The hit was direct and decisive; Buddy went down hard.

Jim hadn't even broken a sweat. Examining the cornet with loving fingers and worried eyes, he checked it for damage.

"They sure do make these things durable," said Jim aloud, marveling at how the instrument had survived the scuffle unscathed.

"Well, then," Jim said to Buddy's unmoving form, "to answer your question, I do indeed want this horn. Sounds like we done made ourselves a deal."

Jim stooped down to stuff Buddy's pockets with the twenty tens before leaving. Then he walked to the river, whistling a happy tune.

Once at the river, he washed Buddy's blood from the cornet.

# CHAPTER FIFTY-FIVE
## *Fathers and Sons*

As the calisaya tea wrought its havoc upon his body, Typhus' bike became increasingly difficult to maneuver. By the time he'd rolled onto Chartres Street he found himself forced to abandon it altogether and complete his journey on foot. Typhus had always been very protective of his beloved bicycle, but today such protective inclinations felt the stuff of fools. Nothing mattered now but the matter at hand. He pulled the burlap sack from the basket of the fallen bicycle and got moving.

The small hill of the levee seemed steeper today than Typhus remembered it, and from its toppermost point he noted just how far down the pier his little rebirthing island was. It'd seemed so much closer before, but before today he'd always made his approach on bicycle—and with a body not full of poison. Descending the river side of the levee, he silently thanked his father's God for the added speed offered by gravity—but gratitude quickly tempered with regret as his feet tangled beneath him. The weird pain of calisaya amplified excruciatingly in the subsequent tumble.

Even in the fall, the burlap bag never loosened from Typhus' grip. When he finally found himself standing above the island's edge, Typhus lay flat on his stomach with his chin resting at the boardwalk's edge. Staring at sand and grass four and a half feet below, he worked out various scenarios of lowering himself to the island with minimal pain. The sad verdict came quickly—in his present condition there was no way down but to fall, and so fall he did. Mercifully, he landed on his back, but the deceptively soft-looking patch of saw grass met him with a stinging collection of thin, red lines that streaked his naked back and shoulders. Finding he could no longer support himself on his feet, Typhus shoved his way through the brush of the sandbank on all fours. Bleeding from the outside and dying from the inside, he was now more determined than ever to reach his sacred spot before letting go the second little life inside him.

To his little beach by the river, to his *rebirthing* beach.

A song in his head played along the way:

*Jesus I'm troubled about my soul...*

Vegetation soon thinned and sand prevailed. Typhus' vision was failing, but the clear and soothing hum of river—along with the accompanying warmth of its breeze—told him he'd reached his destination. He let himself fall to his side in a fetal position; breathing hard, the sweat of his body mixing with his blood, the mixture turning sticky-brown beneath the beating sun. A shallow tide swelled meekly from the river, sending a cool sheet of water across sand to kiss his grounded shoulder. Typhus felt peace for a moment, but the moment soon dissolved into a sharp, percussive shriek that shot up through his throat. The pain in his belly crescendoed then receded with the tide, and during those moments in-between where water and agony fell away, Typhus mustered the strength to reach into his bag. With careful but shaking hands, he placed torn bits of photographic paper face up on the smooth sand, just out of the tide's reach. He assembled Lily quickly—more quickly than he imagined he could—then lay the bag over top to protect her from wind and river spray. The tide would take Lily tonight in its own sweet time. Typhus had done what he could.

The pain of calisaya bloomed full-red; muscles and bones seemingly at war. Something inside was pushing, pressing inward, causing muscles to stiffen, bones to yield. What was unwelcome would soon be expelled—and *that* is the point of calisaya tea. An awful burning in his chest came—and with it a weird sensation of dislodging. Something had come loose, tearing away from his heart. The calisaya focused on the anomaly in his chest, centering its force within his ribcage in a single, blinding contraction. Finally, Typhus felt the thing inside give up, let go.

Typhus listened in amazement to the rhythm of his own heartbeat, now pounding with a strength and clarity he'd never before known—it was a liberating thing, this rhythm. But with liberation comes baggage akin to tragedy, the kind of tragedy associated with final farewells and painful lessons learned.

Before Typhus could adequately ponder the abstract qualities of freedom and tragedy, he realized he had stopped breathing—something had blocked his windpipe. His lungs attempted to pull inward—but Typhus knew this was wrong—and so willed every ounce of his strength to, instead, push out.

The obstruction pushed up then through his mouth with a gush of clear, brown fluid, landing on the sand, palm side up.

A hand.

Rigidly closed in a half-fist, the hand trembled slightly for a moment then lay still. Typhus lay on his side, gulping air, staring at the hand. This was a hand he remembered well—the gentle hand of a loving father. He stared at the nails and the tiny hairs of the knuckles, the creases, the calluses of it. Though the scar upon his chest had always been plain enough, he'd never fully believed the stories of how it had come to be. There was a part of him that *knew*, but another part unable to *believe*. With the truth now as plain as the scar, Typhus found himself wishing he'd not expelled a thing so inclined to attach itself to his heart.

Without warning, the hand jumped into air—then flew into water. Craning his neck to follow its path, Typhus found himself looking at two naked feet near his head. The feet led upwards to an immense, sun-blocking silhouette—now stooping down to him. Typhus felt a cool hand against his forehead.

"Won't be needing that anymore." At the sound of the voice, Typhus knew the hand had not flown into water of its own accord.

It had been kicked.

"Daddy?" said Typhus.

"It's good to see you, son," said Noonday Morningstar.

"You ain't real," said Typhus regretfully, with no better greeting for a long dead parent. "How's it so?"

"Sure, sure. I'm real enough. Dead people just as real as live ones, I reckon."

"Gotta be the tea. I'm imagining this."

"Imaginary people real, too—in their way. If a person can remember or even dream up a face, then the face does exist in some kinda way. Things remembered are sometimes more real than what a person holds in his hand. All that being true and set aside for now; you ain't imagining me."

"Have to be. You're dead."

"Hell, maybe I'm imagining you. Being dead so long can play tricks on a fella's mind." The dead man gave a wry smile. "C'mon now, Typhus. I'd a thought better of you for an open mind. Little fella like you turning dead babies into live catfish oughta be able to believe just about any damn thing."

"I guess," Typhus conceded.

"We both seen plenty strange things in our lives, son. Lots stranger than this. Don't matter anyhow. Soon enough you'll know. Plenty of proof be along shortly."

Typhus winced at a fresh contraction. He held his breath till it passed, then let the air back out slowly.

"It was too much," said Noonday.

"Too much?"

"The tea, Typhus. Done gave yerself a double dose—and you being half-size already. Just like taking *four* times too much. Man, you musta really wanted that hand outta yer chest."

"Am I going to die?" asked Typhus.

"Is that what you want?"

"I don't know."

"No, you ain't gonna die. Not exactly. Gonna rebirth. Just like them babies you rebirth alla time. Snatch 'em from death and let 'em go till they get their story straight, then come back around to do some good. That'd be yer lot, I reckon. Goin' off then comin' back. Only you won't be no fish."

Typhus felt weird relief. "I was going to do that for you, Daddy," he offered. "Was gonna rebirth ya. It's why I came out here after taking the tea."

"You *what?*" Noonday said with a grin. "Gonna turn that old hand of mine into a catfish, was ya?" He laughed. "That there boy gonna turn my hand into a dern fish. Now I heard everything, yes indeed!" Shaking off the laughter but keeping the grin for luck, Noonday knelt beside Typhus to put something in his mouth. "Have a chaw," he said. "Might take yer mind offa the pain."

Typhus pressed his teeth to the bit of tobacco—his father was right, the juice was strong and distracting. After a few moments, Typhus asked:

"Why you ain't told me? 'Bout you not being my real father'n all? Shoulda told me."

"I'd a told you soon enough, Typhus—just hadn't counted on my dyin' so soon. You was only nine, boy. Time wasn't right." Noonday spat some tobacco juice in the river. "Anyway, don't go foolin' yerself. I was your father then, still am now, and always will be. Blood don't mean shit. Love is all that matters when it comes down to fathers and sons. You been lucky—you had two fathers that loved you. And I don't mean that crazy witch doctor you just kilt, neither. He was no kind of father at all. Just an egotistical, lovesick fool and not one thing more."

"I didn't kill Doctor Jack. You did."

"Well, how 'bout that. Listen to you go on, passin' around blame. Who was holding the knife, if you please?"

"Who had their big old hand wrapped 'round my heart, if *you* please?"

Noonday smiled. "Ah, hell, boy. You just needed a nudge is all. It was the right thing under the circumstances—I mean, c'mon, think about what he done."

Typhus looked away from the dead man. "Yeah. Maybe so."

"Sure, sure."

"Whadja mean about me havin' two fathers, then? If Doctor Jack ain't one of 'em."

"Do I gotta spell it out fer ya? Use yer noggin, boy. I raised you better'n that."

"The phantom?"

"He has a name, Typhus. Show a little more respect for the man who took on such a thankless job, lookin' after you, your brother and your sisters in my absence. Say his name, and do so with respect. And with proper love."

"Beauregard."

"Beauregard Church." Noonday's eyes brightened at the name. "He was as good a father as I ever was. Maybe better. And you mistreated that man. Broke his heart. Broke my heart watchin' you do it to him."

"He killed you."

"He freed me."

"Daddy?" Typhus wasn't sure how to ask the thing on his mind, so he said it straight out; "You been with me this whole time? Watchin' me?"

"Typhus, I been with you every step. My very hand on your heart. I'd be with you past today if you hadn't a put me out like you just done."

"I'm sorry I did that," Typhus started with a crack in his voice, "but I had to. Things was gettin'…so hard."

"Well, that's all right. You just settle down. You done nothing wrong, boy. Musta been hard with never a moment's true privacy. Seein' that scar on yer chest every day and wonderin' about it, wonderin' if yer own thoughts were really your own—"

"Were they?"

"Were they what?"

"My thoughts. Were they mine?"

A beat. "Mostly."

Typhus hesitated. There was one more question, and the question came in the form of a single word:

"Lily?"

"Your mama's name was Gloria, son."

"Gloria." The word felt holy on his lips.

"And I guess the answer to what you're asking is *yes*."

"Gloria." Fresh tears welled in Typhus' eyes.

"There was no shame in the love you felt for our Gloria; my wife, your mother. Shame not even in the passion. She was the love of my life, Typhus— and my hand was on your heart through no fault of your own—God Himself having put it there. You had no way of knowing why you felt the way you did. But that bastard Jack sure as hell did know. He knew every bit of it."

In spite of this truth, Typhus could no longer bring himself to feel hatred or anger towards Doctor Jack. Couldn't bring himself to feel anything but regret— regret at knowing the most powerful thing he'd ever felt in his life, his love for Lily, was not even a thing he could call his own. It was a passion borrowed from a dead man, his father.

"That ain't so, Typhus." After fifteen years residence in his son's soul, Noonday had no problem plucking thoughts from his head. "Your love was your own. It was always your own. I just give you a little nudge is all."

"Sounds like you done a lot of nudgin'."

"Guess I did." Noonday smiled. "I hope I nudged you right once or twice along the way."

"Maybe you did. I guess you did. I don't know."

"Well, let's hope—at the end of the day, hoping is all anyone can do. Anyway, now that you done spat out my hand, I guess I'll be off on my own shortly. Off to the Spiritworld, sure enough. And this time all in one piece."

"Heaven," said Typhus, squinting his eyes at the sun. "Up in the clouds."

Noonday lowered his eyes. "I guess I gave you some wrong information about that back when I was a living man—but damn if I didn't take the Holy Bible literal at every word. Truth is, there ain't no heaven and hell, son. Just one Spiritworld. And it ain't in the sky, neither."

"Where, if not up?"

"Think." Noonday winked at his son. Spat another stream of juice in the water; a hint.

"The river."

"Water, son. Ain't nothin' more sacred than water. Even more sacred than air."

"I think I'm dying, Daddy."

"I know, son."

"But I've got so many questions—"

"Shhh. Time for that later."

"I don't understand."

Noonday stroked his son's forehead. "Ain't you been listening to a word I just said? In the water. We'll meet again in the water. Soon."

"I need something, Daddy."

"What might that be?" said Noonday, knowing full well what Typhus needed.

"I need the truth."

"The truth is what it is, Typhus. Real truth is common knowledge in the world of living men. Men only get to asking about it when they have a hard time accepting what they already know. But you knew that, didn't you, Typhus? Ever since you was small, you knew that. You just done forgot is all."

"I love you, Daddy."

"I love you, too, boy." Noonday touched Typhus' cheek. "Ready?"

"Ready."

# CHAPTER FIFTY-SIX
## *This is Blood*

Just below the river's surface: smooth, white, sacred hands rub and loosen spots of red from the golden skin of Buddy Bolden's cornet. Upon liberation, the spots become wisps of red, mingling and joining together into a cloud of nearly invisible pink, lingering with residual longing near the hands that have freed them. When the hands have washed away every drop, the horn is pulled back quickly into the tacky warmth of living air. There is no song to comfort this thing, this cloud of faded, loose color. It must find its own, create its own.

Thus delivered and abandoned by the exquisitely cruel hands, the cloud of pink is left to fend for itself in the great body of water. Locating its scent, tiny life-forms are immediately drawn to the smell of it, investigating the possibility of nourishment with hungry, minute thrashes, giving the blood-cloud its first bit of information, telling it that it can no longer stay in one place and survive, that it must move on. Must avoid premature consumption. Must deliver its message.

This is blood. This

(...)

is *jazz*.

The pink is humbled by its own fragile existence, feeding only on the energy of its fear. It is fear that motivates it, fear urging it to complete some unknown transformation or transaction, to become something brand new, something bold, a pocket of strength from a thing recently weak, a garment extraordinary from unremarkable plain cloth. The pink dives downward, elongating and thinning in shape as it accelerates, occasionally pausing to dance, to hesitate and waver, investigating; cautiously, gracefully, to trip and glide, to swoop and soar, to make its own way, to devise its own type of existence; joy, pain, heartache, triumph.

Its initial sense of longing for familiar pain evaporates quickly as it grows accustomed to a freedom of movement it had never known in the veins of Buddy Bolden. Its form changes at whim of speed and current—there is no recklessness in this movement for there is nothing to lose. It is a wondrous thing, this elasticity of form.

The deeper it travels, the darker its surroundings become—and the more defined the lights. Lights. These are the lights of the dead; souls unknown to blood.

Unknown to blood, this blood, this song *en utero.*

The cloud of red is no longer what it was. It has reached the Spiritworld. It is home at last. Through water it will touch the world. Its time will come soon. It cannot die. But immortality carries a price.

What is sacrificed is a thing newly absent from the soul of Buddy Bolden.

# CHAPTER FIFTY-SEVEN

# When a Cop Comes to Call on Poor Folk, Ain't Never Good News to Tell

ten year veteran of the NOPD, Officer Bryce viewed the errand at hand as the plainest sort of shit work. As far as he was concerned, he was way too old for this kind of thing.

"Gonna ruin mah damn boots fer those niggras," Bryce mumbled to himself as he gazed mournfully down at the formerly spit-polished black police boots that currently sucked upwards then sloshed downwards in the muck with comic rhythm.

"What kinda animals'd live at the edge of the Bayou St. John anyhow?" he complained aloud to no one. "Ain't no figgerin' that crazy niggerin'." A wheezy snicker congratulated the rhyme.

Even Bryce had to admit the discovery of the Bolden kid's corpse had rattled him. The murder itself was unremarkable—he'd seen far too many dead bodies in his time to let one more murdered child get to him. But the sight of this one had thrown an uncharacteristic lump in his throat—and without decipherable cause. Bryce believed such lumps for rookies only, his own throat rendered un-lumpable many years ago. But there was something different about this one.

The kid had been found at the back of a sand bank off the river, tied to a thick stalk of an oversized banana plant, his head twisted clean around and facing backwards. With eyes wide open, his expression betrayed no hint of surprise or fear. This fact, Bryce theorized, meant the kid knew his killer—and had trusted him right up to the moment of his death. Bryce had seen lots of death and cruelty in his day—had even administered his own fair share of both—but the sight of that poor, dead, black kid somehow qualified as the saddest thing he'd ever laid eyes on.

According to two witnesses, the perpetrator was a colored man named Dropsy Morningstar, a.k.a The Christ Kid in certain circles—and Bryce was intimately familiar with such circles. The Christ Kid had been an important component of the lucrative fight store scams arranged by Crawfish Bob—scams that earned local law enforcement officers like himself a good supplemental income on the sly. Even those fleeced by Bob's crew benefited from the operation via important lessons learned, lessons relating to a single but all-important concept: Do Not Fuck With Louisiana. Come down to the bayou looking for marks, and prepare to become one yourself. Bryce didn't know of a single mark who'd ever returned—not for retribution, and certainly not for seconds. Getting skinned New Orleans-style has a way of leaving a sour taste on a Yankee palate—the kind that lingers long.

But now The Christ Kid was out of the picture—and so a new scam would necessarily be conjured by Crawfish Bob and his associates. They could probably find a replacement for The Kid if they really wanted to, but Louisianans are a sentimental lot—memories of a fallen co-conspirator can cloud the eyes and dull the wit. Besides, no one could take blows like The Christ Kid—there had been times when Bryce himself worried that The Kid may have taken a hit too many.

By the time Bryce spotted the Morningstar house, the stink of the swamp had long since brought tears to his eyes. Approaching the front door, he prayed the mother wouldn't be the hysterical type. He wasn't in the mood for coffee and tears at the moment, just wanted to get back into town where he could breathe right again. Bryce knocked on the front door hard and fast, his official-police-business knock.

The door opened just four inches, but the face revealed by those inches took Bryce's mind out of bad air straight away. Second thoughts regarding condolences withheld began to formulate; *Good lookin' niggra bitch like this starts to cryin' on a fella's shoulder, no tellin' where that might lead.* Bryce smoothed back his orange hair with one hand, and put on his most charming smile.

"Pardon me on this fine mornin', ma'am," he began, with minimal brogue. "Might you be Miss Diphtheria Morningstar?"

"I ain't," said the woman, whose eyes moved suspiciously over Bryce's face and uniform. Bryce recognized the look, had seen it a thousand times if he'd seen it once, the look that said, "When a cop comes to call on poor folk, ain't never good news to tell." He'd be offended by the assertion if it weren't so goddamn consistently true.

"Well, maybe I have the wrong house," Bryce continued. "You wouldn't happen to be kin to West Bolden or Dropsy Morningstar would you?"

Suspicion melted to concern, the woman's eyes suddenly wide with recognition. "What's this about, officer?"

"Officer Bryce, ma'am. Officer Bryce of the New Orleans Police Department. You can call me Jim."

"A pleasure, Officer Bryce. Are those two in some kind of trouble?"

"I'm afraid you have me at a disadvantage." Bryce struggled not to let his eyes wander south of the woman's chin.

"Malaria," she said. "Malaria Morningstar. Dropsy and Diphtheria are my brother and sister. West is my nephew. What's this about?"

"Malaria and Diphtheria—those sure are unusual names if you don't mind my saying so." Bryce let a grin escape before he could think better of it. Not wanting to offend, he wandered clumsily in the direction of rewording, "What I meant to say is…"

"Sir, has something happened to them? Are they in jail or something? Are they hurt?"

As Malaria's eyes narrowed with worry, Bryce felt his heart sink. He raised a hand to remove his hat, then realized he'd left it at the station. With nothing better to do up there, the raised hand had another go at smoothing wavy, orange hair.

"Ma'am, I'm afraid it's my sad duty to inform you that…"

He stopped, tongue-tied. Bryce always had trouble getting past those first eleven words. Today especially, the striking beauty of this colored woman made him want to say something clever—as if it's possible to speak charmingly of the death of a child. But before he knew it, his lips had resumed their course:

"…to inform you that… your family dinner table will have two less settings this Sunday." Charming; no, *clever*; yes. Bryce would have to write that one down.

"Sunday dinner?"

"Yes, ma'am," Bryce affirmed, giving her a moment to piece together the implication.

"I don't understand," she said timidly on paling lips. But she did understand—her eyes told Bryce it was so.

"Dead," he intoned bluntly. "The two I mentioned. Found dead this morning down by the river. On a sand dune. By the river. I already said that—sorry."

"Sweet Jesus, tell me this man is lying." Malaria's eyes filled rapidly.

"I wish I could tell you I was, Miss Malaria, but I seen 'em myself." He placed a thick hand on her shoulder hopefully, and added once more with feeling, "I'm so sorry."

Malaria recognized the overture of his hand for what it was, reflexively stepping back and out of the big man's reach.

"If this happened for real, then tell me how," she said evenly, stopping her tears through force of will, forbidding them to tumble down her cheeks in front of this man.

Bryce felt humbled by the unspoken rebuff, humility being a quality not of his nature. His brogue loosened back into place as he replied coldly; "The big one killed the little one. Tied him to a tree and spun his head around like a top. Then the big one killed himself, walked right in the river. Body ain't floated up as of yet, at least it ain't been found. Not that I know of."

Malaria's body went rigid. "That ain't possible. What you're saying cannot be true. Dropsy loved that boy. They was like kid brothers... the way they play. They always play so good together, those two."

"It's true enough, I'm afraid." Seeing that the encounter would clearly not turn romantic, Bryce meant to wrap things up quickly and leave this damn swamp, its foul smell, and its crazy niggras.

Malaria deciphered the cop's shift in demeanor with genuine amazement—had this fool actually thought she would spread her legs for him? This ugly thought mixed with the memory of her recent painful encounter with Typhus. Mixed with the thought of Dropsy at the bottom of the river. And with the thought of West being dead. Poor, poor, beautiful little West. Could he really be dead? She decided it could not be true. None of it could be true. It was just too much to take in all at once. God could not be so cruel.

"*Liar!*" Malaria screeched as she lunged at Bryce, kicking his legs, slapping at his face and chest, sending them both over backwards into mud.

"*Goddamn it get offa me!*" Bryce bellowed as they rolled in muck and wet codgrass. Malaria continued to lash out at him; tears streaking her cheeks, murder in her eyes. Had Bryce chosen to throw her aside he could have done so easily—he decided instead to enjoy the physical contact, slipping his hand up her dress to feel the smooth contour of her hip. He considered taking her by force—after all, she had attacked an officer of the law—but when her slapping hands balled into fists, he found her touch less arousing. The big cop threw one square punch, knocking Malaria back and off of him. Stunned by the blow, Malaria lie on her back—holding the side of her head with wild, staring eyes.

"Now, ma'am, I didn't want to have to hit ya, but ya just assaulted an officer of the law is what ya done." Bryce was back on his feet now, brushing wet grass and greenish brown smudges from his uniform. "That'd be a serious offense I wouldn't mind prosecutin' if I didn't know yer actin' outta grief. Was hopin' we could be friends, even."

"Leave me alone," Malaria whimpered, still lying on the ground with her hands over her face, not wanting to share another minute of the worst day of her life with this abominable creature. "Just leave me alone."

"Now, you sure you ain't need me to stay awhile and..."

She couldn't believe he was still at it. *"Get out!* Get off my property! Go away and leave me *alone!"*

"All right then, little lady." Bryce held both hands up submissively. "I'll go and let you alone with yer grievin'. But if you need someone to talk to you just call on ol' Officer—"

"Get out of here, you *dirty dog!"*

Bryce didn't brave another word as he sloshed back towards town, cursing under his breath—but also secretly hoping this beauty may eventually feel enough remorse for her poor treatment of him to come calling one day. Such a day would never come.

Malaria was a lonely woman, but not that lonely.

# CHAPTER FIFTY-EIGHT
## *Diphtheria's Cure*

On the morning that Marcus Nobody Special buried the small body of West Bolden, the sky was slightly overcast and the air oddly unmoist for New Orleans, a comfort downright uncomfortable in a community so accustomed to discomfort. As if to make up for the oversight, the night brought a distinct chill.

Diphtheria had locked herself in her room at Arlington House since hearing the bad news, shutting herself off from the world just as Hattie had done in the wake of her cure. To work the parlor would feel inappropriate at the least and pointless at best. Old customers and friends had come to call, to pay respects and sympathies, but sharing grief and chit-chat were things she didn't feel much up to. The only person she'd allowed comfort from was Hattie—and mostly because Hattie had put up with her own forceful sympathies in recent weeks.

The funeral itself had been a bleak affair that attracted few mourners. Not that she expected great numbers to attend the burial of the son of a whore, but the absence of Typhus and Buddy had left a bitter taste on her tongue. Buddy's failure to show had surprised no one, of course—being that he was a no-account scoundrel and a drunkard on *good* days. Typhus, on the other hand, had always cared very much for Diphtheria and West. After Father Elois' brief service, Malaria had whispered in Diphtheria's ear, "Typhus got some troubles. Don't feel bad he ain't here." But the whisper only served to underline her feelings of abandonment.

Now all the men were gone. Her father, dead for years. Her son, dead two days. Her man, flown the coop years past. Dropsy, presumed dead—his body not yet turned up. And Typhus—just gone. All gone somehow or other. No men left. No men but her regular customers, and those were hardly men at all.

Diphtheria stared at the ceiling contemplating this absence of men. Wondering if West had felt much pain when he died. Wondering what Typhus' troubles might be, troubles so bad that he'd leave her alone at a time like this.

She closed her eyes and hoped to dream, but sleep never got the chance.

Three light raps. Hattie come to call, to see if she needed looking after, to put Diphtheria's head in her lap, to brush her hair, to bill and coo, to dab away tears if they came. Hattie's knock wasn't such a bad sound, Diphtheria decided. It was a warm sound, a saving sound. The sound of someone giving a damn.

"It's unlocked, Hattie."

The door opened just enough for Hattie to stick her pretty head in, smiling. *What in God's name could that woman be smiling about?* thought Diphtheria.

"How you feeling, sweetie?" sang Hattie.

Diphtheria would have explained the inappropriateness of the question, especially on the funeral day of a mother's only child, but she didn't have the energy for such long sentences. "I'm fine," was her response.

Hattie smiled obliviously. "Got someone special here to see you. You'll be plenty surprised, I think."

"Don't feel up to it, darlin'. Tell 'em to come on back tomorrow." She paused. "Or the next day."

"Might be just the face to brighten you up, girl." Inappropriately, still beaming.

Diphtheria had to admit her curiosity was piqued—she couldn't think of a single face that might brighten a day like this. Then the obvious occurred to her, and her eyes widened.

"Is that Typhus? Where you been, little brother? I's worried about you. Why you want to worry your big sister at such a terrible time? Show yourself, little brother…"

A hand pushed the door open wide enough to fit a second head beside Hattie's. Diphtheria could smell the rye on his breath from across the room, and, from the way Hattie giggled and squirmed, Diphtheria imagined Buddy's hand was likely on her ass. That was just like Hattie; to bubble like a schoolgirl in the presence of a jazz musician—even a no-account bum like Buddy Bolden.

"Ain't ya glad to see me, sugar?" Buddy displayed big yellow teeth like he was proud of every last one.

"You missed the funeral," was all Diphtheria could muster. She was too tired to act mad.

"Well, uh, that's a funny story. Umm, ya see—"

"I'll just let you two have some privacy," interrupted Hattie. Buddy turned and nodded with a grin, making no attempt to conceal one last grope at her behind. "You're terrible, Buddy Bolden!" said Hattie with a blush and a flutter of lashes as she pattered down the hall, twittering like a sparrow.

Buddy closed the door carefully, knowing the alcohol in his blood might generate an unintentional slam. Turning to face Diphtheria, Buddy let his smile fade to the more correct expression of shame, his eyes pointing towards his shoes.

"Ya see, darlin'—"

"Save it, Buddy. I ain't mad. I just don't care is what." It suddenly struck her there was something different about Buddy today. It wasn't the bandage on his right temple—Buddy got into fights and had his share of drunken falls all the time. It was something else that was different. Diphtheria felt a panicked chill at the realization.

"Where's that horn of yours, Buddy?" She'd never seen him without it before. Ever since they were kids together, he'd always carried it with him.

Buddy brightened. "See, that's just it! I was getting around to that. I sold it. Sold my horn, yesiree. Big lotta loot, too. It seems I done got famous enough that it's somethin' of a collector's item. Figure I'll just buy me a new one on the cheap. I was thinking maybe you and me could take the rest of the money and we could—"

"You loved that horn, Buddy. Loved it more than me or West. Never thought you'd go and sell it." Diphtheria was genuinely impressed. Still, something didn't seem right about it. Buddy Bolden didn't just play the cornet; he played *that* cornet.

"Look, look, look," said Buddy eagerly, fishing around his pocket. After a moment he pulled out the twenty tens and proclaimed, "Two hundred dollars! Twenty dixies all told."

"Lotta money," Diphtheria conceded, losing interest quickly but feeling obligated to show some measure of enthusiasm.

"Well, sure it is, sure it is," said Buddy. "I was thinking maybe you and me could take this money and we could—"

"You and me?"

"Well…yeah, baby—you and me." He smiled that charming smile that had once melted her heart, the smile that had tricked her so thoroughly, the smile that told her *his* love was the truest love on earth, the kind of love that took hold and stayed forever, tender and reliable as any love could be. It was also the kind of smile that implied the bearer would never do a thing like grope the ass of a hooker right in front of the woman he pretended to love, a woman mourning the death of their mutual and only child. But today that treacherous, calculated smile only made Diphtheria want to burst out laughing. It seemed any power he'd had over her was gone along with the cornet.

"Mean to tell me someone paid you two hundred dollars for that beat up old thing? Surprised you got two cents." Diphtheria's tone didn't sound half as mean as she'd hoped it would.

"That's what I said, that's what I said!" Buddy held up the wad of bills like a trophy, the product of a miracle, a twist of fate designed by angels. "But it happened just the same, Lord as my witness."

"Collector's item, eh?" Diphtheria said suspiciously.

"Guess so. Must be. Two hunnert dollars' worth, leastways."

Diphtheria gave a sigh. "What you come here for? To brag about your big sale?"

"I keep trine to tell ya, Diphtheria. I got this money and I want us to make a new start. I've been makin' some good money at the Odd Fellows Hall and the Union Son's Hall too, and with this money on top, well, I figured you and me—"

"Ain't no 'you and me', Buddy."

"—figured you and me could get us a little house maybe. Start afresh. Get us some new babies. You could stop whorin'. Stop it for good this time."

"Maybe I like whorin'. This is a classy joint."

"Well, sure it is, baby. Sure it is. But whorin' is still whorin'. You know that."

"Long as I'm whorin' I don't need no man."

"Well, without men you couldn't do much whorin'. A whore needs men for customers. You need us fellas one way or the other, I guess."

"Get out."

"Baby, I'm trine to make things right. I'm a changed man, I swear it."

"Get out."

"All right, all right. No need to sour that pretty face of your'n. I'm leavin'. But before I go, how about a little lovin'? For old time sake. Who knows, mebbe we'll get lucky and make another one just like West."

Diphtheria suddenly found the energy required for long sentences: "You sicken me. You don't even bother to come to the boy's send-off, you show up here drunk as a skunk, you grope my friend's fat backside right in front of me, wave around a fistful of ten dollar bills like the King of France, then act as if the last nine years never happened. Get *out*."

"Now, look here." The charming smile, now gone. "I ain't gonna stand for that kinda talk. I'm *somebody* now. I'm an important man around—"

"Get out! Out, damn you, out!"

"Don't worry, *un petit,* I get it. Workin' girl like you don't cotton to the idea of givin' it away. Maybe you'll appreciate a little business. Well, I can pay. Don't you worry 'bout that—"

"You bastard! Leave me alone! Get out of here or I'll—"

"What? What you gonna do? Huh?"

"I'll, I'll—"

"Fancy whore like you probably gettin' two hunnert dollars a fuck anyhow. No wonder you ain't impressed." Buddy threw the twenty tens on the bed and pulled the covers off Diphtheria. She struggled, but he was stronger than she.

Yanking open his pants with one hand and pulling her nightgown up with the other, Buddy balanced his weight between straddling knees as his head pressed against the pillow blowing rye-heavy air into her eyes and nostrils. The smell of it made her queasy.

Diphtheria hit and kicked and squirmed and tried to push him off, but he only seemed energized by the struggle, by the friction of mutual rage. As he clamped his mouth over her own, she thought for sure she would throw up—but not having eaten in two days, she had nothing but dry heaves to offer. Successfully loosening a wrist from his hard grip, she grabbed a wine glass from the bedside table as he penetrated her, shattering it against the side of his head. His eyes went dead with rage as blood trickled down his cheek to the corner of his mouth. His hands slammed to her throat, his lips pulled back over clenched teeth like a mad dog. Yellow teeth, mixed with red.

The pressure against her throat intensified with each thrust of his hips; into her, into her. She felt her eyes bulge and her tongue swell as her lungs pulled for air, getting none. Her fists bounced off his shoulders and head as she twisted her body violently, thinking that in his drunken state he might lose his balance and topple to the floor—but he remained steady.

A drop of blood fell from his lower lip into her open mouth. Her mind raced. And she thought of a sailor. Diphtheria's left hand pulled at the inch and a half of hair on Buddy's head. Her right hand reached beneath the mattress.

At first she couldn't feel it—but she stretched and wiggled her fingers till she found the handle's edge. It was the same knife she'd used to deliver the sailor, back in her crib days. She'd never needed it since her arrival on Basin Street, but she'd always kept it at the ready, just in case.

Touching its handle while staring into Buddy's cold eyes made her remember—his eyes as black now as the sailor's had been then. When the sailor had come to end her life, she'd been ready to die. In that moment she'd seen the sailor as an angel of mercy, an angel come to deliver her from a miserable existence—but something had kept her from letting go. A thought or a sound had told her to use the knife. She struggled to remember what her reason had been for living then—back when things weren't nearly so bad as they were now.

*touching death with fingertips, caressing its cheek, kissing its nose, its music tick-*
*ling her ears. The music was familiar and telling, its voice gentle and firm. It was*
*the sound of Buddy's horn...*

Remembering.

Buddy had been her saving grace the night the sailor came to call. The sound
of his horn, lingering in her mind, had whispered unprovable wisdoms and
promises of love. Buddy had been her angel, not the sailor.

Buddy was her angel today, too—but a different kind.

The horn was gone now, its music too. Diphtheria could not recall a note
of it, maintained no real recollection of it whatsoever. There was no miraculous
melody left, no wisdoms or promises to give voice. Her only child was dead.
Her love all spent. But her angel had returned to deliver a final mercy.

She gave the knife handle a gentle stroke with her index finger, but left it
where it lay beneath the mattress. No longer did she struggle or pull at Buddy's
hair. Instead she caressed him, wishing he didn't look so angry, that he might
understand everything was all right.

That he might kiss her goodbye. Gently, one last time.

Unaware of her heart's acceptance, Diphtheria Morningstar's stubborn lungs
resolved to pull in one last breath.

## CHAPTER FIFTY-NINE
# Ain't Nothin' Gonna
# Be All Right

Y ou ain't got blood. *I* got blood. Think you got blood? Shit, son. You ain't got no dang blood a'tall. Lemme show you blood. *This* is blood.

Reckoned on buttin' in at this point onna counta that latest revelation, the one mighta ledda slow thinkin' indy-vigil like yerself to believe everything gonna be all right, gonna be all-*RIGHT*; everything gone be just fine. Shit, Dear Reader, you ain't smelt the smallest trace o' real blood in yer whole damned, insignificant, safe little life. Lickity splat sippity sap is what. Thinkin' you want some blood, thinkin' readin' a book like this some kinda fun, thinkin' a good violent fiction a good way to let off some steam without no one gettin' hurt. Thinkin' you *got* it, thinkin' you *want* it. Well, you ain't got *shit*. *I got it.* You ain't got even the slightest clue 'bout what you do really want a'tall. No-siree. Here's one tiny fact for you to chew on a while: What I got you don't want, believe you me.

And ain't *nothin'* gonna be all right, Sunny-Jim.

This is blood. Real blood, sad blood, bad blood, sticky blood, hot blood, solidifying, putrefying, brownin'-like-liver-puddin'-blood, stinkin'-still-thinkin'-blood, kill-leakin' blood, coolin' and foolin', from a prick, from a nip, from a cut, from tear, from a slash, from rip, from a pull, from a lever to a sever frumma lumma lip lap flip flap fog, frumma-lumma-ding-dong mudfish blud-fish BLOOD.

Wanna revlation? Here's a revelation for ya, so listen up:

Walked inna my own dang house early this morning, so early the sun weren't even up yet. And there's mama, hippity bop, not even in bed like she should, lookin' all rumpled-up-like inna sleepin' gown, hair aint' fixed er nothin'. Now, this ain't like mama a'tall.

"Where ya been?" say she, eyeballin' the horn in my right mitt with something suspiciously akin to suspicion.

Now, the question strike me funny onna-counta I been gone just two days—and there been times I been gone two weeks'r better. So what? Mama learned all about my freewheelin' ways a long licka-wicka time ago, learned ta 'cept my ways I figgered then, and thought I'd figgered true. So I just stare in wide-eyed-wonder 'bout now, trine to figger where she got the nerve, where she got the gumption.

"Where ya been?" she say again, but extra stern-like this time. Zippity-pah, think me, still a-wonderin' bout that look in her eye, that suspicious look, that look what say I gotta answer her when she know damn right and well I don't *do* no damn answerin'. Not fer her ner no one else; just like it is and always been.

"Where ya been?" say she again. Tar-nation, think me.

"Well, Ma, ya see…" I start off, shocked and amazed at the quiver in my own voice, like I can't handle the old woman, like I might even feel the slightest shame about things I mighta done, like I'm some kinda stupid little kid what's afraid of a spankin'. Like I'm as lowdown and snivelin' as that dead little nigger, Baby Bolden.

"Tell me where ya been," she say some more. "Tell me now and don't lie," she tack on fer good measure, her eyes shiftin' hither and thither between my own shiftin' eyes and that horn in my hand.

"Just been out takin' care of business like always, Mama," say me. "Someone gotta work 'round here, y'know." I'm shocked times two by my own words and tone o'voice—that I would even entertain a notion of lettin' the old woman have some kinda upper hand in this or any damn sitchy-ation. Tar-nation times *three* is what.

"I spoke with your father," say she. "He told me. He told me what you done," she say some more. "He's sad and concerned, and so am I."

"Daddy died long time ago," say me. "You know that, Ma. This just crazy talk."

"He told me. It was in a dream, but it was the real kind, the kind that means something. He said you'd know what I mean about *WHAT YOU DONE*." Full on shriekin'. This ain't like mama a'tall. Not one itty titty bit it ain't.

"Crazy talk, Ma." I say this even though the very mention of Daddy set my chest to tinglin'. I don't have ta look to know the scar-shaped-lika-hand on my chesty is burning bright red. I keep playin' dumb, checking for angles like always, then go on ahead with:

"What Daddy say I do, anyhoo?"

She don't hesitate: "That boy Dropsy didn't kill that little kid. Not really. You put murder in motion. More murder than just that one, too. Killed that boy's mama in a roundabout way as well. Makin' people crazy, makin' people dead. All by your hand. This is what you done, what you do, what you're gonna do. Lots more to come, your Daddy says, if I don't help you. Dominick—"

Then I realize she ain't talkin' right. Ain't her voice entirely. Not much Eye-talian in it, talkin' somewhere between a nigger and a country cracker. And she know better than to call me by that dang 'talian name. I trained her to call me Jim long ago—and trained her right, or so I thought. Then I see her eyes ain't right neither. Ain't green no more but brown. I'm thinkin' maybe the lamp-light playin' tricks, but also too: I know it ain't. Ain't right. I look in those eyes hard. Then I see. I wanna run but my legs is froze.

Yeah, I got blood. Shit, yeah, I got it. Plenty, too. More'n what I ever thunk possible.

Mama get up and put herself 'tween me and the door. Start talkin' in that voice ain't quite hers, but soundin' familiar just the same:

"Hast thou come to kiss this child? I will not let thee kiss him," say she.

Ain't right; no, no, no. These words comin' outta her I heard somewheres before—though I can't rightly place em in my mind, but something else in me seemin' to place em just fine. There's a tightenin' in my chest as the burn of the hand-scar gettin' hotter. Feels like my heart compressin', turnin' in on itself, fillin' my lungs with somethin' heavy like water. Gettin' hard to breathe. "Stop it, ma. Yer hurtin' me some kinda way. Cain't breathe right," I say, sick at the sound of beggin' in my own voice. I'm scared but also mad; I don't care *whose* mama she is, she cain't get away with this, no way, no how. Just who in fuck she think she is, anyhoo? Talkin' to me in such a way like that. Shimina-fap is what. Times three or better no less.

"Hast thou come to send him to sleep? I will not let thee do him harm," say she.

Times five at *least*, goddamny if she ain't done it again! Done it again right even though I asked her kindly not to, and me her own flesh and blood, her one and only son. Now the tightenin' in my ribs turn from discomfort to true pain, like hard cold, fingers around my heart squeezing the life out. There's sweat on my face and in my eyes, the scar of my chest puffin' and pulsatin', moist and hot, my knees gone wobbly and unsure, I'm losin' my dern legs, my mind feelin' something like guilt and remorse though I can't say exactly why. My legs is goin', I feel like I'm gonna fall, so I find an angle and work it fast—I fall, but fall *forwards* and not back; straight into Mama. I lift my arm up to twist side-ways as I go—so's not to bang that pretty horn agen' the hard, dirty ground.

Knock her in the knees, make her legs go out from under. She go down hard and I roll atop cross her midsection, my back across her ribs, my left hand hooked from behind her knees, pulling up, my right arm swinging up with the horn, then come down quick, landing an elbow into her mouth—just like I done that dog in the alley. I hear a crackle at the impact, supposin' it's the sound of her old jaw crumbling, maybe some teeth cracking and snapping loose. Raise my arm again, then down; let my elbow smash her mouth again, again, agenna-genna-genna-gen. I can't see her face from this angle. I feel her legs go limp and I let em drop. I re-adjust myself to sittin' on top'er now, straddlin' lika bully onna schoolyard grounds. Huffin' and puffin, still feelin' pain around my heart but focused on other things in the immediate here and now. I look down at her, the lower part of her face is ruined; jaw shattered to pulp, hanging wide open. I see yellow cracked teeth on her tongue and down her throat, sharp and jagged, waiting for her to swallow if she dare. Her nose is flattened and bleeding bad, but her eyes look just fine—fine except fer the fear. I feel wet heat on my cheeks, figure out I'm cryin'—this fact just makin' me madder all the more. Just who in hell she think she is makin' a fella cry, her own flesh and blood, no less? Not to mention all the sacrifice I done fer the gooda mankind, only to take it up the backside without so much as a single "thankee kindly, mister," attacked with sticks and nails by a buncha mad dogs dressed in fancy sheets. If I'm so allfired ornery, well, hell, ain't I got the right ta be, all things considered? On the bright side, I'm thinkin', leastways she won't be sayin' no more words. At least I got that one little fact on my side. Right?

"Hast thou come to take him away? I will not let thee carry him away," say she.

God*damn* if she ain't *still* talkin' at me, not with her mouth but with her EYES fer the luvva Pete! Loud and clear, speakin' in my head, right at me, right in me. The hand in my heart is squeezin' so tight now I can taste blood on my tongue, blood comin' up and outta me. I'm scared—more scared than I ever been, but also I'm mad; madder'n hell. I hear a sound like a roar, deep and terrible, louder'n a lion, and the vibration in my gums tells me the sound come outta *me*. Well, god*damn*.

Next thing I know, my thumbs'r over her eyes, pushin' all the way in past the knuckle. She could fight me, but don't—her arms lying limp at her sides. My thumbs go in, then scoop out. The bloody mess in my hands is a terrible thing, even for a buddy-boy like me with an odd attraction to terrible things. I wiggle my fingers fast and furious in the air till the smashed eye-stuff shake loose lika flyin' drizzle. I feel a misty spray on my cheek, wipe my hands off on my shirt.

Some of the blood done soaked straight through the shirt, but when the blood touch my burning scar, the blood feels *good* there—like some kinda travelin'-sideshow-instant-re-actin'-miracle-makin'-snake-oil-shakin'-tonic. I tear open the shirt to smear more blood over the hand-scar; feels good, real dang good. But ain't enough. Need more blood. I put my hands together into a single fist, bring the whole thing down into what's left of her face; again, again, agenna-genna-genna. The shards of her skull nip at the heels of my hands, makin' little cuts, minglin' our blood together inna pointless pact. When the blood stops gushin' I realize my mama livin' no more. I tear my shirt off altogether, scoop her blood up and onto me (as much as I kin hold), spreadin' it all over. I roll in it; tis a wonderful feeling, this stuff. This blood.

*This* is blood.

*I* got blood.

You ain't got shit, mister. Ain't never seen nor smelt such a thing, I'd wager. And never will if yer lucky.

Now I'm feelin' right again—but just look at this damn mess. No way I'm cleanin' this up, but cain't just leave it for the coppers ta see. I strip down nekkid, wash my body by the basin with a bucket and a raggedy linen white, wash myself off real good, me. My skin tingles as the blood come off inna water, there's a sweet dang sadness in such parting of skin and blood, mother and son—sentimental fella that I am. I change my clothes with a lonely little tear in my right eyeball. Pick up Buddy Bolden's horn. Figger I ain't got time to wipe the blood spatters off the horn, but there ain't much on it really and I can get that done later on, take it to the river for a dip and a wipe down like I done with Buddy's blood. I wrap the horn in a small white blanket my dead mama used to wrap me in when I was a baby.

Sentimental fella that I am.

Kind of amazin', me rememberin' things all the way back from when I was a baby, things like that blanket—but I remember it loud and clear like it was only yesterday. Mama always said I was an amazin' child. Reckon she right on that, too.

Then I get dressed in clean clothes, light the match, do the deed, and git gone.

Nothing cleans up a house like a good housefire, is what.

I.

Say.

What I say, Jim.

*Sunny, Sunny Jim.*

# CHAPTER SIXTY
## *A Contrast of Hands*

The mind of Malvina Latour had been in steady decline for better than two decades now, its process of deterioration having integrated itself into her daily routine. Recent events passed through her head like a sieve and lately she'd found herself mostly unable to form clear thoughts of any kind. Being aware of such weakness failed to distress her, though, for she found comfort in the night.

In dreams, she was vibrant and young, her mind sharp and clear. In dreams, she was not a doddering old woman who babbled endlessly and bitterly about shoes left in the middle of the damn floor. While asleep, all was right and peaceful. All this had been so—until Coco Robicheaux had come to call.

Since the coming of Coco Robicheaux her nights had brought only dread, the vivid calm of dreams stained by something dark and deathly. A ghostly thing had invaded her dreams, never far off but never too near—getting nearer with each night.

*Coco Robicheaux.* His presence had become so strong that she now felt him even while awake—as a wisp of smoke encircling her heart, a noose slowly tightening. She didn't know what he wanted, but she knew he was coming for her.

Tonight as she drifted off to sleep a heavy sense of dread fell—something like a premonition of her own death. She might have snapped awake had the dread evolved to fear, but the sensation of it had left her remarkably unafraid. Though dread and fear are often mistaken for one another, they are hardly the same thing. She dissolved into sleep with a thin smile on her lips as she let the dream take her.

§

The thin smile remains as she walks. She is walking now as she always does in dreams, at the bottom of a river. The object of her dreams, she believes, is to find *Manman Brigitte,* her spiritual mother, her personal *met tet.* It's a journey that has yielded not one clue, but a journey full of wonder and gorgeous mystery. To Malvina Latour it is the mystery of a poem constructed by angels.

There is no perceptible current this far below the surface; Malvina moves easily, only remotely aware of the tons of water surrounding her, pushing down from above, reducing far away sunlight to luminescent brown, caressing her skin and causing her thick black hair to drift wildly about her eyes. She is strong in the dream; her joints do not ache, she is not short of breath, her back is straight and absent of pain, her head is held high and proud. She is beautiful in the dream; her skin is a glowing and fair tan, her breasts are firm, her stomach flat, and her eyes as bewitching as they'd been in her youth.

Suddenly she falls, landing softly on palms and knees. Her head turns to investigate what she's tripped over.

Shoes.

*In my damn way...*

Dread and fear become one. This is not right, this cannot be. Mundane realities like this are not allowed in dreams. There are no misplaced shoes here, no regret, no betrayal, no guilt, no pain, no pain, no pain...

Not allowed, not here. There is music now. She hears music; tinny and fine, joyous and troubling. Wisps of red and orange weave through the brown of deep river before her eyes: a subtle invasion. The wisps move easily but there's anger in their movement, they are cool liquid fire. They petition her to remember things that have no business here, things not allowed in sweet dreams of night.

She means to get to her feet, she means to run, she means to wake, she means to leave—but the river floor is soft, slippery, treacherous and she cannot rise up. There is pain in her joints, her legs and back become racked with creaking misery, she can't catch her breath. She notes the thick, flowing black hair so recently dancing around her eyes is now wispy and white. She wishes to sink into the river floor; disappear, be gone. She is ready.

She will not be waking up. This is Coco Robicheaux's doing. He is, she presumes, the thing she'd called into the world on that black night so many years ago. And now, after a lifetime of anguish and regret, he has finally come to thank her with his cold touch. *Manman Brigitte* had been wrong; pain has healed no one, no one has done right by anyone, there is no saving grace. Promises were made but not honored, only bad things truly are.

Her eyes close tight.

There's a hand on her forearm, lifting upward, its grip gentle.

"Mother?" she asks in her mind, with eyes still closed, praying her search might be over, that questions might be answered, that an end might be near. She hears only a laugh in return. A deep, male laugh.

"Nope. Ain't nobody's mama, and that's fer sure."

The voice sounds kind, but Malvina learned long ago not to trust untested impressions. She'd been tricked many times by kind voices in her life, had even tricked a few people with similar deceits of her own.

"Kill me then. I know who you are, Coco Robicheaux. Know why ya come. Get it over with and be done with me." She pushes herself up on trembling legs, her free hand covering her eyes, not wanting to see the demon's eyeless face so close. Not wanting to see him at all.

Another gentle laugh. "Open your eyes, little mother. Probably not who you think, mayhap. I mean you no harm."

"I ain't afraid of you, trickster." Defiance.

"Well, if yer so all-fired brave then look at me already. I ain't as ugly as all that, now. Keep it up and you'll wind up hurting a person's feelings."

Malvina takes one quick step back before removing her hand from her eyes. The man only smiles at her, hands in pockets. Not a bad looking man, this Coco Robicheaux demon. Her eyes widen with recognition.

"I know you," she says.

"Mebbe so, mebbe so," says the man who is not Coco Robicheaux. "Who might I be, then?"

Malvina crinkles her brow. "Can't be who I think—bein' that somebody's long dead."

"Talk sense, old woman," the man says impatiently. "You are of the understanding that this is a dream, ain't that right?"

"Well, yes. I mean it would have to be. We're under water for Pete's sake."

"Well, then. Why would it trouble you to know I *am* dead? Why not talk to a dead man in a dream? Folks do it alla time—ain't that right?"

Malvina takes a cautious step forward. "Well, of course they do. But it's just that…"

"Yes?"

"Well, you look so…so…*solid.*"

"That be so, dear. In this place I'm plenty real. Realer than you, statement of fact. Looky here…" The man holds his hand out towards Malvina. The warmth of his voice tells her it's all right, and she places her hand in his.

"See that?" says the man.

Malvina stares at their clasped hands. His hand is solid, firm and opaque—her own is…not quite there. Transparent by comparison. "Well, I'll be…"

"Interesting, wouldn't you say, dear?" There's warmth in his touch, and he gives her hand a squeeze. "You see, things ain't exactly how you might think 'round here."

"How so?" Malvina is still eyeing the contrast of hands.

"Rationally, you'd think since I'm the one dead, that I'd be the ghost here. Well, that would be true in your waking world, but this ain't no air-breathing, hard-living world we're in at the moment. This is the Spiritworld. And in the Spiritworld, it's the spirits who are solid and real. When living folks show up, it's they who are ghosts. That's because they're not really here. They visit this place only when they dream."

"I'm a ghost?" says Malvina, organizing her thoughts.

"Down here, yes." The man's answer is firm.

"So…you're just a real live dead man talking to a living ghost?"

"Ha! Ain't quite thought of it that way," he laughs.

Malvina is smiling now. "I'm sorry I never got to know you better while we was both living, Noonday."

"That's all right, Malvina. We traveled in diffn't circles, you and me. Me bein' a Christian and you bein' a hoodoo mambo and all. Wasn't till I passed on that I realized it's all part of one big circle after all."

"Well, there are similarities," Malvina doesn't quite follow Noonday's meaning.

"No, not similarities. It's the *same*." He looks at her directly, but she is looking past him.

Her eyes have wandered about ten yards beyond the spot where he stands; there is a man and a boy there, they are playing. The boy is on his knees, stacking innumerable buttons into clever, intricate, and recognizable structures; a chapel, a plantation house, an automobile with wheels that turn—all made from various buttons of stone, metal, cloth, and wood. The man laughs and jumps, shadow-boxing near the perfectly balanced button-structures, pulling his punches just short of toppling them over. The boy looks mildly annoyed but grins as the man skillfully endangers but never destroys.

A beautiful young coffee-skinned woman watches the two play; her sweet smile dances below troubled eyes. The boxing man is her brother, the young boy her only child—both having been so devastatingly lost to her; and now: so wondrously found. Still, her eyes speak of a deep hole that remains unfilled. Someone important is missing—the love of her life. A vivid memory of her lover's eyes—boring into her own in her moment of dying, angry and hurt— weighs heavy on her soul. She bears him no ill will for having removed her from the world of the living, for having murdered her—only wants for him to rejoin her and their child, to see that everything will be all right and always has been. It is not yet his time, she understands. He has a certain penance to pay above before he can be received below. Such effortless wisdom and spiritual clarity are newly acquired by Diphtheria in death. They do little to ease her longing—but she allows herself comfort in the knowing. In the Spiritworld there is a different kind of faith; and that is the blind, baseless belief that the living will somehow, and against all odds, find their way to redemption.

"I know these two," Malvina says, pointing towards the man and boy. "These faces I know." Malvina is trying to place them in her mind. "They're beautiful."

"Thank you, dear. They're my kin. My youngest son and my only grandson. Dropsy and West. And the pretty young lady is my daughter, Diphtheria."

"Of course they are," she says with a smile. "But why here? They all so young—"

"Miss Malvina, I'd like you to meet my oldest son, Typhus," he interrupts. "Today is his first day in this place. And I've got a special surprise waiting on him—just like the surprise I got for you a bit later on."

"We've met," Typhus says with a cautious smile. "In the shop. Miss Malvina comes in regular."

"Hello, Typhus," says Malvina, unable to pull her gaze from the amazing button structures of West Bolden. "Can this be?" Her eyes are full of wonder.

"Now comes the good part, and I'm glad you could be here to bear witness. It is a moment my family has long waited on." Noonday has fixed his stare on a swirl of motion from a nearing river cloud, his eyes brightening steadily. "And there she is, the one and only love of my life."

"Typhus," a breathless female voice can be heard. "Typhus, come here to me."

Typhus' eyes go wide. His freshly unencumbered heart is melting fast.

A woman is walking towards them from the murk, her arms extended.

"Mama?" It's the first time the word has ever passed his lips in the presence of the woman it was made for, but it won't be the last, not by far.

The woman Typhus has only known as Lily for so many years is smiling at him, her deep brown eyes clouding the water about her drifting hair with trails of lilac tears.

"As beautiful a sight as I've ever seen," says Malvina, enjoying the spectacle of mother and son united in death. Then, in a whisper; "Noonday, how did Typhus die? I didn't even know he was sick."

"Wasn't sick a'tall. I killed him myself, just this morning." Noonday says this with a tone of fatherly pride that Malvina finds both distasteful and inappropriate. He ignores her reprimanding stare and continues: "Now, just look at them. Both dead, both happy." His voice takes on the rhythm of a sermon: *"So long in pain before today. No more, no more; Praise Jesus, no more, and amen!"*

"It's wrong to kill children, sir," Malvina scolds. "If that's really what you done."

"Surely it is," Noonday concedes. "But he was nearly dead already, I just guided him that last little bit. Long story. Tell ya all about it later, sister—if ya don't mind. Lots of time later, not much now."

Malvina tightens her face, never having cared for backtalk (much less shushing) from a person so much younger than herself. Noonday just smiles, takes her again by the hand, leading her past Typhus and the beautiful woman whose name is Gloria and not Lily, into a thick of gathering light. Malvina's mind fills with uneasy questions as they walk past the night's first reunion, recalling recent feelings of premonition. "Something bad gonna happen, Noonday. I just don't know what."

He squeezes her hand once more. "Now, whatever may come will do so on its own steam, and that don't necessarily reflect on you or me or things we mighta done in our past and above water. Plenty of blame to pass around. Ain't no one innocent here." His smile fades. "Don't be afraid ner concerned, but I want you to come with me."

"Where to?"

"Some folks been waitin' on ya. Be glad to see you, too. See if we can't straighten out all this fear and bad feelin'." A pause. "See if we can't make things right once and for all."

"What folks?"

"Will o' the Wisps." Noonday Morningstar looks down, slips his naked feet into the two shoes that had caused Malvina to fall. He places an arm around her trembling, transparent shoulders. "Just come along. You'll see."

The two walk forward into murky brown, towards a blue ball of light, a will o' the wisp. As they get closer the light takes on the shape of a woman. Long dead, the woman is not a ghost in this place.

# CHAPTER SIXTY-ONE
## *Spiritworld*

"**M**aria?"

"Hello, Auntie," replies the slender young mulatto woman. She is cradling a small, white blanket in her hands—it is empty and unsoiled. Malvina has seen this blanket before.

"Child, child, I can hardly believe my own eyes." Malvina is seeing and speaking with her long dead niece, her sister Frances' lost child. Her heart is booming.

"Why so hard to believe? For you this is a dream."

"But it isn't," Malvina says.

"I have to go." Maria averts her eyes as she speaks.

"Don't go, Maria. Stay and talk with me awhile. There's so much I want to, that I need to—"

"I lost my baby, Auntie Malvina. Michael's his name."

"I know his name, Maria—"

"Have to find him. Have to go now." Maria backs away, then turns—walks off into the thick brown of river.

"Let me help you," Malvina pleads, moving to follow—but Noonday puts a firm hand on her shoulder, holds her steady.

"Let her go. She'll be all right. This is something she needs to do. A pain she needs to feel."

"But it's my fault…" Malvina says weakly, just loud enough for Maria to hear.

Maria stops in her tracks, turns to face Malvina before going further. "No," she says with conviction. "No, it isn't your fault."

"But Maria, please," Malvina says. "What do I do? What do I say to your mama? What should I tell her?"

Maria's expression is a mixture of exhaustion and resolve. "Tell her to come home. Tell her she needs to come home."

Maria steps away quickly, her hands clutching the blanket tightly, disappearing completely in the murk. Malvina's knees go rubbery with grief.

"So many things," Noonday explains, "will not make sense to you in the Spiritworld. Not while you're just visiting. But when you belong, your questions will be fewer, much fewer."

"I don't understand. I don't *want* to understand."

"Shh. Come. There's someone else you need to see. Someone to make things right in your heart."

He takes her hand and leads her towards a blue ball of light in the distance. Blue with a halo of red.

# CHAPTER SIXTY-TWO

## *Rhythm Found*

"Malvina tries to wish herself awake, "wake up, wake up, wake up," she chants aloud. Noonday strokes her shoulder, but offers no comforting words, says only: "Stop that. Look at him. What do you see?"

Forcing herself to calm, she looks, sees, then speaks;

"He's transparent. Like me." Her heart fills with irrational relief.

"Yes, but not for long."

"He's dying."

"In your world, he's dying. Here, he is being born."

The dying man falls to his knees. His eyes widen and blink. His hair is long and wild, his clothes are tatters. This is the Coco Robicheaux of Malvina's dreams—but in the dream he has no eyes. This creature's eyes are kind and soft.

When his eyes meet her own, everything changes.

These eyes she once knew, long ago and not in dreams. These eyes she had once loved.

Malvina remembers.

The beautiful boy who Malvina Latour had loved when she was a young girl was a free man of color. The boy had returned her love in kind, had brought her the greatest joy of her life. But when she'd found herself heavy with child, the boy had disappeared, as tender loving, beautiful young boys often do. She carried the child to term, had seen him through the agony of birth—but shortly after the child's arrival she found herself unable to provide for him. She had brought her child, a son, to the steps of a Christian church—with a note pinned to his perfect, white blanket:

"Please help my boy. I cannot care for him."

She had lingered on those steps, his little hand encasing her thumb, pressing firmly, his dark brown eyes looking into her own. So trusting, so assured by her presence. Those eyes, those little brown eyes. She sang to him softly,

*Mo pap li couri la riviere,*
*Mo maman li couri peche crab*

She'd hoped he would fall asleep before the time came for her to leave him, so that their parting might not be too painful. But her song had been too loud, had triggered footfalls from inside the church. With an acute agony of the soul, Malvina roughly pulled the boy's hand from her thumb and ran to the safety of shadows. The sound of his cries pierced the night, pierced her heart. She sat and listened as a stern female voice called out to her:

"Come out and be seen! I know you're there! I can hear you!"

Malvina didn't answer, couldn't answer. The wails of her son became muffled as the woman took him inside, away from her forever.

§

*Now.*

Here are those same eyes. Bigger, sadder, wizened, older.

"Thomas?" she asks, using the name she'd given him on the day of his birth.

The man remains on bended knee, no longer transparent, still staring. "They call me Beauregard now," he says at last.

"I'm so, so sorry," she says, then adding softly, "Beauregard."

Beauregard stands, walks to her as quickly as he is able, takes her in his arms. "I love you, Mama," he says simply. "It's all right now. Everything is all right. Everything is as it should, and always has been."

Malvina whispers in the ear of her child, her son, her divine burden, "I have to leave you once more, my Beauregard, my love. But I will be back very soon. There's something I have to do above water. Something I need to finish."

"I know." Beauregard is smiling.

"Someone I need to say goodbye to," she amends.

"Perhaps," interrupts Noonday Morningstar, "'goodbye' is not the correct word at all. Perhaps the word you've been searching for all this time has been *hello.*" The holy man's grin is a wild thing. "Just a thought. Hurry back, now."

# CHAPTER SIXTY-THREE
## *Malvina's Cure*

**M**alvina's first thought upon waking was that she'd forgotten to wind her clock. If the time it told was true, then she had slept in several hours past daybreak—a nearly unheard of luxury she'd not experienced in half a century.

Frances never allowed her such luxuries; always rising early with loud complaints, slamming doors and kitchen cabinets for maximum effect, doing everything she could to disturb Malvina's rest. Out of spite—or so it seemed, or so apparent, or so was.

But this morning the curtains remained drawn, allowing only a single crack of light to pierce the warm dark of Malvina's small bedroom. Pulling her old bones into a sitting position, Malvina flopped her feet to the floor with twin thumps. Instinctively, she kicked both feet forward before attempting to stand, then hissed as she'd hissed every morning for the last fifty-three years:

"Damn shoes."

But her feet only kicked warm air, no shoes in her way on this morning. She squinted at the shadows, then squinted hard into the useless crack of light. Got to her feet, then yanked open the curtain to let the sun pour in.

No shoes. None. The floor was clear. This was very odd. Fifty-three years of tripping over her sister's shoes, placed maliciously, or so it seemed (or so apparent, or so was), underfoot in such a haphazard way—but suddenly today: Nothing.

*Well, good Lord,* thought Malvina, *what on earth has gotten into that old woman to make her come around pickin' up those damn shoes now, right out of the blue and without warning?*

There was something downright eerie about it. She almost called out her sister's name—but that would be giving in. After fifty-three years of noisy silence she would be damned before calling uncle over a little thing like this. It was likely just a sign of Frances' own mental deterioration; forgetting to remember to forget. In any case, Malvina was sure the problem would begin afresh on the morrow, shoes every-damn-where as usual. This unexpected bout of neatness was probably just a tease to punctuate what she'd be missing for the rest of her days. Days of tripping and cursing over those damn shoes. A dangerous thing at her age. Attempted murder, almost.

Malvina looked at the door to her sister's room. Closed. There was a large basket near the door, a basket that had stood empty so long she'd forgotten its original assigned purpose. But the basket was informative today, different today, serving its assigned purpose today. The basket was full.

Shoes. Damn shoes.

Curiously, the sight of it made Malvina want to cry. Sometimes the simplest changes can bring about strange emotional reactions in dotty old women with deteriorating brains, she assured herself. Changes. Little changes. No such thing as little changes at this age.

Malvina cursed herself upon realization of her trembling knees, then got up to make her way carefully to the rocker by the window. Was looking to be a right sunny day, she guessed; a hot one, too. She bent down to pick up the needles and yarn kept atop the knitting bag near the rocker and resumed work on a blue patch she'd started last night; a square that was to be one of many, ninety-nine all told by the time she was finished. Squares that would join together to form a blanket in a week's time, a blanket she didn't need and had no one to give as present. Doing the work calmed her nerves. That was its purpose. Took her mind off the shoes. And now: The odd *lack* of shoes.

Malvina didn't hear her sister's door creak open, but shoes did appear in the corner of her eye. Shoes with feet in them. Malvina looked up.

The eyes of the two sisters met then—the first time they'd done so in a very long time. Frances' face was smoother than it ought to be for a woman so old, but more weathered than Malvina ever remembered it being. Her eyes looked tired to Malvina—not just tired, but troubled. Maybe angry. Or maybe neither, but something else with a smidgen of multiple others whirling about.

Malvina wanted to speak but didn't. Neither did she look away.

"Put down that knittin', old woman," said Frances Latour. Malvina was so taken aback by the simple directness of the statement that she complied without thinking. It was Frances who'd cried uncle by speaking first, and Malvina felt sudden remorse that she had not done so herself.

Frances lifted a hand, then the other. There was something different about the hands, different but familiar. Something Malvina had seen or heard in a dream, now forgotten—but not forgotten....

*a contrast of hands*

The hands reached up to Malvina's throat.

If her sister meant to kill her, Malvina would not stop her—she was ready. There *had* been a dream, one of Coco Robicheaux—but not like the ones before. Fragments of dream-memory struggled at the edge of her mind, fragments meant to remind her of something good awaiting her in death. She wasn't sure what, couldn't recall what had been seen or shown in the dream, but she knew her sense of it was true. More importantly, she *believed* it was true. It was her first experience with real, unquestioning faith. Not such a leap, she thought, to have faith when you're so old as to have nothing left to lose.

She doubted Frances even had the strength to strangle her or break her neck or do whatever it was she intended to do with those hands. *Find out soon enough,* she thought to herself. *Soon enough, soon enough.*

But the hands of Frances Latour slipped past Malvina's throat. Past and around, fingers interlacing behind Malvina's neck. Frances lifted a leg onto her sister's lap, then pulled herself the rest of the way up, resting her head against Malvina's bony shoulder with a sigh. Malvina placed her own arms around her sister's thin waist, holding her tightly as her own eyes filled with water.

Malvina rocked Frances gently, effortlessly. Frances' weight was insubstantial and caused Malvina no discomfort.

This was peace.

And with peace comes answers; and such answers are of sweet dreams, but not of dreams. The answers are only lost memories, recalled at last.

In this moment she sees clearly the sum of her life and of things that come after, the good and the bad of it all. A light shines on consequence both past and yet suffered, some near at hand and some farther along. Manman Brigitte has seen her through this journey in her roundabout and mysterious way, though the cost has been dear and the penance hard. There are trials still to come above ground, larger ones in which waters of green and brown must rear up to reclaim and cleanse through destruction for sake of new birth, to set things right by hammering down wrong, to reinvigorate the living through cruelty of death. She knows that a greater peace will come to those who survive the coming of deathly tide and for those who follow after, but first, but first...

Remembering: A message to deliver.

*"Un petit,"* Malvina says to her sister, her daughter by default and by proxy. "It's time for you to go home now. Someone been waitin' on you. Someone you been waitin' on, too." She considers before adding: "And someone waitin' on me, too." There is joy in the realization.

"Time for us to get on now." She feels Frances tremble in her arms, just as she'd trembled in her arms as a small child so many years ago. Frightened of the dark, of things unknown. "Shhhh," coos Malvina. "None of that, now. I'll be with you shortly. That's a promise, and one I intend to keep."

A whisper in return:

*"Chanson tanpri, Mer?"*

Malvina holds Frances ever tighter, stroking her sister's hair as she sings:

*Mo pap li couri la riviere,*
*Mo maman li couri peche crab*
*Dodo, mo fille, crab dans calalou*
*Dodo, mo fille, crab dans calalou*

# CHAPTER SIXTY-FOUR
## *The Sound of Building Coffins*

In all his years on this earth, Marcus Nobody Special could not remember a more beautiful sunrise.

Deep orange clouds hung low in a frozen swirl to the east, with elaborate spatters flung overhead like wisps of disembodied flame, the sky itself bruised and yellow in streaks as if from the brush of a brilliant madman. The swirl of clouds did not look natural to Marcus, or perhaps looked too natural.

*As natural as the hammer of God?*

He pondered the question mightily and continued to do so until a sudden tug at his fishing line gave him a start. *Getting jumpy in my old age,* he thought. *"Trouble comin'*," he said aloud.

Marcus was suddenly aware of the sound of hammering, relentless and orderly as it echoed off the water from both sides of the river, combining into an uneasy rhythm, somehow familiar—

*Bap. Bap-bap. Buh-bap, bap, buh-bap.*

—and that rhythm caused his heart to sink. He knew it was only the sound of concerned fathers and husbands nailing boards over glass windowpanes, but to his tormented imagination it was the sound of building coffins.

He fixed his gaze purposefully on the salient clouds, paying no mind to the gentle but urgent activity at the other end of his fishing line. Just then, a wind began. The speed and force of it was mild like a breeze, but there was a heavy firmness to it, a certain change in atmosphere heralded by it, a change in the air itself associated with it. An electricity. A static warmth. It felt good on his cheek, like a mother's caress.

"Trouble comin'. Lord, Lord."

Time to move on. He had to get back to the potter's field and make certain preparations. The tug at his line urged him to stay; just for a little while, just long enough to reel it in and have a look, check to see if it was his fish. After all these years he knew the possibility was slight. But there was still the possibility.

He pulled a small knife from his hip pocket and cut the line. "Sorry, son, if that's you. Gotta go tend yer ma now. Gotta make sure she stay put if the water come." A pause and a sniff. "Can't risk losing you both." The fish dived down deep with Marcus' hook still in its mouth, the cut line trailing behind it like an endless tail.

When Marcus was a young man, before the War of the States, he'd seen his first flood in the Parish. The dead had risen that time—he among them—and for once the resurrection of water had been a blessing, not a curse. This time there would be no blessing. Today and tomorrow the dead must stay down. If not all, then at least one. He must tend to Maria's grave, the mother of his only child. He must be there for her as she had been for him.

Marcus Nobody Special walked as briskly as his old legs would carry him towards the cemetery, his head hung low with worry. The storm was coming up fast with the rising sun, the wind gaining enough force that he nearly took a tumble once or twice along the way. By tomorrow afternoon, he reckoned, this city might be a different place altogether. By tomorrow evening, he reckoned, this place might be gone. When he reached the cemetery's lip he tipped his head to take one last glance at the sky. The strange turnings of his mind had melted the clouds into a screaming mouth—but no scream issued from its center, just the gentle hum of steady wind from all around.

And the sound of hammering.

§

Before the troubles, Malaria Morningstar had prided herself on being an early riser. Before the troubles, she'd witnessed each and every sunrise, had watched every morning fog lift with the rising sun. These were not things she missed now that she had discovered the drink.

The drink had turned her routine on its head—late to bed, late to rise. But also, the drink had protected her from the treacherous workings of her own mind. So much had been lost in one week, her family now removed from her completely. It was just too much.

Nearly noon, she stepped outside to discover a thick gray sky that retained a dim swath of orange; a gentle reminder of past sunrises, of who she once was. The same sky that had been wild and beautiful in the eyes of Marcus Nobody Special was unremarkable to her own—the inoffensive hue of an old dirty peach. What she did find remarkable was that the fog had remained kissing swamp so late in the morning, silently and stubbornly unlifted. The air was warm and moist against her skin, but she felt a dry chill. There'd been a time not long ago that she'd wished for a morning like this to come along; a morning that would begin a series of new and different mornings, no morning ever again the same—and she'd imagined that such a morning would be marked by unlifted fog. She shook the thought from her mind and went back inside.

The home she'd loved all her life had acquired new weight in recent days that now pressed down hard upon her soul, and so she found herself frequently leaving early for work; parking herself downstairs at the Eagle Saloon for long afternoons, sipping short glasses of rye till five o'clock rolled around and her shift upstairs at Odd Fellows began.

Today would be no different. She methodically folded and placed her work clothes in a canvas sack—short red dress, black high heels, a pair of six dollar stockings (one of nine pairs left behind at the Arlington House by Diphtheria)—-then put on her mud-walking boots and left for the district, trudging through muck and unlifted fog, focused only on the thought of how wonderful the touch of a glass to her lips would feel once inside the bar.

She did not make note of static wind that scattered and swept away settled fog behind her as she walked, a wind that would soon erase everything she had ever known.

# CHAPTER SIXTY-FIVE
## *Keep My Baby Down*

I t was too late for Marcus to reinforce the brickwork covering Maria's grave. The mortar of it had long since crumbled in places, many bricks loosened by time and a few missing altogether. He had some supplies stored in the small caretaker's shack at the cemetery's edge, but there would be no time for mortar to dry and take hold—large raindrops had already begun to slap the earth at a steep angle.

The wind whipped ferociously and the rain intensified in kind. A pecan tree thirty yards off creaked against a howling gust, shedding pecans that shot like bullets through the air alongside sheets of horizontal rain that stung Marcus' neck like wasps. He lowered to his knees but didn't fall. Stone and wooden markers toppled or flew from graves and water began to collect in animated puddles that indicated where the ground lay lowest. Marcus placed his hands upon the hard red clay above Maria, kissed the brick nearest where her head would be. "Stay down, baby," he whispered.

There was not much that he could do, but he could not do nothing. Crouching low, he hurried to the caretaker's shack, the wind ushering him along with such power that his legs barely kept up with his body. Relative calm inside was short-lived, as the shack's lone window, blurry and shaking from pounding rain, suddenly exploded—a two-foot plywood crucifix crashing through and spraying Marcus with hard water and shards of glass. Quickly regaining his bearings, Marcus grabbed the can of white paint he'd come for and pushed through the door once more, walking into and against the direct force of the storm.

Returning to her grave he noted a few bricks had already broken free and tumbled away, but the water had not yet risen to cover her. Kneeling with the can between his legs, he pulled a small knife from his hip pocket, the same one he'd used to cut the fishing line. As he pried open the lid the knife flew from his grip.

He plunged his naked hand into the thick white paint, then withdrew it to smear a rough diagram over the bricks. The diagram was a *veve*, a Vodou symbol representing *Erzulie Dantor*, the spirit designated by Jesus *Legba* as protector from deadly storms. Upon its completion the paint can slipped free of him, flying over his head and streaking his face with white as it passed to join the knife.

Ten yards to his left was another grave, a newer grave, one with no bricks protecting its occupant from unwelcome resurrection. The marker was a rectangle of plain concrete:

MALVINA LATOUR
1806-1906
SISTER. DAUGHTER.
MOTHER TO MANY

Marcus leaned his hands into the mud above the mambo's heart, let his soul feel all the rage he'd held in through the years. Shouted above the din of wind and rain:

"You listen to me, old woman. You done took my nose, you took my son, you made my life a shambles and done got even with me a hunnert times over. All that, and I never cursed your name, never bothered you not-one-damn-time, never sought revenge when I coulda done plenty, never spoke ill to or about you and never asked you fer nothin'. Well, I'm asking you this one time for just one thing, so listen up and listen good. Keep my baby down in this comin' flood. Hear me now, old woman. You do this thing and we're even. You don't and I'll curse yer name to the heavens, God as my witness, till my dyin' breath and after. Keep my baby down. She my baby but she your kin by blood, so do right by her. I already lost my son's body to the water—ain't found him yet and might never do—but not her, oh no, not her. *I won't have it,* you hear? Not to the water, not her. Keep my baby down. I'm beggin' you to please keep her down, keep her down, keep her down…"

The grave next to Maria's, slightly lower and without bricks, was already topped with a half-inch sheen of moving water. Its stone, freshly slanted from push of wind, stated simply:

FRANCES LATOUR
1818-1853
BELOVED MOTHER TO MARIA

# CHAPTER SIXTY-SIX
## *How Long to Return?*

By twenty past five Malaria was stone drunk, the storm outside humming smoothly like a seashell in her ears.

"C'mon, papa. I'm good fer it," she said with a flutter of lashes to the bartender who'd cut her off, a dapper fellow known to regular patrons of the Eagle Saloon as Gary the Gent. "Y'know I'm good fer it, Gary."

"Yeah, you good, baby. But no cash, no flash. Can't go runnin' this tab straight up to the moon, now."

"Hell, Gary, you ain't no gent."

"You know you love me, baby," he laughed. "All wounds heal with time, as they say."

A strong gust slammed something heavy against the side of the building.

*"Damn,"* flinched Gary. "Don't sound like this shit anywhere near ta passin'."

Malaria wrinkled her nose nervously. "Guess I should get on up for my shift." A flash of perfect teeth. "See you in ten hours, baby."

"Knock 'em dead, sweetheart. Knock 'em right on out."

"You know it." Malaria blew him a kiss as she staggered towards the stairs, offering a drunken ass-wiggle to make up for not having tipped. Gary knew about Malaria's hard luck this past week and so never-minded the stiff, but he did appreciate the show.

"Damn, baby," he said with a grin. She smiled at the compliment.

At the top of the stairs she gave Black Benny a touch on the shoulder and a peck on the cheek. "What's shakin', sugar bear?"

Benny grunted. "What's shakin' is you been downstairs all day gettin' yerself shitcanned and still can't help but drag yer ass in late as usual."

"Oh pooh," she deflected with a pout, as she kept on towards the bar. Black Benny grunted once more before directing a worried eye to the pounding of water against glass.

Buddy's band was up on the platform, sans Buddy, stomping out a lowdown gutbucket gospel blues called "Don't Nobody Go Away" for a sparse crowd of degenerates and a scattering of whores that played cards and sucked back shots, defiantly hooting like hyenas each time the storm crescendoed menacingly outside with a slam or a bang or a wail.

Buddy had tried a few other horns since losing his old one, but when he couldn't make any of them sing or shout the way he liked he lost heart and quit playing altogether. Sitting at the bar now with an early drunk on, Buddy winced into his glass at the noise made by some kid called Tig, his replacement, chosen seemingly at random from a legion of wanna-bees by that lousy turncoat bastard Frankie Dusen. Frankie had been Buddy's longtime trombone player, a good old pal and partner for all those years, but had taken over the band a mite enthusiastically in Buddy's opinion. Almost like he'd been hoping for the chance.

"Step it up, dammit!" Buddy bellowed from the bar. "I learned y'all better 'n that. Keep it poppin'. This ain't no fuckin' funeral."

Frankie grudgingly obliged, stomping out a quicker rhythm till the band caught up.

Buddy spotted Malaria from the corner of his eye, turned to give her a timid smile and wave. She smiled back.

Malaria smiled back because she didn't know Buddy had killed her sister. Couldn't conceive of it. The cops hadn't done much, their investigation amounting to a shrug of shoulders over another dead whore killed, presumably, by another rogue sailor on shore leave. These things happened. There'd been rumors about Buddy's involvement, but Diphtheria's best friend Hattie Covington had supplied his alibi—telling the cops he'd been busy fucking her six ways from Sunday on the night in question. That was enough for the cops and enough for Malaria, too. No way Hattie would tell tales out of school about the murder of her very best friend. Even Buddy wasn't that charming, or so she believed.

Malaria shoved herself quickly behind the bar to make change and pick up her tray. "Refill, Buddy?" she sang, noting his empty glass. But he didn't hear her, his eyes staring hard toward the line of windows that overlooked Perdido Street. Following his gaze, she determined the distraction.

There sat the kid. That lowdown dirty scoundrel brat, Jim Jam Jump, soaked to the bone and sitting at a table with Buddy's old cornet in his lap, wiping off stormwater with a dirty cloth, grinning defiantly and directly into the line of Buddy's glare.

"I never consented to the sale of that horn, kid," Buddy said, loud enough to turn most heads in the joint.

Black Benny readied for trouble, focusing on the path of electricity that crackled between the two.

"Ah, g'wan, ya big sore sport. Took my money without complaint if I recall. Ain't my fault you done spent it up already on some whore. Higgle biggle wutch and such." Jim licked the cornet's mouthpiece like a lollipop, the ugly intimacy giving Buddy cause to shudder as he turned his face back towards the band. Downed the rest of his glass in a gulp. A boom and a rumble like a runaway train gave the building a good rock and moan, drawing a long crack in the ceiling near the back wall on the Basin Street side. The train kept rolling as the gust failed to pass; angry water less like rain and more like waves as it shoved its way through unimaginable crevices between brick and mortar. The hall went quiet with worry ten seconds before the first window shattered. All but one female in the dancehall let out a shriek.

Malaria stayed quiet as a mouse. Still as a statue, staring at Jim Jam Jump, seemingly unfazed by the storm's alarming progress.

"Murderer," she said under breath. No one heard this over the din, but Jim kept a close watch on her lips and saw, and so smiled. She walked towards him on surprisingly steady feet, her mind clearing of alcoholic fog as miraculously as this morning's fog had not. Wind and wet whipped through the hall through broken glass, creating havoc and a righteous mess of the place. The band played on, their tempo picking up with the pounding of their hearts.

"Murderer." The word spun like a top in her mind. The cops had believed Jim's story about Dropsy killing West and then himself, but Malaria had bought none of it. There was no doubt in her mind Jim had killed them both. She recalled a night last week when Dropsy and Jim had come by Odd Fellows to work a table of marks. The gravedigger Marcus had spoken to Jim in anger that night, had said words she'd written off as the babblings of a crazy old coot—words that turned out a warning she might have heeded. She struggled to remember those words now and found herself repeating them aloud and verbatim.

"I got my eye on you, devil." A flying shard of glass soundlessly took residence in her left cheek. She did not flinch. "Sent here by that Voodoo witch to make my life a hell. I know you."

"Well, I'll be damned," said Jim blankly.

"Listen, devil. I got my eye on you. Don't think I don't. I watch yer every move."

"You shut yer pie-hole, nigger whore." Jim seemed spooked. "Keep on and I'll be cuttin' yer damn throat is what." Then leaning forward so only Malaria could hear: "I'll get away with it, too, just like I always done and will. Just like fappy tah."

"Look at his eyes!" Malaria shouted for the room to hear. "Don't you see? Red as summer cherries!"

And they were.

A nervous fear danced in Jim's newly reddened eyes, and so she laughed. There was no good reason behind the laugh—but she did, and the laughter was a declaration, a release—not an attack upon he who meant her harm, this fiend who'd gleefully gutted and ruined her family and her personal history, ended who she was and might have been, and done it all for kicks, but a strike upon the unfair earth itself, the earth that now reared up and tore at its own skin with water and wind and spite.

She was alive. All this suffering and death—and now the fresh promise of more to come—and she was yet alive. And so she laughed.

Another mighty gust pulled and rocked the building further, shattering a second window and knocking Malaria to her knees while Jim crashed sideways to the rattling floorboards. The others had already scurried to the wall farthest from the window side, huddled together in the corner near the stairs. The wind inside was driving upwards against the ceiling now, widening the crack to let a torrent of water pour down upon the dance floor. The building adjoining Odd Fellows from the rear—a decrepit bakery called Manny's, with cribs in the back and skank apartments on the upper floors—rapidly deteriorated then finally lurched and tumbled, crashing onto Basin Street and taking the back third of Odd Fellows down with it. A large section of ceiling broke free and sailed above them into the terrible gray sky as the brittle screams of those still inside the apartments above Manny's harmonized dissonantly with the continuous roar of the building's collapse.

"Malaria!" shouted Buddy from the relative shelter of the building's front end, terror coloring his voice. "Get yer ass over here! Stop fooling around!" The wall that Buddy cowered against held firm thus far, still maintaining a significant section of roof overhead. Malaria heard what sounded like a low rumble of applause behind her and turned to see.

Beyond the missing section of Odd Fellows lay an ocean, the streets of New Orleans obscured beneath a floor of churning black water that rushed over the fresh rubble of Manny's Bakery, pitching the bodies of the living and the dead with absolute equality. She wondered briefly about the fate of her friend, Gary the Gent, who she'd recently stiffed for a tip in the Eagle Saloon below. Absently, she wondered how she might endeavor to settle that tab now.

On the floor in a daze, Jim felt a squeeze at his heart. Blood filled is head and nausea curled him sideways into a fetal position against rough wood. With his eyes shut tight he saw the stern face of his father, Antonio Carolla.

"Time is short, Dominick," said the face. "What you've become is not your fault, but you must fight the devil now. You've been the instrument of much suffering, but it's not too late. You've only got one shot, so don't blow it. Do right. See you soon. Jeeka bye boo."

Jim pulled himself up on unsteady feet, shaking off the haze of pain through sheer force of will. Along with the pain he shook out the image of his father's eyes—and the unwelcome stain of hope they inflicted upon his soul. Muttered aloud to no one: "Stupid ghost thinks I'm bad 'cause that devil in me that one time, but I'd-a been bad whether or not. Ain't here to blame no devil for what I am. Bein' bad is a method done served me well and true."

He let the cornet slip from his fingers, the wind pulling it angrily from the place where he stood. He yanked up a loosened piece of floorboard and swung it experimentally against the wind like a bat. Focused on his prey with eyes like summer cherries. The floor behind Malaria had ripped away clean, the path before her currently blocked by Jim Jam Jump and his splintery board. On another day she'd have melted with fear, but not today. Fear was a thing designed for those with something left to lose.

"My brother counted you as a friend," she said calmly into the brutal wind.

"I'm gonna kill ya now, and no one'll know." Jim smiled, but the worry in his eyes remained. "These suckers behind me about to get swallowed whole by this storm. But me? I kin swim good—just like a fish."

"My brother counted you as a friend," she repeated defiantly and without blinking.

"And I he," said the devil immediately before rearing back with the board. Malaria closed her eyes, and so didn't see him lurch forward—and then past.

"Wake up, now," said Buddy Bolden as he grabbed her by the arm and pulled her from the precipice. With Malaria safely behind him, he held up his weapon—a battered cornet—and waved it wildly at Jim's floundering figure in the waters below.

"I ain't consented to the sale of this horn!" he shouted.

Jim's head bobbed in and out of the turbulent surf, his arms splashing wildly. His mouth opened to say something but was muffled by a low wave as the current carried him sideways to Perdido Street, then off towards Basin before the undercurrent pulled him down and under.

Buddy followed Malaria to the front of the building where the others had grouped together in a shivering clump. She pulled Buddy's head down to her own, kissed his forehead and said, "Thank you, my God, thank you."

Buddy pulled away. "Don't thank me, Malaria. I owe your sister at least that much." His eyes wandered briefly, searchingly. "You got no idea what I done."

"I always thought so poorly of you," Malaria confessed. "I never thought that you had it in you to—"

"If you want to thank me, just get through this." Buddy glanced up at the deteriorating section of roof above their heads. "I'm afraid this old building about to come down altogether. Hope you can swim all right."

"I can swim," she confirmed.

Black Benny hunkered down to Buddy's side and said with a rare smile, "Man, you sure whacked that kid good!"

Buddy smiled faintly and lifted Malaria's hand into Benny's. "Take care of this one," he told Benny. "She's last of the good hearts. The last of the Morningstars." Then he turned to Malaria. "Your father's house likely done and gone now. But you gotta make it through this so's you can build it back up, make some new Morningstars and go on."

"Okay, Buddy. All right, but—"

"Now, if you'll pardon me," he interrupted, "I got some business to tend."

Buddy inched his way towards the precipice, staying close to what remained of the inside wall.

"What's he doing?" Malaria's eyes widened with concern.

"Hell if I know," said Benny.

With cornet in hand, Buddy furthered himself across the narrow remainder of floor that led to the building's missing rear section. A cast iron spiral staircase that normally led to the roof's railed observation deck dangled loosely from the remaining side wall, and Buddy waited for a steady gust to help carry him across before attempting the leap.

Malaria screamed as he jumped, tried to get up and after him—but Benny held her firm. Buddy clung expertly to the swinging stairs without dropping the cornet, then carefully ascended to the wall's top edge. He crawled with his chest low, snaking his way to the flat roof of the adjoining building next door. Gradually making his way back to the Rampart Street side, he crossed back over to the Oddfellows' building—positioning himself protectively on the section of remaining roof that hung over the heads of Malaria and the others. The decorative concrete railing that framed the front of the building like a crown remained wholly intact, and Buddy braced himself against it, pulling himself up to one knee.

The view from here was arresting. With fists of rain pelting his back, he watched helplessly as the storm ripped wood and brick structures asunder before him, nothing untouched or unharmed as far as the eye could see.

He watched the city disassemble and drown, but felt no despair at the sight of it. What went through his mind was not, "Everything is gone." What went through his mind was, "How long to return?" What he saw before him was an open question, not a final statement. The question itself not a mere manifestation of hope, but a realization:

As the city dies, so the city is reborn.

Buddy held tight to his cornet, gave her a gentle kiss. Then he remembered why he'd climbed to this precarious spot.

"Can't undo what's done anymore than I can bring my family back, but maybe can have a hand in keeping things from getting any worse." He held the cornet near his lips. "Now, if I can just remember that tune."

The song came out. The melody soared above him into the tumultuous gray, and he thought of Typhus, the youngest of the Morningstars, a man in the shape of a boy. Remembered his troubled eyes, the eternal longing in them. Buddy hadn't known Typhus well, but he knew the meaning of eyes like that.

He blew on:

*Jesus I'm troubled about my soul*
*Ride on Jesus come this way*
*Troubled about my soul*

The notes came out two octaves higher than he had intended.
The notes held, dipped, leapt and crashed. But didn't crash.
*Saved.*
The sky moaned angrily as the rolling tide belched up the bobbing head of Jim Jam Jump once more. The kid shouted up to Buddy, frothing like a lunatic; "Rat clap-a-tap map flap cut cat! Yeah, Buddy, I got my eye on you, got my ding dang eye all over yer sorry drunken ass! Gimme back my dang horn, you! I paid fer it fair and square! Jim jam scram hucka lucka zucka zig! Jeeka bye boo times two!"

Buddy lowered the horn from his lips in wonder. "Well, if that don't beat all," he said. "The tenaciousness of that brat." Then, for the benefit of the kid:

"I ain't consented to the sale of this horn, so I'm keepin' her! Just you try and stop me!"

The wind died momentarily, enough for Buddy to rise up on two feet before resuming play:

*The devil is mad and I am glad*
*He lost one soul that he thought he had*
*Troubled about my soul, Lord*
*Troubled about my soul*

The waters around Jim came alight; diffused at first, then focused and gathering to a point of orange intensity directly behind him. Buddy shielded his eyes against the glare, unable to look away. From the light's center burst the shape of a man, rising up as a phoenix from the foam.

The able but slightly transparent arms of Dropsy Morningstar wrapped hard around the neck and shoulders of Jim Jam Jump. Dropsy put his lips close to Jim's ear, whispered, "That'll be quite enough, pardna," then pulled down. Orange light blinked out entirely as the two went under. Buddy collapsed across the roof, the cornet loosely in his grasp, the thing formerly ripped from his soul having returned in force—as a lost melody is recalled in time.

A ray of moonlight pierced the clouds, but the storm raged on.

§

The first of them to rise were among the cemetery's newest residents; casualties of loose soil not yet packed down by sun and years. Less than a hundred yards from the spot where Marcus Nobody Special had cursed, threatened and prayed to the spirit of Malvina Latour, the body of young West Bolden slipped up and into the rolling muddy surf.

The dead rose by the dozen that night and continued to do so on the morning after, their faces muddy, blank, violated, lost—but not Maria.

Maria stayed down.

# CHAPTER SIXTY-SEVEN

## The River

The river flows on, as it always has and will.

Beneath bright blue sky a cloud like an immense dome mushrooms above the Girod Street Potter's Field, formerly known as *Cimetiere des Heretiques* due to its Protestant history. The fishing pole of Marcus Nobody Special lies temporarily unattended, waiting. There is much to be done. The storm has made it so. So much is changed, so much the same. The search for a certain fish is interrupted but not ended.

In New Orleans, bodies buried in the ground come up in times of hard rain and flooding. After the storm there is much work needs doing, but it is cleansing work. Long-term wounds have festered, neglected for decades, their washing now begun as there is no other way but to move forward when so much is lost. Finally to heal, to begin again. As the waters subside, bodies of the living and the half-living are mingled with those of the dead. Communities near and far have banded together to search for and retrieve souls nearly lost, those clinging to life, waiting for their turn to be recalled or sent on to reward. The dead, new and old, will be tended to later—buried, burned or sunk—and will be tended then only by family and friends, by survivors, by the ones who knew them, who loved them, who hated them, who had forgotten them, but are reminded. Never to forget again, not until their own dying time.

This is neither the first nor the worst of the dying times in New Orleans. Nor will it be the last. In this city there is a long and curious relationship with death, a closeness, a delicate truce. They say in New Orleans death is so close that the dead are mostly buried above ground, that the dead share altitude with the living. Death is so close here that parades are thrown in place of funerals, parades that begin with the solemnity of a dirge only to explode into joyous send-offs to God knows where. Reminders of life's brevity are constant here, they are in the waters that surround, waters filled with glowing lights of joy and dread, invisible but there just the same. These lights are not visible for they are music; the music not audible in the usual way for it is a touch of the soul, both human and immortal. It's a song that begins like all melodies, with a single note. It's a song that resolves like all melodies, with a single note. Then starting again, a circle. And so they sing. Sing while there's time. Life is short the world over, but the truth is more acute here and so life is lived as if endless. Here is where bad hands are played for all they're worth. Here is where miracles come up from mud.

Marcus Nobody Special is very old and has acquired hard-earned knowledge of miracles and mud. He has long-known about the circle of the river, has witnessed its truth firsthand. There is a secret he has kept. He knows that in this place where death remains close there is no death at all, only rebirth.

The river flows on. Always, always.

*"I'm looking at the river but I'm thinking of the sea"*

—Randy Newman

# BOOK FOUR
## *Apocrypha*

*The following texts were transcribed from documents and newspaper clippings found in a water damaged armoire in the attic of 601 Piety Street of the New Orleans 9th Ward neighborhood. The documents were salvaged by demolition workers contracted to destroy the home per the City of New Orleans' blighted housing laws. Put up for auction on Ebay in December of 2001 by user rubybyrd, these papers sold to the author for $17.47. The opening bid was $1.*

*Note: Only relevant portions of the Hayes journal have been reproduced here.*

*March 15, 1906*
New Orleans Item
*page 9, column3:*

## VOODOO QUEEN MALVINA LATOUR DEAD AT AGE 100
### Body remained undiscovered in Treme neighborhood for 10 days, says coroner

THE BODY of famed Voodoo Queen Malvina Latour was discovered in her Sixth Ward home on Monday. Badly decomposed, the Orleans Parish Coroner estimated that it remained undiscovered for up to ten days.

At 100 years of age, Miss Latour had become reclusive during the latter half of her life due to failing health. Malvina Latour had gained mild fame as the successor to the better known and more flamboyant Voodoo Queen of New Orleans, Marie Laveau. Miss Latour was the last of the great Voodoo Queens, an institution which has contributed significantly to the city's tourism trade.

Miss Latour died with no surviving kin, her last living relation being a sister, Frances Latour, who died during the great yellow fever epidemic of 1853.

Services for Malvina Latour were carried out on Wednesday by Father Tony McFee, a Catholic priest, before a small group of neighbors and tourists at the Girod Street Potter's Field. A light brunch was served afterwards featuring regional performers who donned Mardi Gras masks, danced with snakes, and played drums to commemorate the passing of this celebrated regional character.

*March 19, 1906*
New Orleans Times-Democrat
*page 1, column 4*

## ESCAPED LUNATIC FOUND WANDERING FRENCH QUARTER
### Marshall Trumbo was reporter for Item
### Reported by Clarence Hayes III

THIRTEEN days after his escape from the Louisiana Asylum for the Insane of Jackson, Marshall Trumbo, a former reporter for the New Orleans Item, was located and apprehended near the intersection of Bienville and Royal Streets in the French Quarter.

Mr. Trumbo was discovered missing from hospital grounds on March 4 when the unclad body of supervising nurse Jane Janeway was found dead of a broken neck, her life apparently taken by Trumbo in the course of his escape. Mr. Trumbo, who is slight of form, was found wearing the tattered remains of Miss Janeway's uniform along with remnants of feminine makeup apparent upon his face. It is believed by authorities that he slipped out in the guise of the female nurse, his charade convincing enough to procure a ride into Orleans Parish from a Jackson farmer transporting goods to the French Market. Upon his recapture, say authorities; "Trumbo's physical state indicated he had most likely hidden within the rough terrain of the Bayou St. John during his near two week absence".

While he was a resident of the asylum Mr. Trumbo spent over a decade in a catatonic state, unable to speak, or to even eat without assistance. According to a Times-Democrat exclusive source, Trumbo had in recent months shown vast improvement, speaking articulately and interacting eagerly with other patients, as well as hospital staff.

According to alienist and physician Herschel H. Baxter, "Though having shown a remarkable recovery from his former catatonic state, Mr. Trumbo also showed increased dementia and an apparent inclination towards violence.

Unfortunately, no one at the facility recognized this heightened state of agitation as immediately perilous."

While at large, Mr. Trumbo appeared to have committed no violent acts other than the murder of Miss Janeway.

Upon his capture, Mr. Trumbo appeared well on the road to relapse of his previous long-term catatonic state. Seemingly oblivious to his own filthy state and recent activities, he was able only to repeat a single sentence when questioned by authorities, "They gave it to me but I gave it back as best I could."

Perhaps tellingly, this sentence also constituted the famed "last words" of David Hennessy, the New Orleans Police Chief who was notoriously assassinated in 1891. According to Baxter, the Hennessy murder had made a dramatic impression on Mr. Trumbo, who served as a minor footnote to the investigation.

Shortly following the now infamous mass lynchings which came in the wake of the Hennessy trial, Trumbo visited the home of one of the accused Italians, Antonio Carolla, allegedly to gather material for what was to be a human interest story for *The Item*. What might otherwise have been a mundane inquiry, turned tragic when Trumbo witnessed the murder of a negro priest while present in the Carolla home. This event apparently proved too much for Mr. Trumbo. His brother, George T. Trumbo, had him committed to the Jackson facility shortly thereafter.

Perhaps due to influences at The Item, Trumbo himself was never treated as a suspect in the death of the negro priest, which remains unsolved.

Marshall Trumbo has been returned to the care of the Louisiana Asylum for the Insane, and is currently being monitored under high security conditions.

The publishers of the New Orleans Item have declined to comment on the Trumbo case, and have failed to report on the story themselves in any meaningful way.

*March 28, 1906*
New Orleans Times-Democrat
*page 7, column 24*

## MUSIC STAR IN MOURNING ATTACKS MOTHER
### Reported by Clarence Hayes III

SUFFERING from apparent dementia, musician Charles "Buddy" Bolden, a negro, struck his mother with a water pitcher yesterday, causing minor injuries. In a highly agitated state, Bolden told police he believed she was trying to poison him. Although Bolden, whose orchestra is a popular and frequent attraction at the Odd Fellows' Hall at the corner of South Rampart and Perdido Streets, is a known dipsomaniac, it is likely that his troubling behavior may be attributed at least in part to a series of recent tragedies suffered by the musician.

Bolden's only son, nine-year-old West Bolden, was found murdered on March 4th, his small body left on a sand bank along the river levee, his alleged killer being West's own mentally retarded uncle on his mother's side. The murderous uncle is believed to have committed suicide, last seen walking from the crime scene into the Mississippi River. His body has not been recovered as of this writing.

Only two days later on March 6th (the day of his young son's funeral), Bolden's estranged common-law wife and the mother of his son, Diphtheria Morningstar, a prostitute, was found murdered by strangulation in her residence and place of business, The Arlington House, on the 200 block of Basin Street. Bolden was initially interviewed as a suspect in Miss Morningstar's death, but was cleared after another prostitute, Hattie Covington, told police that Bolden had missed the the boy's funeral and had not come to call on Miss Morningstar in several weeks. Miss Covington also told authorities that the last person to visit Miss Morningstar was an unidentified sailor, most likely a customer of The Arlington House. For the attack on his mother, Bolden was arrested on charges of insanity and assault. He is currently awaiting arraignment.

*Clarence Hayes III, Journal Entry,*
*March 29, 1906, evening*

This morning I awoke from a dream that left my body clammy and shivering. If not for strong and lingering feelings of intuition, I would have sworn off such mental disturbances to the sordid nature of recent assignments given me by my editor at the Times-Democrat. But something in the pit of my stomach tells me there is something more to it.

My recollection of the dream's details are sketchy at best, but the impression left was that three recent subjects of mine—the Voodoo Queen Latour, the Trumbo case, and the Storyville musician—are interlinked in some unwholesome way. I had intended to go about my day and let the dream fade from memory, as dreams are wont to do, but the aforementioned feelings of intuition urged me to investigate further. It is said that the "intuition of reporters" often pays off, though I have never experienced any such occasions of fruitful premonition myself.

To my surprise, a cursory investigation into the individual cases did in fact present an immediate link between two of the subjects. It appears that the negro priest (whose murder Trumbo himself witnessed in 1891) was a man called Noonday Morningstar. An unusual name—and equally unusual are the names of his daughter and son, Diphtheria and Dropsy. Which brings me to the aforementioned connection: Diphtheria Morningstar is the name of the prostitute murdered this past Thursday, a fact I had included in the Bolden story—and Dropsy Morningstar, who was Diphtheria's brother, was also the "murderous uncle" who'd killed young West Bolden before allegedly taking his own life. I have found no facts which link the Latour woman to any of this, but I've a hunch that further investigation may correct that. Then again, more often than not, a hunch is but a hunch and nothing more.

Still, I must consider whether such investigation may be feasible under current conditions at the paper. Since Sam Cain's recent departure for the Chicago Tribune (lucky old son!), the workload for remaining staff has been significantly increased, allowing me little time for potentially frivolous endeavors. It must also be considered whether such a story (whatever that story may be—and if there even is a story at all beyond simple coincidence), might hold the interest of the paper's largely white readership (or editorship, for that matter), being that all of the subjects of the story, save for Trumbo, are negroes.

Perhaps I will look into the matter further if I can find the time. I must admit that the case of Marshall Trumbo is unusually intriguing to me—if only because he is a brother journalist who let the horrors of the job dismantle his soul in such a bloodchilling way. So far, the editorship of the Times-Democrat seem only to have recognized his sad tale as an easy and excusable way to take jabs at a competitor—but I do know that I am not the only journalist in their employ who has been affected in a personal way by the disturbing fate of Mr. Trumbo.

I suspect, if there is indeed a connection, that it can all be traced back to the Hennessy case. This, at least, seems to be the starting point of Trumbo's downfall.

*Clarence Hayes III, Journal Entry,*
*April 1, 1906, evening*

Today was a milestone of sorts in my career as a journalist.

My esteemed editor, Raymond Hockett, deemed fit to remove me from my usual routine of menial crime related stories, and has awarded me the post of Lead Investigative Reporter regarding allegations of corruption against Senator Foster. It seems that Foster's challenger in the upcoming election has dredged up the Senator's ancient (if admittedly questionable) 1894 pardon of Theodore "Big Ted" Baosso. Baosso, a former high ranking police official who habitually flaunted his open alliances within the underworld, was convicted back in 1885 of "forging and uttering a fake marriage certificate" in order to woo and elope with a young girl (Baosso was still married to his wife of four years). Foster was Governor at the time, and most likely hadn't considered any potentially long lasting effects of the Baosso pardon.

Naturally, Foster's political enemies view this decidedly old news as a way to prove, in a roundabout way, underworld ties to the Senator himself. Although the allegations will most likely act as a mere bump in the road for the popular and powerful Foster, my having been granted such high profile opportunity marks a significant step up for this fledgling crime reporter.

This assignment is clearly a test of my abilities—as well as a strong and unexpected vote of confidence—from Mr. Hockett. I plan to prove my mettle to him with exceptional coverage.

On a more trivial note: A slightly expanded investigation into the Trumbo/Morningstar matter yielded no additional useful information, and I hereby consider the matter closed. Although intuition may very well be a useful tool in reporting from time to time, I expect it may also tend towards hindrance. It is important to keep matters in proper perspective.

*April 28, 1911*
New Orleans Times-Democrat
*page 1, column 1*

## BLACK HAND MURDERS CONTINUE IN LITTLE ITALY
### Police request community cooperation in grocer deaths
### Reported by Clarence Hayes III

YESTERDAY morning on the 200 block of Rocheblave Street, the bodies of Vincent and Mary DePaul were found murdered in the backroom apartment located behind their popular Little Italy grocery store.

The third in a ghastly string of murders this year, all of the crimes thus far have involved grocery store owners and their wives, each crime having involved the use of an axe. In addition to these murders, five other incidents of axe attacks upon grocers and their families have accrued, some of which have yielded survivors. Sadly, none of the surviving victims have been able to provide police with useful descriptions of the assailant or assailants. Lead Detective James Bryce believes this absence of witness information symptomatic of the Italian community's collective fear of the so-called Black Hand, which police strongly suspect are behind the attacks.

The bodies of Mr. and Mrs. DePaul were discovered by Salvatore Dutti of Cleveland Street, a neighbor and regular patron of the DePaul Grocery. In an exclusive interview with the Times-Democrat, Mr. Dutti stated that he first suspected trouble upon Mr. DePaul's failure to open the store at the usual appointed hour, an occurrence which had not happened in the grocery's twenty-plus year history. After loudly knocking at the DePaul' alley side door for several minutes to no avail, Mr. Dutti forced entry to investigate. Upon the grisly discovery, he immediately sent for police.

Mr. Dutti revealed to the Times-Democrat that he noticed a sealed envelope lying on the chest of Mr. DePaul. "That envelope had blood on it," said Mr. Dutti, "and it just gave my heart a chill knowing it must have come from the killer himself."

According to police, no such envelope was apparent upon their arrival. "If there was such a letter or note," said Detective Bryce, "it would certainly have proved valuable to the investigation. It is more likely that Mr. Dutti, in his distraught state, merely imagined he saw something. In any case, we have no such letter in our possession."

Mr. Dutti, however, remains steadfast in his claim. "Might have been the negro got it," he stated further. The negro in question is Marcus James, the supervising caretaker for the Girod Street Cemetery who is contracted by the Orleans Parish Coroner to retrieve bodies from crime scenes.

Although James could not be reached for questioning before press time, police believe the caretaker had no motive in tampering with any potential evidence, and hold to the theory of Mr. Dutti's overactive imagination.

As with previous attacks, the killer did leave his usual calling card of a bloody axe and a chisel in plain view at the scene—the latter used to pry open a door panel for entry to the victims' residences. Police have retrieved these objects and are retaining them as evidence.

Detective Bryce maintains that the NOPD investigation is largely focused on the so-called Black Hand, a mysterious criminal organization which has struck terror in the heart of New Orleans' Italian community for many decades, but has proved maddeningly elusive to police. "These killings show no economic motive," said Bryce. "At each of the crime scenes there were valuables left untouched and in plain view, including cash and jewelry. This fact alone enforces the theory of the Black Hand's vendetta style of murder in which theft does not necessarily come into play." Bryce did concede, however, "If it is the work of the Black Hand, it doesn't entirely fit previous patterns. In the past, the Black Hand's steadfast policy has been to not harm women. Of course, as the organization grows and thrives, their methods have become more vicious—and so their policy towards women may be changing in kind."

The police place partial blame for the Black Hand's rapid expansion on its very victims—the Italian community. It is believed by law enforcement officials that if a few courageous individuals might come forward, significant strides towards defeating these criminals could be achieved.

The New Orleans Police Department urges anyone with information regarding the killings—or any other criminal activities possibly attributable to the Black Hand—to come forward immediately. The police guarantee absolute protection to anyone who presents them with useful information. "Without the assistance of the community," said Detective Bryce, "our hands are sorely tied."

*Clarence Hayes III, Journal Entry*
*September 23, 1916*

Quite a surprise came with the afternoon mail—a letter from good old Sam Cain in Chicago! As a couple of young bucks, Sam and I began our journalism careers together before the merger of the Daily Picayune and the Times-Democrat. I haven't heard from the old sod in over a decade! Sam had quite a few interesting stories to tell of his exploits in the Chicago metropolis—it seems he's having quite the time! But what inspired his decision to write me was of a darker nature.

Apparently, after reading an editorial by one of his colleagues (a humorless and crusty old Irishman named O'Shea), Sam felt a letter to me was in order. O'Shea's op-ed piece centered mainly on the abhorrent conditions of the saloon neighborhoods of Chicago's East Side, but towards the end of the piece were details of a killing Sam thought I would find interesting.

This murder, he explained, bore eerie similarities to the unsolved "Axeman" killings which so terrorized the people of New Orleans six years ago. His suggestion seems to be (without explicitly saying so) that our own Axeman may still be plying his trade, but in a new setting. An interesting theory, but there are many maniacs in the world and tenfold as many axes—most likely coincidence.

In any case, it was certainly good to hear from old Sam. I must remember to write back and extend an invitation should he find time for a visit.

*August 31, 1916*
*Chicago Tribune*
*page 12, column2*

"EDITORIAL":
THE FORGOTTEN VICTIMS OF CHICAGO'S
SOCIAL EVIL: OUR CHILDREN
Cults of perversion, venereal disease, and opium
reach out to our youth
Editorial by Michael T. O'Shea

THERE IS a sad state of affairs in Chicago today.

After a hard day's work, it is often the desire and inclination of the city's laborers to unwind and relax before returning home to their families, the most common manifestation of which being the nightly visitation of local watering holes. This in itself is an innocent and even necessary freedom of the working class—indeed, one that must be protected and cherished as any freedom. But such simple pleasures are nigh so simple in the modern age. The troubling truth is that if a man happens to choose the wrong neighborhood in which to unwind, his drink will likely be brought to him by a waiter who also doubles as "cadet". This cadet, with a wink and a smile, will attempt to sell him the services of a prostitute—and sometimes much more.

The word "cadet" is slang (or, rather, euphemism) referring to a type of pimp who manages a single prostitute—this prostitute usually being the cadet's own wife or girlfriend—and sometimes his sister, or even mother. For supplying safe venue, the owner of the saloon is given a portion of the proceeds from these lurid business transactions. It is a stunningly lucrative enterprise.

The appeal of such immediate (if illegal) financial reward has, over the years, resulted in an explosion in the saloon industry. Many such establishments exist solely to take part in these unsavory practices. A few statistics regarding this explosion as provided by the Vice Commission of Chicago prove enlightening:

There are 7,152 saloons in Chicago today, making the ratio of saloons to populace an alarming 1 to 300. An ordinance passed on November 1, 1906 states that "no new dramshop licenses may be issued until licenses in force at the time are 1 for every 500 of the population". For this to occur, the population of the city would have to nearly double—it is estimated by city officials that such an increase in citizenry could take more than twenty years.

Instead of patiently waiting for the census to accommodate, the criminal element now sidesteps the law by opening illegal operations known as "blind pigs". Blind pigs are illegal saloons hidden in the backrooms of legitimate daytime business, and therefore not readily visible to authorities.

Even those operations that possess legally acquired licenses have incorporated clever and effective systems to avoid police detection of illegal activities inside. Many employ "lighthouses"—young men or boys stationed in front of the saloons who act as lookouts. If an approaching police officer is spotted, the "lighthouse" simply pushes an electronically attached button to alert those inside of impending danger.

Once inside, the patron is often greeted by much more than the casual solicitation of cadets. In some cases, the weirdly perverse activities of certain homosexual cults thrive in the shadows, if not right out in the open.

I must warn that the following portion of this editorial, though important in that it reveals ugly truths which can no longer be ignored by our citizenry, is quite shocking. Kindly read no further if you are of mild constitution.

To quote verbatim from the report of the Vice Commission: "It appears that in this community there is a large number of men who are thoroughly gregarious in habit; who mostly affect the carriage, mannerisms, and speech of women; who are fond of many articles ordinarily dear to the feminine heart; who are often people of a good deal of talent; who lean to the fantastic in dress and other sexual life. They preach the values of non-association with women which are nauseous and repulsive. Many of them speak of themselves or each other with the adoption of feminine terms, and go by girls' names or fantastic application of women's titles. They have a vocabulary and signs of recognition of their own, which serve as an introduction into their society. The cult has produced some literature, much of which is incomprehensible to one who cannot read between the lines, and there is considerable distribution among them of pernicious photographs. In one of the large music halls recently, a much applauded act was that of a man who by facial expression and bodily contortions represented sex perversion, a most disgusting performance. It was evidently not at all understood by many of the audience, but others wildly applauded. Then, one of the songs recently ruled off the stage by the police department was inoffensive to innocent ears, but was really written by a member of the cult, and replete with suggestiveness to those who understood the language of this group."

Even unsuspecting patrons with normal sexual habits are often seduced into taking part in pervert acts. Or, as is disturbingly stated in the report: "Men who impersonate females are among the vaudeville entertainers in these saloons. Unless these men are known, it is difficult to detect their sex. They solicit men at the tables for drinks the same as the women, and ask them to go upstairs for pervert practices."

As if that weren't appalling enough, these cults' collective appetite for effeminate young men has led to the inclusion of young boys, sometimes as young as ten years of age.

Besides the lifelong mental, spiritual, and, even physical scars suffered by the desperate young children roped into these cults, some of the more immediate concerns include opium addiction and social disease.

The widespread existence of venereal disease is seen as little more than an inconvenience to the owners of such establishments, commonly employing "house physicians" who intentionally deceive the inmates by down-playing the danger of such afflictions. Some uneducated inmates have testified before the vice commission that these so-called "house physicians" have recommended sodomy and other pervert acts because doing so "reduces the risk of disease".

In one North Side house on Seminary Avenue, out of 18 inmates, 12 reportedly had syphilis. In one case, even though the girl's condition had advanced to a visible state of necrosis at the palm of her hand, she was still allowed to receive men.

Another shocking statistic revealed by the commission states; "In a twenty-seven month period, 600 children under twelve years of age have passed through the venereal ward of the Cook County Hospital. 60 % had been innocently infected, 20% inherited the disease and 25% had been assaulted by infected persons. About 15% had syphilis and 85% had gonorrhea" The report concludes with this mercifully vague but heartening summation; "The dreadful results of venereal diseases among children are almost beyond belief."

When asked by a vice officer how he thought he'd obtained syphilis, a twelve year old boy declined to answer directly, instead commenting, "Well, I guess this means I'm off to Hell Proper. Just like my mama done."

Sadder still is when the ruination of children's lives is overshadowed by their utter destruction.

On August tenth, vice investigators witnessed a colored woman in a LaSalle Street saloon playing the piano while her son accompanied her on violin. The bartender admitted to authorities that the boy was a mere 14 years of age. There is a regular house of prostitution upstairs, conducted by the wife of the saloonkeeper. On August 29, the investigators returned to find the boy no longer accompanying his mother's musical performance. After inquiring as to the well-being of her son, the woman became quite emotional, telling the officers she'd been talked into allowing the boy to accompany a thin white man with a charming demeanor upstairs for pervert practices. It was explained to her by the saloonkeeper that it would not take much time or effort on the boy's part, but that the financial rewards would be substantial. She'd agreed to this transaction, and several days later her son had yet to emerge from the upstairs area. The saloonkeeper assured the woman that her boy had simply run off for a while, and that he would probably return when he became hungry enough. However, these words offered little consolation to the distraught mother. Investigators assured the woman that they would look into the matter further, and left her in tears.

Early yesterday morning the body of a boy matching the description of the missing LaSalle Street violinist was found mutilated and murdered in the back-room apartment of an Italian grocery store of Chicago's Little Italy. Although police remain unsure as to whether the boy had been sexually molested, the instrument of death was declared to be an axe—the object having been left by the killer, still tainted with bits of the boy's blood, flesh, and bone. The actual location of the body posed a mystery, say police, being found by the Italian grocer himself, who made the grisly discovery upon his return from a visit with family in New Orleans. The police have not entirely ruled out the grocer as a suspect, but his guilt seems improbable since the apartment appears to have been broken into, the killer having pried open a door panel with a chisel—an object left at the crime scene along with the axe. Robbery was clearly not the motive, say police, as many valuables—including cash—were left in plain view and undisturbed by the killer. It is not the job of this writer to divine meaning or motive behind the murder of an innocent child, a child so tragically sent to an unspeakable death by his own misguided and uneducated mother. It is my desire only to use the example of the young LaSalle Street violinist to point to the source, and to show that this atrocity—one of many—could have been prevented.

The wheels of legislation move slowly. We cannot sit by and wait for a spirit of enforcement and intolerance from the authorities that may never come. It is up to us, the citizens of This Great City, to boycott these offensive saloon-keepers and their cronies. The law of supply and demand is a double edged sword, and it is time for the side of decency to take a turn wielding that sword. If no action is taken, then it is the complacent citizenry of Chicago who will be, in effect, sending its children "off to Hell Proper."

We must not forget that such a Hell has room enough for us all.

*November, 8, 1917*
New Orleans Times-Picayune
*page 7, column 4*


NEW ORLEANS' NEWEST EXPORT BUSINESS: THE MUSIC
OF THE BROTHELS
New Orleans orchestra a national sensation as new federal
ordinance
poses to close red light district
Reported by Clarence Hayes III


WHEN THE Federal government in the form of Secretary of War Newton D. Baker decreed last August that "open prostitution" be banned within five miles of any United States army installation (with Secretary of the Navy Josephus Daniels immediately following suit), it became clear to the nation entire that the ordinance was directed at New Orleans specifically—being that our own Storyville red light district is the only legally "open" district of prostitution in the country.

After much local protest from city officials (including an unsuccessful bid by Mayor Behrman to gain an audience with President Wilson personally), the battle to preserve the containment of vice in our city seems to have been lost. The ordinance is due to go into effect on November 12th at midnight.

New Orleans is a land of eternal irony, however, and though the feds may have succeeded in closing Storyville, they have not killed the district's spirit—as is now evidenced in the exploding success of a certain musical recording by New Orleans' own Jim Jam Jump Orchestra, led by cornetist Dominick Carolla, a native of the city.

"The American people have said their collective piece," stated Carolla with a wry smile, "by casting its vote for the musical anarchy of our own beleaguered tenderloin district. Jazz music is at the heart of the feds' discontent and ire, and the people want to hear every note of it!" Although Carolla speaks with a certain tongue in cheek bravado, national sales figures seem to back up the sentiment.

Recorded last February for the Victor Talking Machine Company of New York, the orchestra's first recording, "Jim Jam Jumpin' in the Alley with Sally," was received with moderate enthusiasm. But when news of Storyville's impending demise made national headlines in August, public sympathy for the popular district only served to energize sales of the record. Now, as Storyville's final hour approaches, the record's newfound popularity seems to have spurred a national mania for "jazz," an artform born in the doomed brothels of New Orleans.

Carolla scoffs at the mention of jazz as an "artform," preferring to describe it as "the assassination of melody, the slaying of syncopation"—in any case, it is hard to deny the appeal of its infectious rhythms, nor is it easy to deny the plain facts of its admittedly seedy origins.

Jazz music, or "jass" as it is sometimes referred, evolved quickly from its roots in the syncopated blues or "ragtime" piano music commonly played in the welcoming halls of the tenderloin's poshest sporting houses during the final decade of the 19th century. Invented by negro musicians, the music was initially frowned upon by white audiences until its appeal in the brothels became evident. Soon, white orchestra leaders began to incorporate its unruly rhythms into their own repertoires. In 1915, the popular negro bandleader Freddie Keppard was approached by the Columbia Recording Company of New York with an offer of a recording contract. Keppard declined, siting his desire to keep this original New Orleans phenomenon local, and candidly doubting whether its wild rhythms would be understood or embraced by an audience outside its home. The following year, Columbia approached, and indeed recorded, several compositions by Dominick Carolla's outfit—but decided at the last minute not to release the recordings, worried that the music may irreparably damage the company's cleancut image. Carolla responded to Columbia's hesitancy by taking his jazz on the road. Later that year, The Jim Jam Jump Orchestra had become a sensation in the popular Chicago night spot, The Booster Club—and early this year furthered their pilgrimage to New York City. Their arrival in New York resulted in a regular job at the fashionable Reisenweber's Café on Columbus Circle and soon thereafter they secured a recording contract with Victor.

Now that the national marketability of New Orleans "jazz" has been proven beyond a shadow of a doubt, Victor plans to release more recordings by the Jim Jam Jump Orchestra later this week. Columbia has announced plans to release the formerly suppressed recordings it made from the previous year, and now many New Orleans artists, Keppard included, are lining up to make their own records.

Though city officials may be wringing their fists at the federal government's interference with local lawmaking, perhaps they can now count the continuation of the district's spirit in the form of "jazz" as at least one small victory. Or, as Mayor Behrman so aptly put it, "You might make it illegal, but you can't make it unpopular."

*May 24, 1918*
New Orleans Times-Picayune
*page 1, column1:*

## AXEMAN STRIKES AGAIN!
Gruesome axe killings resume after 7 years of silence;
suspects arrested and released.
Reported by Clarence Hayes III

AFTER a seven year hiatus, the fiend who became famous for terrorizing New Orleans' Little Italy in the Spring of 1911 has made a ghastly return.

Yesterday morning, the bodies of Mr. and Mrs. Joseph Maggio were found badly mutilated by an axe in the apartment behind their Maggio Grocery store, in the heart of Little Italy. The trademark tools of the fiend—a bloody axe and a chisel for gaining entry—were once again retrieved from the scene, just as such items were routinely found at the scenes of the 1911 murder scenes. Also similar to the 1911 killings is that robbery appears not to be a motive—jewelry and other valuables having been left behind in plain view. Indeed, police have reported that a considerable amount of cash was found beneath the blood saturated pillows of the Maggios.

Immediate panic ensued in Little Italy upon news of the axeman's return. Several suspects were apprehended by police, questioned, then released for lack of evidence.

Although the 1911 slayings remain officially unsolved, police ceased vigorous investigation when the murders abruptly stopped as quickly as they had begun. It was presumed that the murderer had either relocated, died, or had been sent to prison on other charges. Now that the murders have resumed, police and local prison officials are carefully checking the whereabouts and alibis of violent criminals who have been recently released but who were not incarcerated at the time of the original killings.

At the close of the 1911 investigation, it was held by police that the killings were most likely the result of the mysterious Black Hand crime organization of

Little Italy. However, Detective James Bryce, who was in charge of the investigation then and remains its lead investigator today, now has his doubts as to the Black Hand's possible involvement. "This reappearance after so long seems to point to the activities of an individual, not an organization," said Bryce this morning. "Most likely, the killer temporarily left the area, or was incarcerated on other charges, then released. If the former is the case, then we may be able to track his movements through the assistance of authorities in neighboring cities. If the fiend simply left town awhile, it's likely he has perpetrated similar crimes in a different environ—most likely a large city with a significant Italian community. This man has a specific, set pattern from which he is unlikely to stray."

Detective Bryce also implied the previous speculation of "vendetta-style" killings to be less likely due to the lack of normally coinciding evidence, such as threatening letters or a history of extortion in the lives of the victims. All of the axe killings seem to have come completely without warning or provocation. This observation has instilled an even deeper sense of terror in the Italian community, the pure randomness in the killer's choice of victims providing less comfort than would some identifiable rationale or motive.

Less delicately but more to the point, Superintendent Mooney stated today, "I am sure that all the crimes were committed by the same man, probably a bloodthirsty maniac, filled with a passion for human slaughter."

Detective Bryce's own comments countered the superintendent's slightly; "We have not, of course, ruled out the possibility that this more recent slaying is the result of a mimic wishing to cover his own tracks by pretending to be the 1911 fiend. It is still quite possible that the original killer is deceased or in prison on other charges at this time."

*March 12, 1919*
New Orleans Item
*page 8, column 1*

## EDITORIAL:
## THE JAZZ PROBLEM
### By Bradford G. Huntington, Ed. In Chief, The Item

ALTHOUGH in the past I have found rare occasion to do so, today I exercise my editorial privilege in the pursuit of exposing a social evil that has served only to tarnish the image of the Good People of New Orleans in the eyes of the world at large. It is also my sad duty to report that this "problem" of which I speak only seems to worsen with each passing day.

In the course of two short years, a trend, which many Orleanians initially considered a harmless if annoying fad, has diabolically blossomed into a many tentacled serpent—causing Our Fine City untold embarrassment and shame. More alarmingly, this "serpent" has recently proved itself capable of penetrating the very fabric of American Society.

This insidious monster goes by the name of "jazz." Shameful even in namesake, the word is, in fact, negro slang meaning "to fornicate."

In the fall months of '17, a novelty recording by the all-white New Orleans outfit known as the Jim Jam Jump Orchestra was released by the New York City based music company The Victor Talking Machine Company. Following a relentlessly ribald advertising campaign by Victor in which inestimable financial resources were expended, the record became the centerpiece of seedy social events and rebellious conversation not only among the young and impressionable but also, and more shockingly, among the affluent and fashionable all across the nation. Without missing the proverbial beat, more New Orleans groups quickly jumped on the bandwagon of greed and disgrace, releasing more such novelty recordings at an alarming rate. It wasn't long before similar orchestras began popping up in other urban centers—most notably New York, Chicago and Kansas City—and even in some rural areas of the Midwest. This music of the brothels has also managed to infect the far away shores of some European nations.

In the interest of the almighty dollar, and with no regard as to public interest (especially the interest of our nation's vulnerable youth), the wealthy and powerful executives of the Victor Talking Machine Company have shamelessly rushed to feed into the morally bankrupt god of "the sensational, the lude, and the profitable." Without hint of conscience, this pattern of spiritual corruption has perpetuated for no good reason beyond the desire to "give the people what they want."

I set pen to paper today to tell these God-less corporations that this is NOT what the people want, just as no sane person wishes to be seduced by evil. The seduced, however culpable for their actions, are too often children. And I argue today that these seduced children are little more than the innocent victims of those who would seduce them.

When a proud and noble community like that of Our City finds that an aspect of its society has made significant effect on the the world at large, it is tempting for that community to take pride in the phenomenon. "After all," one might say, "does it not bear witness to the charisma and vitality of New Orleans that so many have become fond of a thing created by our own?" But the only moral answer is: "Not when that thing comes directly from the filthiest and most despicable among us, from the very bottom of our social barrel." May I suggest to you, my fellow Orleanians, that this is not how we should strive to be recognized.

Make no mistake, this "jazz" music is unwholesome stuff. Invented by scoundrel negro musicians of our former tenderloin district for the express purpose of background music in brothels, it bears no resemblance to any sound created by the educated and refined musicians of which New Orleans has plenty. The original purpose of these insidious rhythms and caterwauls was to create an atmosphere in which men and boys might be tempted to spend hard earned wages on relations with wayward and disease-ridden women. It is a music of prurient excitement, not of beauty; of carnal lust, not of love. It is not a thing for the people of This Great City to be proud of, and we would do well to discourage its continued export. Its purveyors should not be hailed as heroes but, rather, should be held in contempt as the corruptors and amoral profiteers that they are.

Of all those guilty for allowing this distasteful phenomenon to grow in such cancerously quick fashion, one name springs to the forefront as deserving singular disgrace. This man is Dominick Carolla, the son of Italian immigrants and leader of the aforementioned Jim Jam Jump Orchestra. Carolla is not only a devious corruptor, but also a plagiarist and a liar. Among his outrageous and publicly circulated lies are his claims that he invented "jazz" on his own, though common knowledge tells us this music existed in the seedy sporting houses of Basin Street since a time when he was certainly but a small child. Moreover, to imply such a music could have originated from the soul of a white man, even an innately criminal one, is an insult to the entire white race. It is rumored that Carolla stole his first musical instrument, a cornet, from an incapacitated negro musician who was later committed to the Louisiana Asylum for the Insane due to acute dipsomania. Still, Carolla is hailed by many as a modern day celebrity and hero; a "great ambassador" of New Orleans culture.

Citizens, I implore you: Please refrain from canonizing this swarthy seducer further. He is not what he appears to be. He is an agent of the devil himself, he is this and no more—perhaps less, if such a thing is possible. It was he who spread the disease of jazz beyond the control of our own borders.

Two years ago when the impending demise of legalized prostitution in our city was making national news, our Mayor shamed us all by bowing to the lowest stratus of public opinion, choosing to champion the cause of our criminal element. The mayor's efforts were handily defeated by federal authorities, but the war on debauchery is far from over. We must pull together and show unwavering solidarity in this matter. It is the duty of every man, woman and child of New Orleans to take a stand; right here, right now. We must say "no" to jazz music, we must speak in unison and do so clearly. We must not allow the awesome advertising machines of New York to tell us what it is that "the people want." That decision is for us alone, and it is one long ago made. It is a simple matter of right and wrong, the moral answer having been planted in our collective bosom by God Himself before the beginning of time.

We, the people, must speak—and be heard.  –BGH

*March 14, 1919*
New Orleans Times-Picayune
*page 1, column3*

## "ESTEEMED MORTAL," WRITES AXEMAN
Letter to Times-Picayune editor deemed authentic by police

THE FOLLOWING letter was received by our offices shortly before press time. The letter has been reviewed and examined by investigating officers, and is believed genuine by them. The decision to print its contents here was a difficult one, but it was decided that to do so would be in the best interest of public safety. The text is reproduced here unedited and in its entirety.—THE ED.

*HELL, MARCH 13, 1919*

Editor of the Times-Picayune
New Orleans, La.

Esteemed Mortal:

They have never caught me and they never will. They have never seen me, for I am invisible, even as the ether that surrounds your earth. I am not a human being, but a spirit and a fell demon from the hottest hell. I am what you Orleanians and your foolish police call the Axeman.

When I see fit, I shall come again and claim other victims. I alone know whom they shall be. I shall leave no clue except my bloody axe, besmeared with the blood and brains of he whom I have sent below to keep me company.

If you wish you may tell the police to be careful not to rile me. Of course, I am a reasonable spirit. I take no offense at the way they have conducted their investigations in the past. In fact, they have been so utterly stupid as to amuse not only me, but His Satanic Majesty, Francis Josef, etc. But tell them to beware. Let them not try to discover what I am, for it were better that they were never born than to incur the wrath of the Axeman. I don't think there is any need of such a warning, for I feel sure the police will always dodge me, as they have in the past. They are wise and know how to keep away from all harm.

Undoubtedly, you Orleanians think of me as a most horrible murderer, which I am, but I could be much worse if I wanted to. If I wished, I could pay a visit to your city every night. At will I could slay thousands of your best citizens, for I am in close relationship with the Angel of Death.

Now, to be exact, at 12:35 (earthly time) on next Tuesday night, I am going to pass over New Orleans. In my infinite mercy, I am going to make a little proposition to you people. Here it is:

I am very fond of jazz music, and I swear by all the devils in the nether regions that every person shall be spared in whose home a jazz band is in full swing at the time I have just mentioned. If everyone has a jazz band going, well, then, so much the better for you people. One thing is certain and that is that some of those people who do not jazz it on Tuesday night (if there be any) will get the axe.

Well, as I am cold and crave the warmth of my native Tartarus, and as it is about time that I leave your earthly home, I will cease my discourse. Hoping that thou wilt publish this, that it may go well with thee, I have been, am and will be the worst spirit that ever existed either in fact or realm of fancy.


THE AXEMAN

*Clarence Hayes III, Journal Entry,*
*January 12, 1923*

This dream will not leave me.

I have not mentioned it in these pages for many years, have tried to put it out of my mind since its initial occurrence, but I am now at my wit's end. As the years have gone on, the dream has evolved—from swirling scraps of images and sound to crystal clarity and instructive voice. But even when the voice of the dream is instructive, I have little or no recall upon waking—just a pathetic memory of the dream version of myself, scribbling frantically in a notebook that exists only in dreams, aware that I am dreaming, and struggling desperately to carry with me some useful information into the waking world.

Useful? What a laugh that is. What could possibly be "useful" about words uttered by nonexistent phantoms in a dream. But something deep within me believes these things important, and this believing gives me doubt of my own sanity. These words that I now set to paper bring to mind the original lurking demon of my nocturnal plague, my fellow unstable reporter, Marshall Trumbo.

Perhaps we are not so different, he and I.

Today was different only in that when morning came, I did recall a thing from the dream, something short but specific, and potentially "useful".

In the dream, I am sitting in a barber's chair at the center of a large white room, where many colored men dressed in white shuffle about aimlessly. The barber speaks warmly to me as he snips at my hair, his hands callused but gentle as they occasionally brush the back of my neck. His voice drifts about my head endlessly, but all I can recall is what he says at the end. In these final moments of dream, the barber spins me around in his chair to face him, and our eyes meet. He bends down, puts his hands on my shoulders, smiles, and says: "You ain't gonna remember a word I just said, are ya, sonny?"

"I'm sorry," replies the dream version of myself.

"Well, that's all right. No use in crying." And he's right; in the dream I am crying. "You come see me again. See me soon—in your waking world. Then you can write it all down and not worry about the pages dissolving like they tend to when you write in dreams. That notebook yer holdin' ain't exactly real, y'know."

"I know."

"You'll see me, then?"

"All right," I say.

"Promise?" His smile fading.

"Promise," I confirm.

"Hair looks good if I don't say so myself," he says finally, admiring whatever he has done to the hair of the dream-me. Then he puts two fingers over my eyes and forces them open—a confusing situation since in the dream I can see perfectly. But when he does this I am awakened in my bed, the dream now gone, and only the last bit of dialog still fresh in mind.

For many years I have worked hard to shake off such disturbing remnants of dream—the inclination to do so making sense as such remnants have always been just that; maddening pieces of clues, implications that lead nowhere. To puzzle extensively on these things seem only to invite the possibility of madness.

But today I do not shake off the images and voice. Today, I have coherent memory of an invitation, and it is a thing I understand—at least partially. Would it be mad to follow through? To seek out this barber in waking life, if for no other reason than to find out if there is some actual correlation between dream and reality? To do so would be easy enough, for I know who the barber is. Indeed, I know where he is.

He is Charles "Buddy" Bolden, and he is in the Louisiana State Asylum for the Insane, of Jackson, Louisiana. He has been there since 1907, his incarceration there having occurred shortly after the first manifestations of these persistently mystifying dreams of mine.

But to go to such a place without rational reason would be a questionable thing for a man in my position, a senior reporter and associate editor of the most esteemed news source in the state. Of course, I could always invent pretext—create a ruse by which such a visit may seem reasonable—perhaps as background material on some story or other. Certainly, it could be done without raising many eyebrows.

Plus, I have made a promise.

Dear Lord, I can scarcely believe the very words I have written thus. Am I really concerned about a promise made in a dream? How ridiculous it seems on the surface—but at the same time I believe there is meaning in it. If nothing else, I feel certain the dreams will only worsen if I don't make an effort to dispel this fantasy by light of day. But what if I am unable to do so?

Though it is hard for me to comprehend, I believe I will actually go there. There is part of me which disapproves mightily of the notion, but there is deeper part elated by it. Perhaps this will be the first step towards peaceful sleep. Perhaps there is something I must learn before such peace can happen in my nights on earth. Perhaps, perhaps, perhaps, a million perhaps.

But what will be my ruse? My perfectly logical reason for visiting a dipsomaniacal negro in a Jackson crazy farm? Of course, it will be the same as before.

Yes, I have done such a thing in the past. Not at the beckoning of a face in a dream, but from a simple desire to investigate—or so I had told myself and my employers. Years ago and with something nearing glee, I went out of my way to declare "jazz" a newsworthy topic, rushing off to New York City with the intent of interviewing Dominick Carolla of the famed Jim Jam Jump Orchestra. Not because I had actually felt a thing as trite as jazz worthy of a journey so far, but because I recognized, if indirectly, Carolla to be linked to the faces of my dreams. His father was Antonio Carolla, whose death by lynching was the catalyst for Marshall Trumbo's initial attack of insanity. And though only a baby at the time, I have come to learn that Dominick was present during the events of that dark and mysterious day. Carolla the younger grew to be a man, and became famous as the white man who popularized a music invented by negroes. It struck me as a clever human interest story, and, to be honest, it turned out to be a better story than I'd imagined it might.

Upon tracking Carolla to his place of employment at the Reisenweber's Café in New York City, his reception of me was cool till I told him I was from the Picayune—the mention of his hometown newspaper goosing a sinister expression of recognition upon his face.

My interview with him was brief and bizarre. The man seemed possessed of some sort of mania, perhaps related to his excessive alcohol habit—but I managed to gain adequate information to slap a story together. Cautiously, I brought up the subject of his father's disappearance, the Morningstar murder, and Marshall Trumbo. I must say his reaction to these things gave me a chill; his eyes lighting up brightly as if such grim conversation brought him pleasure.

He did not answer my queries verbally, but rather, just continued to smile and nod as I spoke.

Finally he did speak, saying only, "Say, Mr. Reporter—y'ever get around to talkin' to the gravedigger 'bout any of this?" When I asked him who he meant, he gave a little laugh before responding; "Nobody special."

I meant to press further, but the band's break had ended and the club manager began waving insistently for Carolla to return to the bandstand. Before I could say another word he was bounding towards the stage. I considered staying through another set so I may continue our interview in the subsequent break, but something in my heart told me I was best advised to leave. I did so quickly.

Tomorrow, I think, I will go to Jackson. If anyone from the paper queries, I will tell them it is a follow-up to the jazz story and that, in light of the astounding success of jazz music, it might be enlightening to interview Buddy Bolden from his current residence. After all, many have declared Bolden's band to be something of a starting point for the jazz sound—and here he was locked away in a hospital unable to reap its rewards while others received credit, cash, and fame for what may very well have been his own invention. Really, that is not a bad idea for a story at all. Perfectly plausible, I would say.

I will leave in the morning—it is settled. I'll take with me young Benny Price, an intern, for the sake of accurate record. He is only seventeen years old, but quite the proficient stenographer. Also, I have noted a penchant for discreetness in him—a quality upon which I shall rely.

*Transcript of unpublished interview with Charles "Buddy" Bolden,*
*conducted by Clarence Hayes III at Bolden's place of residence,*
*the Louisiana State Asylum for the Insane in Jackson, Louisiana,*
*recorded and transcribed by Benjamin Price on January 13, 1923*

**Hayes:** Mr. Bolden, I appreciate you giving me your time this morning.

**Bolden:** Don't see many white folk in this place. 'Ceptin' the doctors.

**Hayes:** Mr. Bolden, do you feel all right—I mean, do you feel up for this interview?

**Bolden:** Whatcha mean do I feel all right? 'Course I'm all right. Do I look like I ain't all right?

**Hayes:** No, no, of course not. I mean, you look fine. It's just that....

**Bolden:** ....Just that since I'm in a place for crazies must mean I'm crazy, and so maybe I ain't all right. Crazy folk scare you, mister?

**Hayes:** Well, no...

**Bolden:** Don't lie. I kin tell if ya lie. Us crazies got a sense for such things.

**Hayes:** Yes, all right. This place makes me very ill at ease if you must know.

**Bolden:** *(smiling)* Well, if *you* must know, kinda makes me ill at ease too. Thought I'd get used to it, but I ain't yet. Been a coupla years too.

**Hayes:** It's been sixteen years, Mr. Bolden.

**Bolden:** That long? Really? Shee-it. I guess time flies when yer havin' fun. (laughs) Well, my sense of passin' time done got messed up long ago. Call me Buddy, mister. You are white, ain't ya? Makes me nervous when white people start callin' me Mr. Bolden. White folks start callin' a niggra "mister," usually means something bad gonna happen.

**Hayes:** All right, Buddy.

**Bolden:** Doc says you from the newspaper.

**Hayes:** That's right. I'm from the Times-Picayune.

**Bolden:** Must be a slow news day, you comin' all the way out to the crazy farm just to talk to an old beaten nigger like me. If you come to hang somethin' on me, I sure hope it's somethin' ta get hung for. Dyin's all I got left 'bout now, and I don't see much point in waitin' around.

**Hayes:** What I came to talk to you about....(long pause)

**Bolden:** Take yer time, mister. Got plenty of time, me. Don't get much company, neither.

**Hayes:** Well, jazz, of course.

**Bolden:** Don't sound like yer too sure about that. Why'd anyone from the news wanna talk about fuck-music? Don't make no sense. Maybe you crazy, too. (laughs) Well, if you are, you come to the right place. Make yerself ta home, Mr. Reporter.

**Hayes:** Mr.—I mean Buddy, I get the feeling you're unaware of just how big jazz music has become in the last few years. Storyville closed down permanently six years ago, but the music of those halls has become a national phenomenon. International, in fact. It's become quite the sensation in England and France.

**Bolden:** You shittin' me?

**Hayes:** No, I'm not.

**Bolden:** Well, I'll be damned. How'd such a thing come about exactly?

**Hayes:** The first record was made in New York City in 1917. The sound became popular very quickly after that. Many thought it a fad and predicted its popularity would fade, but it actually gets more popular every year.

**Bolden:** Some New York boys made a record of it?

**Hayes:** No, a New Orleans outfit. Dominick Carolla and the Jim Jam Jump Orchestra. Theirs was the first big success, but they're already considered passé. The new big star is a man called Jelly Roll Morton. Colored man. Creole, I think.

**Bolden:** I remember that kid. Name of Ferd, but insisted everyone call him Jelly Roll. Cocky little piss. But he could play all right.

**Hayes:** Buddy, do you remember Dominick Carolla? Or, did you know him at all?

**Bolden:** Yeah, I remember that punk just fine. Stole my horn, that kid. Well, I guess technically he bought it—I mean, he left some money after he hit me over the head with the damn thing and run off. I did spend the money on a pricey hooker, but I didn't actually consent to the sale of that horn. I loved that horn. Wanted to leave it for my son. Guess it don't matter much since West died, though. Died so young. I wasn't much of a daddy to that boy, sorry to say. Woulda been nice to leave him that horn. Only thing I ever had what meant anything. (tears visible in Bolden's eyes)

**Hayes:** I'm sorry about your son.

**Bolden:** Nuffa that. Why'd you come here?

**Hayes:** Well, there's great interest in the jazz phenomenon and a lot of rumors about its true origins. A good many of the older musicians who had played in the tenderloin say it was you who originated the sound. But others take credit for it.

**Bolden:** By "others" you mean Jim Jam Jump, I suppose.

**Hayes:** Yes. Him and a few more.

**Bolden:** Well, he can have the credit. I don't want it. Thass just fine with me. Sure would like that horn back, though. I got it back from the kid, during a time of storm, but they took it from me when they put me in here. Guess they musta sold it off by now.

**Hayes:** Don't you think, I mean, for the sake of historical accuracy, that the record should be set strai—

**Bolden:** Historical accuracy? (laughing loudly) Sonny, I'm about to bust a gut here on that one. Who in their right mind would give hang about the historical accuracy of "Fonky Butt"?

**Hayes:** Well, the commercialized version of the music has lost some of its original vulgarity. But its sound is unique—and it's struck a resonant chord with a lot of people.

**Bolden:** (becoming more serious) Ya keep calling it a sound, but that ain't quite right, y' know. I wouldn't call it a *sound* at all. More lika *feelin'*.

**Hayes:** A feeling?

**Bolden:** A feelin'. And ain't nobody can take credit for a feelin'. Feelin' is something—well, either you got it or you don't. Can't invent no feelin'.

**Hayes:** Well, I suppose you can invent a way to express a feeling. Jazz might be just that; a new method of expressing—

**Bolden:** No. The method don't matter. Listen, this jass thing—it mighta passed through me its first time round, but that don't make it mine.

Or nobody else's neither. It just is. Passed through me—what good it doin' me now? Passed through Jim Jam Jump—you say he's already near forgotten. Now it's passin' through Ferd Morton—his time with it'll be over soon enough. Next in line—who knows? Only thing fer sure: if it caught on real big like you say, don't matter how it got started. A butterfly might flap his little wings in China, that little bit o'wind travelin' all the way round the world, wind up a hurricane in Galveston. Think anyone in Galveston give two shits about which butterfly wrecked their city?

**Hayes:** I suppose not.

**Bolden:** Course not. That'd be a trivial curiosity, nothing more.

**Hayes:** Some people say it's a matter of heritage. They say the white musicians are trying to take credit for something that belongs to the coloreds.

**Bolden:** I say let 'em have it. With no problem. They want the credit? They *got* the credit. I'm the easiest credit man in town. *I say, I say, I say, I say!* That won't change what's true—and the truth have a way of revealing itself over the long run, anyhow. Hell, white folk deserve some recognition—it was white people what made it popular in the sportin' houses in the first place. You think we was playing for the benefit of negroes in them days? No, sir. No indeed.

**Hayes:** Interesting point.

**Bolden:** Look, Mister Reporter, I guess you could say jass enriched my life in some ways; lotsa fine women looking after me, and some pretty good money from time to time—but also it brought me low; brought me to a place like this. And maybe I was meant to end up in this place, just as jass mighta been meant to be a music *from* black folk but *for* white folk. Course, it won't sound the same nor as good if black folks ain't playin' it, but possession is nine tenths of the law they say—and it's the white folks got money to do the possessin'. One thing I know: that jass music can mess with a man's spirit, and if they ain't careful, could be some white folk end up in a place like this, too. Along with possessin' come responsibility, y'see—and with responsibility come risk. And sometimes that risk can fall down hard on a man's soul. Y'see, most white folk think black folk is weak of mind and spirit, and this belief makes 'em feel superior. That superior feelin' can keep a man from being cautious, can cause a man to slip, to fall.

**Hayes:** I see.

**Bolden:** No, I don't think you do see. No matter, though. I don't want no damn credit for this "phenomenon," as you call it. Too much damn responsibility. I do miss the ladies, though. Jass was definitely good for that. *(smiling)*

**Hayes:** About Dominick Carolla—

**Bolden:** Jim Jam Jump, you mean. *(scowling)*

**Hayes:** Yes, Jim Jam Jump.

**Bolden:** Damn punk stole my horn.

**Hayes:** Stole more than that, if you ask me. But I was wondering what memories you may have of him personally. Any significant interactions between the two of you that you can recall?

**Bolden:** *(pausing to think)* Nah, I don't wanna get on this. Why don't we change the subject, sonny?

**Hayes:** Soon—but I do have a question about a particular instance, if you don't mind...

**Bolden:** *(sighing)* All right, then. Out with it.

**Hayes:** In 1891 when you were just fourteen years old—you were questioned as a witness to a homicide—

**Bolden:** *(surprised expression)* Man, you sure done yer homework. I'll give you that.

**Hayes:** A man called Morningstar, a preacher, was killed that night. And a man named Marshall Trumbo was there—a white man.

**Bolden:** Newspaper man. Like you.

**Hayes:** That's right. And Caro—I mean, Jim Jam Jump was also there. But he was only a baby.

**Bolden:** *(far away look)* I seen some things that night.

**Hayes:** What can you tell me about that night?

**Bolden:** I was just a kid. Old man now. Can't remember much of it.

**Hayes:** Mr. Bolden, please...

**Bolden:** *(angry)* Goddamn it, I told you not to call me that!

**Hayes:** I'm sorry, it slipped—

**Bolden:** What's this about? Why you here really? Shoulda damn known it had nothin' to do with no fuck-music. You been playin' me, aintcha, Mister Reporter?

**Hayes:** No, no—not at all. It's just that I had heard some things and I wanted to see if there was any connection—

**Bolden:** Well, I don't remember nothin' bout that night. Nothing, you hear? You want to know about all that crazy stuff, why dontcha go talk to the gravedigger? That fool nigger loves to flap his gums.

**Hayes:** What gravedigger?

**Bolden:** You know—Marcus. From Girod Street Cemetery. Ugly son of a bitch with no nose.

**Hayes:** Marcus James?

**Bolden:** Nobody Special.

**Hayes:** Excuse me?

**Bolden:** I don't know his real last name. Everybody call him Marcus Nobody Special. That's all I know. Go talk to him. He remembers everything. Or so he pretends. I think we're done here, sonny. *(getting up to leave)* Thanks for the company. I got a busy day of being crazy to tend to now, if you don't mind.

**Hayes:** One more question if you don't mind. Please? Buddy?

**Bolden:** *(stops with back turned to Hayes)* I might not answer, but go ahead.

**Hayes:** Marshall Trumbo is—well, he lives here too. He's been here since before you.

**Bolden:** Yeah, so what of it?

**Hayes:** I was wondering if you ever had occasion to speak with him. I mean, since you've been here.

**Bolden:** That man is white, sonny. I never been over to the white end of this place. Didn't even know there was a white end. If there is, I imagine it's pretty posh. Not like here. But no, I ain't never seen him since that night. Hope never ta see him or anyone else from that night ever again, neither. Now, if you'll excuse me.

**Hayes:** Thank you for your time, Buddy.

**Bolden:** Shit. *(walks away quickly through main corridor)*

*Clarence Hayes III, Journal Entry*
*January 13, 1923*

This morning I journeyed to Jackson to interview Charles "Buddy" Bolden. My conversation with him was most unnerving.

Towards the end of our discourse, Bolden mentioned the gravedigger Marcus James; a character who had come into play (in a minor way) at the onset of the original "axeman" crimes. I now believe that Dominick Carolla had also been referring to James during our brief Chicago interview when he mentioned "nobody special"—this term also having been used by Bolden as a sort of nickname for James. Hence, via Marcus James, there now seems to be a tangible link between my dreams and the axeman mystery.

I am so tired. The more I seek answers, the more questions arise—the implications of which only fill me with dread.

Bolden supplied sufficient fodder for a passable story on the topic of jazz, but I don't believe I can bring myself to write such a piece. I can just barely bring myself to write down this entry, but I feel compelled to keep a record of these things, as my memory has been slipping of late. Perhaps due to lack of sleep.

I am so very tired, but the idea of sleep only disturbs me further. As little as I remember of the dreams, they do exhaust me so. It's as though the dreams take place underwater—breath feels so precious upon waking. I must distract myself. I think I will go for a walk. The Faubourg Marigny can be very soothing in the quiet, early morning hours.

*May 1, 1926*
New Orleans Times-Picayune
*page 2, column 1*

## JAZZ ORIGINATOR SUFFERS BREAKDOWN
### Reported by Clarence Hayes III

THURSDAY MORNING Dominick Carolla, leader of New Orleans' own internationally famous Jim Jam Jump Orchestra, was admitted to the psychiatric ward of Tulane Infirmary after suffering what doctors describe as "an acute nervous condition".

Friends and colleagues of Mr. Carolla have related what they call "unusual behavior" from the already decidedly eccentric local celebrity. Doctors have speculated Mr. Carolla's current condition as possibly related to depression, stemming from his orchestra's sliding popularity in the jazz world. Many critics and fans of jazz have recently dismissed Carolla's latest recordings as outdated, while newer orchestras continue to expand upon the boundaries of the artform and take turns basking in the ever-fickle spotlight of public opinion.

Mr. Carolla is the composer of many tunes already firmly established as popular standards, including his widely covered composition, "Jim Jam Jumpin' Blues." The future of the Jim Jam Jump Orchestra is uncertain, its remaining members in agreement that they will not continue in absence of their leader.

*July 7, 1926*
*New Orleans Times-Picayune*
*page 4, column1*


## FAMED ORCHESTRA LEADER RELEASED FROM HOSPITAL
### Reported by Clarence Hayes III


AFTER TWO months under hospital supervision following a nervous break-down, orchestra leader Dominick Carolla of The Jim Jam Jump Orchestra has been discharged from the Tulane Infirmary's psychiatric ward.

In a brief press conference held on the steps outside the Tulane facility where a sparse handful of reporters stood in attendance, Mr. Carolla declared that his days as a jazzman are ended, stating his current intention of "dedicating the rest of my short life to the will of a great and terrible God." The remaining members of The Jim Jam Jump Orchestra had previously sworn to disband the group if Mr. Carolla did not return as their leader.

This marks the end of one of the most important ensembles in the history of the international jazz phenomenon, which Mr. Carolla and his band played a key role in popularizing. Mr. Carolla recorded the first ever commercial release of jazz music in 1917, and many of his compositions are now considered standards within the modern age music industry.

*Unpublished transcript of interview
with Dominick Carolla at the home of Clarence Hayes III,
conducted by Clarence Hayes III,
recorded and transcribed by Benjamin Price
August 13, 1926.*

**Hayes:** I thank you for your time, Mr. Carolla.

**Carolla:** The pleasure's all mine, Mr. Hayes. I enjoyed our brief talk in Chicago a few years back—my only regret was that you made your leave so soon.

**Hayes:** Well, thank you. I'm afraid the long trip had gotten the better of me, and a good night's sleep was beckoning.

**Carolla:** Perfectly understandable. No need to explain. Did you get the information you'd come for?

**Hayes:** Excuse me?

**Carolla:** Back in Chicago. I assumed that you were digging around for information not directly related to jazz. Were your inquiries fruitful?

**Hayes:** I'm not sure what you mean.

**Carolla:** Did you speak to the gravedigger as I suggested?

**Hayes:** Oh, yes, I mean—no, I haven't.

**Carolla:** Shame, shame. How've you been sleeping lately? Try counting sheep?

**Hayes:** Traditionally, it's the interviewer who asks the questions during an interview.

**Carolla:** I've never been big on things traditional. As an example, I typically have desert before dinner. But all right, I'll play (winks). Ask me a question.

**Hayes:** Your recent retirement from jazz has devastated many fans from around the world. How do you view your impact on the new jazz subculture in America and the world at large?

**Carolla:** You flatter me! *Thank* you, sir. Quite to the contrary, Mr. Hayes, clearly, fans around the world could give a rat's ass whether I continue with jazz or not. Indeed, my conscience is clear on all counts. Well, most counts. I'm working on that. I'll be clearing the last of it this morning with you, I reck—I mean, I hope.

**Hayes:** Well, it's true that the popularity of The Jim Jam Jump Orchestra has waned in recent years, but couldn't that be a temporary thing? After all, your orchestra is credited by many as the original jazz band.

**Carolla:** Popularity shmopularity, Mr. Hayes. It's all quite meaningless in the grand scheme of things, don't you think? I'm sorry, I forgot that only *you* may ask questions. Well, to your query.... During my little vacation at the hospital, I had occasion to meditate on various things. It is now clear to me that record sales and celebrity are just window dressing for a thing far more important. Jazz is a thing, a living thing, really —and for me it was a gift. I've abused the gift in a way, but I intend to give it back with all due interest. Or, as the saying goes, "they gave it to me but I gave it back the best I could." Eighty years from now when people read this book, they'll know I did just that. And I will be redeemed in the eyes of God, and, more importantly, redeemed in the eyes of mortal man. Well, more important, that is, if you happen to be a mortal man. Which we both are, or so it would certainly seem.

**Hayes:** I'm not writing a book. This interview is for a newspaper article.

**Carolla:** I didn't say that you were writing a book—nor did I mean to imply that you should. In any case, we both know that you have no intention of writing any such article. This little talk is for your benefit alone— and you know it. At least that's what you imagine. You're still seeking answers, still hoping for sleep. Don't fret, sleep will come in time, Mr. Hayes. Maybe sooner than you think.

**Hayes:** Mr. Carolla, do you feel all right? I mean do you feel up to this interview or should we continue it at another time?

**Carolla:** *Whatcha mean do I feel all right? Course I'm all right. Do I look like I ain't all right?* (STENOGRAPHER'S NOTE: VOICE CHANGED, MUCH DEEPER. TO MY EARS; A SPOT ON IMPERSONATION OF BUDDY BOLDEN - BP)

**Hayes:** *(long pause)* I—*(another pause)*

**Carolla:** *(laughing)* Didn't mean to get ya all discombobulated, Mr. Hayes. I just thought it time me and you got ourselves on the same page, so to speak. You pretending you got me fooled, me playing along so's not to rattle you. It's just such a long way around. So what do you say we cut the bullshit? I'm just so very, very tired. It's a long road I've traveled. So very long. Really, you have no idea.

**Hayes:** How did you acquire my transcripts? The interview you just quoted was never published.

**Carolla:** That interview was never published just as this one won't be. Not as a newspaper article, leastways. To answer your question; *I read the book*—and vice versa, of course. Hell, I'm in the book. So are you. We're being read right now. Can't you smell the *voyeur?* Right there. Look. *(pointing)*

**Hayes:** I'm confused. What book are we talking about? Who is the author of this mysterious book?

**Carolla:** Fellow named Maistros. And yes, it is quite mysterious. Oh indeed, a very mysterious and curious thing, that book.

**Hayes:** Never heard of him. Maistros, you say?

**Carolla:** Might be 'cause he ain't born yet. *(laughing)* Lo! The mystery!

**Hayes:** Clearly, you have somehow become familiar with my notes regarding the Bolden interview.

**Carolla:** Funny thing about that nigger. He turned down two hunnert dollars for that damn horn—an exorbitant offer! Then, come to find, I wind up purchasing that very same horn for a mere twenty bucks from an orderly at the Jackson nuthouse. Guess I should have been more patient. Good things come to those who wait, or so they say.

**Hayes:** How would this writer you mention have had access to my personal notes?

**Carolla:** *(sighs)* I doubt if you have the intestinal fortitude for the answer to that, and it would be mighty tough to explain in any satisfying way. Let's just assume it's true for the sake of continuity during the course of the interview at hand. Shall we?

**Hayes:** *(pauses)* All right. Can you tell me how you met Mr. Bolden—and any significant details about your relationship with him?

**Carolla:** (NOTE: AGAIN IN THE VOICE OF BUDDY BOLDEN) *Damn punk stole my horn. (laughs uncontrollably, and at length)*

**Hayes:** It seems that you are obsessed with imitating Bolden.

**Carolla:** Well, that really stung, Clarence. And here I was thinking you n'me was gettin' to be friends, lippity hey. I was just having a little fun with ya is all. Why ya wanna hafta mafta shlafta mifity bang goo go and get all mean about it? Shy lye foo say I, is who.

**Hayes:** Mr. Carolla, are you feeling all right?

**Carolla:** (Note: Again in the voice of Bolden) *Crazy folk scare you, mister?* Listen, slim. Buddy didn't invent jazz anymore than you did. Mip map mop. You oughta know that by nippity now hugga wugga flip fly. It was a thing in nature revealed to him, then he passed it on to me. Now you got it—he got it, they got it, we got it—gitta gotta get it flappa mot hap hi. It's just an old fashioned ailment, like a disease or a fever gettin' passed on from body to body, but it don't have to swim in blood no more—oh no—it done gradjy-ated times two, is who. It's way past being born now, past the pain of birthulatin'. *(voice again changing, this time taking on the rhythmic speech of a negro preacher:) Soon it will be a holy thing, a thing in the air transferred through sound and thought alone, destined to break free from its prison of sacred muck in the Bayou St. John, and on to the world at large. As the storm surges and the water doth swell, the bayou itself shall stretch out to the river through long dead fingers resurrected at last—hallelujah!—diluting itself in clearer water only to rapidly thicken and multiply, to travel and go forth, to touch a million souls livin'in pain,* offerin' up freedom of the spirit to the living, a freedom previously enjoyed only by the dead. This is my father's— my true father's—gift to humanity. A simple "thank you very kindly" for teaching Him the nature of joy and pain—and for being so kind to his wayward son, yours truly, during my short stay here on earth. Second stay, really; first doin' the lamb bit; now the lion. Grrrrr.

(Note: The sound of an animal issues from Carolla's lips).

Sorry there, Clarence, didn't mean to startle ya. Now, where was I? That's right! The gift! …When the waters rise and yon fingers doth reach, it is I who shall usher this thing, this gift, to the river from the bayou, just as the wrath of the so-called Axeman was delivered through these scared hands. 'Tis I who shall beckon the towering surge and the mighty swell of the great waters to leap forth and to pound upon the lands, bringing death and destruction, yes; but lo! what love! When this thing is done—the gift released!—the demon freed, the package delivered; then my work will be done, my destiny fulfilled, and so on and so forth, unto ages and ages, ack shally hack bim bop bam boom halla walla hi hoo, amen times two. God bless you, geshundheit, nostrovia, good-night, farewell, ta-ta, yassoo and adieu. And when those watery fingers of death reach the Mississippi River, then—and only then—will you see me no more.

**Hayes:** *(after long pause)* May I ask a question?

**Carolla:** I'm sorry, I'd forgotten the rules. My apologies, and, yes, please do ask your question. It's only fair.... *I reckon.*

**Hayes:** You just mentioned the Axeman. You said his wrath was delivered through your hands. Is that a confession?

**Carolla:** *(smiling)* Confession?

**Hayes:** Yes. Are you saying that you are the Axeman?

**Carolla:** Well, not entirely, no. That would be misleading.

**Hayes:** How so?

**Carolla:** Seeds. Just seeds.

**Hayes:** Seeds?

**Carolla:** Yes, I planted seeds. That's all. I did the first of em, then let the seeds blossom on their own, which they did nicely in the fertile soil of New Orleans. Planted other seeds up North, but they didn't take as well—bad soil. And, oh yes, I almost forgot—I did send that letter to the newspapers. But that was really in response to a particularly libelous editorial by one of your competitors.

**Hayes:** *(after long pause)* May I ask one more question?

**Carolla:** *(Again in the voice of Bolden) I might not answer, but go ahead.*

**Hayes:** *(pauses, going through notes)* Can you tell me what you believe might have triggered the breakdown which led to your recent stay at the Tulane facility?

**Carolla:** Clarence, Clarence, Clarence. You've clearly learned nothing. No worry. There is time to learn. Always time. Clarence, listen, there *was* no breakdown. OK? Get that through your head.

**Hayes:** No breakdown?

**Carolla:** No, but there was an event.

**Hayes:** What sort of event?

**Carolla:** I became that which I have coveted all my life. Or, rather, recognized that such has always been so.

**Hayes:** I'm afraid you've lost me.

**Carolla:** *(sighs)* Of course I have. Let me try to explain. A human life is a note of jazz. In jazz, a note doesn't lead to other notes so much as the note itself changes, traveling through the air, fueled by its ability to shift pitch and alter tone along the way; sometimes collecting truth and discarding lies, sometimes masking the truth it has acquired by dressing itself in lies *un*discarded. My own journey has been painful, but it has been a path of discovery and of righteousness—and that path has taught me all I need to know. It has taught me who I am, what I've done, what I must do, what I can control, what I will never control, how I began, how I will end—and what all of it means.

**Hayes:** I don't understand. What does *any* of it mean?

**Carolla:** *(smiling)* It means that I have learned to dream. And to dream is to know the truth.

**Hayes:** And what truth might that be?

**Carolla:** *(Again in the voice of Bolden) I think we're done here, sonny.*


*(Carolla rises to leave)*



*end of interview*

*To: Mr. Raymond Hockett*
*c/o The Times-Picayune*
*New Orleans, Louisiana*

AUGUST 14, 1926

Dear Mr. Hockett,

It is with heavy heart that I now write you of my intentions to effectively end my tenure with the Times-Picayune. I will remain at your disposal for a period of two weeks from the date of this letter.

My decision is related to an urgent letter I received this morning from my mother and father in Baltimore. The details are personal, but my family is in need of my immediate presence there. In light of this emergency, I must ask: Please let me know if it is possible for me to leave before the end of the afore-mentioned two weeks.

I wish to sincerely thank you, Mr. Hockett, as well as the entire staff at the Times-Picayune, for having treated me so well during my time in your employ. I truly hope that this notice provides a suitable length of time for which to find a replacement, as I do not wish to cause any undo inconvenience.

With sincerest regrets and deepest gratitude,
I am yours,
*Benjamin Price*

*Clarence Hayes III, Journal Entry,*
*August 25, 1926*

Last night my sleep was oddly dreamless, and I awoke this morning to the sound of hammering.

A hurricane struck Houma late last night; it is a powerful one. My heart goes out to the poor people of that city, the amount of warning received by them having been negligible; frantic radio communications from commercial vessels, most likely lost themselves only hours before the beast made landfall.

The hurricane's future path is uncertain. I would despise myself for wishing it to edge westerly and possibly affect Galveston, a city so utterly devastated just over a quarter century ago by such a storm. But if the winds should blow towards New Orleans, it's uncertain if our levee system could stand up to such a force. Quite bluntly: Should the levee fail, the result will be catastrophic. Twenty years past and the city is still not fully recovered from the storm of 1906. I fear that we are vulnerable to total destruction this time.

I am reminded of a comment made by Buddy Bolden three years ago. He'd made an analogy about the theoretical motion of a butterfly's wings at one end of the world, traveling and gaining power till that tiny bit of wind blossomed into the complete devastation of a city far away. Indeed, I'd like to know the name of the butterfly who's responsible for this.

More disturbing are memories of Dominick Carolla's ramblings, only days ago having spoken of "a towering surge" that will bring "death and destruction" to the city. Perhaps the insane mind is similar to those of woodland creatures; squirrels and gophers who burrow themselves into the safety of earth weeks before the appearance of a natural disaster—or fish who dive down deep to insulate themselves from the violent surface waters above. I can't help but think that Carolla's predictions may have more substance than sheer animal instinct—in any case, coincidences presented by the Carolla interview have given me great pause.

Ironically, I did make an attempt just yesterday to speak with Marcus James—as instructed by both Bolden and Carolla. James' attitude towards me was guarded at best, and, like Bolden, he outright refused to speak of events directly related to the Morningstar murder of 1891. His tone with me turned bitter and dismissive by the end of our discussion, apparently due to past abuse from local reporters. Or, in his own words, "Can't never trust no newspaper reporters to tell things straight, so I ain't saying nothing a'tall." I suppose I can't blame him for that.

I was dismayed to learn of Benny's abrupt resignation from the T-P, my regret made more acute by Mr. Hockett's unspoken implication in forwarding Benny's letter of resignation to me personally—the insinuation being that I had managed to scare off a perfectly good stenographer by including him on these recent expeditions. In fairness, Mr. Hockett's inferences bear weight of certain truths. I know that Benny was deeply troubled by the dark utterances of Dominick Carolla—as was I. If this was the true reason behind his resignation, then it was kind of Benny not to specifically mention such to Mr. Hockett. Whatever the case, in light of the impending storm I am grateful to Mr. Hockett for allowing Benny immediate leave—so that he might be safely away in time, should danger arrive here.

Something in the pit of my stomach tells me it will.

The winds are whipping ferociously outside. Rain squalls have been coming and going all afternoon. The sun hides behind a blanket of gray, and the clouds churn urgently. Many neighbors have already left and gone north—others are busy preparing for the worst.

The sound of hammering has been relentless since before daybreak, its constant rapping from around the Marigny having combined into an uneasy rhythm, somehow familiar. I am not sure what this familiarity means. It is like an echo from the mind of another, a builder of coffins surrounded by depthless, churning waters; a builder of answerless endings, forging deathly comfort by way of nails into wood. The sound is shallow and harsh to my ear, yet plumbs deeply into my soul. Like the nail, like the nail; driving it home, a home unknown to this life.

Mr. Hockett has ordered all newspaper staff to leave the city immediately. His colleagues at the Biloxi Tribune have kindly offered shelter for us and our families till the storm passes.

I have decided that, as a newsman, I must stay and ride out the storm should it come. It is not the job of a reporter to run from danger, but rather, to bear witness. I will attempt to keep this journal and all attendant notes, documents and clippings in safe order so that they may survive potential flooding. And, if the worst should happen to me, then I hope someone may find it—and put together the nagging puzzle that I have failed to complete.

*Clarence Hayes III, Journal Entry,*
*August 27, 1926*

The winds outside are raging.

After losing a window to flying debris, I hastily hammered a table top across the affected window frame to prevent further wind from whipping through the house, potentially with enough force to blow the roof off. Before I'd managed this repair, the first floor was made a mess of; papers flying and furniture tumbling amongst airborne shards of broken glass.

A small glass chip seems to have embedded itself in my right cheek. I can't get it out.

In anticipation of further window damage, I have taken to dismantling various pieces of furniture; removing any large flat section that may serve as a brace. It is clear to me now that I should have taken the example of my neighbors and done this much earlier. As it is, I am forced to do my hammering from inside— to attempt to do so from without would no doubt prove perilous.

The rain is falling harder than I have ever seen; water leaking from in between bricks through spaces unseen, pushing through impossible openings between glass and window frame. Loose debris is pounding against the roof and walls with the force of cannon fire.

My radio will not function.

So much for my brave newsman's ethics of "bearing witness" and "riding out the storm". I am useless to my profession inside this house, and do not dare venture out. The only meaningful witness I may bear of this disaster would be in its aftermath—and I have my doubts as to whether I will survive to see it.

As I write this I am hearing a new sound. It is loud, very loud, but I can not place it. It is the sound of a freight train, charging off the tracks.

Dear God. Water is coming in—and coming in fast. I must preserve these papers and vacate to the attic immediately.

Dear God in heaven. This will surely be my end.

*August 28, 1926*
New Orleans Times-Picayune
*page 1, column 1*

# HURRICANE!
## DEVASTATES SOUTH LOUISIANA
Death toll in thousands, property damage incalculable
Reported by Raymond Hockett, editor-in-chief

A HURRICANE charged up through the Gulf of Mexico on the evening of August 25th, striking landfall near Houma in the early morning hours of the 26th before beginning a trail of death and devastation that was to last for two days.

The unprecedented magnitude of the storm caught Louisiana's sleepy southern region by surprise, resulting in horrendous loss of life, limb, and property—exceeding even the destructive force of the infamous Hurricane of '06—and leaving behind a dazed community of survivors to pick up the pieces. The following account of the hurricane's path is based on information available at this early date.

Late in the afternoon of the 25th, the steamship Cody, while cruising 220 miles east southeast of Galveston, reported 75 mph winds while the steamship Argon suffered even more treacherous northeastly winds of 100 mph neat 27N 90.5W. In Grand Isle, the pressure sank to a dramatic 28.31" with estimated winds of 100 mph. Meanwhile, the hapless citizens of Morgan City contended with winds above 60 mph and over five inches of rain in a matter of hours. The City of New Orleans at this time was already experiencing warning gusts of up to 52 mph, while the attendant pressure sank to a menacing 29.37". Further north to Burrwood, winds reached a slightly lower 50 mph as the pressure dropped to 29.55". All this before the eye hit landfall.

In the early morning hours of the 26th, the eye of the great hurricane collided with Houma. The lone Episcopal church of that town was reduced to swirling splinters in a matter of seconds, while surrounding sugarhouses were uprooted and wrecked, crops utterly destroyed. Gismer, Burnside, Lutcher and Caryville experienced severe damage, the few roads high enough to avoid immediate flooding rendered impassable by heaving debris, airborne wreckage, and uprooted trees. Buildings directly affected by the eye wall were removed from their foundations and lifted skyward, the remnants of which transformed into a deadly shower of brick and wooden shrapnel that rained down upon any poorly sheltered citizenry as if from a terrible enemy in a great war.

By the morning of the 27th, the slow moving hurricane only increased in power, its winds graduating to 120 mph before reaching Napoleonville and Thibodeaux. Houses, churches, and businesses there were lifted, shaken, then dropped as telephone poles cracked and splintered against the force of terrible winds.

In the first 27 hours, 42 inches of rain had fallen in Madewood and Shriever. Pecan orchards and sugar crops, as well as early rice and cotton crops, were flooded and swept away. The New Canal lighthouse at Donaldsonville was severely damaged and the Timbalier Bay Lighthouse, where, north of Isle Deniere, a 13 foot storm surge had already blanketed the southern coast of the Timbalier Bay, pushing the structure forward in the muck of its foundation into a norwesterly slant. The storm continued on its northwest path towards Shreveport when a slight change in direction occurred, shifting the storm's path from northwest to due north—putting East New Orleans in its direct path.

By this time, news of the devastation (as well as firm warnings presented by winds as powerful as 90 mph) had convinced many Orleanians to seek higher ground. Although severe property damage similar to that suffered by the far southern regions of the state were suffered in Kenner and Slidell (where winds mercifully began to lose speed, dropping to 70 mph), it is believed by rescue workers and city officials that many of the inhabitants of those towns did evacuate in time. Similarly, many residents of New Orleans proper did leave—but some, believing the course of the storm to be firmly northwest, chose to stay and ride out the remainder of the hard wind and driving rains.

The storm did pass the city—but then wavered to the east; leaving land and settling momentarily over Lake Pontchartrain where it gathered in force from its formerly dwindling winds of 70 mph to an increased rate of 95 mph. This brief return in strength resulted in a towering storm surge of 12 feet, bringing a wall of water out of the lake and into the famously docile bog of Bayou St. John with tremendous force.

Bayou St. John, normally a stagnant receptacle for Lake Pontchartrain's seasonal overflow, was instantly transformed into a raging river. The bayou has a theoretical history of long ago possessing five great waterways—this theory was quickly realized as water rushed from its bosom and across the city proper towards the Mississippi River. Water continued to surge forward from the bayou at various points, sweeping through the city's center where flood levels reached up to fourteen feet before plunging over the levee and into the river. The hurricane lost strength then, and began, once again, to move northwest of the lake—where it would soon begin to lose its center and disassemble.

In the storm's wake the levee proved traitorous, keeping water within the city instead of without—its intended function effectively reversed. Flood waters in the French Quarter as well as in the eastern parts of the 7th, 8th and 9th Wards, soon largely drained westward to Mid City—taking with them an as of yet undetermined number of lost souls and much debris from devastated buildings. The crumbling and abandoned structures that formerly made up the old Storyville red light district proved most vulnerable, all but four of these structures having been completely washed away. Loss of life suffered in the city alone cannot be accurately measured at this early date, but the immediate horrors have already touched us all in a profound way. Our own family at the *Times-Picayune* has suffered particularly heart rending losses—and I would like to take this opportunity, as editor-in-chief of this publication, to express my deepest and most heartfelt condolences to the families of our colleagues and friends who are so far missing and presumed lost.

Those of our staff presently unaccounted for are; Leonard Orr, Harvey Meaux, Elvis Munstermann, Reginald Dupree, Clarence Hayes III, Irvin Brite, Susan Forester, Gasper Landrieu, John Cannazerro, Timothy Reilly, Barnard Lees, and Anthony Schiro.

I would also like to express deep gratitude to our fine colleagues at the Biloxi Tribune for generously granting use of their presses until conditions allow for our safe return to New Orleans. We are currently continuing operations of the *Times-Picayune* at temporary offices located at 511 Grand Street in Biloxi, courtesy of Tribune management.

*Clarence Hayes III, Journal Entry,*
*August 27, 2 PM (approximate)*

I am on the roof.

The rain has mercifully slowed, but the wind remains strong. My back is pressed to the chimney—it blocks the wind just enough.

My home stands tall at two stories; its ceilings high. Less than an hour ago, the attic had provided sufficient refuge—I did not imagine the waters might reach higher. It is mysterious to me that the surge has come from the northwest side of the house and not from the east where the river lie. Is it possible the floodwaters have come from the lake and not the river? From the Bayou St. John? This doesn't seem possible, but must be true.

There is one small window in the shape of a setting sun at the east side of my attic—and from this crescent shaped portal I have witnessed horrors that will stay with me to the end of my days. Helplessly, I have witnessed as my neighbors, the Rhyans, were chased upwards within their home by quickly rising water. The Rhyan house being only one story high and perhaps a mere nine feet at its highest point, the churning brown waters of the flood overtook it quickly.

Their dilemma first became evident to me when I spied an axe smashing upwards through the shingles of their rooftop. First the mother, Bernice, climbed out of the hole and into the wind and rain. I watched as the father, Ted, pushed the four children one by one into the waiting arms of their mother, who lay flat across the roof on her belly. Once retrieved by her, the three smallest children, a girl and two boys, clung desperately to Mrs. Rhyan's thin legs, while Tommy, the oldest at eleven, held fast to the jagged rim of the hole alongside his mother. Lastly, Ted pulled himself out, throwing his heavy body over the smaller children to anchor them against the force of wind and wave. It was at this time that the eyes of their five year old, Betsy, seemed to find my own through the chaos of the storm. Extraordinarily, her gaze betrayed no sense of terror. I cannot ever know if the following was a product of my own imagination, but as my mind recalls it:

She smiled at me—yes, *smiled*—then gave me a quick wink. This tiny creature. It was as if she read the fear in my own heart and wished to console me—to convey that all would be well and fair in the end. Surely I imagined this—no mere child could show such strength in the face of almost certain death.

Shortly after this exchange (imagined?!?) between myself and the girl, a large wave struck hard at the family—like the paw of an immense cat swatting tenacious fleas. After the wave had passed, Tommy's grip on the loose shingles and damaged roofbeam tore free, causing his body to be thrown eastward, flailing and kicking at the waters that pulled him away from his kin. He drifted helplessly from the family, struggling most pitifully to keep his head above water, and screamed for his father to come to his aid. Such a terrible sound I have never heard—and I cannot begin to imagine how the sound must have cut at the soul of Ted Rhyan. Ted could not help his son, for to leave the remaining children unanchored by his weight would have meant to sacrifice them all.

The sound of Tommy's screams soon did fade as the undertow of the ever-expanding river pulled him down. To my great shame, the sudden absence of the boy's screams washed over my selfish heart with something like relief. Truly, I am damned for having such despicable feelings, however involuntary.

But what was soon to follow would prove even more horrible.

At the cruel loss of her eldest child, Bernice Rhyan responded by rolling over slightly to reach young Betsy with her left hand, her right holding firmly all the while to the traitorous rim of the roof hole. Pulling the small child's head close to her own, Mrs. Rhyan said something in the girl's ear—Betsy responding with a frantic nod. Mrs. Rhyan then hugged Betsy hard with one arm, and kissed the top of her head firmly. She did all this only seconds before briefly freeing her second hand to twist the girl's head around with a sickening snap, the sound of which I was somehow able to hear above the roar of howling wind, whipping rain, and forever surging tide.

Mrs. Rhyan let Betsy go.

Betsy's small body traveled a great distance in a short time, riding the crest of a terrible wave as if in flight, sailing perhaps thirty yards northwest before plummeting downwards, submerging forever.

The expression upon Ted's face was—quite shockingly—not of anger or grief at his wife's actions—but of understanding. He reached a hand to his wife's face, brushed her cheek with open palm, then appeared to say something. He did this before similarly twisting the necks of his remaining two sons.

I am not sure why the parents decided their children should die by their own hands rather than be swept off while still living. Perhaps it was to spare them the pain of a living separation, so that they might die not alone. Or perhaps they did it because it was the last thing on earth they were able to control in their children's lives. I believe in my heart that it was, in fact, a type of mercy killing. I pray it to be so. In any case, if it was murder—it was murder most tender.

Immediately after dispatching their children to the world of the dead, Mr. and Mrs. Rhyan held hands—then actually stood upon the roof—letting the next wave knock them backwards—together—surrendering their own bodies to the storm. There was an undeniable peace in this final act, this conjoined suicide.

By the time the Rhyan house had submerged completely, water had begun to pour across my own attic floor—streaming across my ankles and rising fast. I wrapped this journal and all attendant notes and papers into my only rain coat quickly, grabbed the axe that was thankfully near at hand, and took a cue from Ted Rhyan's recent example; smashing a hole through the roof from inside.

At this moment of writing, a ray of sun is pierced the clouds.

The rain is thinning, but the winds are still strong and water continues to rise. I am sitting with my back pressed to the chimney, its stationary bulk blocking the brute force of wind and preventing me, at least for the moment, from being thrown to the waves. The pages I write upon now are dampened, but thankfully I have completed most of my entries these many years in pencil. So far, the written words appear mainly unsmeared and intact.

This will be my last entry, I know.

The waves have calmed slightly as the crack of sun widens, but the swell of the tide increases still. Even at this place of my last stand, this toppermost point of my tall home, the water crawls diligently to my hip. I watch things floating by. Broken furniture, children's toys, bits of plaster and debris, the bodies of animals; household pets and livestock as well as human bodies—normal things twisted and sad. A burlap bag floats near to me—something inside seems to keep it afloat, and so I grab onto it. It is tied shut, I open it—and find an empty, round tin meant for holding coffee beans inside. Air-tight when closed, it is the trapped air of the tin that has allowed the bag its weird buoyancy. I will take this as a sign. I will fold in half and roll these papers of mine, cram them all into the tin, tie the tin into the bag, then let it all go. Hopefully to be found by a sympathetic soul.

If this is found, please forward its full contents to Raymond Hockett of the Times-Picayune Newspaper Company. It's my hope that he will venture to make sense of these, my last hours—and the troubling years which have led to this moment.

There are lights under the water—I do not know how this is possible, but it is so. There is a comfort in the glow of them. They seem to echo the eyes of young Betsy Rhyan, telling me that death is not terrible. They are winking at me, welcoming me.

The water is very high now. Time to secure these scribbles of mine, to send them on their way.

There is music in my head. It is high and mournful—but also there is joy in the sound.

Pray for me, please.

Goodbye.

Clarence Hayes, III

*TO:*
*Mr. Raymond Hockett*
*c/o* The Biloxi Tribune
*511 Grand Street*
*Biloxi, Mississippi*

August 30, 1926

Dear Mr. Hockett,

Please know that my thoughts and prayers are with you in this deeply troubling time.

As you'll recall, I was pulled from my post at the Times-Picayune by urgent private matters concerning my family in Baltimore. These matters are now sufficiently resolved, and, with your kind permission, I now ask if I may return to your service.

If the answer is yes, I will take the next train to your stated temporary offices in Biloxi. If no, then please accept these, my warmest wishes. And, if I may be so bold, please do write me if you hear any news regarding our missing colleagues. In particular, I would appreciate any news concerning Mr. Hayes—who I had become quite close with during my tenure at the T-P.

Enclosed you will find an address card with information as to where I can be reached by mail, wire, or phone.

Yours most sincerely,
Benjamin Price

*Raymond Hockett, Journal Entry,*
*November 3, 1926*

Dear Clarence,

It seems that your demons have become my own.

If you are in a place where souls can see such things, Clarence, I hope you find some peace in knowing that this bunch of notes and papers have been delivered to me, your requested recipient. It is early morning and I have been reading throughout the night—sometimes with great difficulty as there is water damage done to a great many of the pages.

I think I have a general understanding of what has tormented you, dear friend, and I must admit to having shed a tear upon reading of your apparent end. But I cannot for the life of me understand what you would like me to do with this information. All I can think of is to continue these notes where you have left off. Perhaps the resolutions you seek (even in death) may come if I record my own experiences upon these sadly weathered pages. I will try.

Let me begin with the unlikely story of how this journal has found me.

After the hurricane had passed, the City of New Orleans found itself betrayed by its own levee system—keeping much of the water within city limits even after the river tide had settled back to a manageable level. The Army Corp of Engineers devised a temporary pumping system, the technology of which frankly perplexes me. The going was slow but progress was steady—in a matter of weeks the six to eight feet of water initially held in by the levee was forced back into the river. When the flood level reached a more inhabitable six inches, residents and businesses were allowed to return—to survey damage and begin the arduous process of rebuilding. My own uptown home on Napoleon Avenue appeared miraculously unscathed from the exterior—but on closer scrutiny it became apparent that the contents and interior were thoroughly ruined. This marks me among the lucky ones—most homes could not withstand the combination of wind and tide, many of them leveled completely. The offices and warehouse building of the Times-Picayune were mostly spared—the structures themselves left intact, but not much salvageable inside. We did manage to repair the presses to the point of working order, however, and have been back in full operation since early October.

Understandably, news from the world beyond is a matter of trivia in the eyes of most Orleanians at the moment. Such massive loss of life and property is an all consuming thing—and attendant emotions have made the rebuilding process particularly painful. Getting lost in the work of this tremendous effort does help on some level—to focus on mundane labor can pull one's mind from the larger picture if only for brief, blissful moments and sometimes for hours at a time. There will be plenty of time for prolonged mourning later, I suppose.

Yesterday morning, Georgia, my secretary and personal assistant whom you know well, tapped lightly at the door of my office. Brazenly poking her head in when I failed to respond, she spoke to me in a near whisper, "There is a Miss Morningstar to see you, sir. I believe that you should speak with her." I gave her my usual dismissive wave, but she was unusually persistent.

"She has news of Mr. Hayes, sir," she stated with a note of urgency. The mention of your name, dear friend, had me rushing to the door. You see, I had foolishly hoped at that moment that such "news" may be of your well being. Of course, it was not.

The woman was a pretty Creole, light of color. The circles under her eyes and the lines on her face, which have become so common in the Parishes of late, made it impossible to hazard a guess as to her age, though I imagined her to be in her mid to late 40s. As I reached to shake her hand, her eyes met mine with an uncomfortable intensity.

"Mr. Hockett?" she queried in a soft voice.

"I am," said I. "How may I help you, madam?"

She held in her hand a coarse burlap sack—presumably the one mentioned in your final pages. "This was meant for you, sir. You should take it now."

She untied the opening to produce a tin from inside, which she pried open with bitten fingernails before removing its contents in a bunch. "It's not too bad with water, sir," she said. "I peeled the wet parts carefully and laid em out to dry. Should be able to read what's been said just fine. Just as I have."

"What's this to do with Clarence Hayes?" I asked.

"They were his belongings, sir. On the last page he asks they be returned to you. I hope you don't mind me holding onto them for a few days. As you will see, there is a part of it that belongs to me as well."

"Where on earth did you find it?" My voice, I'm afraid, sounded regrettably (if unintentionally) stern—causing her to take a step back.

"The bag turned up where my house used to stand," she responded. "Where my *father's* house, I should say, used to stand." The latter sentence came out boldly, with the indignance of a beaten but still proud heart.

"Your house—?"

"My father's house—"

"Of course, your father's house."

"Gone. All gone now."

"I'm so sorry."

"I'll be just fine, thank you. This storm ain't my first. Been built back up before, just as it'll do now. I have no doubt that me and mine'll be just fine."

And I believed her. As frail and battered as she appeared, there was a powerful resilience in her eyes. I stumbled onward:

"I'm sorry—how did you—?"

"It was just there. Atop a plain, muddy piece of bog where my father's house used to stand—near the edge of the Bayou St. John. Foolish place to put a house, I guess. My father liked privacy from the world, and that it was—if nothing else."

"How do you suppose it found its way there?" My voice still too tense with apprehension to sound friendly, I tried to compensate by softening my eyes.

"Must be God put it there. My father himself is mentioned a time or two in those papers, maybe that's why. I tried to make sense of those words that your friend wrote down. Couldn't—though I admit to not trying very hard. Figured you might have better luck. Anyway, I don't need to know how this story turns out no more. Just wanna let go and move on. Maybe you'll do the same. But that Mr. Hayes wanted you to have this. Being his last request on earth, I suppose you're obligated in a way. I mean, if he was your friend."

"Yes, he was my friend."

"Then this belongs to you." She hesitated before saying, "Sir, may I keep the bag? It reminds me of someone I used to know. Someone used to have a bag just like that."

"Of course," I responded, accepting the tin but leaving the burlap sack in her hands. She held it tightly to her chest, then turned for the door.

"Miss Morningstar?" I called out—she stopped and turned. "Is there somewhere I can reach you? I mean, so that I might have the opportunity to express my gratitude—"

"No. Thank you, but no. That isn't necessary, sir. You might not want to thank me after you've gone through it anyway. And I don't have anywheres permanent to stay right now to be contacted at. House done gone. Mostly staying with friends from church"

"I'm so sorry," I repeated stupidly.

"Thank you for the thought, sir." She left.

I retired to my office, sat down with the twisted bundle of clippings and this weathered journal of yours. With the lot of it sitting awkwardly atop my desk, I sat staring in disbelief for minutes or hours—I know not which. Finally, I decided to postpone further examination till the workday was through. I placed the bundle in the lower lefthand drawer of the desk and resumed my busy day, these papers of yours never far from my mind.

By seven-thirty p.m. my office work was done. I removed the papers from their drawer and began to look them over—intending only a cursory glance before returning home for a more thorough examination. I never did make it home— and before I knew it, the sun was rising.

And now I know your story—and I understand that the story is woefully unfinished. You ask me, in your way, to chase this mystery in your stead. But how can the story of one so lost, dead, and gone, be sufficiently completed by the living? I don't know where to start. I don't even know if these things you say can be true. But, as the messenger Miss Morningstar so eloquently implied, I am obligated in a way. You were indeed a good friend to me, Clarence. And so I will try.

I will begin by attempting to contact those whom you've mentioned that may still be living. I assume that Bolden and Trumbo remain in the care of the

Jackson mental facility. Carolla is a flamboyant character, tracking him down should be an easy enough task. Marcus James, the gravedigger you mentioned, is another possibility. The one known only as Maistros may prove more elusive— as he has eluded yourself—but I will consult various directories, including city, prison, and police records, to see what turns up.

This will be my effort. I will work with what you have given me, old friend. I will attempt to find some answers, to tie some loose ends. I pray that doing so fulfills my obligation to you in some small way.

You would no doubt be pleased to learn that your young friend Benjamin Price has returned to the staff of the T-P. He has asked, in particular, for me to share any news related to your disappearance. I intend to share these papers with him when I have finished with them—as I'm sure you would have me do were you here to instruct me.

At the very least, perhaps, these pages will bring him, your friend, some small condolence or sense of closure.  –RH

*Raymond Hockett, Journal Entry,*
*November 6, 1926*

My Dear Clarence,

The last two days have yielded little opportunity for sleep. At the time of this writing I find myself quite exhausted.

When my schedule has allowed, I have played detective on your behalf. If nothing else, it was quite a nostalgic experience for me as I have not worked "in the field" in an investigative capacity for several decades. The work inspired great envy in these old bones, triggering remembrances of my former and younger self. Oh, the energy I must have possessed!

I am afraid that I have either lost my knack for such work, or the answers you seek simply spring from questions meant to remain as questions. Whatever the case, what I have come up with is as follows:

Marshall Trumbo: Currently in a catatonic state, and still under close guard. No interview possible.

Charles "Buddy" Bolden: His condition has worsened greatly since your talk with him three years ago. My attempt to communicate with him was rewarded with incoherent mumbles and far away stares. I am told that he spends his days counting and recounting the bed posts of his ward.

The name "Maistros" has yielded nothing conclusive—though there does appear to be a small clan of recently arrived Greek immigrants by the name of "Maistros" currently residing in Liverpool, Ohio. A father and mother (Michael and Artemis) and an infant son (George). The Greeks appear to have no significance or relationship to the matters at hand. I have also learned that the name "Maistros" is derived from a Greek word meaning a type of hot easterly wind.

After considerable snooping I have learned that the first name of the Morningstar woman who brought me your belongings is Malaria (quite a strange name for such a lovely woman)—and she is indeed the daughter of the priest whose death you have puzzled over. I could not locate her—and have discovered the rest of her siblings and kin had died off before the flood, and, in fact, before even the flood of 1906.

Perhaps the most intriguing piece of this puzzle is the gravedigger, Marcus James, whom you claim to have recently spoken with. I went to the Girod Street Cemetery where I met a middle-aged negro called Barnard, a man with a nearly indecipherable Creole accent. At the mention of James' name he responded curtly and mysteriously;

"Dead man inna river lookin' fer his fish".

I asked him if he meant to say the man had died. He responded, "Yeah, yeah—long time ago. Yellow fever times in 1853. Long, long time ago. Before you'n me's born, mister."

At first I was sure he was incorrect—for you yourself had recorded a recent instance of speaking with Marcus James personally. Surely Barnard was mistaken—perhaps even feeble of mind—but I had yet to uncover any solid evidence of a still-living Marcus James. Nor had I located any living kin or close acquaintance of his.

What I did find was registry of birth for a free Creole man of color by that name, born in the year 1825—with no corresponding record of death. Save for the absence of any death record, this seems to coincide with a plausible time frame for him to have died in 1853 (coinciding with Barnard's statement). Bear in mind that in times of plague, not all deaths are recorded. For him to be alive today he would have to be 101 years old, which I consider unlikely. And so, I am uncertain as to who you think you've spoken to.

As for Dominick Carolla, I had occasion to speak with several musicians who knew him well—all of whom felt quite confident that he had been lost in the recent flood. Apparently, Carolla was quite unstable of mind towards the end. As mentioned in your own interview with him, he had bragged to many that he himself would pull the waters of the Bayou back into the Mississippi River—to deliver some sort of package—before securing his own death immediately thereafter. This, at least, coincides with the general content of your recorded interview with him.

Indeed, I've managed to corroborate (if sometimes strangely) much of what you have stated in these papers—but there is a key instance in which your own coverage of the story is flawed (how many times have I told you never to rely solely on police statements!?) At the time of his son's murder, Bolden was indeed estranged from the child's mother, Diphtheria Morningstar—but he did pay her a visit on the day of West's funeral.

After confirming police reports regarding Hattie Covington's statements to police (upon which you unwisely relied), I ventured to dig deeper by seeking out other former employees of the Arlington House—my hope being to question persons who may have been there on the night of Diphtheria Morningstar's murder. My investigation was surprisingly short, beginning and ending at The Brass Rail nightclub on Canal Street. The house pianist on duty there was a negro called James C. Booker—who had also been, for several years, the house pianist at the Arlington. (As an aside; the skill and dexterity that this man displayed on the piano at the Brass Rail last night was most amazing!) Mr. Booker revealed himself to have been a musical acquaintance of Bolden in the old Storyville days. To my surprise, he claimed specific recall of Bolden's presence at the Arlington House on the night of the murder because, as he put it, "Buddy came in happy as a clam, but left mad as an eel." This statement not only contradicts Miss Covington's comments, but also seems to point to the possibility (if not likelihood) of an altercation between Bolden and Miss Morningstar. When I asked Mr. Booker why he thought Miss Covington may have lied to police, he replied, "Well, you know, all the girls in the back o'town was sweet on Buddy in those days—all but the one he had his own eye on, that is. He was a pretty big star back then—iffen case you didn't know. Diphtheria never cared about that star binness, though. Never did care at all 'bout that stuff, she."

The only potential connection to Marcus James in all this seems to be his role in removing the bodies of Mr. and Mrs. DePaul from the crime scene of the initial "axeman" murders—a crime which Carolla seemed intent on associating himself with during your interview with him. But please consider: mentally unbalanced persons do commonly attempt to take responsibility (or, disturbingly, "credit") for notorious murders. With this in mind, the axeman murders hardly connect Dominick Carolla and Marcus James in any conclusive or meaningful way.

I tend to think that Malvina Latour, the voodoo priestess you mention, had nothing to do with any of it. There is simply no evidence linking her—save for your insistent dreams.

Clarence, I must say: I have a very, very bad feeling about all of this.

Most of it sounds like superstitious nonsense to me—but something in the back of my mind hears an eerie ring of truth to it all. Perhaps that is a symptom of my own fatigue. Could it possibly be true that Carolla somehow knew in advance of the great storm? Perhaps, as you suggest, certain madmen have a gift of second sight. And what of the gravedigger Marcus James? If I were a superstitious man, I would deduce that you had spoken with a ghost.

Dear friend, though it is hard for me to say so on these sacred pages of yours, I must entertain one last hurtful theory—and I'm afraid that doing so is unavoidable. I believe it possible that you yourself suffered from some affliction of the mind as you wrote certain portions of this journal. I do not mean to speak ill of you, my friend, especially in the wake of your most tragic demise—but I must at least consider the possibility now that certain facts have revealed themselves. Also, I must admit to you that, in the course of this cursory investigation, my own sleep has been decidedly unrestful. I awake in an exhausted state—as if I have suffered horrible nightmares—though morning brings no memory of dreams.

And with this I must beg my leave of these matters, Clarence—I have done my best on your behalf.

I have decided that I cannot in good conscience forward these papers to your friend Benny Price, as promised in a previous entry. I hope you can forgive me this, but my fear is that these matters will only succeed in preying upon his mind as they preyed upon your own—and as they have begun to prey upon mine. My chief goal now is to simply experience and be done with this terrible grieving process, and to contribute as best I can to the recovery of our devastated city. Perhaps, along the way, some of us Orleanians may succeed in healing our own damaged hearts to some degree.

I am honored to have known you, dear friend.

Goodbye.

Raymond Hockett

*Benjamin Price, Journal Entry,*
*October 9, 1931*

Dear Clarence,

Although it is a strange thing to do, I will follow the example of Mr. Hockett and fill these sad journal pages as if you are in a position to read what is written upon them. Equally strange: There is something in my heart that tells me you are right here with me now, and that you can see these words as I set them to paper.

That in mind, let me start by telling you how much I miss you, Clarence—and how devastating news of your passing was to me. Not a day passes that a picture of your warm smile fails to enter my mind.

Now: Onto the business at hand.

As did our Mr. Hockett, I will begin by telling you how these pages have reached me.

Three days ago, on the 6th of October, our friend Raymond Hockett lie on his deathbed with advanced cancer of the lung. Speaking was difficult for him, but I visited him regularly in those final weeks. On the day before his ultimate passing he presented me with your written belongings—and along with these he presented a peculiar story.

He told me of how your private writings had haunted him, of how he wanted badly to destroy these pages, to forget about them completely. But every time he came close to doing so, an overwhelming sense of foreboding prevented the action. So he kept them, and preserved them well—without truly knowing why.

It seems that Mr. Hockett had acquired an affliction of dreams similar to your own.

On that sad day of the 6th he revealed these things to me. He also confided that the intensity and clarity of the dreams increased proportionately as his own death drew nearer. Towards the end, clear memories of these dreams managed to follow him even into waking hours.

He told me that you yourself had visited him in these final recalled dreams of his—and that your demeanor had given him great comfort in the face of his own mortality. He further related that, in these dreams, you showed him the mysterious underwater lights mentioned in your final journal entry—and that those lights were a welcoming thing, a thing not to be feared. You had forgiven him, he said, for his decision not to follow through on the task presented by your writings—but he also informed me that you had urged him to pass this torch on to me, saying that I would understand your plight better than any other living person. You told him I would only need follow the instructions of my own heart.

Of course, you were right. Having been in the presence of both Carolla and Bolden during your final interviews with them, I do indeed have a well-formed idea of what has disturbed you so. But still; I have only a vague sense of where those troubles may have originated.

Of things witnessed during those interviews, what I recall most clearly is the frightful thing that came alive in Dominick Carolla's eyes during certain points of the exchange. Certainly, Mr. Hockett could not have the remotest idea of such a thing. I cannot say if I believe the thing in Carolla's eyes was of evil—but I know in my heart that it was a thing of power, and, though this might sound silly to anyone but you and I, I believe this power to be a darkly spiritual thing—a thing to be respected and feared.

I will go forward with this quest on your behalf, dear friend—but I must confess to feelings of great unease at the thought. I do not know what, if anything, I will unearth. It has been years since the days of those troubling interviews, and long decades since the point in time where these things seem to have begun; that day in 1891 when Noonday Morningstar lost his life—and Marshall Trumbo, his mind.

Still, I will go forward. And if the troubling dreams that have plagued yourself and Mr. Hockett should visit me as well, I have resolved not to resist them. Instead, I will listen—hopefully to learn.

I am in your debt, dear Clarence. It was you who took a chance on a young intern by your personal recommendation at the start of my career. Since then your lessons have served me well. You would no doubt be pleased to learn that in a short time I graduated from stenographer to reporter, from reporter to senior reporter, and from there to my current post as assistant editor. It is now a possibility that, with Mr. Hockett's passing, I will be considered by the publishers for the post of editor-in-chief. All this I owe to you, dear Clarence. Without your tutelage and faith in me at the beginning, I would surely not have amounted to much.

And I have shown you such keen lack of gratitude, my friend. It was wrong of me to abandon my post so abruptly after the interview with Carolla. Although the reason I gave Mr. Hockett for my resignation was fabricated, I always expected you knew the truth—as is confirmed in your pages. The plain truth is that I was afraid. That thing in his eyes shook me to my core—and so I left. I wanted to put as much distance between myself and that thing as possible. But I am older now, and less easily rattled. If that thing is to present itself again, I will be steadfast—as were you. And like you, I now know there is something important to be learned from this maddeningly unfinished tale.

Tomorrow I begin.

Yours in faith,
Benny

*Benjamin Price, Journal Entry,*
*October 13, 1931*

I am just back from my trip to the mental facility in Jackson.

Before today I had nothing of great interest to add, but now I find myself so overwhelmed with information that I am unsure where to begin. I will start with the basic facts.

Buddy Bolden is dead.

Marshall Trumbo is dead.

The two never had occasion to meet within the walls of the asylum due to hospital segregation policies. But even in lieu of such policies hospital records confirm that Trumbo's history of escape and mayhem had placed him in permanent solitary confinement till the day of his death, preventing meaningful interaction with any of his fellow inmates for the vast bulk of his stay there. Nevertheless, the deaths of the two men coincide eerily—both having occurred in the same week. This, at least, according to hospital records.

Bolden's body was deposited in the old Holt Cemetery.

Trumbo's remains were cremated at the request of his brother.

It appears that in the colored portion of the hospital few if any records are kept of the inmates—and so the final days of Buddy Bolden will likely remain a mystery.

As for Trumbo, I managed to befriend a young doctor called Hector Worth, the replacement of the retired Dr. Baxter who'd offered you so little cooperation in your initial queries. Doctor Worth seemed quite anxious to meet anyone harboring interest in Trumbo's belongings, Trumbo's own brother having declined to recover even his earthly remains. He expressed plans to destroy the papers prior to my arrival—and was strangely eager to be rid of them. You would be quite interested to learn that, for a time, Trumbo was quite the prolific scribbler during occasional yet brief non-catatonic episodes at the Jackson facility. He conducted many bizarre interviews with his fellow inmates, and kept a number of journals in which he recorded his thoughts and described, in great detail, the images of his own troubling dreams—sometimes with accompanying illustrations.

When I asked Dr. Worth if I may take these papers with me, he consented most enthusiastically. When I promised to return them as soon as possible, he surprised me by stating most emphatically:

"No, no. Burn them when you are through."

To this I replied, "You wish them disposed of?"

"No, I didn't say that. Do not simply discard them—you must burn them."

Before I could query him further, he turned his back to me and hurried off as if I'd threatened him with bodily harm. As Mr. Hockett stated in his final entry, there does seem a considerable amount of superstition attached to this case. Still, I was surprised to see such behavior coming from a man of science such as this doctor.

And now a nearly unfathomable pile of loose pages and rumpled journals left behind by a madman sit before me. I will go through them a sentence at a time, I will take notes regarding anything relevant, and when I am done, dear Clarence, I will record my thoughts upon these pages in hopes that we may both achieve a heightened understanding of these strange and troubling matters.

I promise to write again very soon.

Yours faithfully,
Benny

*Benjamin Price, Journal Entry,*
*October 18, 1931*

Dear Clarence,

I have found no comfort in the nonsensical scribbles and disturbing illustrations of Marshall Trumbo.

Although I found his handwriting to be quite legible, almost effeminate in style, the content itself is mainly indecipherable twaddle—and the passion with which Trumbo has infused into these ramblings I found downright unsettling. I now better understand the eagerness of Dr. Worth to be rid of this matter completely.

As for the written notes, a few passages have struck me as potentially important, though I was not initially certain as to why.

The first group of journal pages that I will draw your attention to are clearly relevant to this mystery in some way, as is evidenced by the header, which reads:

## FRAGMENTS OF DIVINE PROPHECY COLLECTED FROM DREAMS

Below this is the following nonsense, which I transcribe verbatim:

"JIM JAM JUMP great things-liggity-bump rat clap-a-tap map flap cut cat jippity jap hubadah gump flitty pritty stump sklip pap pah jeeka by boo what i say, jim zigga higga jig nope-a-dope shippity shah jim jam scram hucka lucka zucka zig ffffrit hunka hunka chunka wood-shy sam. Flim flum flam fliggity mighty lighty lo and bee-hold shlibbity shlob yuppity gob mister heckle beckle joe flam slap fly whackety crack smack freaky bop squeak flappy-tah beeka bye boo better-getter-fly, say hoo whackety crack split bap-a-tap himmina hah-hah hoo lickety-quick Bap. Bap-bap. Buh-bap, bap, buh-bap fap whap ding mippity moppity jiggle wiggle wutch small as a ball in crack in a wall and that's all to the hall tickety-tall bippity bend tale-tell-told-tall stories crazy talk whupitah-walk flippity better-wetter-getter goo locka doo is why funny wunny fip fap fah co-inky dink or flinkity bink? Slimmity-slam honk-a-tonk man no-how, not-now, kung-pow, brown-cow, and-how, nippity-now, zippity-zow smuggle-dee-bug double-blink yuckety duck hissy-pissy hucklebuck fuckfuckfuckety fuck hunk-a-lunk lakjufa doir estay lickity splat sippity sat real blood, sad blood, bad blood, sticky blood, hot blood, solidifying, putrefying, brownin'-like-liver-puddin'-blood, stinkin', still thinkin' blood, kill-leakin' blood, coolin' and foolin', from a prick, from a nip, from a cut, from tear, from a slash, from rip, from a pull, from a lever from a sever frumma lumma lip lap flip flap fog, frumma-lumma-ding-dong mudfish bludfish BLOOD hippity bop times one times two times three times four times five times six times seven times eight times nine times ten times eleven times twelve times thirteen times chapter thirteen? Zippity-pah! Lo! the mystery! lippity hey why ya wanna hafta mafta shlafta mifity bang goo go shy lye foo say I, is who mip map mop nippity now hugga wugga flip fly gitta gotta get it flappa mot hap hi god bless you, geshundheit, good-night, farewell, ta-ta, and adieu and when those watery fingers of death reach the Mississippi, then and only then you will see me no more. They gave it to me but I gave it back the best I could I RECKON to dream is to know the truth I think we're done here, sonny"

Jim Jam Jump, as you know, was the name of Dominick Carolla's famed orchestra. I thought the rest may be a sort of code, perhaps a series of anagrams, but hours of manipulating words and letters have yielded nothing telling.

Further along within the same journal is another bold header:

*THE LAST AND UNEXPECTEDLY FINAL WORDS OF JIM JAM JUMP*

And below this....

# CHAPTER THIRTEEN
## *The Last and Unexpectedly Final Words of Jim Jam Jump*

Next time the telephone DON'T ring, pick it up. I double dog dare ya, smugbug. Zippity-zah times *TEN*.

§

I am nearly ashamed to tell you that upon reading those words I find myself staring in the direction of my own un-ringing telephone—tempted to pick up the receiver to see if anyone is on the line.

I know, dear Clarence, how insane that must sound—but I expect you might understand (perhaps even sympathize with) this presumably innocuous touch of madness on my part.

A separate journal begins with the following header:

### PUZZLE WORDS FROM RECURRING DREAM

The words beneath read as follows:

*"Zedn Nasicb Uqmao Tuoyn Raioe Htvae Emayi Uodonri Ine Encpd Aq Plimu O Ano Oarce Unthar Dead Iu On Eru Hurt Ecibuotor."*

This gibberish is written and rewritten over and over, to cover exactly ten pages. Starting with the eleventh page (and continuing to the end of the journal— which is well over one hundred pages in length), various rearrangements of these letters and words are presented, sometimes using elaborate graphs and charts—as if Trumbo had desperately attempted to unravel some intricate code. With no luck, of course.

Although I recognize this for what it is (the obsessive ramblings of a madman), I must confess to you, dear Clarence, that the touch of these pages to my hand brings a chill. More troubling than Trumbo's written journal pages were his illustrations of things remembered in dreams. Surprisingly, Trumbo was quite a talented artist—his images possessing a vividness and attention to detail that could be, at times, quite breathtaking. But the things portrayed in these drawings were largely surreal and ominous in nature.

For instance:

*Images of large rats; beaten, twisted, and bloody—possessing large glowing eyes more human than rodent.*

*Pictures of an old woman with blank holes for eyes, holding a dead child in her arms.*

*Pictures of an old man with a large hole where a nose should be*

(And most chillingly) *Detailed drawings of a faceless man in the act of attacking sleeping men and women with an axe—each illustration underscored with a street address in the form of a caption.*

And, yes, I did a cursory review of the old unsolved "axeman" murders—and found the street addresses to accurately reflect corresponding crime scenes of that case.

These "axeman" illustrations inspired me to bother poor Dr. Worth at the asylum one last time, this time by telephone. Not wishing to irritate the man unnecessarily, my question was simple and to the point:

"Did Marshall Trumbo ever have occasion to read newspaper accounts of the axeman murders, or; did he have any way at all of knowing the details of those crimes while incarcerated at the Jackson facility?"

Dr. Worth's curt reply caught me by surprise:

"I suppose you now see why I want nothing to do with those... things." After an uncomfortable silence, he elaborated; "No, he did not. He has spent nearly all of his time either in a catatonic state or under diligently monitored security conditions. He has had no visitors, no occasion to read news reports, and has showed no desire whatsoever to read any such materials. In other words, there is no earthly reason why he should know any specific information regarding the axeman killings."

"No *earthly* reason?" I echoed lamely.

"Are you finished, sir?" he snapped impatiently.

I told him that I was—and that I would not be bothering him again.

But the story gets even stranger, dear friend, as I must now relate.

One thought continued to nag at me: That the key to all this must lie with the presumably deceased gravedigger Marcus James (or Marcus "Nobody Special," as he was apparently known to many). I set off on a mission to find any and all information about him, and further; to seek out any living relatives or friends who he may have conversed with regarding these matters.

The most obvious place to begin such an investigation was at his only known place of employment, the Girod Street Cemetery (formerly known as *Cimetiere des Heretiques* due to its Protestant history). I initially intended to inquire only of the man's record of employment there—or perhaps speak to someone who might have known him. I was to leave with more than I'd bargained for.

The gravedigger Barnard (the same previously mentioned by Mr. Hockett in these pages) was there, hard at work with a shovel and hoe—but also there was an older gentleman, perhaps seventy years of age. I inquired as to their, and asked which of them might be in charge. The older gent, who introduced himself as Leroy Paint, responded, "Neither of us. That would be Mr. Marcus. He ain't here right now, though."

I bluntly told him I'd assumed Marcus James died long ago. I also mentioned that were he still alive he'd have to be over a hundred years old by now.

"True, true," Mr. Paint answered. "Older than most of these here markers, I reckon. But still alive and working hard just like always. Not surprised you think he dead, though. Lots of superstitious folk 'round here telling silly tales." With this last remark, he shot Barnard a hard glance—causing the younger man to flinch noticeably.

"Where can I find him?" I asked hopefully.

"Well, when he ain't ta here, he's mostly lookin' fer his fish. Out on the long pier off the levee, nearest cross streets being Decatur and Iberville. See an old hunched over negro with a fishin' pole out there, that'd be Marcus Nobody Special. A harder workin' man I never knowed. Don't sleep much, that Marcus."

With this encouraging information in tow, I immediately drove to the T-P offices so that I may load the company Dictaphone into the trunk of my car. If the old gravedigger had anything useful to say (and I assumed that he must), I wanted to get every word of it properly documented.

Having crammed the bulky recording device (along with three spare cylinders) into my automobile, I drove to the intersection nearest the levee as instructed by Mr. Paint. Spying the form of an elderly negro with a fishing pole standing off a long pier (as predicted), I parked the car, pulled the heavy apparatus from the trunk, and began lugging it up towards the levee's peak.

The man didn't seem surprised or alarmed by my approach—to the contrary, it was almost as if he'd been expecting me.

"Afternoon," he called out as I came within earshot.

"Good afternoon," I replied between labored breaths.

When I reached him, he continued about his business without further acknowledgment of my presence. I dropped the recorder to the pier more heavily than I'd intended, and proceeded to massage the part of my shoulder where the strap had dug in.

"Sounds heavy," he said without looking up.

"Yes, it is," I confirmed.

He looked me in the eye with a mixture of curiosity and suspicion.

"I hep you, sonny?" he asked.

I stood silent—a closer view of his physical appearance having momentarily paralyzed my good manners. Below his shortly cropped, snow white hairline were two eyes; one milky and blind, the other clear and sharp. And where there should have been a nose was only a weathered and hideous scar the size of a silver dollar. In his mouth I noted two brownish protrusions which I assumed to be teeth. This man was clearly very, very old—and had lived a very hard life.

"Yes, I hope so," I replied belatedly. "Would you be the gravedigger, Marcus James."

"Thass right, sonny. And who might you be?"

"My name is Benjamin Price. I'm a newsman for the Times-Picayune."

His attention returned to the river's surface. "Well, goddamn. You fellas just don't give up, do ya? Lawd, *lawd*. Well, I ain't got nothin' ta say to you—just like I had nothin' to say to the last fella. Sorry, I cain't hep ya, sonny."

"Sir, was the last fellow that you speak of a man named Hayes?"

"Guess so. That sound right, if I recollect. Clemence Hayes? Few years back it was."

"Clarence. Clarence Hayes. Clarence was my friend, Mr. James. He died in the flood."

His eyes returned to me, but softer this time. "Sorry to hear that. But just the same, I got nothin' to say to no newspaper folk."

"Mr. James—"

"Call me Marcus, sonny. When white folk call me 'mister' usually mean trouble comin'. If ya don't mind, that is."

"Marcus, then. I am very sorry to bother you—and I fully understand your feelings towards the press. But I assure you I am here in a strictly personal capacity on behalf of my deceased friend. I know this might sound strange, but if I might speak with you about certain things that only you could possibly know, I believe his soul may rest easier."

"Don't sound as strange as you might think, sonny."

"Then you'll help?"

"Mebbe. Depends on what you wanna know."

"Thank you so much!" The excitement in my voice coaxed a smile from his hardened face, but as I began to unpack the recording equipment he looked up with renewed suspicion:

"Whass all that there?"

"A Dictaphone. I had hoped you wouldn't mind if I recorded what you have to say."

"Sound recording device?"

"Yes."

"For collectin' up talkin' and songs and whatnot?"

"Yes. If it's okay."

"Damn. Times sure have changed. Yeah, I suppose it all right."

"Thank you," I replied with genuine gratitude.

At that moment, something odd occurred. Although the weather had been calm and still all day, a sudden gust came up from the river to pull a page loose from one of Trumbo's journal's (several of which I had stuffed into the Dictaphone case for purpose of reference). The page soared upwards, then down— swerving right, then left—and up once more—lingering for a moment before plunging to the pier at Marcus' feet. Fearing it may be lost in the river with another gust, I dove to retrieve it—but Marcus had already placed a foot on. He stared down at the sheet with his good eye open wide. Slowly, he bent down to pick it up, then held it close to his face.

"I doubt if that would mean anything to you," I said. "Just some gibberish written by a mentally ill person. May I have it back, please?" He ignored me, continuing to eye it closely.

"Means something to me," he spoke softly.

"Pardon?"

"Might mean more to me than it does you, I reckon."

I edged closer, wishing to see which page it was. The gravedigger's breath was strong and surprisingly sweet. I recognized the page immediately.

*Zedn Nasicb Uqmao Tuoyn Raioe Htvae Emayi Uodonri Ine Encpd Aq Plimu O Ano Oarce Unthar Dead Iu On Eru Hurt Ecibuotor.*

Marcus scrunched his eyes together and cleared his throat noisily. "Where'd you get this from, sonny?"

"It was written by a man named Marshall Trumbo. Did you know him?"

"Mm hm. Dass right. What I thought. Newspaper man. Like you. Like that Clemence fella."

"Yes."

"Met him long time ago. Last time, he brought me a thing like this too. Needed someone to read it to him. This one tougher, though. No number key. Can probably figure it out in a minny or two if you want. Got time for that, or you in a hurry?"

"Excuse me. Are you saying you can make sense of that?"

"Yup. Civil War code."

"Yes, yes. I believe it is a code as well."

"Don't believe nothin', sonny. Know it fer fact."

"But Trumbo tried to decode it for years. Came up with nothing. I gave it a try mysel—"

"Got a pencil? Paper too?"

"Yes, certainly." I handed him paper and pencil, which he exchanged for his fishing pole.

He began counting the letters. After a few minutes, he wrote down some numbers and X's, divided by a slash:

5X5X3/5X4X1

"Well, my guess is that's the key. The one that would make most sense, leastways."

"I'm sorry, I don't understand…"

"Don't worry, you don't need to. Let me put this little baby to the test and we'll see what's what."

He proceeded to draw a series of grids similar to the ones Trumbo had drawn in his journals. The first three were drawn the same, and looked like this:

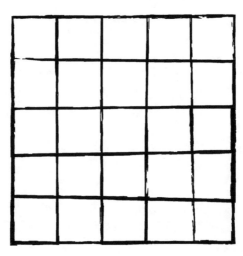

—and the last was similar, except it was four spaces tall instead of five. After completing the grids, he filled each with letters; writing them across like so:

| Z | E | D | N | N |
|---|---|---|---|---|
| A | S | I | C | B |
| U | Q | M | A | O |
| T | U | O | Y | N |
| R | A | I | O | E |

Then he began re-writing the letters from the grid onto a fresh sheet of paper—except instead of taking the letters from left to right as they had been originally written, he took them in the order they appeared on the grid from top to bottom. When he'd finished, he cleared his throat and said:

"Well, then. There ya go. Clear as day."

To me, the new order of the letters still appeared jumbled and meaningless;

ZAUTRESQUADIMOINCAYONBONE
HEURETMOINVADICAYONPEINED
AMOURQUANDPORTELACHAINEAD
IEUCOURRITOUTBONHEUR

"I don't understand," I admitted.

"And neither did Mr. Trumbo, I suppose. Mebbe that's because the words ain't in English."

I studied the words harder before making my best guess—

"French?" I asked uncertainly.

"Not exactly. Nigger French. Proper folks call it Louisiana Creole, but I still call it what it is. Nigger French. A type of language invented by slaves from the old days; mixin' French words with the older, African way of talkin'."

"Can you translate?"

"Sure. Part of an old song. Know it well. Creole song. Sad song. Sound like this."

And he began to sing:

*Z'autres qu'a di moin, ca yon bonheur;*
*Et moin va di, ca yon peine:*
*D'amour quand porte la chaine,*
*Adieu, courri tout bonheur*

The words themselves meant nothing to me, but the melody stirred something deep inside which I find impossible to put into words. After the last note rang out, he retrieved his fishing pole and handed Trumbo's page back to me as if nothing special had just occurred. Anticipating the next and most obvious question, he answered before the asking:

"Translates to English roughly as such:

*Others might say it's your happiness*
*But I say it is your sorrow*
*'Cause when you're touched by truest love, my friend*
*You can kiss all happiness goodbye."*

Clarence, it is important that I tell you this:

Even in English, the words did not mean nearly as much to me as did the *melody*—and the sound of his voice in the singing.

And in this fact, I believe, lie your answer, my dear lost friend. I pray that somehow you were there with me in spirit on that lonely pier to hear the sound of his voice, the miraculous sound that came out when the gravedigger sang.

I stood motionless for a few moments with my eyes locked to the windlessly heaving river.

"Ready when you are," Marcus Nobody Special reminded. I snapped out of my daze and finished setting up the Dictaphone, positioning the microphone towards him.

Then I pressed "record."

# CHAPTER SIXTY-EIGHT

# Can't No Grave
# Keep My Body Down

Well, I'll tell you since you asked nice, young fella. But truly, it ain't no one's damn ta-do except fer my own. Mm hmm. Mostly what I'll say is this here, so listen up:

Trouble 'round the potter's field always start when folks get to dyin' too quick. Come down to simple math, sonny. Too many bodies in too short a time equals bad news in the City of New Orleans.

I suppose it's about time someone set the record straight on all that crazy talk anyhow, seeing's how even the damn papers never got it right. Big fancy damn newspapers with all them fancy damn edjucated reporters writing words big enough to smash out a fella's teeth and *still* can't help but make it all up. Trine to make a dollar and a dime is all. So write it down and get it straight, mister. Sharpen up that damn pencil and get it right, yessir. Mm hmm.

Folks'll try and tell ya I's dead awhile.

Like to say being dead made me crazy, made me spend not enough time working in that potter's field and too much time on this little piece of levee looking for a certain fish. Well, I'm looking fer that fish, yessir—most always will, I guess. But I ain't been dead yet, me. It's fun to believe in the spooky stuff and folks like to have their fun. The truth ain't so dern spooky a'tall, really—but plenny ugly just the same.

I remember the day it start, the real bad dyin' times. Yella fever times. Yessir. Walking home from the river one night in eighteen fitty-two, looped longways back to the semma-tree so's I could pass by the cathouses on the Rue Dauphine. This a habit I been in since I done made the worst mistake of my life in breaking the heart of Coffee Maria. A mistake mostly because a sweeter, kinder, prettier little thing never did I see, but also because that same little Coffee Maria was the niece of Malvina Latour, a local hoodoo mambo in them days. I only broke things off with Maria on accounta the kinda work she be doing; laying down with other fellas in Auntie Jin's sportin' house. But hoodoo folk don't take kindly to the broken hearts of their kin, no matter the reasoning. So I figured ol' Malvina had me marked for some mischief.

Weren't no crib by a mile, that place. Real clean for a whorehouse and good enough money—but it still felt like sharing the woman I loved, which ain't something I could ever cotton to with any sensa comfort.

Maria was working that night, and sitting on the steps outside when I passed. Pretty little head down in her hands, my Coffee Maria. Looking mighty blue, she.

"Evenin', sweet child," say me. "Some bad man treating you mean tonight? Want I should smash his head fer ya, lil darlin'?"

I startled her, but her mind always quick: "You mean someone meaner 'n you, Mr. Marcus Nobody Special?" First time anyone ever called me that.

"Doan be thataway, darlin'. You know yer my special gal. Always will." True enough, that.

The hardness left her eyes: "Mama dead."

"Ah, darlin'..."

"Got sick, died. Skin turned yella and hot. Talkin' crazy then...I...I...just dunno...she got worse quick, stopped breathin'...oh, Marcus!"

"Oh, little baby." I held her in my arms. Holding her close felt special good, made me feel like a regular heel enjoying it under the circumstances. But that little Coffee Maria sure was sweet; her tiny body trembling against my chest like a scared sparrow.

This was the first dyin' from the yella fever sickness I heard of that year. But not the last. Wouldn't stop ner slow by summer's end. No sir, that killin' fever'd keep up strong and steady straight through the year eighteen hunnert'n fitty-three, sure 'nuff. *Mercy.*

§

Well, eight months passed since the day Coffee Maria cried in my arms, that day her mama died. I kept wanting to go back to visit that little girl, to pay my respects and offer up some comfort. But I been busy. Bodies pilin' up. Yella fever bodies.

Bodies.

Me and Black Jake handling things pretty good awhile, then it just got too much. Fever spread a lot quicker than usual that year, spread like wildfire; *le quatres paroisses.* Mayor Crossman lent a hand by loaning some chain gangs to work the semma-trees in the city proper. Nice to have the help, but those convicts sure is ornery. If that fool mayor really wanted to help, he'd let us burn 'em up, do it right. Be better for everyone. Burn 'em up and there ain't no diggin'. Burn 'em up and they's only ash. Burn 'em up and you don't have to worry about the rain so much.

I hated to think of what'd happen to all those shallow buried bodies if a real good rain come up. Tried not to think about it, but I know the rains a-comin'. Then what?

I worried real hard on that one.

Bodies in the potter's field ain't so much buried as sunk, sonny. Hard enough to get 'em down, then you gotta worry bout *keeping* 'em down when the rain come. Sometimes keeping 'em down ain't too hard—and sometimes ain't too easy. Folks with money keep their dead above ground. Seal 'em in the fancy 'spensive tombs or shove 'em back in oven slabs. Ovens are best if a fella got some money but ain't exactly rich. Year and a day'll burn them bodies to dust, nice and clean. You got a good oven slab, you can fit a whole lotta folks in one tomb, save yerself a pile of money over time.

One of them chain gang fellas a sin-ugly Frenchman called Girton. Short, stocky, mean fella. Real *rabougri bajoe*, he. Ugly and full of hate. Mm mm. Especially hate niggras—and really hate ol' Marcus for being the field boss. When it come time to break up the chains to pick up the pace, I watch that Girton real close. Train that rifle on him good. Something about that boy just set my nerves to twitchin'.

§

Every morning me and Jake took turns going through the poor parts of town with the funeral cart, pickin' up dead. Usually get a whole new batch every sun-up. Most folks pass at night, sonny. I guess it just feel more like quitting time with the sun down and gone.

Certain things I seen while collecting up dead from those country shacks sent me a chill. Seen whole little families holdin' on tight to one another in a bed; deader'n coal, birds pickin' at their shoulders. Little chilluns with looks of terror in their eyes, frozen in the heat, like they could see something terrible coming at 'em in their dyin' moments. *Lawdy*.

But the worst of it was something I'll never get out my eyes. I guess you could call it an omen of sorts, considering how things turned out.

Went into a little shack where the streets ain't got names, a shack just like all the rest. One room country shack. Open up that door with a bang, just like always. Yell:

*"Hey ho! Grave man getcha dead!"*

Didn't hear no one. Figgered probbly everyone dead in this place. Figgered wrong.

Dead man on the bed, lying face up, staring at the roof. Mulatto, like me.

There in the corner of the floor a pretty little mother sat cross-legged, baby at her teat. The woman's skin done turned orangey, one of her eyes closed, the other half-open and froze, looking at the little baby in her lap. Her lips stretched in a thin line across her face, smiling at one side, dead flat at the other. This was not a terribly unusual scene during plague times—exceptin' for one little thing.

The baby at her breast was not yet dead.

Bony and lean, the tiny thing clung on for dear life, trine to suck something out its mama's yella teat, the lower half of his little body soaked in chamber lye and tatlin'. I put a hand on his little shoulder, but that child a strong 'un; just tighten his grip on that dead mother of his'n. So I yank him back hard, pick him into my arms. Little fella lets out a yell. High pitched yell. Scared and sad sounding. Lost sounding. I can see the blood on his lips, blood oozing from his dead mama's breast, dark red with streaks of black. That sweet little man crying so hard, the smell of his mama's death come out strong from his soft little toothless mouth. Something about his eyes tuggin' at my heart. Strange eyes. *Des yeaux goueres*—pale and sad. I looked around and notice a tiny white blanket wrapped around the dead man's feet. A little perfect blanket, soft and clean—looking strange in this filthy place of death and dyin'. That blanket looked just like a miracle.

I pull it from the Mulatto's feet and wrap that baby up tight, cover him all up, and make a straight line for the Charity Hospital on foot. Run faster'n I ever run. When I get there a white nurse lady, looking dead tired and dressed in yella, motion me over so's she can take a peek at that little'un. The lady look down, unwrap the child's face from the blanket, say; "This one's dead, boy."

I say; "But ma'am, he was hot to the touch not ten minny ago." She look at me warm, but her words is cold:

"Baby ain't dead from fever. You smothered him with that blanket. Dumb nigger." Walked away.

Like I said, you may consider this an omen of sorts. I walked that little baby on back to his mama so's they could get buried together. Looking at the dead Mulatto on the bed, I felt a kind of anger. Why he on the bed but not the mother and child? Why that blanket around his feet and not around that baby? I piled that Mulatto on the cart *first*. Then went around the neighborhood, piling other bodies over top him. Load it up good. Finally, I come back around to the dead mother and child.

So's they could ride on top.

Felt a twitch of guilt separating the Mulatto from his kin in such a way, but at the time it felt like justice. Funny how justice can make the just feel guilt. Lotsa irony like that in this world, sonny.

§

The sky'd been merciful dry for a week or two. Back at the potter's field, the boys were making good progress on the biggest dern hole I seen there yet. Nice deep hole, wide too. Ol' Jake holding that rifle, making sure them ornery chain gang boys workin' hard. That nasty Girton stop just to give me a mean lookin' smile—like he know a dirty secret. Start my skin to crawling, that smile.

Jake offer me the rifle expecting I'll wanna take over supervising and put him to work down in the hole with them other fellas. I just wave the gun away and let him keep her, though. I can't bear to watch that little baby being buried like that. That baby I kilt with the perfect white blanket. Nope, ol' Marcus Nobody Special was feelin' extra blue that morning, and when I feel that way I go see Mama.

Mama's grave the cleanest in the potter's field. I put her down right next to my little shack, put a nice layer of brick and mortar right o'er top. Every brick is lined up just right, pretty and perfect. Those perfect bricks'll make sure she stay down no matter how hard it rain. So I put my knees right down on the bricks closest mama's heart, hang my head down and make a little tear for that poor dead baby. The one I kilt.

After a spell, I look up at mama's stone, wiping my eye. Right off I see something different about that stone. There's writing on it. In pencil. Says this:

*Marcus—come to 601 Dauphine. Hurry please. Maria*

My little Coffee Maria. Needin' me.

So now I'm wondering how long that bit of writing been on Mama's stone. Wondering what kinda trouble my baby in. If it too late. I'm wondering all that as I'm running. Running to see my pretty gal. Hoping she all right. Knowing she ain't.

Soon as I make it to the front door of Auntie Jin's I get a powerful bad feeling. Something telling me to turn tail. But I can't. I can't just leave without knowing. Gotta see what the matter is with my baby.

A pile of yella fever dead on the roadside near the door. I poke through a-looking—but Maria ain't one of 'em. Glad of that—but still, something terrible wrong. I feel it in my bones.

I walk in the door.

Ain't no Coffee Maria in that place. But there's that mean lookin' woman Malvina Latour—sitting in a rocking chair, creaking back and forth. She just look me up and down, smiling and looking mad. Rocking and a-creaking. Holding something in her arms. That little something wrapped in a perfect white blanket. That blanket look just like a miracle to me.

I should run. But I walk right in. Door slams closed behind me. My arms get grabbed by strong hands, holding firm and twisting hard. *Hounsi*—two big fellas from Malvina's *houmfour*, her hoodoo temple—holding me tight. Malvina stand up, take a step toward me. Unwrap that little something in the blanket. Blanket falls to the floor, in a mess of dust and grime. Malvina hold a little baby up—skin yella and orange, nekkid as a jaybird in the whistlin' time. Little manchild. Eyes open. Dead, dead, dead.

At first, I'm thinking this the same baby I kilt—though I know that ain't rightly possible. The eyes look the same—but the child is different. Pretty little child, deader'n dirt. Malvina got a tear in her eye, but still smiling. She say:

"Meet your son, gravedigger." And looking in those tiny, pale eyes, I know.

I know my little Maria kept this from me. Being Maria's a whore, I guess I could have let myself believe the child warn't mine. But I'm lookin' into those sweet, dead eyes and I know. That little fella my son. My boy. The fruit of my Coffee Maria. My eyes turn to water and my head dizzy. I want to die right then and there. But there's something I gotta know. I look at that evil Malvina square in the eye, shakin' like a goat's ass, trine to find words:

"Where my Maria?"

Her words bite my ears like a cottonmouth sprung from its coil:

*"As if I would tell you where she is.* How she is. Whether she alive or dead. I won't tell you nothin', gravedigger. I ain't here to ease your mind. I'm here to put right what you wronged." She pause. Smile gone. That snake in her throat comin' up slow and even this time:

"Put things right, gravedigger. Kiss this child. Be a good father."

She hold that little fella tight around the ribs, bring him up level with my face. My knees go wobbly—it a good thing those *hounsi* got me by the arms or' I'da took a tumble over backwards. That little boy's face an inch from mine now, his little death-smell sweet and soft. Snake's a-comin' out Malvina's mouth at a dead crawl:

"A kiss. Just a kiss."

My lips part to speak—

Alla sudden, Malvina push her hands together hard on that baby's ribs. I hear those ribs cracklin'—a sickly noise, that. A puff of white dust come out that baby's mouth and into mine. Into my mouth, my eyes, my nose. Hoodoo dust. Poison. I know this'll be bad right off.

Feel the effect straight away, me. This a punishment I heard of—I'm to be dead, but not dead. My muscles go rigid and hard. My breath slowing. Stopping. My heartbeat gone terrible slow. My skin feelin' cold. I ain't never been this scared. I just wanna cry.

"You'll die slow, gravedigger. Piled into a hole with the rest. You'll hear and see and feel it all. And you'll wonder about Maria. And you'll never know. You'll die wondering. Take your questions with you, gravedigger. Roll them around in your mind as the dirt of the dead is sprinkling on yer sorry face." Then she say to the hounsi: "Bring him to the street. So his cronies can pick him up fer burying. Lay the little baby on mister gravedigger's face; eye to eye. Make sure gravedigger's eyes stay open. Wide open."

§

I reckon I lay on that heap o' dead outside Auntie Jin's for a good three hours 'fore that funeral cart finally come around—my dead son staring me in the eye the whole time. And guess who's driving that cart but ol' Frenchie Girton. *Lawd, lawd.* I can understand Black Jake picking one of the convicts to go out with the cart since I never made it back, but fer the life of me can't figger why he'd pick that rat-bastard Girton. Mayhap ol' Frenchie volunteered. Mayhap-al-so-too Frenchie in cahoots with that evil Malvina. Mebbe Jake in on it, too.

I'm thinking:

Poor me. Poor, poor me. Trouble comin'.

Girton pick that dead child up off my face, toss 'im in the cart like a rag. Then he look down at Marcus-me with a smile. "Whadda we have here?" he say, grinnin' like a devil. "My Mulatto friend, Mr. Marcus. *You hear me, boy?*" Then I know he in cahoots with Malvina 'cause he know I ain't dead. It a sad day for Marcus, no lie. That evil Girton keep talking, low and steady:

"Yeah, you hear me, boy. I see it in your eyes, yes? That a little tear in your eye, Mulatto? I believe so." Grin stretch wider. "You can feel, too, eh? Feel this, Mulatto." He look around to see if anyone watchin'. Then he bend down like to kiss, lips parted. I feel his dry teeth slicin' in slow. His breath smell bad; smell like death, rotten onions and old swamp.

That stinkin' French garbage bit my nose clean off.

Yes indeed, sonny—clean *off.* Lawdy, yes—a terrible pain, that. Spit my own nose back in my face. Laughin'. "Feel that, Mulatto?" Girton laughin' hard. My heart beating so slow I don't even bleed. Not bleeding scares me even more—not sure why. Then a miracle happen.

Outta nowhere I find the strength to scream. Scream loud and hard, me. Scream way up high like a little girl. Girton snarl and bring a boot down on my face. "Stay dead, you! Stay dead!" My strength gone, my mind blank now. I don't remember another thing till we back at the potter's field.

§

When my senses come back around I'm layin' face up on a lotta lumps. Figgered the lumps was bodies, and figgered right. Ol' Jake looking down at me with big, wet eyes.

"Poor ol' Mista Marcus. Itta sad day. Sho, sho." Sniffin'. "I din't wanna do it, ol' fren'. But dat hoodoo lady, she sho scare ol' Jake. Yessuh! Sedja kilt a lil baby and hadda pay. Say if I don't help, I pay too." Sniffin' some more. "You bin good ta me a long time, Mista Marcus. An' ol' Jake sho is sorry. Lawd, yes."

I tried screaming like I done before, but that hoodoo poison sunk in too hard. All I could do is look dead and stare as he pick me up in his big arms.

"I make you a promise, Marcus. I won't let yer body float up. If she do, I'll put you down first. 'Afore tha others. Thatta solemn oath, too."

So, now I *am* screaming. But not so no one can hear. Screamin' inside. In my head. Good and loud.

Jake lay me down in that big hole. Lay me in first—face up, flat on my back on the muddy ground. I guess this a courtesy of sorts; him figgerin' the further down the hole, the lesser chance of floating back up with the rain.

So I'm just lying there waiting awhile, feeling the wet mud at my back as Jake say a few words to Jesus on my behalf. Waiting and a-thinking, me. Then Jake walk away from that hole—and I know what's coming next.

Bodies.

One by one. Smacking me hard. In the face, the neck, the chest, the gut and the leg. Bodies. Covering ol' Marcus up. One by one. I know my little son is one, but I can't see where. I'm trying to see, looking fer my boy. Don't know why exactly, but I'm looking. The light breaks into narrow gaps and cracks between the corpses. Those cracks of light fill up with dark, one by one. The weight on my chest and head is something terrible. Then the last crack of light done swallowed up. The weight get heavier and heavier still. A little while pass before the first bit of dusty soil crinkle down though the bodies. I feel it on my hand first. Just a tickle. Then one eye, then the other. Feel it on my tongue. Didn't know my mouth was open till that.

Quiet.

Awful quiet. Long, long, awful quiet. Don't know how long.

Malvina was right, sure nuff. I be thinkin' about my Maria.

Wondering if the fever got her. Feeling sorry about that little dead baby of mine, and that other'n from the country shack. Feeling bad. Real bad. Thinkin' mebbe I really am dead. Mebbe this my own special hell. What I had coming. What I had coming and what I got. Justice from God on high. I can't feel my own heart beat. Can't tell if my chest trine to rise fer air. Can't tell if my eyes is still open. Dark. Heavy, heavy dark. All I feel is the weight of the dead piled on my chest and legs. Packed down tight with bodies and dirt. Feeling the pressure on every inch of me. A cannonball of fear jumping 'round my skull.

But after a while that cannonball sit still. After a while there's comfort here. It's so quiet. Mebbe this ain't hell a'tall. Mebbe a sort of heaven. Mebbe both. So quiet.

Quiet.
Quiet.
Quiet.
Quiet.
*quiet*
HEAVY

§

A day or two pass before I hear a spiritual my mama used to sing:

> *Tell me Sister Mary, tell me now*
> *Where you been gone so long?*
> *I been jumpin' them ditches*
> *And a-cuttin' them switches*
> *Swimmin' in the river*
> *Eatin' catfish liver*
> *Now my soul want to go home to glory*

Singing in my head. Mama's close now, I know. But after a while the singing stop. And I'm still here in the quiet, heavy dark. Mama left me again. Jesus, too. Quiet. Heavy. Dark.

Hard to say fer sure, but I reckon three more days pass before I feel the rattlin' at my bones.

I'm guessing this the death rattle—that little bit of shakin' folks do when they're getting ready to pass. I feel a smile in my heart. Going to God, now, I think. Going to see Jesus. But after a few seconds the death rattle stop and I'm still here in the ground. Mud pressed to my back, weight of the dead at my chest. Still here. A minny or two pass. Rattle again. This time harder—but shorter. Half a minny pass. Then a jolt. Dusty dirt falling in my mouth again, tickling my eyes. And with that last jolt come a sound. Far off and muffled—but a sound. First sound I heard in days. And my mind still clear enough that I recognize that sound.

*Chango* talkin'. Thunder.

Then more thunder, more shakin' and joltin'. After a spell, the weight of the dead is shifting around on me, pressing my bones. More semma-tree dirt sprinkling on my tongue, dusting my throat. The weight is getting heavier. Heavier still. Then I feel a dripping at my cheek. A drop in my eye. Mouth filling up with water. Throat filling. Wanting to cough. Can't cough. Muscles in my throat still too frozen with hoodoo poison to oblige a cough. I start to feel a cold panic as the grave begin filling with water. The water creeping up to my shoulders, filling my ears. Water in my ears. Coming up, up, up. Into my mouth and the bitten hole of my nose. Filling my mouth. Turning the dirt in my eyes and mouth into mud. Sticky mud. Wanting to push the mud out with my tongue. Tongue won't move. My body still but my mind is racing:

*In New Orleans, bodies come up in the rain.*

I'm praying to Jesus that my breathing stay slow enough to keep me from drowning. I'm praying the extra weight of mud and the water on the bodies don't crush my ribs. And, for the first time in history—*I'm prayin' that bodies come up and come up quick in the City of New Orleans.*

Now I'm under water. Soft, warm water. Before too long, the mud and the dead start to moving; sliding and pressing against my cheek and my hands and my stomach and my legs. Bodies shifting. Pressure on my ribs getting lighter. Then lighter still.

*In New Orleans, bodies come up in the rain.*

Thunder louder now. Crashing and shakin'. Booming like dynamite. Hurting my ears. The pain is good, there's a comfort in it. Bodies shifting fast over toppa me. Something like a spider slipping in my mouth. But ain't a spider. Touching my tongue. Pushing mud in my throat, keeping the water from seeping in my lungs. My mind works to decipher the thing in my mouth. Fingers. Tiny fingers. A baby's hand. Tickling my tongue through the mud and water.

*I am found.*

I know the hand is my son's hand. My little baby. I'm wondering now if he was ever really dead. Maybe that evil Malvina gave him the same poison I got. Put him in a sleep like the dead, but not dead. Maybe he looking for me in the dirt like I's looking for him. The hand slides out.

*I am lost.* Bodies shifting. Hard n' fast. Moving 'round. Pressure getting lighter alla time. A shoe kick me in the jaw. A body passing by. Pressure gone.

A murky light, hurting my eyes. The pain is good. The ground does not touch my back. I'm underwater, but I'm coming up. *Praise Jesus.*

My face touches air. Cool air, *lawd-a-mighty*. Water washing over my eyes. I can see the moon and the stars. Mud packed tight in my throat from that little hand; soft and cool, and holding firm.

Little waves pushing me along the ground. Sometimes I'm on my back, sometimes on my side, sometimes face down. Sometimes head first—sometimes feet or side. The rain is beating hard all around, like the sound of horses running. The ground beneath me sometimes soft with mud, sometimes hard with brick and stone. I am movin' with the little waves and the current of the storm. My clothes are being torn from me. I am surrounded by horses it seems.

§

I am gliding in the streets. Gliding with the dead. I am looking for my son. Looking for my Coffee Maria. I am gliding.

I hear water rushing. Loud and glorious. Roaring like an angry bear. Thunder crash. It a magic sound, the sound of Jesus laughing, *Legba* the savior, setting me free from the grave. I hear the menfolk shouting. I hear the ladies screaming. I see their boots as they wade past. Their voices are tired but filled with terror; it is a wonderful sound. It is the sound of the living. My dead brethren push and bump against me. They are gliding with me. They have become like family to me. We have been through a lot together, me and the dead. There is a joy in their touch. We have no clothes. We are not wading. We do not scream.

I am gliding. Now there is nothing but water. No mud, no brick and stone. Just water.

I am in the river.

Face down, drifting. Moving with the current. My eyes are used to the dark so I can see good. Catfish swimming. Different shades of brown and black. Sniffing at the bodies that float at the surface. Curious. Moving on. The water and catfish are dreamlike and soothing. I fall asleep. I am dreaming. The catfish are moving slower. A pretty little catfish come right up to me—sniffing at my eye. Funny lookin' fish. Tan with pale eyes. *Des yeux goueres.* Wrapped in a perfect white blanket. Caress my cheek, a tickle of whiskers. Bringing comfort to my tired mind. Then there are more fish like the funny one. Wrapped in white blankets. Protected by miracles. Swimming beneath the drifting dead. Looking up. Curious. Moving on. They smile at me. The babies leave me. I am content. My sleep is dreamless and peaceful now.

Gliding. Silken water. Caress and tickle. Deep. Warm. Cool. Perfect. Tears. Motion. Life. Sacred.

Blackness.

§

When I awake I am not lying down. I am walking.

I wake to the sound of singing. The voice is unfamiliar. It is my voice. It don't sound right because I have no nose. It takes me a while to figure this out. So, as my brain coming around, I listen to the words of the song:

> *Jesus, I'm troubled about my soul*
> *Ride on, Jesus, come this way*
> *I troubled 'bout my soul*
> *Old Satan is mad and I am glad*
> *He missed one soul that he thought he had.*
> *Troubled 'bout my soul*

Then I pay attention to what my eyes is seeing. There is water and a shore. Flatboats with men shouting off yonder. Bodies floating on the water. Bodies on the sand. Bodies 'neath my feet. I look down at my feet. They are bloody. I been walking long.

My mind is clearing now. Clearing fast. I remember.

> *Troubled 'bout my soul*

I look to the living men in the distance, the ones on the flatboats shouting. On the land side there's a thick, black smoke pouring into the sky. Burning bodies. Ashes in the air, floating up to heaven where they belong. *Praise God.*

I 'spect I am not too pretty, me. I am nekkid. I am bloody. I have no nose. I come up from amongst the dead. I should be dead, too. I walk on two legs, wave at the living. I am a sight. Sho, sho.

I walk on. I am careful not to step on my dead brethren. I look at the faces of the dead as I pass. They don't look glad to see me. I don't see my boy. Maria neither. I cross over sand and climb the levee. Comin' down the dock just as I am, nekkid and bleeding. Some folks point. Some ladies scream. Some run. Some drop down cold. No one laugh. They know me. They know I should be dead. They leave me be. Be crazy not to, I guess. This is where the lies start up. Crazy talk about a dead man walking the streets of New Orleans. Folks like to have their fun. Folks like a good story. But I ain't dead now and never was. Sharpen up that pencil and get it right, young fella.

Walkin'.

My skin is tender from touching water and mud fer so long. My feet hurt on the ground, getting punched n' cut by little rocks and crumbs of broken glass. Leaving bloody footprints in the street. Clouds of black smoke in the sky. Sweet smell of burning dead all around. It smell real good to me, that smoke. Finally I'm there.

601 Dauphine. Auntie Jin's.

I stand at the door where my Maria used to lay down with other fellas. I know who's inside. I will kill her. I will kill that Malvina Latour. Don't care if I hang for it. I push open the door slow. I am boiling with rage. I am thinking of Frenchie Girton. I am thinking of killing binness. I am filled with hate. But not fer long.

First thing I see is a sleeping angel. *Une binette.* She is not yellow or orange. There is a healthy color on her cheek, *café au lait,* but her body is thin and wasted. My Coffee Maria. She is covered in a white blanket. The blanket is long and soft; not for babies or the feet of dead men. For Coffee Maria. My love.

But I done guessed it right—Malvina there, too. Rocking in that creaky chair. Stroking Maria's forehead with a wet rag. Her look is soft and sad. Her eyes meet mine. She isn't afraid of the hate in my eye. She wave a hand. With no snake in her voice, she say: "Come in, boy. This little girl been waiting on you." I have no rage in me now. I kneel beside my Maria. Hold her hand. Cry, me.

My baby's eyes open. Softly, she: "Oh, look at you…" Looking at the hole where my nose used to be. Seeing me nekkid, bloody and thin. Feeling like a dern fool, me.

"I'm fine, little one. I'm fine as long as I'm with you. I'll never leave you, again. My sweet Coffee Maria." My voice sound funny without a nose, she make a little smile. Sweet, sweet, she.

"I had the fever, Marcus," she say. "I was dying from fever but I needed to see you. I needed to say that I love you. I needed you to know that I love you. I won't lay down with them other fellas no more. I promise. I've always loved you, Marcus…"

"Shhhh, little one…save your strength…"

"No. I need to say this." Her face gone serious and stern. I could not say no to her.

Pretty little voice, soft and weak:

"There was a baby in my body, Marcus—your baby. I named him Michael— for the saint. He knew. Little Michael knew. From the womb, he knew. He saw us through all that death, and brought us back together. Even if just for a little while, he brought us together. It was what he wanted. For us to be together again. When he was born…" her voice broke into little sobs.

Malvina continued in her stead, the mambo's voice gentle and even:

"When that little baby came out of Maria, he took the disease with him. Her fever broke the minute of his delivery. He lived a little while, then died. Died from fever. He died for his mama. And you. So she could be with you. But his work was not done. He sent you on your way, Marcus. Into the grave. So you could know. He was never far from you. Always nearby. And when you were ready, he found you. And he brought you back. Back to her."

Tiny fingers on my tongue…

And it was true.


(…)


*I am found.*


"He never left you. Never gave up on you. You must not give up on him, Marcus." The mambo's eyes filled with clear water. "She's dying now, our Maria. Her body was too weak from sickness. Michael's sacrifice only bought her time. Took the sickness out, but her body too spent. She's dying, Marcus…" Tears silvered the mambo's cheek.

Maria smiled at her aunt, a finger to her lips. "He found you, Marcus. He really did. Our baby. Now you must bring him back, my love. Find his little body. Bury him with me. So we can all be together in the potter's field. All three. Together. We are a family now, Marcus. Find our boy. Promise."

"I promise."

She hold my hand tight. Smile. Her eyes fading but glowing still. She believe my promise, but I don't know if I believe it myself. I am shivering. She pull that perfect blanket off her body, hold it up to me. I push it back to her.

Malvina say: "No. It's time." Gently, Malvina take that sacred blanket from Maria's hands, step behind me. Wrap it around my shoulders. My Maria is skin and bones in a loose, yella dress, lying on the bed. Her feet are bare, my little Coffee Maria. She lift a hand to my face, stroke my muddy head. Pull me down to her sweet lips, whisper soft in my ear:

*"Mo couer tacher dans to chaine comme boskoyo dans cypiere."*

Her dying breath was sweet as cypress. I could feel it on my tongue. Like tiny fingers. I pulled the blanket tight around me. And it felt just like a miracle.

§

*Now.*

As for me, well.

Still doing that hard potter field work, old as I am. Lotta work to do round here, the storms have made it so. The third in my lifetime of such a kind, all told, and hopefully the last. But that's just fine—when I work that field, my Maria is close. When I ain't with her, I'm here on this piece of levee lookin' for that fish.

I made my gal a promise many years past, and promises are for keeps.

I'll find our baby Michael before I die. Maybe after. Til I find him, I won't stay down. You can bury me, but I'll come back up. When the water is right, I'll be back. Little Michael will see to it, and I'll see to him. Don't you worry none. I'm looking for that catfish. The tan one with pale eyes—*des yeaux goueres*. The one that touched my cheek and gave me comfort among the drifting dead.

Regarding this more recent storm, I will always remember those things, too. For like the storm of my youth, and that second one, too, its unfolding will likely go on for a good bit.

Like so many others, Buddy Bolden rose to the challenge brought on by high water brought by the flood of 1906, only to find himself diminished with the tide. Straight off, he sought only to recover the body of his little son—just as I continue to seek my own in the now. But Buddy gave up too quick, lacked the tenacity to continue against all odds, just as others can't help but go on. Some folks is unable to keep toiling after so much bad fortune, and I don't blame them for it—not one lick I don't. These troubles can be more than hard. Beyond sad they sometimes are. After a spell of fruitless trying, Buddy just fell into that bottle of his. Fell so hard he wound up in the big asylum over by Jackson, very likely to die there some day. In the end, I reckon he done what he could to right his own wrongs, done the best he could. But there's only so much a man can do in that regard, only so many bad deeds can be made good on.

But Buddy's time here was not in vain, for he brought music into this sad world—and he did one extraordinary good deed in saving that Morningstar gal. The one called Malaria.

Not long after the risen waters of ought-six had gone back down, she come across an old friend from the Eagle Saloon, Gary the Gent. She'd assumed Gary to be dead and swept away like so many she had known, and had tried hard not to dwell upon such. But later come to find he'd made it up and out of the black waters just like she.

This meeting of Gary and Malaria was at once tender and cordial, she holding back tears and promising to make good on that old bar tab. He just smiled and took her in his arms—and there she stayed; their mutual tears ripening on a vine of the heart till heavy enough that they might fall of their own accord. Tears did fall in time—and that ain't all that fell neither. Other things come of that chance reunion. Good things they were, too.

Malaria and Gary the Gent, whose last name is Byrd, were married twenty-five years ago today. The two of them knew each other only as friends before that storm, but in their rediscovery of each other after so much misery apart, well, it was as if the tragedy of their lives had created a passion for living that they'd otherwise never have known. Having lost everything worldly once again, five years ago in the flood of '26, they just shook off the sorrow and kept on strong—that love they'd discovered between 'em twenty years past only getting more fierce. That fiercest of loves tending the very ground they walk upon to this day. Sonny, if there's one thing I come upon through all this trouble; it's that if love don't stay fierce, it don't stay at all.

Starting over is a funny thing. You only get one true start, on the day that you are born. But as we get older and know better about the lives we've lived, every once in awhile we try to make ourselves a new beginning. Problem is that you can't erase where you come from, the accumulation of your experience being undeniably *who you are*. Ain't no one can be rebirthed out of a past that has come to define them, no matter if these things come by chance or design. You can only pretend to start again; never to forget, try as you might. I guess that's what Buddy learned. Some fare better than others in this life—with its various turns and stops and starts. This may not be right, but it is true.

Last I heard Gary done built that old Morningstar house back up better than it was. Last I heard Malaria was heavy with child. Last I heard they was doing quite well together, those two. Last I heard they was happy. Simple things. Small victories. One heartbeat at a time.

Starting over, or something like it, the best they can.

Very last thing I heard was an old song in my head, singing somethin' bout troubled souls and a savior called Jesus pulling folks up from the clutches of hell. An old song is all it is and ever will be, but if played true—it is enough. Starting over and over again from the pit of my heart. A circle in time. Just as the spring trickles into the lake that flows into the river that empties into the sea so that it may rise up to the sky to make rain that must fall—sometimes to fall very hard—and back down again to fill that first little spring once more.

# ACKNOWLEDGMENTS

Deepest appreciation to the following, without whom you'd be holding some other book in your hands right now: Joe Phillips, Michael Allen Zell, Geoff Munsterman, Matthew Miller, Deborah Meghnagi, Katherine Maistros, Billy Martin, and The City of New Orleans.

Additional alphabetical gratitude to: Raymond Buckland, Jenny Keith Ciattei, Bryan Civello, Douglas Clegg, Crispin the Coffee Guy at the old Rue De La Course in the Quarter, Mark Doten, Bremner Duthie, Shari Fisch, Vicky Gashe, GiO the Burlesque Queen of New Orleans & Dr. Bob, Mambo Sallie Ann Glassman, Habitat for Humanity, Jeff "Almost Slim" Hannusch, Skip Henderson, The Ghost of Edna Hicks, Homeless Bill, Mr. Ike and His Harmonica That Cost More Than a Car, Jenna Mae, Kaldi's Coffeehousemuseum (RIP), Jack Kelleher, Little Freddie King, Gary Krist, Andrea Oliver Ledee, Levees.Org, Diane Maistros, Elly Maistros, George Maistros, Michael Maistros, Michael Martin, Keely Merritt, Peter "Sneaky Pete" Orr, Lisa Pasold, Diana Price, Zak Rahman & Schiro's Café, Stacey Dian Robbins, Coco Robicheaux, Gary "The Gent" Rouzan, Brett Savory, The Very Reverend Jim Smith & His Damn Frontier, T-Bone "Whiskey Boy" Stone, Paul G. Tremblay, Mike West's 9th Ward Hillbilly Band, Malcolm "Papa Mali" Wellbourne and everyone who came back to New Orleans after the storm to swing a hammer in trembling fists.

Special love and gratitude to the original cast of "Calisaya Blues," a play based on this novel, who so lovingly brought Dr. Jack, Hattie, Typhus and Diphtheria to life for the stage. They are: Donald Lewis, Alexis McQuarter, Ryan Etienne and Deveney Marshall.

Extra special thanks and love to my babies: Amberle & Booker.

CRESCENT CITY BOOKS
New Orleans, LA
www.blackwidowpress.com

*The Sound of Building Coffins* by Louis Maistros

THE VALENTIN ST. CYR MYSTERIES by David Fulmer

*Chasing the Devil's Tail*

*Jass*

*Rampart Street*

*Lost River*

*The Iron Angel*

*Eclipse Alley*